ALL DAY AND A NIGHT

Alafair Burke's books include her Samantha Kincaid series, two standalone thrillers, and her highly acclaimed series starring NYPD Detective Ellie Hatcher, the previous title of which, *Never Tell*, was a Kindle bestseller. A former Deputy District Attorney in Portland, Oregon, Alafair is now a Professor of Law at Hofstra Law School, where she teaches criminal law and procedure.

Praise for *All Day and a Night*:

'If it was me on the slab at the coroner's office I would want Ellie Hatcher on the case. Burke's detective is one of the best in the business and this take on New York City could only come from a writer who knows its darkness and light so well.' **Michael Connelly**

'Spring loaded and razor sharp, *All Day and a Night* is a surprising and compelling thriller. But Alafair Burke has given us something more gripping than just a crime novel. Her story is about women, their drive, their compassion, and their public and private battles for success and acceptance.' **Ivy Pochoda**

'Gripping . . . a propulsive thriller.' *Publishers Weekly*

'For fans of Lisa Gardner and Tess Gerritsen, and readers who enjoy tough female police officer protagonists and complex plots.' *Library Journal*

All Day and a Night

ALAFAIR BURKE

FABER & FABER

First published in 2014
by Faber & Faber Limited
Bloomsbury House,
74–77 Great Russell Street
London WC1B 3DA
This paperback edition first published in 2015

First published in the United States in 2014
by HarperCollins Publishers
10 East 53rd Street, New York, NY 10022

Typeset by RefineCatch Limited, Bungay, Suffolk
Printed and bound by CPI Group (UK) Ltd, Croydon CR0 4YY

A CIP record for this book is available from the British Library

ISBN 978-0-571-30233-8

For John DeWitt Gregory

What would people think if they could overhear their own conversations?

"I don't know how many times I have to explain this. I go to work all day. I'm there . . . all . . . day. If I want to come home, have a beer, watch the tube, and go to sleep, it's because I'm exhausted. It's not . . . about . . . you."

"You love to throw that in my face, don't you?"

As Helen shifted in her sleek white leather swivel chair to stay alert, she could see herself posting a surreptitiously recorded excerpt of this couple's therapy session on the Internet. She imagined both husband and wife listening to it online. She pictured them saying to each other, "At least we're not like that."

"Seriously, Susan. On what planet did I just throw something in your face?"

"That you work. As if I don't. You were the one who got out pen, paper, and calculator and figured out that my salary barely covered daycare, not to mention the housekeeper on top of it. So I gave up one job and got two in return, but—no—*you're* the one who works all day."

Helen took a deep, slow breath. It was one of her

regular tricks during sessions. Most people didn't notice. If they did, they'd interpret it as a sign that they should do the same. But what a deep breath gave Helen was a surge of oxygen to keep herself from nodding off. Now where were these two in the volley of husband-wife-husband-wife?

"Fine. You want me to stay home? I will." Ah, it was the husband's turn again. "Because I would kill to have more time with Aidan. Except I'd get out of bed before ten o'clock. We'd occasionally turn off the television and get some fresh air. Maybe I'd actually take up cooking instead of watching celebrity chefs three hours a day."

"Oh, like you don't leave the office to work out in the middle of the day. Or drink at lunch. Or come home stinking of booze when you supposedly had a meeting. But that's right: you're the one who would kill to have more time with Aidan."

Helen scrolled through her client notes on the iPad resting on her lap. Aidan: was that a son or a daughter? She couldn't remember. Call her old-school, but crap if she didn't miss the days of handwritten notes on lined paper. But the iPad, she'd learned, made her type of patients feel less studied. Less examined. Less broken. An iPad made them feel like they were with their caterer or interior decorator, not a psychotherapist.

"What the hell is wrong with you?" Back to the husband again. "I've told you—I'm expected to do client development. And, yeah, I exercise. Last time I checked, we belonged to a gym three blocks from the apartment that offers daycare if you're in such dire need of a break from our child. Maybe then you wouldn't feel so bad about your body that you won't let me f—"

"Don't you dare, Jack. Don't you fucking dare."

"So it's okay for us to hurl the word at each other when we're fighting, but God forbid I use it to point out we don't have a sex life anymore."

And there it was: sex. There it always was.

Helen knew that sex was only . . . sex. She knew that great sex wasn't enough to form the foundation of a lifelong partnership. She knew that bad sex could mean anything: a lack of emotional intimacy, an absolute lack of physical attraction, or a "mismatch in activity preferences" as she'd learned to call it, as when one person wanted sweet talk in front of the fire while the other wanted (or needed) the kinds of dirty, dirty things that were legal only because no one had imagined them in time to try to prohibit them.

But no sex? No sex at all between two people trying to run a shared household, and raise a child together, and put up with the rest of the world day in and day out without seeking intimacy from another person? Sex couldn't make or break a marriage, but Helen had learned one thing about sex in fifteen years of marriage counseling: it was a hell of lot easier to put up with another person's shit when you were having it on a regular basis.

"On that subject," she interrupted, "when I saw you

3

last week, I suggested that the two of you try to set aside time to work on that aspect of your relationship." She had the script down pat: reserve time for each other, separate from stress, be your own best people for one another and see what happens. But she, Susan, and Jack all knew what she meant: get down to marital business. "Were you able to do that?"

Silence. Silence, like bad sex, could mean anything.

Helen had two children of her own with whom she'd like to spend more time. Yet here she was, at four-forty on a snowy Sunday afternoon, listening to Jack and Susan West fight. Those names. So perfect, like out of a soap opera. Somehow their appearance matched their perfect names, too. Yet they fought, like almost all of Helen's patients. They fought about everything—money, work, childcare, jealousies, and, perhaps most of all, betrayal, whether actual or perceived. They fought because life can suck and a lot of people needed help to cope with the person who was supposed to help them cope.

The truth was, Helen knew she wasn't at her best these days in that area. She had forced Mitch, after all, to see one of the city's most respected counselors, and a year of hard work hadn't saved their marriage. And so now she and Mitch were paying for two households, which meant money was tighter, which meant she now took weekend appointments, which meant she had to tune back in and pay attention to Jack and Susan and a fight that felt important to them, but which she knew was utterly mundane.

4

Where were they? Right. The subject of sex, followed by this moment of silence. Helen had been here many times before.

She was about to deliver her typical advice to try again when she saw Susan and Jack exchange a glance and then look away. It was Susan who smiled first, followed by Jack, whose smile turned into a laugh. And then the two of them were laughing together.

"Is this a reluctance to talk to me about your physical life together?" Helen asked. She knew from experience it wasn't, but she wanted them to choose to share the moment. So many patients came to therapy and spoke only about the worst aspects of their marriage. Discussing the better moments—however rare—helped people get past their resentments and visualize the ability to reconnect.

Susan spoke first. "It's stupid, really. I—I bought lingerie. If you could even call it that. It was—well, it was really tacky." She looked again at her husband.

"It wasn't tacky. Okay, it was trashy, but I mean that in a good way."

"It had this flap that . . . I'll spare you the details, but I started laughing, and Aidan heard us and walked in. His poor brain is probably going to be scarred. For the rest of his life, he'll flinch when he sees kelly-green lace." The woman was blushing. "Anyway, it didn't actually happen."

"Did you not notice my little home-improvement project yesterday?" Jack asked.

5

The smile began to fade from Susan's face. Helen knew that the couple—once again, like everyone else—had a tendency to keep score when it came to household responsibilities.

Jack explained before the tone of the conversation soured. "The door. I put a latch on the bedroom door. I thought you'd notice last night and we'd maybe resume where we left off. When you didn't say anything—"

"No," Susan said, still smiling and blushing. "I totally didn't notice. Really? You did that?"

Apparently in the bartering economy of the West family, hardware installation was roughly equivalent to trashy lingerie.

Four-forty-eight. Close enough to the fifty-minute mark for Helen, especially when the clients were two seconds away from getting down and dirty. "Why don't we continue this next week?" If she made really good time, she'd be home to watch the red carpet coverage with the kids. It was the first Oscar night since the separation and, though the kids hadn't mentioned it, she knew they'd have something special planned.

Helen was still tapping out her session notes on the iPad when she heard a buzz from the building's front entrance. Now that money was tighter, she not only had weekend sessions, but she made do without an assistant.

"Yes?" she said through the intercom.

"Dr. Brunswick? I think I left one of my gloves up there."

She didn't see a glove on the couch, but she'd allow Jack to search for himself. She buzzed him up, cracked open her office door, and resumed typing. A minute later, she heard the hinges on the door creak.

"I didn't find it, Jack, but feel free to—"

The man standing in her office wasn't Jack West.

"Where's Jack? Sir, you need to go right now. See this?" She touched her iPad screen. "I just alerted security. They'll be here in seconds. You really should go." Would the man know she was bluffing? She thought she sounded firm, or had her voice quaked?

"You don't even recognize me?"

All these years, she had listened to normal, ordinary people like Susan and Jack West dissect every moment of their normal, ordinary lives for a reason: because she had Jessica and Sam, and she used to have Mitch. She had a family to go home to. She had a life she loved. As fascinated as she was by people with more serious troubles, she had learned she didn't want her own thoughts to live among theirs. She wanted her thoughts to be as normal and ordinary as she could keep them.

But now this man—this stranger—was in her office, and she knew she was looking at the face of hopelessness. And then she saw the gun.

PART ONE

THE FRESH LOOK

I

Ellie Hatcher was a gambler, even though she'd been raised to believe that gambling was reckless. *Foolhardy,* her mother would call it (because Roberta Hatcher wanted to pretend that she grew up in an old-money world of Tudor manors surrounded by show horses, instead of a no-money world of aluminum-sided houses encircled by cyclone fences). Worse than foolhardy, to risk money on games of chance was arrogant. Smug. To think that somehow the randomness of the universe would align in your favor was . . . unseemly.

But the way Ellie looked at it, a bet wasn't *gambling* if she knew in advance that she held the advantage. Gambling, in Ellie's view, was an investment banker with an eight ball of coke at the Venetian Hotel letting twelve hundred dollars ride on some random fat kid playing junior-league softball in Minneapolis. To gamble was to believe in luck, or fate, or the gods. Ellie, by contrast, believed in her own skills, and felt no guilt taking money from people whose own skills (or beliefs in imaginary blessings) couldn't match up. Some months, she earned more at the poker tables of Atlantic City than in her paycheck from the NYPD.

Ellie played the odds, but only when she knew the odds were in her favor. And she damn sure was *not* going to lose today's bet against her partner, J. J. Rogan.

They were in an interrogation room of the homicide squad of the 13th Precinct. Seated at the small aluminum table was a woman named Laura Bendel, who had dialed 9-1-1 three hours ago, screaming for an ambulance to save her husband. Ellie and Rogan had already listened to the recording of the call:

> *9-1-1. What's your emergency?*
> *Oh my God. The blood. So much blood.*
> *Please, help.*
> *Someone is hurt?*
> *Seth. My husband. Please, oh my God. I*
> *need help.*
> *Why is your husband bleeding, ma'am?*
> *He's cut. In the . . . stomach, I think. Oh my*
> *God. I—I think I stabbed him.*

The dispatcher did her job, textbook style. The name. The address. Keeping Laura on the phone, as calm as possible, until officers arrived.

Just as the dispatcher's conversation was textbook, so was the scene. A spilled Macallan bottle next to the upturned coffee table. Broken lamp. A button from Laura's torn designer blouse on the hallway runner leading to the threshold of the kitchen. The wood knife block knocked to the floor, the light-gray marble now smeared with Seth Bendel's blood, thanks to the ten-inch gourmet chef's blade protruding from his gut.

The responding officers found Laura weeping over her husband's dead body, her hand still holding the phone she'd used to call for help. "I didn't mean to. I'm so sorry, Seth. I'm so sorry. I love you. I love you." It took them fifteen minutes to calm her down enough to tell the story: he was beating her once again, and she only meant to scare him. He charged at her—hard. The knife was in her hand. Now he was dead, and she was heartbroken.

Rogan was buying the tale. Ellie wasn't. They had a hundred bucks riding on it.

Right now, Rogan's was looking like the stronger hand. A civilian aide had just entered the interrogation room to deliver four pages of medical records from Bellevue Hospital.

According to the records, Laura showed up at the emergency room with a bloody nose two months earlier, claiming that she had "*walked into a door*"—quotation marks courtesy of the attending physician, whose notes indicated his skepticism: *Followed suspected-DV protocol.* Ellie knew that if a doctor believed that domestic violence was the true cause of injury, the doctor would ask the patient directly and encourage her to report it, but would call the police independently only in the face of actual evidence of a crime. That evidence was lacking in Laura's case, so, once the doctor confirmed that Laura's nose wasn't broken, he sent her on her way with an ice pack, antibiotic ointment, and a pamphlet about domestic violence.

"What is that?" Laura asked, eyeing the documents in Rogan's hands. "Is that about me?" The two first fingers of her right hand continued to stroke the front of her throat, still red from the black Armani belt she claimed Seth had used to choke her before she wrestled free and grabbed the knife. Even after hours of hysterical crying, she was still gorgeous. Long, shiny blond hair. Clear, porcelain skin. Bright green eyes. High cheekbones. A knockout by any measure.

Ellie saw the sparkle in Rogan's eye. He was counting his hundred bucks already. Not that he needed the money, but Ellie's partner was almost as competitive as Ellie. Almost. "We got the medical records from Bellevue for last February's bloody nose. Why didn't you tell the doctor that it was your husband who punched you?"

The question might have sounded hostile to a casual observer, but Ellie knew Rogan was giving the woman a chance to recite the obvious explanation. Ellie could barely suppress an eye roll as she listened to Laura's version, once again textbook. She covered for her husband for all the same reasons most women covered for their abusive lovers: she was afraid of him, and for him, and because she loved him, when he wasn't hitting her.

Ellie was still reading the emergency physician's notes.

Rogan had seen what he'd wanted to see, and now she was processing the rest. She pulled her cell phone from her jacket pocket and pretended to see a text message on the screen. "Sorry," she said. "Gotta deal with this."

She moved to the corner of the interrogation room and pulled up Facebook. Sure enough, like seemingly every other thirty-two-year-old man, Seth Bendel had a profile. Better yet, he was an active poster and hadn't bothered with privacy settings. She scrolled down the page to last February's activities. Bingo.

"Your emergency-room visit was on February 14th," Ellie said, tucking her phone back into her pocket.

"Was it?" Laura asked. "I couldn't remember the exact date."

"That's Valentine's Day. Did you and Seth do anything to celebrate?"

She gave a sad smile. "We used to, when we first met. But once we were married, we had an anniversary to celebrate instead. Seth always says Valentine's Day is more of a Hallmark-card holiday for people who don't have the real thing. Amateur night."

Rogan's eyes had moved to Ellie's jacket pocket. He knew something was up.

"The ER doc who treated you made a note: he saw you snap a cell-phone picture of your injured face before he cleaned you up." Ellie's best guess was that the doctor added the notation to aid the prosecution in the event

Laura subsequently changed her mind and decided to press charges.

"I thought I might need it someday. Plus it was just something to remember. I take pictures of my food, too." Laura laughed nervously at her own self-deprecating comment.

"Or you wanted to be able to show Seth the lengths to which you'd go to ensure you had power over him. That you would tell people he was beating you. That you had evidence. That you would ruin him."

"I don't understand," Laura said, complete with a confused head shake.

"I would have been pissed too if my husband spent Valentine's Day drinking at the Soho Grand with all his unmarried work buddies." She placed her cell phone on the interrogation room table in front of Laura. Rogan craned his neck, trying to get a better view of the screen. From his vantage point, he would only be able to see that it was a Facebook profile, but that would be enough for him to figure out that Ellie had found a flaw in Laura's story.

"Right here, Laura." Ellie pointed to the relevant post. "A 'check-in' at the Soho Grand bar on February 14th at 11:10 p.m. He didn't even bother covering his tracks. Did he tell you he got stuck at work? *Sorry to miss Valentine's Day, babe, I'll make up for it?* Or was he the type who didn't even bother to call? You just sat there in your living room—maybe even in a new dress—wondering where he was and why he didn't pick up his cell or answer your texts. Then you checked his Facebook page. Look, one of his buddies was even nice enough to tag everyone so you could see whose company your husband chose over yours."

"The time on the hospital report must be wrong," Laura said. "He came home drunk. Picked a stupid fight, like always. Then he punched me."

"Speaking of his drinking, I notice from all these many pictures your husband posted, he seemed to favor martinis."

"What about it? I don't know why you're treating me this way," Laura protested. "You told me I was here voluntarily. That I'm not under arrest. And now—"

Ellie looked at Rogan and could tell he knew it was over. "I'm trying to give you a chance to keep it that way, Laura. Just hear me out. See, he always seems to be drinking martinis in these photos. Meanwhile, this woman standing next to him in every single group shot on Valentine's Day—according to the tag, her name is Megan Underhill, works with your husband at Morgan Stanley, went to Harvard, *very* attractive by the way. She appears to favor a dark drink served in a highball glass. Could even be Macallan, like the bottle I saw thrown on your living room rug tonight."

"Sometimes he drank martinis, sometimes he had scotch."

"Fine, let's say your husband's beverage choices ran

the gamut. No big deal. But here's the more curious thing. This very attractive woman named Megan? She's not as attractive as you, if you ask me, but she's different, especially in her coloring. Olive skin. Black hair. That dark-plum lipstick she's wearing in these photographs wouldn't do much for blondes like us, and yet it would appear to be a perfect match to the lipstick I noticed on the rim of a highball glass in your kitchen sink."

"This is crazy," Laura said. "I had a drink myself when Seth first started to pick at me tonight. Sometimes it would calm everything down if I would just tell him I needed to take the edge off—like I was taking the blame for whatever imaginary slight set him off. And maybe I wear the wrong colors for my skin. I didn't realize this was a makeover session." She looked to her ally Rogan for help.

"Fine, then," Ellie said, crossing her arms. "Just tell me where I can find that lipstick in your apartment. Or your purse. Or, you know, wherever you keep your makeup."

"Um, I don't know where I put it."

"Okay, so how about the name of the color? Or the brand? Anything you can give us to help clear up the confusion."

Ellie flashed a glance at Rogan. He knew—when was he ever going to learn?—that she'd been dealing from a stacked deck all along. At her side, she rubbed her thumb and index finger together. *Pay up, partner.*

*

Less than an hour later, they had Laura's confession on videotape. The woman was still blaming her husband for his own death, but instead of self-defense, she claimed that the discovery of the lipstick-stained highball glass had sent her into an uncontrollable rage. A battered woman might have had a shot getting past a prosecutor, but not a jealous wife. Laura would be indicted for murder, no question; a jury would handle the rest.

Rogan was handing Ellie a crisp new set of twenties from his wallet when John Shannon emerged from their lieutenant's office to witness the transaction. "Looks like a nice wad of dough you guys got there."

Ellie could already see where this was heading. The most effort Detective John Shannon ever put into the squad room was cracking wise. With money changing hands from Rogan to Ellie, his wee brain was probably overheating from the collision of potential barbs: Would it be the attractive female detective earning her money the old-fashioned way, or yet another comment about Rogan's family wealth? Lucky for Ellie, more often than not Shannon had a way of opening the door for her go-to retort.

"You mean like those wads of dough you snarf down every morning at Krispy Kreme?" She tapped out a "bu-dump-*bump*" on her desktop. "I'm sorry, man. You just make lame cop-eating-doughnut jokes so . . . damn . . . easy."

"When you got it, you flaunt it," he said, patting his

oversized belly. At least the guy had as good a sense of humor about himself as he expected in others. Ellie saw his gaze move to the squad room entrance. "You don't see your man enough at home, Hatcher? He's got to come see you in *our* house? I owe him a follow-up report, so I'm heading for the can till he's out of here."

The *he* in question was Ellie's boyfriend, Max Donovan. She had only just gotten used to the word *boyfriend* to describe a relationship between two level-headed grownups when the nature of that relationship suddenly changed three months ago. Now they lived together. And at this minute, he was—as Shannon noted—coming to *her* house.

Max knew better than to greet her with a kiss, hug, or even a handshake in the squad room. Once he reached her desk, he simply said, "I must not have heard the music."

"Music?" she asked.

"Of whatever ice cream truck had Shannon hauling ass."

Ellie laughed, but Rogan shook his head in mock disappointment. "You two are morphing into the damn Wonder Twins, is what you're doing. You realize that, don't you?"

"The Wonder Twins didn't actually morph into one," she corrected. "They touched each other to activate their individual morphing powers. One could transform into water and its various states; the other changed into animals. *Form of—*" She held up her fist for Rogan's return tap, but all she got was a death stare.

"Don't *make* me join Shannon in the men's room. You don't want to know what that man is capable of in there."

Max feigned a shudder. "So I need to run something past you in my official capacity as a representative of the New York District Attorney's Office's Conviction Integrity Unit."

"Conviction integrity unit" was the preferred prosecutorial language for a specialized unit that reviewed what defense attorneys would call either "innocence cases" or "wrongful convictions." Ellie knew that Max viewed his recent appointment to the unit as a sign that the elected district attorney, Martin Overton, was looking at him as a potential supervisor.

Max took a seat in the worn, wooden guest chair next to their face-to-face desks. "And before you get too worried, it's not a claim from a defendant, and it's not a claim about you. This is about a conviction that was locked and loaded eighteen years ago: a serial killer named Anthony Amaro. Problem is, we got an anonymous letter. The author claims that Amaro is innocent and that the same guy who killed six women twenty years ago is still at it."

He reached into his briefcase and pulled out, not a letter, but an eight-by-ten photograph of a woman's face. He handed it to Rogan, who gave it a quick look and passed it to Ellie. "And supposedly the latest victim is Helen Brunswick."

2

Helen Brunswick is looking up at the camera from beneath a "Life Is Good" baseball cap as she accepts a face lick from a chocolate Lab. Someone who had never seen the photograph before would have placed the woman in her mid-to-late thirties, but Ellie knew she was forty-five. Ellie also knew that the cap had been a Mother's Day gift from the woman's ten-year-old daughter, Jessica. The dog's name was Gus. The photographer had been Jessica's fourteen-year-old brother, Sam.

Any New Yorker who hadn't been in a recent coma had seen that same photograph of the slain psychotherapist. It seemed to be the favorite of the local journalists who had been captivated by the case. Rogan undoubtedly knew the same basic facts that Ellie had gathered from the media coverage, but that didn't stop Max from covering the fundamentals. "Park Slope shrink. Two kids. Recently separated. Six weeks ago, she didn't come home from a counseling appointment in time to meet the ex-husband. No answer on her cell. No pickup at work. The ex finally made the six-block walk from their brownstone to check on her, and found her body in her office. Two shots. Signs of a struggle, but no forced entry."

Like any high-profile case, Helen Brunswick's had brought out the armchair detectives who scoured the Web for information about the victim, her husband, their kids, and all potential enemies. In the process of a divorce, initiated by the husband. Not quite enough money to keep up the standard of living the couple had once shared. Last Ellie had heard, the doctor-husband had been forced to hire security to escort the kids between his Upper East Side apartment and their Brooklyn private school undisturbed.

"Two responses," Rogan said. "One, everyone knows the husband did it. Two, last time I checked, any place six blocks from a Park Slope brownstone can't be in Manhattan South, which means this has nothing to do with us."

Rogan was twisting the cap on his Montblanc pen, always a sign that he was growing impatient with a conversation and didn't care if people noticed. Ellie was about to encourage Max to get to the point, but remembered all the times she'd insisted that he not treat her like a girlfriend at work. She owed it to him to hold up her end of that bargain. If this were any other ADA, she'd give him a few more seconds before piling on.

"I mentioned our Conviction Integrity Unit. Our job is to look at all innocence claims that come in on any case our office prosecuted. Eighteen years ago, this man, Anthony Amaro, pled guilty to the murder of a prostitute named Deborah Garner." He handed them another photograph, this one a mug shot. The displayed date of birth put Amaro at thirty-one years old at the time. He had a round, flat face, and the line of his black, slicked-back hair was already beginning to recede. He appeared to stare straight through the camera. "At the time, it was believed that whoever killed Deborah Garner also killed five other women in upstate New York—all shot, all with ties to the sex trade. Their bodies all carried the same signature, specific enough to connect the cases together: broken limbs. Always after death."

"Sounds like the kind of person who might read about a big case like Brunswick and ask a random buddy to send an anonymous letter claiming a connection," Rogan said. "Oh my goodness, he must be innocent."

"I promise, it's more than that. Usually, in the Conviction Integrity Unit, a cursory glance makes it clear there's no issue. We know everyone in prison claims he's innocent. This one? The lawyers are pretty torn."

It dawned on Ellie that Max would not describe his colleagues as "torn" without considerable deliberation. "When did your office get the letter?"

"One month ago, tomorrow. We've been tight-lipped on it—with everybody."

Moving in together had been a bigger leap for Ellie than for Max. Besides the lingering question of whether marriage and children were in their future, they had the added complication of entangled jobs. She and Max had promised each other to be utterly scrupulous not to blur the lines between the professional and the personal. In her position as a detective, she had yet to encounter a situation where she couldn't talk about her work with her ADA roommate. Apparently, the reverse wasn't true.

"And it's not just the letter that concerns us. As much media attention as the Brunswick murder has gotten, we managed to hold back some details."

"The signature," Ellie said. "Brunswick's limbs were broken?"

Max nodded. "Both arms. And not in a struggle. Postmortem, just like Amaro's victims. When Amaro was prosecuted, it was a fetish unobserved—or at least unrecorded—in any prior homicides. And now we've got the same postmortem injuries inflicted on Helen Brunswick, and we've got someone out there writing letters about information that was never made public. We're going to need follow-up. The only question is: Who's going to do it?"

Ellie was intrigued, but Rogan, apparently, did not need time to mull over a response. "Brunswick's not our case," he said. "Neither was Deborah Garner."

"Not originally," Max acknowledged. "But what we want is a 'fresh-look team.' These innocence claims are—well, they're a little schizophrenic. Obviously, we want to make sure we got it right, but there's this theory that we develop a form of tunnel vision. Psychologically, we want the people who have been arrested, especially the ones who have already been convicted, to be guilty. We *need* them to be guilty, so we can continue to believe that the system doesn't make serious mistakes. A fresh look means bringing in new people, unassociated with the original case, to look for evidence of innocence. A fresh look is supposed to be neutral. I'm the most experienced ADA in the office with no personal connection to the original detectives and prosecutors on the Deborah Garner case, but we need an investigative component, too."

Ellie had never seen Rogan look so annoyed with an ADA, and, unless she was mistaken, his irritation didn't stop with Max. She couldn't blame him for wanting to avoid the assignment. Revisiting Amaro's conviction meant second-guessing the work of the people who put him behind bars.

"Sorry," Rogan said, "but we need to clear cases on the board." His eyes were fixed on the squad's white board. Now that they had Laura Bendel's confession, they could change her husband's name from red to black ink.

Max cleared his throat, and Ellie knew immediately she wasn't going to like whatever came out next. Maybe she had her own form of tunnel vision, because she wanted to believe there was a good reason for Max to pull them into this.

Rogan's gaze moved suddenly from the white board to the far corner of the squad room. Their lieutenant, Robin Tucker, was leaning halfway out her office door. "Why are you two still here?"

"Sorry, Lou," Ellie said. "ADA Donovan was just running something past us."

"No, duh. Who do you think has to approve something like that? And I got a Brooklyn South captain on the phone wondering why his guys haven't heard from you on Helen Brunswick. Increase the words per minute, all right? From what I hear, you've got a lot of work on your hands."

3

Carrie Blank tucked her skirt beneath her crossed legs once again, hoping it wasn't too short for a job interview.

"Ms. Moreland will be with you shortly," the receptionist assured her.

Oh no. Had the shift in her chair registered as a sign of impatience? Carrie didn't want the receptionist to tell Linda Moreland that the potential new hire was pushy. "Oh, no problem at all. I'm happy to wait."

Crap. Had that sounded sarcastic? Or too sycophantic?

She felt dampness building inside her silk blouse. Why was she so nervous? She knew precisely why: because last week her former-professor-turned-famous-criminal-defense-lawyer Linda Moreland had phoned her out of the blue, asking if she had any interest in representing the man who was as near to the boogeyman as Carrie could imagine.

Carrie remembered the first time she heard about a serial killer in their city.

An eighth-grader named Doug Bronson—the kids

called him Dougie-Bro—had been absent for more than a week. Even at Bailey Middle, a week was enough time for school administrators to start asking questions. Pretty soon, Mrs. Jenson was pulling guidance-counselor duty, visiting each class to explain that their fellow student was moving to Baltimore to live with an aunt.

Carrie could see the frustration in Mrs. Jenson's face as she reported, without elaboration, that Dougie had "lost his mother." The school board, she announced, had decided that it would be "inappropriate" for students to repeat any rumors they might hear beyond the fact that Dougie's only parent had died. Instead, students were "encouraged" to report any such "gossip" to the principal's office. Mrs. Jenson didn't bother suppressing a closing eye roll—because, right, students at Bailey were known for reporting their peers to the principal.

Predictably, the announcement Mrs. Jenson had been forced to make immediately led to desperate and frenzied discussion of the *real* story about Dougie's departure. His mother, they soon heard, had been murdered. And not just her. There were other victims, but the police were keeping the case quiet—supposedly so the killer wouldn't know they had made the connection, but more likely, in the eyes of kids from Red View, the Keystone Kops didn't want everyone to see they were a helpless joke.

In an escalating war for the latest updates, it was Monique Davidson who broke the juiciest tidbit. Carrie remembered how Monique, with her giant hoop earrings, ballcap turned backward, had huddled anyone she could gather on the school's front steps. The bell was about to ring, but no one cared. The coy teases of "You won't believe this" and "No wonder Dougie left town," delivered between pops of chewing gum, were too delicious to resist.

Dougie's momma was a ho. The reason the *po-po* didn't care was because the victims were all prostitutes.

Not to be one-upped by Monique, other kids came forward each day with new information, each report more gory and lurid than the last. Dougie didn't even know who his daddy was; his mom had gotten knocked up by a john. Dougie had an uncle in town, but the state wouldn't let Dougie stay with him, because he was the one who was pimping out his own sister.

Then, by the ninth grade, there were rumors about the other victims—three, then five, then six, then ten, then forty. The police thought the perpetrator might be a cop. Or maybe it was a teacher. Some of the victims had their eyes plucked out. Or their stomachs cut open. Or their genitals mutilated. Why hadn't the adults realized what would happen when they instructed children not to talk about a killer in their midst?

Carrie and Melanie had formed a pact to stay together on the walk to and from school, enlisting Bill for additional protection whenever possible. They ducked into storefronts at every sighting of a container van, which struck them as the perfect vehicle for abduction and torture.

The two girls were still virgins, but they also knew they were among a dwindling minority—and Melanie had let first one boyfriend, and then another, get to third base. (In fact, Carrie suspected a few stolen steps past that, though remaining technically short of home plate.) At a time when they were just starting to think about their sexuality, the idea of women being killed for selling it made their bodies seem dangerous. And intriguing.

When Carrie's mother finally overheard the girls whispering after school about the latest link in the gossip chain—a new victim—she decided she needed to intervene. She told them that the victims were *at risk*. They had a *perilous* lifestyle. They weren't *good girls*—like *them*. And because Carrie's mother was Carrie's mother, she could not resist admonishing them to let this be one more reminder of the importance of working hard in school and going to college.

But as much as Rosemary Blank tried to maintain the protective bubble she had inflated around her daughter, Carrie had always known that the realities of their life put her one tiny little pin-pop of a bubble away from the hardships of Red View. The walk between their house and the Burlingame Mall inevitably took her to Sandy Avenue, where sometimes the men slowing on street corners mistook two fourteen-year-old girls for fresh meat on the block. Carrie herself had been to Doug Bronson's house more than once in the sixth grade. His mom hadn't *seemed* like a prostitute. And if rumors could be trusted, Trina Martin—who used to stick up for Carrie when the older middle schoolers made fun of her honor-student ways—had started giving bj's in the high school parking lot for money, defending the practice because it "wasn't really sex."

And then there was Carrie's own sister, Donna. Or "*half* sister," as her mother consistently corrected. (And that was when she was feeling generous. "That girl," "bad seed," and "your father's little accident" were some of the other terms that were known to flow effortlessly from her tongue—and that was in English. Carrie could only imagine the meaning of the Chinese words her mother often mumbled under her breath when Donna was around.) Donna—ten years Carrie's elder and a high school dropout—was another subject her mother tried to wall off from the Blank home. But for the first sixteen years of her life, Carrie had overheard snippets of her parents' fights about her half sister: *drinking*, a friend who was a *bad influence*, a phone call from police, posting bail, *drugs*. These were words Carrie had been raised to fear.

And now she had words about dead women to add to the mix.

As much as Carrie's mother had tried to convince her the killings had nothing to do with them, all Carrie knew was that she was becoming a woman in a place where someone was killing women. Without any real information to make her feel safe, Carrie's imagination—sometimes boundless—filled in the blanks. Then, her senior year of high school, the danger wasn't only in her imagination.

Donna was dead.

Her thoughts were interrupted by the *click-click* sound of four-inch heels on the hardwood floor of the small waiting area. She looked up to see a pair of well-moisturized, muscular legs beneath a skirt three inches shorter than hers. It was her former professor, Linda Moreland. Carrie was surprised that such a busy lawyer would even remember her, but the woman had called Carrie three times in the last week to discuss the possibility of joining her law practice. When Linda initially explained the nature of the case Carrie would be working on, Carrie nearly hung up. But proving how effective a lawyer she was, Linda had not only persuaded Carrie to accept the appointment but had Carrie convinced that the assignment was inevitable.

"So tell me, Carrie: Are you ready to make those SOBs find out who *really* killed your sister?"

She rose from her chair, trying to conceal her nervousness. Was she really considering working for Anthony Amaro's lawyer?

"*Half* sister. But, yes, I'm very glad you called."

4

The newly comprised "fresh look team" rode together from the precinct to the New York County District Attorney's Office at 80 Centre Street—Rogan at the wheel of the fleet car, Ellie riding shotgun, Max in the back, no sound except Rogan flipping radio stations.

As they were heading up the courthouse stairs, Rogan announced that he'd left something in the car. He tapped Ellie's arm before turning back: "Just say what you need to say. I'll be up in five."

As soon as the elevator doors closed, Ellie said what had been on her mind for the last forty-five minutes. "You had to pick me? Of all the detectives in the NYPD? And you didn't even talk to me about it. You went to our lieutenant."

"I honestly thought you would be excited."

Her eyes widened. "Excited? About reinvestigating a case that other cops already closed? About stealing an active investigation from the detectives who've been working Helen Brunswick's murder for weeks? Do you know what kind of position that puts us in?"

"If other detectives aren't doing it right, you should want to fix it."

"Why are you assuming someone did something wrong? That's the risk of this kind of second-guessing. Not to mention that we *live* together."

When the elevator doors opened on the tenth floor, he led the way, in silence, to a conference room, and then shut the door behind them. "I thought about running it past you first, but I know how you feel about special treatment. This is how I would have handled it with anyone else."

"But you didn't dump this on anyone else." She looked around at the boxes covering the conference table. From the notations on the whiteboard, she could tell this had been the Conviction Integrity Unit's workspace for the Amaro case. "You dumped it on us."

"I wouldn't call it dumping, and the choice was completely on the level. You guys have worked a serial case before. You're both new enough that you don't have connections to the original players. And I didn't think you had that 'us versus them' mentality; I thought you'd be willing to work outside the chain of command, reporting to the DA's office. You're both pros, and the whole office knows it."

"A lot of people in the department are pros, Max."

"They don't have your background, Ellie."

"You mean living with an ADA? Working outside the chain of command, as you put it?"

He shook his head and forced a calm smile to his face. "Please don't twist my words around. If you really want to know the truth, I picked you to work on this—*you*, specifically—because I know you're the very best."

"That sounds a lot like special treatment."

"No, it sounds like the truth. I know you, Ellie. I know your background, and I know the empathy you have for victims. You've told me how your best memories of your father were down in that basement, playing jacks and serving as his sounding board for the competing theories."

The father he referred to had been a detective, the basement was in Wichita, and the competing theories had been about a sadist who tortured and murdered women and children.

Max closed the distance between them and rested a hand on her shoulder. "You saw the compassion your father had for those victims. And that compassion—that relentless desire to get to the truth—is part of who you are now. You don't play politics, Ellie, and you don't take shit from anyone. Not even me." This time, his smile came naturally. "So, yeah, you're absolutely right: I picked you for a reason. You're the kind of person I can trust to do the right thing. And so is Rogan."

"But, like you said, your decision was about me. How do I explain that to Rogan?"

"You don't. This isn't about personalities. If Anthony Amaro is innocent, that means someone left a serial killer on the street. And Helen Brunswick might just be the tip of the iceberg. There could be more victims, and Amaro will have spent eighteen years in prison for no reason. This is the most important job I've ever been asked to do as a prosecutor. To do it with anyone other than the two of you? *That* would be showing you special treatment."

They heard a tap on the door. "Hey," Rogan said. "Wasn't sure I had the right room."

They both knew he was testing the waters. Ellie took one more look at Max. He wasn't going to budge.

"This is the place," she said, taking a seat. "Max was about to fill us in on what's in these here boxes."

The six cardboard file boxes formed a line across the rectangular top of the mahogany-veneer table. At the head and foot of the table stood matching white boards on wheels, both covered in an array of neatly printed, multi-colored ink.

"Our team figured we'd leave our work to help get you started."

Rogan had already erased one of the boards by the time Max finished speaking.

"Hey, I get it," Max said. "I can leave if you want."

Rogan pulled the top from one of the boxes and handed it to Max. "No way those stupid color-coded bullet-points were your handiwork. Show us what you've got."

"Six boxes of files: one for each of Amaro's victims. That one"—he pointed to the box in front of Rogan—"is our office's entire file on the murder of Deborah Garner, including all police reports." Ellie could see that the various Redwelds and manila files barely fit inside. "It's also the most complete. Although the other five cases were all closed, Amaro was only charged with, and only pled guilty to, one crime: the murder of Deborah Garner."

"Why just her?" Ellie asked.

"To start with, it was the strongest of the cases and the one that led to Amaro's arrest. Garner was also the last of the six victims. Think about the timing. Eighteen years ago? What was happening with criminal law in New York?"

Rogan made the connection faster than she did. "New York passed the death penalty," he said.

Max pointed at Rogan. "Exactly. Deborah Garner was murdered two weeks after the death penalty went into effect. Pataki campaigned on the issue, and signed the law that Mario Cuomo wouldn't. The courts have put a hold on it since then, but at the time, the fact that New York State was going to start executing people was big news. Deborah Garner was the only victim killed after the law went into effect, meaning it was the only case that was death-eligible. The threat of lethal injection was enough to leverage a guilty plea from Anthony Amaro in exchange for a life sentence, no parole. She was also the only victim in our office's jurisdiction. The others were all found in Amaro's hometown of Utica."

"That's up near Albany, right?" More than a decade

after moving to New York from Wichita, Ellie was like most city residents and had only a vague sense of the state's geography beyond the metropolitan area.

"Closer to Syracuse, but yeah, up there. If I had to guess, there was no point in another county going after Amaro for additional convictions. He was already behind bars forever, and—"

"And they were only prostitutes," Ellie added. They all knew the reality. Last year, she'd worked a case with a Los Angeles homicide detective who told her that either everyone counted or no one did, but in her experience, some people seemed to count a lot more when it came to prioritizing the resources of the criminal justice system. "Any other commonalities?"

"Certainly not in appearance," Max said. "The victims ranged in age from twenty-five to forty-three. Heights from five-one to five-seven. Some were thin, some were heavy. All white, but complexions and hair colors were all over the map. All shot, but all with different guns."

"Meaning he was smart enough to dump the weapon with each kill," she said. "Cheaper to buy replacement guns on the street than risk getting nailed with ballistics evidence."

Max continued his summary. "Same postmortem injuries. There was geography, of course: the five victims killed before Deborah Garner were found in Roscoe Conkling Park. And we're talking about a relatively tight time frame. Six women killed within seven years."

Ellie was realizing the enormity of the task awaiting them. Two presumably competent homicide detectives had been working on the Helen Brunswick case for weeks without an arrest. The other six cases were ancient—the original investigators most likely retired or dead by now—and involved victims at the fringe of society, where witnesses tended to be few and forgetful. "You haven't mentioned DNA," she said.

Max shook his head. "No DNA. At least, not at the time. Is there anything to be found today? We don't know, but we've got NYPD looking at the Garner evidence and the state crime lab analyzing the Utica cases."

"Isn't that a little premature?" Rogan asked.

"It was Martin's call." Martin Overton was the elected district attorney. There were four levels of managers between him and Max. Max's comment about this being the most important case of his career was taking on new meaning.

Rogan still hadn't sat down. Now he stepped away from the table, leaned against the conference room door, and crossed his arms. "Did your boss stop and think about what you're supposed to do if the labs actually find something new?"

"Martin has made it very clear that this needs to be a transparent process. Any exculpatory evidence will get turned over to the defendant."

"He's worrying about his next election," Rogan muttered. "The pendulum has officially swung."

When Ellie first put on a uniform, city residents would regularly flash her a thumbs-up. Crime was down, the streets felt safer, and zero-tolerance policing was all the rage. Now, after years of decreasing crime and increased security, voters had revolted against any elected official who publicly supported the NYPD's stop-and-frisk practices. They kicked out the long-serving Brooklyn DA for failing to protect defendants' rights. And now Martin Overton appeared to be acting more like Anthony Amaro's defense attorney than a prosecutor.

Ellie wanted to hit rewind and tell Max he should know better than to parrot his boss's talking points to them. Instead, she tried to translate Rogan's comment. "Does Martin understand the problem of jumping straight to the DNA?"

Rogan still looked like he was trying to press his body through the closed door and escape unnoticed. "These were working girls, Donovan. The science is so good now that the lab is bound to find something that was undetectable all those years ago. Just because some john leaves behind a drop of saliva, that doesn't exonerate Amaro."

"No, but our office strongly believes that something like that—in combination with this letter—would need to be looked at closely."

"Right, because of a transparent process." Rogan stepped forward, reached into the open cardboard box, and removed a file folder. He flipped it open on the table and stopped on a color photograph of a woman's corpse.

Her face was gray-white and bloated, her pale, dry lips starting to droop. "This woman had a name: Deborah Garner." He kept flipping and landed on an image of Deborah Garner's partially nude body splayed on dirt. All four of her limbs had multiple fractures, leaving them with a wavy appearance. "Eighteen years ago, someone who had your job and someone else who had our job assured someone who cared about this woman that at least her killer would never see another day of freedom. This isn't about transparency or process. This is about whether the kind of man who could do this to a woman—to *six* women—gets a second shot, just because some fishing expedition turns up DNA from a sloughed skin cell overlooked twenty years ago."

Ellie knew Rogan was right, but found herself saying, "We're getting way ahead of ourselves." Barely into the assignment, she was already playing mediator. "Maybe we'll get lucky and the lab will find Amaro's DNA. What about the letter? Did that go to the crime lab?"

"It was the first thing we did. I think we hoped to find something linking it to a sick practical joke. Maybe a leak with the medical examiner to a wannabe comedian. Instead, we're still at a dead end: the envelope was self-sealing, the stamp self-adhesive. No prints. It was post-marked eight days after the Brunswick murder, mailed from Manhattan. That's all we got. Now the reality is setting in, and we're wishing we'd made better use of all this time."

42

"What about the therapist, Helen Brunswick?" she asked. "No physical evidence there, either?"

"You'll need to get all the details from the Brooklyn detectives who've been working the case," Max said. "My understanding is that they have plenty of trace evidence—hairs, fingerprints, skin cells—but with no certainty that any of it necessarily belongs to the killer. They just heard back yesterday that none of the profiles hit in the DNA database."

On television, these things happen in a matter of minutes. Even in a high-profile case, it had taken six weeks for the lab to run DNA through the database.

Rogan finally took a seat next to Ellie. He tapped his neatly trimmed nails on the tabletop. "The fractures alone would never have been enough to connect Helen Brunswick to these old cases," he said. "So it's really about the letter; whoever sent it knew about her injuries. And they wanted to make sure someone made the connection to Anthony Amaro. Brunswick's husband found the body. That means he had eight days to figure out he was the primary suspect and respond accordingly."

"Is the husband still talking," Ellie asked, "or has he lawyered up?"

"Last I heard," Max said, "he was still cooperating. But you should check with the detectives at the 7-8 first. They know you're taking over."

"Great," Rogan said. "I'm sure they'll be thrilled to hear from us."

5

Carrie picked the exact wrong time to leave work.

Had she bolted from the building as soon as she quit, no one would have heard the news, and so no one would have been paying attention as she walked away with nothing but a purse, a briefcase, and maybe one extra bag filled with her most important office possessions. Alternatively, she could have waited out the other attorneys. She'd pulled enough all-nighters to know how quiet the place eventually got—albeit well after midnight, and that gunner Theo Mayers seemed to linger past two on a regular basis.

But, no. Carrie stupidly decided to break the news about her change of employment at seven o'clock. She had picked that time because she could definitely count on catching her mentor, Mark, to tell him personally. But then she wasted two hours in her own office, backing up personal files onto a thumb drive and wadding newspaper around picture frames and her beloved crystal elephant—the one she'd won in a raffle and had kept simply because it was the only thing she'd ever own from Tiffany.

At least when she walked out she should have gone

44

incognito—maybe taking the stairs down to the thirty-second floor (land of the printing department, an obscure collection of state legislative histories that didn't fit in the firm's library, and an unused gym) before hopping onto the elevator. Instead—again, stupidly—she had walked out of Russ Waterston in the largest possible way: just before ten p.m., when most associates leave, while juggling a purse, briefcase, two plastic bags, and a potted philodendron.

By then, everyone had heard the news of her departure, and so everyone watched. People used the term *walk of shame* to describe the seven-a.m. subway ride in last night's seductress outfit, but the ten-p.m. walk of shame at Russ Waterston was far, far worse.

Carrie could see it in their faces as they watched her: HER? Really? *She* is quitting? Seriously? So it was with great relief that her walk of shame had been interrupted by a call from Bill. He was in the city. It was short notice, and it was late, and he totally understood if she didn't have time, but he'd love to meet for a drink.

To Carrie in that moment, it felt like she'd been saved.

The heel of Carrie's pump got stuck in the cobblestone as she exited the taxi at Ninth Avenue and Gansevoort. Normally she would've changed into more practical shoes to meet a friend this late, but she tried to look her best where Bill was concerned.

At thirty-five years old, Carrie still had never been to

45

Europe, but as she navigated a route between the postage-stamp-sized bistro tables at crowded Pastis, she pretended she was in Paris, just off the Saint-Germain-des-Prés. Bill waved to her from a table in the back corner. He rose and greeted her with double kisses. "*Bonsoir*," she said cheerfully.

"One of these days, we're going to make it there," he said.

"You remember." She could feel herself smiling for the first time all day.

"Of course."

She and Bill had always had a special bond. He played big brother to Melanie, too, but he and Carrie used to sneak away by themselves. They would stay up late on the merry-go-round, well after the park was closed, and spin each other slowly as they talked all about the wonderful things life held for them in the future.

They had never been a couple—at least, not since a one-week period of "going steady" in the fifth grade. Over the years, they had flirted on and off, and had even stumbled into bed together more than a few times, but they always agreed that trying to build a romance wasn't worth risking their friendship. She would call him her closest friend, and liked to think he'd say the same. Now, perhaps for the first time in their entire lives, they were both—at the same time—on the verge of changes that could be exactly what they had been waiting for.

Bill was drinking water, as usual. Ignoring the intimidating French wine list, she asked the waiter for a margarita on the rocks, with salt. Tonight she wanted the hard stuff.

She was dying to tell Bill about her new venture, but didn't want to squelch their first in-person celebration of his good news. She couldn't believe it had been more than three months since they'd seen each other. When had they both become so busy?

"But the question is," she posed, "when is the state of New York's lieutenant governor going to have time for a European tour with a lowly little attorney from his childhood?"

"Stop it. The work's far more mundane than you'd want to know." But as he described his passion projects—a training program on community policing, statewide prekindergarten for all, job preparation for parents on welfare—she could tell he was loving every moment of his new position.

Sitting here with Bill, while he was having such a special moment in his career, made her feel better about her own decision to work for Linda Moreland. Things were working out for both of them. When they were kids, their shared fascination with law and politics had bonded them. Melanie had always been smarter than Carrie, and probably Bill, but she never found a focus for her innate academic ability. Bill and Carrie, on the other hand, were the only high school students they knew who watched *Meet the Press*, scoured the op-eds of the *Nation* and the

National Review, and knew more about Bill Clinton than they did about the New Kids on the Block or the Backstreet Boys. Back then, after a couple of wine coolers and too many spins on the merry-go-round, they would sheepishly admit their most wild fantasies—Carrie's to sit on the Supreme Court, Bill's to be the president of the United States.

Compared to where most people got with their dreams, and where the two of them had started in Red View, they'd done pretty well for themselves.

Perhaps because they were each in a unique position to know how much the other appreciated the success they'd managed to achieve, he felt free to share his current frustrations. The head of the state assembly was too stupid to understand basic law that governed the real life of street policing. Public employee unions were too entrenched to understand that the state could not afford to keep up with the rapid increase in retirement benefits. "Plus, I finally sold the condo in Rochester, at a huge loss, and now I find out that the place I bought in Albany might have termites. They need to do a second test. Maybe it's just the porch, but it could be the whole house. Sorry. I think that's what they call First World problems."

"I think I'm having one of those moments myself," she said. She took a gulp of her second margarita and slammed the glass on the table. "I quit Russ Waterston today."

He nearly spit out his water. "Isn't that the job you called your *happy place*?"

That sounded so ridiculous now, but it was with good reason that Carrie had always felt lucky to work at Russ Waterston. For fifty-seven years, the boutique law firm had managed to attract top-ten-percent graduates from the elite five: Yale, Harvard, Stanford, Chicago, Columbia. Carrie had shared a hallway with law review editors in chief, Supreme Court clerks, and Solicitor General externs. It was still hard for her to imagine, but her first job out of law school (when she *finally* graduated) was to join the best legal thinkers and writers in the world for what was arguably the most rarified legal practice imaginable: federal appellate work.

"I know. It's a big deal," she said.

"So . . . what's next?" he asked. "From what I read, people only leave that place if they're about to accept their own judicial appointment. And if that's what's going on here, I'm going to take back all that Podunk state government stuff I just rambled about, because obviously I should be president by now."

"No, it's nothing like that." She was about to tell him everything about Anthony Amaro and his plea for Linda Moreland's involvement, but she really didn't want to make the night about her. "A former law professor of mine has a tiny practice. Postconviction work in criminal cases. More responsibility. More specialization. I'm happy about it."

"Good for you."

She knew she could count on him not to point out, as

her law firm colleagues surely would have, that working for a solo practitioner was not exactly a step up—or even a lateral move—from the job she had left.

"Good for both of us." She clinked her margarita against his water glass. There was a pause in the conversation, and she found herself asking, "Do you ever feel guilty?"

"For being so ridiculously good-looking?" he said. "All the time."

"You know what I mean. Every time I talk to Melanie, it's like I almost want to apologize," she said. "Maybe she's different with you. I always wonder if she resents me. Like we both wonder whether I really earned it."

The three of them were all clumped together in high school, always within a few hundredths of a point in their GPAs. Melanie, Bill, and Carrie, the three star pupils whom any of their teachers would have pegged to make it out of Red View. In the end, Carrie was the one who got the biggest scholarship any of them had ever heard of, and she always suspected it was because of Donna's death.

He shushed her and rubbed her forearm. "That's not fair. Besides, that stupid prize didn't even matter. You and I are where we are today because we were willing to look beyond the only narrow slice of life we knew and deal with the larger world. I'll always be there for Melanie, but let's face it: she never made that leap."

She knew what he meant. At one level, Melanie had to grow up faster than either of them when she'd delivered a baby boy three months after their high school graduation. But in many ways, she was still stuck in that same place.

Carrie, on the other hand, sometimes felt like she and Bill had each lived three lives since then. She arrived at Cornell believing she'd won a golden ticket, only to discover that the other students were way beyond her academically. She was already struggling in her second semester when she got the phone call on March 17. Her father had pulled the refrigeration truck in front of the grocery store, just like normal. Then he stepped out of the cab and walked directly in front of an oncoming SUV. The company was blaming the fatal accident on her father's own negligence, claiming that he was tired and distracted because of a prohibited moonlighting gig he'd taken on the side.

Carrie always suspected, but her mother would never admit, that her father had taken the second job because Carrie had told him about some dormies' upcoming plans for a spring break jaunt to Cancun. She had mentioned it only because she was shocked at the ability of eighteen-year-olds to whisk away on a beach vacation, but it would have been just like her father to do whatever he could to help her fit in with her new peers.

Suddenly, Carrie had to worry not only about her classes, but now about her mother being able to keep up with rent, car insurance, and utilities. She took a waitressing job. She went home more often. Her GPA dropped.

Within a year, she had lost her scholarship. She moved back to Utica with three semesters of mediocre grades under her belt.

She lost the golden ticket. It would take her ten years in total to graduate from college.

Bill was the one who helped her get on her feet and back in the classroom again. He was the one who got her to see: it's a marathon, not a sprint. While Carrie was at Cornell and Melanie was changing diapers, Bill had spent his postgraduation year in rehab, battling a drug dependency he had successfully hidden until then, even from her. He managed to turn the setback into a new beginning, committing himself to helping other kids who were trying to get clean. He followed his father into law enforcement, continuing to speak openly about his past struggles. At his induction as the youngest chief of police in Rochester's history, he talked about the terror and the thrill of holding a crack pipe for the very first time. He brought the audience to tears and was invited to serve on the governor's advisory council on public safety issues. Then last winter, he had been appointed lieutenant governor when a stroke disabled the previous officeholder.

His path may not have been direct, but he was exactly where he wanted to be: serving as a statewide public official. There were already whispers about him running for governor in eight years. "I'm happy for you," Carrie said.

"Then why do you sound so sad?" he asked. "All this talk about Red View and high school?"

She shrugged. "You're right. It's dumb. Just the drama of leaving the firm. I guess it has me feeling melancholy."

Bill was probably her closest friend. So why couldn't she tell him that she had walked away from a perfect job to represent Anthony Amaro?

As they hugged goodbye outside the restaurant, it hit her: it was because she was wondering whether she'd made a terrible mistake.

6

Ellie came home to find Max standing on the sofa, holding a tape measure vertically against the living room wall. She kicked off her pumps, headed straight for the fridge, and grabbed two bottles of Rolling Rock. She patted Max on the calf as she took a seat on the edge of the couch and popped off the bottle caps—one for her, one waiting for him, once he finished whatever the heck he was doing to the wall.

"Does an open beer mean you're not angry anymore?"

She and Rogan had spent the afternoon wrapping up the paperwork on the case against Laura Bendel, with a plan to jump into the fresh-look investigation the next morning. They had also agreed that the assignment was now theirs, regardless of how it came their way, and all they could do was make the best of it.

"I was never angry, Max. I was frustrated. And worried that this case could be a disaster."

"And now?"

"Honestly, I feel the same. But I know you at least believe you chose me for all the right reasons."

"I wish you'd take my word on that."

She took a long pull from her bottle, searching for a change in subject. Max hopped down and scribbled *108"* on a legal pad on the coffee table.

"You're not considering a pet giraffe, are you?" she asked. "Those things live more than twenty years, you know. Major commitment. And think of the food bills. And the smell. Not to mention the weird looks when you walk him on his leash. There goes your anonymity."

"You know, a normal person would simply ask why I was measuring our wall."

"No fun in being normal."

"Then maybe you should be the one with the pet giraffe."

"There would be some benefits. We could sell rides to kids on the street. And imagine if someone broke in and saw Mr. Longneck waiting in the hallway. Or maybe we'd get a girl, so I could tie little pink bows to her horns. I seem to recall that when baby giraffes are born, the mothers kick them over and over again so the little cuties learn to stand up on their own. Probably a parenting lesson in there for us human types."

He leaned behind her to begin measuring the length of the sofa.

"Fine, you win. What's up with the measuring?"

He smiled and gave her a quick kiss. "I'm finally getting around to hanging those photographs." He jotted down another number, picked up the second bottle of beer, and clinked it against hers.

She said, "Oh, right." But her initial blank expression was a giveaway: she had no idea what he was talking about.

"Those pictures from Montauk?" He pointed to three framed photographs leaning against the side of the couch. "We agreed we'd hang them on this wall?"

Now she remembered. They'd taken them together on a weekend beach trip last summer, and Max decided to have three of them printed and framed: the train station, surfers on the waves, and—something else. All she remembered was finding room for them in a closet when they were still in the phase of unpacking boxes. Now that they'd been in the apartment for three months, and she knew precisely where to find her clothes, shoes, and other essentials, she was used to the place as it was. If she lived alone, those photographs would remain in the closet until the next time she moved.

That was one of many differences between Ellie and Max. Before their joint move, he had lived for eight years in the same Nolita apartment. It was on a high floor of a doorman, elevator building. At least by the time Ellie saw the place, it was neatly decorated with coordinated furnishings like the dark-gray sectional sofa she was sitting on, and the modern coffee table with the glass top that was now ringed with two watermarks because she'd forgotten, once again, to use coasters. Max even had lime-green throw pillows that managed to match the decorative vase perched on the cabinet beneath the television.

Max had taste.

Ellie? She had good taste when it came to food and people. She had *a* taste—not sure everyone would say it was *good*—when it came to her clothing. But in terms of decorating, she had no preferences whatsoever. She'd never had the luxury to make choices.

In Kansas, she'd always lived at home. The scholarship awards she'd cobbled together on the Kansas teen pageant circuit had barely covered part-time tuition at Wichita State. Then, when she'd followed her brother, Jess, to New York City, she had been one step above transient, moving from one ratty sublet to the next, waiting tables to cover rent.

Her first year on the NYPD, she had a brief respite from the constant shuffling when she'd accepted her then-boyfriend's invitation to let her sublease expire and stay with him. The boyfriend was an investment banker, and his apartment looked it. But it had been decorated, inch for inch, by a designer hired for the job, so it didn't reflect his taste, let alone Ellie's. Ellie had never even thought of the place as her own. In an entire year, she never got to the point of answering the apartment phone or getting a copy of the mailbox key. It was more like she'd been crashing there a lot. When the boyfriend made it clear that he didn't understand why Ellie insisted on working as a cop when she could be not-working as an investment banker's wife, she knew she had to get out.

It was her brother, Jess, even less stable than she, who

had come to the rescue. One of his three million friends was about to give up a rent-stabilized place in Murray Hill to try to make it in Los Angeles. The tiny, dingy place on East Thirty-eighth Street was nothing fancy, but it was affordable, and hers, and even had a separate bedroom. As for decor, though, she could list the pieces of furniture on one hand: a sofa that had been left behind by Jess's friend, the old leather trunk that doubled as a coffee table, a chair that found its way back to her place after being marked for disposal from the Midtown South Precinct, a dresser from Goodwill, and a mattress set she'd bought new because the one thing she had really missed while she'd been subletting place to place was a bed that was truly hers.

All five pieces of her furniture collection were still on Thirty-eighth Street, where Jess was now the sole occupant. Being in an apartment filled with Max's belongings was perfectly acceptable to her, but Max was constantly looking for ways to make the place *theirs*—hence, the current photograph-hanging project.

She looked at the notes he had jotted down. "You need *math* to hang pictures on the wall?"

Now he was measuring the frames themselves. He took the paper back from her and wrote down more numbers. "You do if you want them to be level. I tried to get the wires even on the frames, but the middle one's a little lower, so that nail needs to be a quarter inch higher than the other two. And to space them evenly over the length

58

of the sofa, we need a gap of two and three-quarters inches between each picture."

"You're giving me flashbacks to eighth grade geometry. I got daily hall passes from Mr. Rundle in exchange for bringing him back a Snickers from the vending machine."

"Admit it: if these pictures were hanging in a line and weren't perfectly even, it would drive you crazy. And then your way of fixing the problem would be to shift the nails around the wall until you were satisfied. If we ever moved the frames, the wall would look as if it had been burrowed by a groundhog."

True, which is why she would have left them in the closet.

As he measured the final photo, she could see that it was one she had taken of the old-fashioned gas pumps outside the Spring General Store in East Hampton. She remembered the smell of fried chicken on the store's front porch. She remembered why Max had insisted on taking a weekend trip to walk the beach at Gerard Point: he wanted her to see the beauty in a place where she had been forced to kill a man shortly after she and Max had met. He had been the one to print out the photographs in black-and-white and have them matted and framed as her "housewarming" present.

Remembering the sweetness of the gesture, she felt the tension of the day begin to slip away. She thought of the promise she'd made herself when she had accepted Max's invitation to live together. This time she wouldn't just be a roommate. She would try to become the kind of woman who might be able to build a life with another person.

She set her nearly empty bottle on the coffee table and picked up a hammer. "Tell me where to make some holes, boss."

But as she steadied a nail at the center of a tiny "x" Max had marked on the wall, she silently wished that he had been this methodical about his plan for the Anthony Amaro investigation.

7

By the time Carrie got home, she was infused with three and a half margaritas. Not a regular drinker, her first instinct was to pass out in bed. But as she kicked off her heels inside the front door, she couldn't ignore the mess piled in the corner: her briefcase, two overstuffed plastic bags, and the philodendron—the leftovers of her surprisingly abrupt goodbye to Russ Waterston.

She felt restless. Wired. Unfocused.

Fortunately, she had her own approach to therapy.

Carrie remembered receiving her first journal, a gift from Mrs. Jenson. Because Mrs. Jenson doubled as a guidance counselor and English teacher, most of the students didn't take her seriously in the classroom. She was good about referring kids to the free lunch program and asking if they were getting enough sleep, but she didn't instill the kind of fear most of the kids at Bailey Middle School needed to persuade them to do their homework—or to show up for class, for that matter.

The first twenty minutes of Mrs. Jenson's class on Mondays were reserved for "journaling," as she called it. Her only rule was that their pens had to keep moving on the page. No thesis sentences or five-paragraph formulas required. Just free-flowing thoughts. If students wanted those thoughts to remain private, they could fold the pages in half within the notebook, and she promised not to read those. Most of the kids treated the enterprise as a joke, filling the pages with fart jokes and hallway gossip, and then dog-earing them to test Mrs. Jenson's word. But for Carrie, those twenty minutes a week were the only peace she ever seemed to find—away from her mother's expectations, the taunts from other kids, her studies. Away from everything.

One Monday, Mrs. Jenson asked Carrie to stay after class. She heard a high pitched "oooooh" from a boy in the back row. Next to him, a girl added, "Good girl's in trouuuu-bull." It didn't take much goodness to be a *good girl* at Bailey Middle.

Mrs. Jenson waited until the room had cleared to relieve Carrie's fears with a reassuring smile. "Everything's fine. I just wanted to give you something." She unlocked her top desk drawer and removed a journal the size of a hardbound library book. Carrie ran her fingertips across the cherry-red, faux-crocodile cover. She gently opened the snap closure to discover the first blank page, marked with a thin black velvet ribbon. She imagined expensive chocolate. "In case you ever want to write when it's not a Monday in class," Mrs. Jenson explained.

The teacher must have seen Carrie's reluctance. "Take it," she said. "Someone did the same for me when I was about your age. My journal didn't just make me a better writer. It probably saved my life."

Now Carrie was thirty-five years old, and "journaling" remained a constant habit. She even bent a page in half on occasion, just to remember how special it felt at fourteen years old to put a secret into undeniable words—to see it in black ink on white paper—without having to share it with anyone else.

She reached into her briefcase, removed the most recent journal, and wrote down everything she hadn't said to Bill:

> It wasn't the fact they were watching me that made me so uncomfortable. It was the fact that I knew how shocked they were that I was leaving—and the reasons for their shock. Anyone perusing the firm's attorney profiles would have spotted me as the one who was luckiest to be there.
>
> The hardest part was telling Mark. How long had it taken me to get used to calling him Mark instead of Mr. Schumaker? When we met, he was an alumnus doing Fordham a favor by serving as a moot court judge my 3L year. The topic was the constitutionality of GPS searches. I felt so awkward, participating in the contest even though I was ten years older than the other students. But he told me

afterward that my brief was one of the best demonstrations of appellate advocacy he had ever seen from a young lawyer. I was shocked when he invited me to interview.

Mark never hid the fact that my personal background had played a part in his decision to go to bat for me. My written work had been good enough to get me through the door. But he told me it was my answer to the question "How have you dealt with any adversity in your life?" that got me the offer.

I nearly made the mistake of declining to answer, never wanting to be anyone's charity case. But then Mark pointed out the backgrounds of the other recent hires: the son of a senator, the niece of the White House chief of staff, nearly everyone from private schools from kindergarten on. There's no such thing as merit separated from biography, he had told me. The only question is whether you're going to let your biography hold you down or help you up.

Tonight, I had to remind him of his words when I broke the news that I was leaving to work for a big-haired, big-mouthed, grand-standing lawyer like Linda Moreland.

He had laughed at first, assuming I was joking. Just the previous week at P.J. Clarke's,

*we had caught a glimpse of Linda screaming at
Nancy Grace on the television. Mark made a
joke about the two of them being the Road
Runner and Wile E. Coyote of the criminal
justice system. He was surprised to learn that
just a few years ago, Linda Moreland had been
the visiting professor in charge of CUNY's
criminal trial advocacy program when I was a
1L there, before I transferred to Fordham.*

*But last week's surprise didn't come close to
matching his shock when I told him that I was
leaving Russ Waterston to work for the woman.*

*It's like you said, I told him. Biography is
part of merit. I know that, objectively, working
for Linda Moreland is a step down from a job
at Russ Waterston. But she has a case that I
just can't walk away from. This is the case that
made me want to be a lawyer. It's like it was
meant to be.*

She felt the warmth of the tequila still in her stomach,
definitely still in her brain. The words were flowing,
straight from her mind to her fingers to her pen.

*I have always believed that Donna was differ-
ent. "She was exactly like those other girls,"
my mother used to say. Even my father, when
he was still alive, told me that there were things*

about Donna that he wished weren't true—things that put her in danger.

But I'm not a child anymore. I know the difference between wishful thinking and instincts rooted in fact. Not only was Donna different as a person; her case wasn't like those other victims'.

I have spent my whole life trying to do what was expected of me, never taking risks. I panicked tonight at dinner because I was scared I had made the wrong decision, but big decisions require risk, and this was a decision I made from instincts—instincts that I have never really learned to trust. But from Utica to Cornell, back to Utica, to Cortland State, to CUNY and Professor Moreland, to Fordham and Mark Schumaker and Russ Waterston: It was all leading me to this job.

I will finally find out what happened to my sister. I will find out who killed Donna.

Carrie closed her journal and tucked it into her briefcase. She did not know it yet, but for the first time since she received a red, faux-crocodile notebook from her seventh-grade English teacher, her journal pages would no longer remain private.

8

Helen Brunswick had been murdered in Park Slope, considered by some to be the paradise of New York City. Its name deriving from sprawling Prospect Park, the neighborhood drew to Brooklyn upper-middle-class families who might previously have opted for Manhattan's Upper West Side.

The 78th Precinct that serviced Park Slope was on Sixth Avenue, just off of Flatbush, a couple blocks south of Atlantic. This was considered Prospect Heights, not Park Slope. There was a time, just a few years ago, when that geographic third of a mile represented a far larger cultural gap. When Ellie thought of Park Slope, she immediately conjured a stereotype of well-to-do mommies pushing strollers between natural-food co-ops, book clubs, and baby-and-me yoga classes. Prospect Heights, by contrast, was known for an eclectic mix of ages, incomes, and races. But now, thanks to an influx of big money from the Barclays Center and Atlantic Yards development project, younger, richer, whiter people were pouring into the area.

Even the precinct house looked the part. A nice, neat, five-story cube of stone and brick, the building seemed more like a public library or historic boutique hotel than a police precinct.

Ellie paused as she reached for the front door's handle. "We're sure we don't have a friend who can help smooth over the introduction?"

"Sorry."

They'd been on the receiving end of what was about to happen. Feds took over a local angle. Once it had been the state police. The worst was when cases were reassigned to another team based on nothing more than budgetary considerations. Whatever the reason, they both knew what it was like to be pulled from a case. And they both knew it was hard not to blame whoever was taking over, no matter what the circumstances. But here they were, about to take away a high-profile case because some obscure unit in the district attorney's office had said so.

They told the civilian aide at the front desk they were there to see Detective Tommy Santos. Ellie had asked around about him before heading out to Brooklyn. He was a fifteen-year veteran. Supposedly hardworking, the older of the two partners. The smarter, as well. Straight arrow. Married. Kids. Church. He had promised to be available to meet with them.

Before the assistant was out of his chair to show them the way, they heard a loud voice from the squad room. "I got 'em, Roxie. They're getting the luxury treatment. I got a room booked and everything. Champagne on the nightstand."

So that's how this was going to go.

But when Santos greeted them, he seemed utterly sincere. "You two here to steal the front page from us, huh?" Once again, it was the kind of sentence that could easily be construed as snide, but the visual cues told a different story. Santos approached them with outstretched arms, then offered each of them a vigorous handshake. Even his eyes smiled. If not for the bumps in a nose that Ellie guessed had been broken at least twice, she wouldn't have imagined a confrontational side to the man.

The reserved room turned out to be an interrogation room down the hall. No champagne in sight.

"Sorry Mike couldn't make it." Michael Hayes was Santos's partner. "He's interviewing a witness in federal custody down at MDC, but I can tell you everything you need to get started." Ellie had spent more than enough time dealing with the bureaucracy of the Metropolitan Detention Center to understand why they weren't waiting for Hayes.

"We appreciate the cooperation," Rogan offered. "We all know how it feels to have a case reassigned midstream."

"No kidding, midstream. Like pissing into a urinal and realizing it's the queen's china. Got to cut it off quick, you know. Sorry, no offense."

"None taken," Ellie said.

"This won't even take long. A lot of cases, what you read in the paper isn't even close to what we're actually working. This one? Media's got a lot of the story right. Helen was exactly what she seemed: respected therapist, good mom, no problems until the divorce. Not like what usually lies behind the front page, you know?"

They did know. Crime reporters loved to spin tales of good versus evil: innocent people minding their own business until they ended up in the wrong place at the wrong time. The more tawdry papers used words like *fiend*, *lowlife*, and *scoundrel* for the perpetrators; *honor student*, *devoted husband*, and *beloved mother* for the victims. But more often than not, the truth behind those cases was more complex. Honor students could be bullies. The apparently devoted husband could be frequenting prostitutes on the side. And sometimes beloved mothers sold drugs to other beloved mothers at the health club to help cover private tuition. Wrong place, wrong time, but more complicated than the fairy tales would suggest.

Santos was saying that there was no evidence that Helen Brunswick had been living a secret, more dangerous life.

"I gotta admit," he said, "even I kind of lost it when we saw the kids at the house. You guys—you look young, but you know how you get used to it. So imagine an old guy like me. We see the two kids crying with their dad when he gives them the news. And then we check out the apartment and it's all done up. Decorated. It was supposed to be a real family night."

"Watching the Academy Awards?" Ellie had read that detail somewhere.

"Yeah. I guess the parents always made a big deal out of things that they could all enjoy together at home. Any kind of *event*—Super Bowl Sunday, election night, the Grammys, Golden Globes. They'd dress up and decorate. Cast ballots or make little bets. You should have seen the lengths these kids had gone to." Ellie could tell he was reliving the moment in the Brunswicks' townhouse. "It was a Sunday, and the dad—Mitch Brunswick, he's an endocrinologist—I guess they're for diabetes and what-not. He was scheduled to bring the kids back to the mom that night for a custody swap. But an evening drop-off wouldn't leave time to set up for the award show. So Mitch brings the kids to Brooklyn early, right when Helen heads to the office for her weekend appointments, and the three of them all work on the preparations together— even though Mitch isn't staying. Those poor kids, man. They were devastated."

"When was Helen supposed to be back?" Rogan asked.

"Her last appointment was at four o'clock. An hour appointment is actually only fifty minutes in therapist time, plus a few minutes to wrap up, plus the walk home, so she had told the kids five-thirty at the absolute latest. The kids even made a signature drink, no booze. Anyway, at five forty-five, Mitch starts calling Helen's cell phone." Santos acted out a phone with his fingers against his ear. "The kids start worrying when red-carpet time starts

71

without Mom, but as the hour hand moves, Mitch admits he started getting angry, thinking she was doing this to blame him for her having to work extra hours on the weekend. By the time the opening monologue starts without her, he's fed up. He leaves the kids alone and walks up to her office. Gets no answer on the outside buzzer. Has to stand around on the street until a screenwriter who uses the top floor as a writing space shows up with a key. Screenwriter tells him to fuck off—he's not letting anyone into the building—until Mitch pulls out his ID. Shows him that his last name matches the plate on the building for Dr. Helen Brunswick. Tells the guy he's free to call the police if he's worried it's not legit. They walk into the office together and find her body on the floor. Two bullets in the chest."

Ellie hadn't realized from the news coverage that another person was there when Mitch Brunswick had discovered the body.

"You're absolutely sure he was with the kids the whole time before he connected with the screenwriter at the building?" Ellie asked.

"Absolutely. One of the first things we checked. The kids backed him up, plus he was sending e-mails from his iPad while he was at the house. He used the wireless network there to send them. It was only fifteen minutes later that he showed up begging to be let into his wife's office."

"When did you realize the victim's arms had been broken?" Rogan asked.

"You could tell there was something wrong just by looking at her, like she was a doll whose arms had been removed and placed on backwards."

"So Mitch Brunswick would have been able to draw the same conclusion when he found the body." Rogan's thought came out like a statement, not a question. If they could prove Brunswick was the one who wrote the anonymous letter to the district attorney's office, they might be able to wrap this assignment up quickly.

"Obvious. Like, two-plus-two-equals-four obvious," Santos said. "But we assumed it was something that happened in a struggle. Or you start wondering if she'd been tortured. Then the autopsy results came in."

"You held back the fact of the postmortem fractures from the public," Ellie said. "But what about the husband? Did he know that detail?"

"We didn't tell him, that's for sure. And there would be no way of knowing from looking at the body. When someone's heart is beating, blood forms around the bone break. But if the injuries are inflicted postmortem, they call it 'effectively bloodless,' because there's so little blood. No, it takes the autopsy to know that. Unless, of course, he was the one who did it."

"But you've got his timeline locked down," Rogan said. "You think he hired someone for the job?"

"Wouldn't be the first husband to go that route. And maybe, for good measure, he had them replicate the MO of an old serial killer case from upstate New York."

"Sounds a little far-fetched," Ellie said.

Santos gave a look to Rogan, like, *How do you put up with her?* It suddenly dawned on her that, just as they had asked about his reputation, he may have done the same with them, in which case he could have heard about her relationship with Max.

"And the alternative isn't?" he asked. "A serial killer got away with six murders eighteen years ago and suddenly decided not only to reappear, but to let the DA's office know about it with a letter? No way, José. Not to mention that theory only works if Anthony Amaro is innocent. The man confessed, and to no less a cop than Buck Majors."

"Who's Buck Majors?" Ellie asked.

Another look at Rogan, but his face was blank too. "Boy, they weren't kidding about a fresh look, were they? When it came to closing cases, Buck was the man. The department used to have him dole out lessons on how to remain in control of the box. A master interrogator. A legend. He could get a guy to confess, and then thank him for the privilege. If Majors said Amaro was guilty, he's guilty. Hate to break it to you, but the DA's putting you through the wringer, all because of some ridiculous letter. He doesn't want the liberal elites who have taken over this city to accuse him of ignoring *exculpatory evidence.*" He spoke the term like it was an obscenity.

"Trust me on this: stick with the husband. He's playing like he's full of regret about the breakup, but he's got a girlfriend. Even popped the question, but when she got a look at his finances, spread thin between two houses and paying alimony, she got cold feet. Man wants to put a ring on it." He held up his left hand. "No more Helen means only one roof to pay for. We've just been waiting for a break."

"And now we come along and take it from you," Rogan said. "I think if I were you, I'd be a lot more upset about that."

The same smile that had greeted them returned as Santos reached into his suit jacket and retrieved a folded page from his pocket. "Opened this right before you called. Check out the letterhead."

The Law Offices of Linda Moreland, Esq.

It was a notice of representation, alerting both the NYPD and the New York County District Attorney's Office that Linda Moreland was now the attorney of record for Anthony Amaro. Attached to the letter were copies of a motion to vacate Amaro's conviction and a demand to review the entire investigative file and all prosecution records to search for evidence exculpating her client. A separate demand requested access to all records documenting any confessions elicited by NYPD detective Buck Majors. The letter was signed by *Caroline Blank, Associate*.

Ellie had never heard of Caroline Blank, but she was

definitely familiar with Linda Moreland. She'd made a national name for herself in a short time span by taking on claims of innocence by defendants who had already been convicted.

"The woman believes every inmate is innocent and every cop's a criminal." Santos refolded the letter neatly and tucked it into Rogan's front jacket pocket. "Have fun with that 'fresh look' investigation. Before you know it, you might be famous."

9

Carrie Blank pondered the documents spread across the table in front of her. When she'd arrived this morning at the Law Offices of Linda Moreland, LLC, she had found them thrown together in a cardboard box, pages facing in eight different directions, some folded in half or thirds, some paper-clipped or stapled together for no obvious reason. After two hours, she had arranged them in reverse chronological order.

The most recent was the letter Linda Moreland had received ten days earlier from "the client" (would she ever get used to thinking of Anthony Amaro as *the client*?):

> *Dear Ms. Moreland,*
>
> *I just saw you on television from Five Points Correctional Facility talking about the case of Jerrod Carter, who is also currently inprisoned here. When you said the name of the "DETECTIVE" who supposedly got him to confess—Buck Majors—I nearly cleaned out my ears to make sure I heard you right.*
>
> *I have now conversed with Jerrod Carter about his case. Most importantly, we have*

compared notes about Buck Majors and our so-called confessions. I have come to believe that your work for Jerrod Carter was meant to bring you to me, or visa-versa. Please hear me out, because I promise you will be interested.

A couple weeks ago, I recieved a letter claiming that a female doctor was killed in Brooklyn, alledgley by the same way I was alledgd to kill my alledgd victims. I can't send you the exact letter since its all the proof I have, but here's the important part: "Helen Brunswick, murdered in Park Slope. The newspapers aren't saying, but both her arms were broken AFTER she was killed, just like with the ladies you supposedly murdered. Now what are the odds of that, and how come the NYPD doesn't want you to know?"

Please. I have had this letter all these days with no idea what to do until I saw you on TV and ~~talked~~ conversed with Jerrod Carter about Buck Majors, who lied about Carter's confession—and mine. And on top of that, I was nailed for killing six people (TO BE CLEAR: I KILLED NO ONE!!!) based only on my one so-called confession from this "detective."

The confession was BOGUS from the start. Take a look. You will see. Look at the words Buck Majors used when he was supposed to

*be quoting my so-called confession, and then
compare those words to the so-called confession he got from Jerrod. You mean him and
I—two guys that never met each other until we
were in the joint, who got arrested three whole
years apart—we just happened to use the
SAME EXACT WORDS???* **No way!**

*Please help me. A real killer is out there, and
it's not me. And while he's been out there all
these years, I have been in here, and I missed*

*- Seeing my mother when she was dying and
asking for me*

- Her funeral

- My sister getting married

*- My neice and nephew (twins) being born,
learning to talk, starting school. They do not
even know they have an uncle because they
would not understand*

*-Everything else I might of done as a young
man to make myself better and stay out of jail
and be a regular person*

*I know I made mistakes. I was no angel,
and I admit (and told Buck Majors) I hired
prostitutes sometimes. But I did not kill any-
body. Please believe me. Look at the words of
the confessions. There is no way. My original
attorney, Mr. McConnell, was a good man, but
he was more worried about saving me from*

the needle than proving my innocence. I didn't know then that I'd be better off dead than pullng LWOP for crimes I did not do. There's a reason they call it "all day and a night."

I look forward to your response.

Sincerely,

Anthony Amaro

Amaro had included a hodgepodge of attachments with his letter, random pages of miscellaneous documents he had collected over the years. Carrie's first task this morning had been to file a motion to vacate Amaro's conviction. They knew they didn't have sufficient evidence yet to exonerate Amaro, but accompanying the motion was a request for a *subpoena duces tecum* to the Utica and New York City police departments for all documents associated with Anthony Amaro's case.

She had also reached out to Harry McConnell, Amaro's original defense attorney on the Deborah Garner case, and learned that he was retired from practice. She left a message for the daughter who now ran the office, hoping she might be able to fill in some of the blanks. Now Carrie was creating a more specific list of requests to file with the police. While Linda's many years as a courtroom defense lawyer made her great in front of a jury, big-firm practice had made Carrie very, very good at looking at pieces of paper and figuring out which other pieces of paper were likely missing.

She was pulled into the present by three quick raps at the door, followed by the appearance of Thomas's cheerful face. "You sure you have everything you need in here?"

In here was a squat better suited as a janitorial closet than a lawyer's office. Thomas's eyes darted around Carrie's makeshift workspace in curiosity.

Yesterday, she had thought of Thomas as simply the receptionist, but now Carrie realized that, until today, he had been the only full-time worker at the Law Offices of Linda Moreland, LLC, other than Linda herself. From what Carrie could tell, Thomas was Linda's secretary, scheduler, and personal barista. When Linda had introduced them yesterday, Thomas beamed as Linda recounted a story of him producing a backup tube of her go-to shade of lipstick when she couldn't locate hers before a recent CNN interview.

Linda Moreland had been a true one-lawyer shop, but now she had so much work she needed a second lawyer — enter Carrie. When she offered Carrie the position yesterday, she had also offered to let her delay the start-time until she secured "proper working space." Carrie had been the one to decide she wanted to start right away, and now Thomas had added *Take care of Carrie as she worked out of a storage closet* to his list of responsibilities.

"Thank you so much, Thomas. Really, I'm fine."

"She's got me calling the building manager to nudge

him about the space down the hall she's expanding into. Obviously it's more urgent now that you're here."

At Russ Waterston, lawyers billed their time in six-minute increments, so there wasn't a lot of in-office small talk. "Well, thanks for doing that. But I don't mind this."

He didn't close the door, though. "I never thought she'd hire a full-time lawyer. She has a bunch of investigators she likes to work with. And she's used contract attorneys when she's busy; and she likes to employ interns. I think it reminds her of teaching. But I guess something happened with the Jerrod Carter case that led to all this new work?"

"Something like that."

"Because I know she thinks that case is a big one, with a big payout. Like, that's why we—well, *she* was going to be able to take more square footage in the building. I mean, he's been in prison for fifteen years, and now there's new DNA pointing to someone else. The problem is, Carter confessed. Or at least, he supposedly did. So Linda's been digging into the detective's history. Turns out he was extremely successful getting murder suspects to confess. He was considered one of the very best by the NYPD. Linda thought maybe he was a little *too* good. Buck Majors. That's his name. Except the cops all called him Dime. Know why?"

Carrie did know, because Linda had explained the connection between Jerrod Carter and Anthony Amaro to her before Carrie had even agreed to yesterday's job interview. But she could see that Thomas was eager to tell her. She raised her eyebrows.

"They joked that he should be named Dime instead of Buck—like you couldn't be questioned by him without doing a 'dime' in prison. That means ten years. So Linda had already been digging around about the detective, wondering if he'd earned his big reputation by lying or beating it out of them or something."

So far, everything Thomas had said could be gleaned from information Linda had discussed during talking-head gigs about the Jerrod Carter case. She noticed Thomas's eyes darting not so subtly around her table full of documents.

"Anyway, that's all I know. But, I'm not a lawyer or anything, so—I'll leave you to be."

Carrie had seen how Linda treated Thomas the day before. She was friendly and full of praise, but when it came time to talk about the job and Carrie's responsibil-ities, she had closed her office door, even though Thomas was the only other person around. She was so focused on her own priorities that she had never noticed the obvious: Thomas wanted to feel like a real member of the team.

Thomas beamed when Carrie spoke up before he closed the door. "The reason she needed another lawyer is because there's a pattern. It turns out that, in case after case, Majors claimed that the defendants confessed with phrases like 'You got it right' or 'That's how it happened' or 'I didn't mean to do it.' Linda's still trying to find more police reports and trial transcripts, but she says that at least one of those phrases appears in about two-thirds of the detective's confessions. And it was actually Jerrod Carter and another inmate who initially spotted the similarities between their two confessions to Major. Or, rather, their *supposed* confessions. So now she's also representing the other inmate. His name is Anthony Amaro."

She showed him the letter Amaro sent to Linda, seeking her help.

"All day and a night," he said. "You know what that means, don't you?"

"I do." She hadn't until she'd looked it up online. A life sentence was "all day." "All day and a night" meant a life sentence without parole. "I'm focusing specifically on the Amaro case, while Linda continues to track down other questionable confessions obtained by Majors. She's finding more potential clients every day who are going to challenge their convictions."

"Wow. That's amazing. Because Linda has built this huge platform, and is, basically, famous. But, you know" — he looked down the hallway, just to make sure no one was around— "we're small," he whispered. "And, like, I was wondering how she was going to pay for that space. And, well, for you." He laughed nervously.

Ah, and for him. He'd been wondering whether Carrie was here not as an addition but as a replacement, as the only other body Linda Moreland could afford.

"Not to worry," Carrie said. "From what I've been

84

reading, Buck's new nickname should be 'Multimillion Bucks,' as in, the millions of dollars he's going to cost the government for trusting him."

They heard the front office door open, and, just like that, Thomas was back at his post.

A few minutes later, there was another tap on the door. Linda pulled a step stool from against the wall and used it as a chair. "Sorry about the ghetto digs. More importantly, sorry to make you get started on your own. That stuff at Cardozo took longer than I expected."

She had already explained that she was giving a lunch-time lecture at Cardozo Law School, followed by a meeting with the director of their wrongful-conviction clinic. She had been hoping to peel off some of their students to work for her in exchange for school credit.

"Any luck?"

"Nah. They want a level of supervision we can't provide. I need working bodies, ready to go."

"Well, I've been chipping away." She told her about the *subpoena duces tecum* she had filed.

"Sounds like good work. But I'll warn you, this isn't like the civil cases you're used to. You can't just ask and expect to receive. They'll claim confidentiality of police personnel records, protection of witness and informant identities, ongoing investigations, every piece of bullshit. Sometimes you've got to find another way. I've got a contact in the crime lab. He tells me the police got a letter

85

similar to the one Amaro received at the prison, but have they said one word? Of course not."

"They're just ignoring it?"

"Not entirely. They're having the labs take another look for DNA evidence. They're probably hoping to find fresh evidence against Amaro so they can bury the letter without anyone being the wiser, but my contact will tell me one way or the other."

"How do you have a source there?" Carrie realized how naïve she must sound to someone with Linda's experience.

"Because I show him more respect than the prosecutors do. The ADAs treat the science types like puppets, expecting them to regurgitate whatever rehearsed testimony might impress a jury. But I've learned that if you treat them like professionals, they'll be fair on cross-examination. They'll acknowledge the limits of their evidence. I've spent years cultivating relationships. The last thing these people want is to contribute to a wrongful conviction. They won't tell me everything, but they'll tell me when something doesn't smell right."

Carrie noticed that Linda's voice was calmer—less shrill—than during her television appearances. "Has anyone ever told you that you seem so different in person?"

Linda's laugh was deep and warm. "Oh, all the time. And thank God for that. 'Linda' on TV is a persona. In this job, you've got to be a fighter. Cops and DAs have the built-in superhero thing. There are eight different flavors of *Law and Order* on constant cable replay, depicting them as the good guys. I do what I need to do to help our clients. I try to channel every person's inner rebel, that small part of us willing to recognize the terrifying truth that sometimes cops and DAs get it wrong—and, even worse, sometimes they really don't give a damn."

10

You ready to talk?" Ellie asked. According to her watch, they'd been in the car for five minutes. They had already hit the Manhattan Bridge, and her partner's only words had been "Not yet," muttered when she started venting about Linda Moreland. Since then, he'd been surfing the radio. He'd been briefly satisfied by the tail end of Stevie Wonder's "Isn't She Lovely," but once the song ended, he'd gone back to channel flipping.

"Stupid department-issue p.o.s. Impala. Should've taken my ride. Terrestrial radio is tired."

At least he was using his words now. Ellie was ready to press him for answers. "So, I assume the paucity of decent music on FM isn't what's actually eating at you. Is this about Santos? I thought he handled the case reassignment pretty well under the circumstances."

Rogan didn't respond.

"Or the stuff he said about Buck Majors?" she asked. "We knew we'd have to double-check the Amaro investigation. If anything, the fact that Majors had a solid reputation makes it more likely Amaro's guilty, which seems like good news to me."

Still nothing.

"Look, I talked to Max about this whole 'fresh look' thing. He wants to believe he picked us because we'd do the best job, but I don't blame you for feeling like it's my fault."

He shook his head. "It's not that. Though, don't get me wrong, there is a *that*. But *this* is about Linda Moreland."

"Oh, she's the worst. I see her enormous head on TV and I want to throw it out the window. The television. Her head, too, if that were possible."

He turned off the radio but didn't say anything.

"And that *voice*," Ellie added. "It's like getting stabbed in the ear with a metal skewer. I don't understand why cable channels give her a platform. How is she possibly—"

Rogan cut her off. "They give her a platform because she feeds a certain part of the population their red meat. It's no different from what politicians on both sides do. Hell, Nancy Grace and Jeanine Pirro have gotten rich and famous railing against criminals. Linda Moreland has simply turned the tables and is railing against us."

"Yeah, but we're the good guys." She blinked her eyes and flashed a smile, but Rogan wasn't in a joking mood.

"Her audience would disagree," he said.

As far as Ellie was concerned, Linda Moreland's representation of Amaro was just one more log on the fire—a loud, annoying, camera-hogging log, but a minor irritation in the big picture.

Rogan, on the other hand, seemed more than inconvenienced.

Her attempt at humor having failed, she tried another tack. "In the end, Rogan, she's just another lawyer. And I hate to say it, but she's getting results. She's made a name for herself by proving that sometimes the system gets it wrong. No one should want to keep an innocent person behind bars."

"Did you hear me say I wanted innocent people in prison?"

"No, of course not. It's—"

"My problem with Moreland is she's not just about correcting mistakes. I get it—every once in a while, an eyewitness gets it wrong, or the forensic evidence is flawed. But that's not how Moreland operates. She's not just out to free her clients, because they can't afford to pay her. It's not enough for her to prove someone made a mistake. The only way she gets bank is by pressing claims of misconduct. In the only story she knows, her clients are perfect little angels, victimized by cops and prosecutors who don't give a rip whether they have the right guy or not. I *know* you can't be cool with that."

"Whoa, I wasn't *cool* with her. I was saying that dealing with her is no different from dealing with any other defense lawyer. Every time we get a confession, we know some lawyer's going to accuse us of coercion. Every time we do a consent search, there's the inevitable claim that we're 'testilying.'"

"I'm telling you, Moreland's different. There's no line she won't cross. She'll watch your house. Check your finances. She will get up in your shit. With her it's personal."

Then Ellie realized this was personal for Rogan, too.

"You're speaking from experience, aren't you?"

He paused, then nodded. "She was basically behind that whole IA mess."

Not long after becoming her partner, Rogan had made a vague reference to a time when he had to cooperate with Internal Affairs against a previous partner who was dirty. This was the first time she could recall him mentioning it since.

"The bad guy was a captain with the Ballers," he explained. "Went by the name of Snowball, supposedly because of a white birthmark on his face, but mostly because he was the head of a major cocaine crew. He ordered a hit on the boss of the Grant Avenue Gunners, a rival crew that was encroaching on his territory. The vic also happened to be the son of a one-season, benchwarming halfback for the '82 Washington Redskins. His father's Super Bowl ring was his proudest possession. I was the lucky detective who found that ring inside a Gucci loafer at the back of Snowball's closet. At trial, the banger who pulled the trigger testified that I coerced him into naming Snowball as the man in charge and must have planted the ring. He also said I told him that I worked for the Gunners and would kill him and his entire family if he didn't take down Snowball."

"Sounds like something out of a bad television show," Ellie said. "No one would believe that."

"Except his lawyer—a younger, less famous Linda Moreland—went looking for corroboration. She had an investigator take pictures of my car and house. She had financial records showing—how did she put it? *Assets inconsistent with my NYPD salary.*"

Ellie remembered how Rogan had quashed her early curiosity about his Cavalli suits and Patek Philippe watch. "When a brother's got some extra spending money, he must be up to no good. Is that about right?" It was only after the entire squad room watched her try to pull her foot from her mouth that he explained the true source of his outside income—an inheritance from the grandmother who had married a well-known R&B singer.

"Up until then I was still sort of trying to keep my money situation to myself, coming to work in cheap suits trying to blend in."

"You in a cheap suit? Did you compensate by sleeping in silk pajamas?"

He smiled, but quickly became serious again. "Once my finances were out at trial, IA had to get in on the action—looking me over, as well as my partner. Turns out I had an explanation for my extra cash, but he didn't."

She knew the story from here: Internal Affairs assumed Rogan had known about his partner's corruption, and he had no choice but to cooperate. To a lot of cops, anyone who worked with IA could never be true blue.

"I'm sorry, Rogan."

"IA was bad enough, but having to testify in court in front of some lowlife gangbanger about my mom and my grandmama and my life? I can honestly say that I hate Linda Moreland."

She had already felt guilty about getting Rogan dragged into the whole "fresh look" thing. Now he was so upset about Linda Moreland, he had just missed the turnoff from the FDR Drive for their precinct.

"We're just getting started on this," she said softly. "It's not too late. I could put it all on me—because of living with Max and everything. Just say the word: Do you want out?"

"Oh, *hell* no. But let's just say I won't cry when we prove that Anthony Amaro is as guilty as he looked eighteen years ago."

"That means explaining who wrote that letter to Moreland and the DA's office, which means finding Brunswick's killer."

Rogan hit the wigwag lights on the car dash and increased their speed. "That's why we're going to the Upper East Side. Let's track down Mitch Brunswick and see if we share Tommy Santos's not-so-warm-and-fuzzies about the grieving ex-husband."

11

Carrie's list of documents to request was seven pages long by the time her cell phone buzzed against the table. It was Melanie.

"Hey, Melanie."

"Are you all right?"

No "Hello." No "Hey, it's Melanie." Just: "Are you all right?"

"I'm fine. Why?"

"I sent you an e-mail this morning. It bounced back —"

"About what?"

"What do you mean?"

"The e-mail. What was it about?"

"Oh, it was — it's this dog. On a couch. He jumps up there but the owner has it booby-trapped." Carrie remembered how much Melanie had wanted to be a pediatrician. Now she seemed to spend her days forwarding YouTube videos. "You've got to see it. Trust me, it's hilarious. Anyway, I sent it to you, and then it bounced back with an automated message saying to contact the firm for details. Then I called your office and your secretary picked up and said you weren't working there anymore. Is everything all right?"

That was the world Melanie knew, because it was the world they had grown up in. If you had a job and then you didn't have that job, then something must have gone terribly wrong. People lost jobs; jobs didn't lose people.

"Everything's good," she assured Melanie. "Believe it or not, something pretty amazing came along. I'll give you all the details when I have more time."

"You're not glossing it over, are you? You can tell me if you got fired. I mean, I just talked to you last weekend, and now you're out of there? No notice or anything?"

"It's not like that with law firms." Russ Waterston was not the kind of place that wanted lawyers to stick around once they announced they were leaving. Short-timers had no motivation to work and every motivation to poach clients. "I swear, everything is really good. I'm working for a lawyer named Linda Moreland. She does postconviction criminal—"

"*The* Linda Moreland? Oh my GOD!"

Carrie had to hold her cell away from her ear.

"I see her on *Headline News* and TruTV all the time. How did *that* happen?"

"She was the one who called me. She was running a criminal advocacy program at CUNY when I was there. I transferred to Fordham, but she remembered me from the essay I wrote for the program."

"You mean Linda Moreland just called you out of the blue and offered you a job because she remembered you

95

from an essay you wrote years ago? You must have made one hell of an impression."

"The essay was supposed to explain why we were interested in criminal law. I wrote about growing up in Utica. How afraid we were—you know, like a boogey-man out there might grab us at random. And then it wasn't random. He got Donna."

"It still seems weird that a story about being a kid from Utica who lost a half sister she barely knew would be enough to get you a job." Coming from anyone else, the comment might have sounded cruel, but Carrie and Melanie had been glued at the hip since first grade. They had fallen out of touch during Carrie's time at Cornell, and then Carrie was so ashamed for allowing that gap to form that the distance continued to grow further, even after Carrie moved home. But within a few months, Melanie heard from Bill about how hard Carrie was working to help her mother. And Carrie heard from Bill that Melanie had kicked Tim out of the house after yet another arrest and was taking care of their toddler alone. They found their way back to each other and made it through the rough spots. Carrie had gone back to school. Melanie had taken Tim back yet again. Their lives were on different tracks now, but would always be entangled. At this point, she thought of Melanie as a sister.

She had wanted to talk to Melanie about the Amaro case in person, but saw no way to avoid the subject now. "Well, it makes sense, considering the nature of the job.

She's gotten to the point that she has too many clients to handle alone. One of the other defendants is Anthony Amaro."

"Anthony Amaro? You have to be kidding me." Carrie had to hold the phone away from her ear again. This time, though, Melanie's excitement was more outrage than enthusiasm. "You had a good job, making good money. And now you're working on something like *that*?"

"Work *like that*? You sound like my mother, when she used to say that girls *like us* didn't need to worry."

"Oh, I can't even *imagine* what Rosemary's going to say."

Melanie had always been afraid of the force called Rosemary Blank. "My mother is in favor of anything that proves that her daughter is a success. Linda Moreland is exactly the kind of go-getter she wants me to be. She opened her own firm. She has eight exoneration cases under her belt. She's a new breed of celebrity lawyer. She doesn't try cases—she wins them through postconviction claims of innocence. This is putting all that esoteric appellate work I did at Russ Waterston to good use."

"Sounds like you're practicing your talking points for your mother."

Carrie laughed. "Yeah, a little. Okay, a lot, definitely."

Carrie heard another call beeping through. She recognized the number of the law office she had been trying to reach.

"Just a second, Melanie." She switched to the new call. "Carrie Blank."

"Carrie, hi. This is Kristin McConnell. You left a message about an old client of my father's, Anthony Amaro."

It was the daughter of Amaro's original defense attorney. "Thanks so much for getting back to me. We're representing Mr. Amaro on a petition for postconviction relief and were hoping to obtain any files your father might have. I know it's a long shot but—"

"I can have everything ready in an hour."

"Seriously? That's amazing."

"Long story. You'll have a messenger pick them up?"

Carrie looked at the pile of Redweld files. She could use a break. "No need," she said. "I'll pick it up myself."

She thanked Kristin again and clicked back to her call with Melanie. "Sorry about that."

"I get it. I know how valuable your time is." All these years later, Carrie could never tell when Melanie was being self-deprecating and when she was being passive-aggressive.

"Anyway, thanks for the concern, Melanie, but I'm happy about this new job. I'm getting *paid* to find out the answers to all those questions I've always had about Donna's death. She was an addict, but I'll never believe she was a prostitute. As Amaro's lawyer, I can get access to everything."

"But at what expense? He was the guy we were hiding

from. And now you're going to help him? He's a *mur-derer*. He killed your *sister*."

"*Half* sister," she said, chopping at the first syllable like her mother used to, though Melanie didn't seem to see the humor. "Linda Moreland says he didn't do it, which means the real killer is still out there."

"And what if it turns out Linda Moreland is wrong?"

12

Rogan pressed the button for the ninth floor.

"Am I crazy or is this the same building you and Donovan almost rented at some point? I know it was somewhere up here."

They were in Yorkville, the far east side of the Upper East Side, just a block from the East River, but a serious hike from the Lexington Avenue subway line. Traditionally, it was one of the most affluent neighborhoods in Manhattan, the site of the real Gracie Mansion and the fictional Michael Corleone's penthouse. But, these days, Yorkville was also the site of some of the more-affordable(ish) new high-rises in Manhattan, which is how Max's real estate agent had ended up pressuring them to consider a unit in this behemoth rental building. Ellie had forced Rogan to make a detour on the way back from a witness interview in Harlem to check the place out. After saying thirteen times that it was "fine," he finally conceded that the walls were thin, the construction shoddy, and the entire building too "cookie cutter," validating her own antipathy for it.

For Mitch Brunswick to have moved from the prewar townhouse he'd shared with his family to a "starter" rental in Yorkville was a serious step down in the New York City real estate hierarchy.

Ellie recognized the man waiting at an open apartment door when they exited the elevator. He had been photographed countless times, usually trying to shield his face, since his wife was murdered in March.

"Dr. Brunswick?" Rogan asked. "We're the detectives your office called about."

Brunswick's answering service had explained that the doctor had shifted his office hours to "increase patient convenience." They took it as code for taking more weeknight appointments to increase the size of his practice. Rogan had made the call to give Brunswick advance notice of a home visit. Now they each introduced themselves.

"Oh, I assumed it would be Detectives Santos and Hayes."

"Of course," Ellie said. "Can we have a word inside to explain?"

He stepped aside to allow them in. A chocolate Lab jumped from the sofa to give them a quick sniff and then resumed his position.

If Rogan had declared the building itself cookie-cutter, she could only imagine his assessment of this particular apartment. The living room looked like the lobby of an airport hotel, the generic furniture most likely circled from a catalogue.

Just as they'd agreed in advance, Ellie laid out the

reasons for the reassignment of his wife's case—at least the version they had decided to give him. "We could sugarcoat this, Dr. Brunswick, but I'm sure you're more aware than anyone that several weeks have now passed without an identified suspect. We've been asked to take a new look at the case."

"You *are* sugarcoating it if you say I've not been treated as a suspect. Every attorney friend I have tells me I shouldn't be talking to the police. I'm home right now because my patients are leaving in droves. My own neighbors step out of the elevator when they see me coming, pretending they forgot to pick up their mail. Yet here I am, opening the door for you, hoping I can convince someone—*anyone*—that I didn't do this. Maybe then you'll actually start looking for whoever killed Helen."

So many suspects think that cooperating with police will make them look innocent. In reality, talking to law enforcement is a one-way street. Lawyering up is a sure sign of guilt. But without real evidence of innocence, too much cooperation can look even worse.

"Since you're shooting straight with us," Rogan said, "why don't we just come out and ask: Why *shouldn't* we suspect you?"

Mitch looked up at his perfectly white ceiling and shook his head. "I don't know. Honestly, I understand how they're making it sound. Hell, not just how it sounds—how it *looks*. I get it: every time I read a story about a woman getting victimized, I say the same thing—

it's got to be the husband. And when I realize how I must look to the outside world—"

Ellie thought he might cry, but he pressed his lips together, focused on a spot on the blank white wall behind them, and continued. "I'm the asshole who let a sixteen-year partnership with a smart, beautiful, intelligent woman—the mother of my children—slip away. I'm not making excuses. We just—it sounds clichéd, but we grew apart. I never stopped caring about her; I never stopped respecting her. But I got to this point—and, Jesus, I feel so selfish trying to justify my feelings. If I could change any of it, on the off chance it would prevent what happened to Helen, I'd do it in a second. But I know the reality of the situation, so I have no choice but to try to explain how it got to the point where I look like a murderer. It's what a lot of couples go through: the kids come along, you're both still working, you start snapping at each other more and more. Eventually, we were distant enough to create room for a third person. I assume you know about Lisa. Now I understand why people warn you: don't talk to the woman next to you on a plane; head straight to your room instead of the hotel bar after that presentation at a medical conference; avoid temptation at all costs. But once I met Lisa, it was too late. I realized we only get one life. That's what I said to Helen during one of our last stupid counseling sessions. God, what a lie that was, sitting there twice a week, when I was already in love with someone else. There she was, trying to save the marriage, while I was just biding my time, trying to break the news. I told her—we only get one life, and we're both still young enough to have another fifty years of happiness. It happens that way sometimes: people move forward and start over again. But then some monster murders the mother of my children, and I'm on the front page as the d-bag willing to kill her for a clean break. I'd give every day I have left to bring Helen back, I swear."

"But, now that Helen's gone," Ellie asked, "isn't it true that you have a better chance at that happy life you wanted? No ex-wife in the picture. Only one household to support."

"You sound just like Santos and Hayes. Look, I thought Lisa and I were of one mind about starting a life together. But I guess she assumed I could leave my wife and still have the three-story townhouse and disposable income. She loves me. She loves the kids. But she's a surgeon with her own money and didn't want to marry a man who had to pay so much in child support and alimony that he took an apartment an intern would rent."

"But now that there's no alimony—"

"You're wrong. Lisa had a problem getting married given my financial situation, but we were still very much together, just without the entangled finances. It's not like she wanted her own kids, and not everyone needs the piece of paper, you know?" Oh, did Ellie ever know . . . but the last thing she needed to think about now was her own situation. "Now that I'm the guy who supposedly killed his wife to be with her? Let's just say it's a little frustrating that people think Helen's death somehow helps me be with Lisa."

Rogan was out of his chair, pretending to pace near the dining room table, which was covered with files and notebooks. "What's this over here?"

Mitch looked up at the ceiling and shook his head. "Great. So I can either look uncooperative by asking you to leave, or come clean and tell you that I broke medical-privacy laws by going through Helen's patient files."

"And why would you do that?" Ellie asked.

"Because to my knowledge, no one else had. Santos and Hayes saw Helen as some kind of fluffy romance counselor. They seemed to assume that just because her practice wasn't in the center of Crazytown, her patients couldn't be dangerous. And that's the irony—Helen told me she was interested in psychology in the first place because of the real sickos. But once she was doing the actual clinical work, it was too heavy. Depressing. Instead of helping her patients, she was scared of them. So she went into private counseling to get away from—from that darkness. But I'm convinced her killer is in here. He knew her as a therapist. That's why he went to the office."

Guilty men didn't pore over a table full of files in their off hours.

"So who should we be looking at?" Ellie asked.

He sighed and shook his head again. "I don't know

yet. There's the couple where the husband is a teacher accused of sleeping with a student. He seemed to think Helen made him sound like a child molester, which of course he is. Then there's the husband who finally admitted the reason he was coming home late; he was sneaking back into the restaurant where he works to pilfer money from the safe. Maybe he was worried Helen would tell someone."

Neither theory sounded compelling, and he knew it. He suddenly swept a pile of files off the table. "Damn it!"

Rogan caught Ellie's eye, as if to say, *The man's got a temper.*

"I'm sorry," Mitch said, bending over to pick up the papers. "I don't know what else to do. I can't live like this forever. I keep thinking about Sam and Jessica. At some point, will even *they* begin to wonder?" He extended the files in his hands toward them. "Please take these. Maybe you'll see something I missed, or you can dig back further and find more patients, from the past. When she was getting her Ph.D., she worked with people who were seriously mentally ill. One of them could have tracked her down."

Rogan crossed his arms. "We'll promise to take a look at every theory."

"Call a Dr. Alex Sumner. Please. Do you know him?"

They both shook their heads.

"He's a psychiatrist. I think he serves as an expert witness in a lot of insanity cases. We saw one of those courtroom sketches in the newspaper a few years ago, and I remember Helen telling me he was one of her professors during her internship. It was at Cedar Ridge Behavioral and Psychiatric Care. Even back then, I guess he was such a big deal that he'd travel across the state in different clinical rotations. That's how she got to work with him."

"And you remembered his name all these years later?" Rogan asked. Ellie could tell her partner was still searching for a revealing slip of the tongue, something to confirm the other detectives' suspicions.

"No, I remembered the case. It was awful. The nanny who killed the children?"

They both nodded their recognition, but Ellie's mind was somewhere else. Something about the connection between this Dr. Sumner and Helen Brunswick was bothering her.

"Helen and I were saying it was every parent's nightmare. Then she made the comment about knowing the defendant's psychiatric expert from her early interest in abnormal psych. I was grabbing at straws yesterday, Googled the case, and found Sumner's name. I left a message with his office, but I guess . . ." His voice trailed off. He guessed that busy psychiatrists didn't return phone calls from suspected murderers.

Ellie realized now what had been nagging her. The internship he'd mentioned hadn't been listed on his wife's credentials, apparently because she hadn't completed it.

"Where did you call Dr. Sumner?" she asked.

"At his office."

"I mean, where *geographically*?" she clarified. "He's in the city?"

Mitch nodded.

"But before, you said your wife was able to work with him because he traveled around the state."

"Yeah, that's right, because at the time, she was still in her internship at Cedar Ridge."

Rogan saw where the conversation was heading. "And Cedar Ridge is where exactly?"

"Upstate. Just outside Syracuse."

"Which direction outside?" Rogan asked.

"Um, I guess east? About thirty miles?"

Ellie looked to Rogan for a lesson in New York State geography, but he was moving on. "What exactly was your wife studying with Dr. Sumner up there?"

"At the time, she was specializing in the treatment of people who manifested antisocial and criminal behavior. She never spoke much about it, other than to say it got to be too much for her."

Ellie was doing the math in her head. Helen Brunswick would have been starting a postgrad internship right around the time someone was murdering women in Utica.

They waited until the elevator doors closed to speak.

"East of Syracuse," Ellie said. "That's near Anthony Amaro's territory, right?"

"Yep, thirty miles east makes it closer to Utica than Syracuse, in fact."

"And it sounds like she was working with the heavy-duty nutjobs. It's conceivable that one of them has been stalking her all this time."

"Nearly twenty years. That's a long time, Hatcher."

"Could be someone who was hospitalized or on his meds in the interim. Something could have retriggered the obsession. Come to think of it, her murder coinciding with the end of her marriage made Mitch look guilty." The elevator doors parted, and she continued to speak as they made their way to the building's exit. "But if someone was watching her, the breakup could have been the event that convinced her stalker to make a move."

"There's a far simpler explanation: he knew his wife's past—at a loonybin in Utica, right around the time someone was killing the women of Utica—and that's exactly why he hired someone to replicate Amaro's MO when he took her out." He held the lobby door open and she stepped outside.

She was still processing Rogan's response when a man with a camera stepped in front of them and snapped a picture. He was faster than the well-coiffed woman with the microphone: "Detectives, why were you speaking with Dr. Mitch Brunswick?"

Ellie held her forearm up instinctively against the bright light shining above the cameraman, but the television correspondent kept yelling questions. "Why has the district attorney's office assigned a fresh look to the case?"

Ellie felt Rogan pushing her toward the car. How did the media know so much already? As she fell into the front seat, she heard the reporter's final question: "Is it true that you have evidence connecting Helen Brunswick's murder to the crimes of convicted killer Anthony Amaro?"

Rogan jumped into the driver's seat and gunned the engine. Once he pulled away from the curb, he looked at her and frowned. "And boom goes the dynamite."

PART TWO

VICTIM NUMBER FOUR

13

The law office of McConnell and Associates was typical of a small partnership in New York City: shared space with a few other lawyers in the same predicament added up to one floor in a respectable building with a respectable-looking communal staff. Kristin McConnell's office exceeded expectations, however. Given that the original McConnell, Harry, had been Amaro's court-appointed lawyer, Carrie would not have been surprised to find peeling paint and loaded mousetraps. But now that the man's daughter, Kristin, was in charge, Carrie recognized a large canvas on the interior wall as the work of a contemporary of Jackson Pollock.

Beneath the artwork were two large cardboard boxes, marked neatly with labels that read: "Anthony Amaro, 8/5/96."

"You must be Carrie." Kristin looked to be Carrie's age—mid-thirties—but handled herself with a confidence that Carrie was still searching for.

"I called you on a lark," Carrie said. "I can't believe you still have records this many years later."

"Like I said on the phone, long story. The old man didn't believe in throwing files away, and he retired before getting around to computerizing the documents. I swore to him that I'd retain all client records for twenty years, and I spend a small fortune on storage keeping my word. I have them filed by date of conviction and do a purge every four months. That's how I was able to get you these so quickly. Honestly, you're doing me a favor by taking them two years early."

"Well, I really appreciate it."

"Amaro's challenging his conviction?" Kristin asked.

Carrie nodded, unsure how much she should reveal. "It's part of a larger project. Major issues with the police department's lead detective."

"I know Linda Moreland's work. Your client could certainly do worse."

Carrie smiled.

"How much do you know about my father?"

"I know he was Anthony Amaro's lawyer."

"That's as much as I expected. I'm probably the only attorney our age who knows what a lion he was in his era. A true voice of the downtrodden. I actually remember this case: he took it pro bono because it was one of the very first cases that was death-eligible in the state of New York."

Carrie was now regretting that she hadn't taken the time to conduct a quick Google search of Harry McConnell. His daughter clearly admired the man.

"The client made a point of saying how appreciative he was of your father's representation on his behalf." Did that sound as stupid in the room as it sounded to Carrie's own ears?

"He worked when he should have been enjoying his last healthy years. His opposition to the death penalty was that strong. At least he was able to see capital punishment go down with barely a whimper before this state ever saw a single execution."

Carrie found herself confused by the direction of the conversation. "I'm sorry if you lost him prematurely."

Kristin shook her head. "No, my father's still living and breathing. He just doesn't remember everything. He had the curse of being told by his doctors early on that he'd lose his memory to Alzheimer's. I don't even know why they bother telling people. What are you supposed to do? I wanted him to retire and spend his last capable days enjoying life. He wanted to spend them in practice, and he forced me to make two promises: one—to keep these idiotic files for twenty years, and two—to tell him when it was time to hang it up so he didn't shortchange his clients. So when you thank me for these dusty documents, just trust me that the second promise was much harder to keep."

Carrie still didn't know what to say. She'd been raised in a family that didn't talk about any of its hardships, and this total stranger was telling her about the difficulties of handling her father's dementia. "Well, hopefully, your father's insistence on hanging on to these documents will be fruitful. I take it you kept up his practice?"

"Nope. Thank God that wasn't the third promise. Personally, I can't stomach criminal defense work. Took me a while to realize that. I represent crime victims, in fact, because no one else does. The prosecutors represent the state, whatever that means. The defense attorneys do whatever they need to do to get the defendant off. I represent the victims—which usually means pressuring the state to do what's right, and pressuring the defendant to pay up and plead guilty."

Carrie was wishing she had sent a messenger to pick up the Amaro files. "Wow, that sounds like a really interesting practice."

"So is Amaro claiming ineffective assistance of counsel?"

The shift in tone was palpable. What had sounded like a mournful daughter's meandering now sounded like an attorney's cross-examination. "No. Um, there's new evidence. It's still coming together, but the claim is that he's innocent."

"Yeah, but we both know that's not a legal *thing*. You have to have a basis for constitutional error at trial. I've learned over the years that these shitbags my dad bent over backwards for are perfectly willing to claim ineffective assistance of counsel when that's the last egg in the basket."

Carrie was done smiling. She bent over and lifted both boxes. Kristin didn't offer her a hand. And, once again, Carrie wondered what the hell she had gotten herself into.

14

Ellie's desk shook as Rogan slammed down his phone. "And that makes oh-for-five," he declared.

As Helen Brunswick's next-of-kin, Mitch Brunswick had waived his deceased wife's rights to privacy, enabling them to obtain her educational records. Based on those records, they knew that in Helen's early efforts to complete a postgraduate internship in abnormal psychology, she had completed rotations at five different mental health institutions in ten months. She had only two months remaining when she decided to withdraw from the program.

Now they were looking for some connection between her studies, the Amaro victims, and her murder. But so far, none of the hospitals would release information about the identity of her patients, or even the general *type* of patients she was treating.

Rogan tapped his nails against his desk. "You realize it's just a matter of time before the press finds out we're calling around upstate mental institutions, asking about Helen."

"I still can't believe those reporters were camped outside Mitch Brunswick's building yesterday. How do you think they knew about the connection to Amaro?"

"It could have been any kind of leak," Rogan said. "Or, frankly, it might've been Mitch Brunswick himself. He's the one who sent us on this wild goose chase. Pretty smart, when you think about it. Read some old newspaper articles about a serial killer's signature. Hire someone to do the job, using the same MO. Then send the letter tying the murder to the old cases, using information no one else would know. Call the press to divert their attention. Then just happen to mention that she used to work the nuthouses upstate."

"I don't know, Rogan. It's not like he dropped that information in our laps. Those files he was digging through were recent. It was only after we blew them off that he mentioned her past in Utica."

Rogan shrugged. "So he's smart. He wouldn't be the first."

"So we keep digging. You haven't gotten *anywhere* with the hospitals?"

"The most information I got was from Alex Sumner, the shrink Mitch mentioned. He said Helen quit the program after getting a dressing-down from the department head for calling the police about two different patients she thought were a danger to the public."

"God forbid she should try to protect anyone."

"Exactly. But there *are* rules about confidentiality, and apparently the powers that be thought she was a little too quick to step outside of them. She decided that dealing with the criminally insane wasn't a good fit for her after all. According to Dr. Sumner, people who do that work have to have—how did he put it?—*empathy for people who don't have empathy for others*. They have to believe there's a hope for change. And Helen didn't."

"So who were those two patients?"

"That's where I thought I was getting somewhere. Dr. Sumner pulled major strings with his hospital contacts and got me the names of the two patients she reported. I made a quiet call to Utica PD's records department." Rogan slid a clipped set of documents across the table. She flipped through the pages as he summarized them. "First patient was Gregory Katz. He told her he fantasized about boiling a woman in a pot and eating the stew."

"Nice."

"Sumner says Helen's call to police violated the ethics rules because there wasn't a specific victim in imminent danger."

"Oh, for fuck's sake."

"So for half a second, I thought we might actually have someone worth talking to. Not a big stretch to think that a guy who wants to boil women in a pot might break their limbs first. But flip the page and you'll see the problem."

It was another Utica Police Department report—a fatal car accident on Christmas Day 1998. Gregory Katz was killed by a drunk driver.

She flashed a thumbs-up. "Go karma."

Rogan slid another pile of documents across the table, this one much thicker. "Second guy was just a kid: Joseph

Flaherty. Not nearly as interesting as the wannabe cannibal. Helen thought he was a danger to a fellow patient at the hospital. According to Brunswick, he was completely noncommunicative and nonsensical when he was off his meds, but obsessive and paranoid when he was on them—accusing this other patient of being the devil and trying to kill his five wives. And, mind you, the kid didn't have any wives."

"And calling police on him broke the rules, too?"

"According to Sumner, it did. This time, she at least had a specific individual she was trying to protect; problem was, the potential danger wasn't grave enough."

"I can see why she wanted to quit." Ellie was flipping through the pages of reports. "What's all this other stuff?"

"The mess that became of that kid, Joseph Flaherty. In and out of hospitals—in fact he's in as we speak—but mostly he's homeless. Twenty-two arrests: criminal trespass, disturbing the peace, basically acting a fool. Four of those calls are noise complaints from the same address. Guess Flaherty got obsessed with some cop and kept showing up in the yard, screaming at the windows until neighbors called the police. He was only a teenager when the Utica killings were happening, so not exactly the profile of a serial killer."

"Not totally unprecedented, though," she said.

"The real problem's the timing of Helen's report. Check out the date." She flipped back to the first document in the pile. Helen had called police about Flaherty on July 5, 1995. Five women had been killed in Utica by then. "And check out the notation at the end."

Patient is on commitment hold, per mother. Held involuntarily, inpatient, full-time for last nine months.

Two of the victims were killed in early 1995. A teen-ager couldn't stalk prostitutes on the streets of Utica while confined to a mental institution.

Rogan was right: the hospital angle was a bust.

"Any luck on your end?" he asked.

While Rogan had been calling treatment centers, Ellie had been reviewing the information they had about Anthony Amaro and his victims, looking for any connections to Helen Brunswick.

"We've got the one New York City victim—Deborah Garner—and the five Utica victims. The first bodies were found in May, 1991, at Roscoe Conkling Park by a family that had taken their cat there for burial. I guess it was Fluffy's favorite place to run off to every time he escaped. Dad's digging the hole, and the kids are crying about Fluffy, when Mom whispers to Dad that she sees a bone in the dirt, and the bone looks human."

"That's one very detailed police report."

She shrugged. "I made up the kid tears. And the kitty name."

"Fluffy? Show some originality."

"Says the man who named his first dog Snoopy. But, whatever. You get the picture. Family calls police. Police dig for more bones and find the remains of two bodies within a sixty-foot radius. They're eventually identified as Nicole Henning and Jennifer Bronson. Henning had been dead longer." To help Rogan keep track, she wrote down their names on a legal pad. "Bronson had a kid, and was reported missing by her brother, but no one called in Nicole Henning's disappearance. Going by when the women were last seen, plus the best guess of the medical examiner, they estimate that Nicole Henning was killed around February of 1989 and Jennifer Bronson in April of 1991." She noted the dates next to the women's names. "Fast forward a year to March 1993. A peach of a mother calls police after it dawns on her she hasn't seen her thirty-two-year-old daughter since Christmas. It turns out the daughter, Leticia Thomas, has a history of prostitution. On a lark, the police take a cadaver dog back out to Conkling Park and find Thomas's body. The ME said she'd been dead a couple of months, max."

She added Leticia's name and "estimated 1/93" to the growing list of victims and dates.

"So the guy went right back to the same dumping ground," Rogan said.

"You could literally throw a stone to Leticia's grave from either of the first two victims'."

"And this is when Utica PD finally admitted they had a serial killer on their hands?"

"Correct. They didn't release specifics yet, but they did alert the working girls to be careful and to let police know if they saw anything or anyone suspicious. They also started patrolling the area of the park where the bodies had been found, hoping for a repeat visit."

Rogan shook his head. "Like the guy's not going to notice that."

Ellie made two small hatch marks on the bottom of the page and then continued her summary. "Fast forward again to April 1995. Another family is at Conkling Park, but this time in the northwest corner. They find what looks to be a human bone."

"Another cat funeral?"

"No cat in this family—at least not to my knowledge. But they did have a dog, who was very much alive. Alive enough to pick up the scent of a dead body during the family hike. The body was identified as Stacy Myer, last seen a week earlier. And she wasn't buried well, not like the first three. More like she was dumped and covered with leaves."

"Because the guy knew the police were looking for him by then. He rushed."

She nodded and made a third hatch mark. "And they probably realized they'd been pretty stupid to do a visual patrol of one part of the park to the exclusion of the rest. So the cadaver dog came back out, and found another body with more advanced signs of decomposition. Donna Blank. Reported missing, also by her mother,

123

shortly after New Year's, a time frame consistent with her remains. Her body was in a deep grave, like the others, but her postmortem injuries were less severe. Both of her wrists were broken, but the limbs were otherwise intact. Hard to know why exactly, but maybe he had to rush with her, too." She flipped the legal pad to face Rogan. "Put it all together: five victims in six years and change."

"The guy accelerated," Rogan noted. "Two victims within a few months in 1995."

Ellie added a fourth hatch mark, and then made some additional notes. "Henning, Thomas, and Myer were known prostitutes, all with vice records, Henning and Thomas with convictions. Jennifer Bronson worked out of a lingerie modeling establishment." She batted her eyes with mock innocence. Back before the Internet had given prostitutes an alternative to working the streets, lingerie modeling shops, massage parlors, and other "jack shacks" provided cover. "Donna Blank worked at a strip club. And her family confirmed she had a drug problem." The line between stripping and prostitution was a thin one when a drug habit needed to be fed. As she added Donna Blank's name to the list, something about it felt familiar, as if she had recently seen it in another context. She tried to pull the moment to the surface, but kept losing its edges.

"You still there, Hatcher?"

"Yeah, sorry." She continued her summary. "Then we

get to New York City, October 1995. Deborah Garner. Picked up from a New Jersey rest stop, found dead in Fort Washington Park."

1. Nicole Henning – 2/89 – prost.
2. Jennifer Bronson – 4/91 – "lingerie model"
3. Leticia Thomas – 1/93 – prost.
4. Donna Blank – 1/95 – stripper
5. Stacy Myer – 4/95 – stripper, prost.
6. Deborah Garner – 10/95 – NYC, prost.

Rogan gave the list a quick glance. "He must have come to the city because he knew that UPD was finally looking for him."

"Bingo. UPD stepped up the visibility of their investigation once Victims 4 and 5 were found. They had the social-service providers plugged in, too, handing out fliers to the working girls, warning them about a killer. The acceleration continued. Three kills in one year."

"Or he was keeping that pace the whole time," Rogan offered, "and the bodies haven't been found. There's no guarantee this is a complete list."

There was so much they didn't know.

Rogan tapped his pen against her notepad. "There's no way Helen Brunswick belongs on this list."

"Two of the Utica victims had prostitution convictions. The county had a counseling and education program that was mandatory with vice-related sentences.

From what I can tell, the program was run at the time by Cedar Ridge Behavioral and Psychiatric Care."

It was one of the hospitals where Helen Brunswick had interned.

"Major stretch. It's only two of the six women, and even if Brunswick had contact with them, how does that make her a target twenty years later, and what does it have to do with Anthony Amaro?"

"You're calling him Amaro again, huh?" she said with a smile.

"That's the dude's name, isn't it?"

"Yeah, but it's not the name you've been using. See those chicken marks at the bottom of the page there? Four times. I counted."

"You count everything, Rainman, and you don't usually need notes."

"I tallied them up to prove I was right. You said 'the guy' four times. *The guy went back to the same dumping ground. Like the guy's not going to notice a police patrol. The guy knew UPD was on to him. The guy accelerated.* That's four times you referred to the killer without calling him Amaro."

"So what about it?"

"Admit it, Rogan. You've got your doubts."

"The guy. The bad guy. The perp. The mutt. The dirt-bag. *Amaro* by name. You're making too much of a word."

"Maybe." She figured it was best not to press the point.

"Speaking of Amaro, I reached out to Buck Majors. I'm waiting for a call back."

Ellie assumed the detective who put Amaro behind bars would want to help keep him there. "Talk about creative names. Buck Majors. Boom-chicka-pow-wow."

"The idea of you and porn together is messing me up. Stop it."

"Hey, does Donna Blank's name seem familiar to you? From before just now, I mean."

"I don't know. Maybe Donovan mentioned it?"

"But it seems like we just saw it in another context, like I had a flash of letters on a page. And maybe just the last name."

She was shuffling through the documents scattered across her desk when Rogan reached over and plucked out the demand for documents they'd received from Amaro's attorney. "Right there," he said. "Linda Moreland's associate is Caroline Blank. You really hang on to every detail, don't you?"

Ellie glanced at the signature and then grabbed for the initial missing-persons report for Donna Blank. Listed as family: Marcia Haring, the mother who called police; Henry Blank, the father; Rosemary Blank, stepmother; Carrie Blank, half sister. "Take a look," she said, pointing at the half sister's name. "Carrie could be short for Caroline."

"One way to find out." Rogan typed "Caroline Blank attorney" into Google and searched for images. He tilted the screen toward Ellie, while she laid a photograph of Donna Blank in front of it.

"The attorney's Asian," he said. "The vic's a white girl. But the attorney looks like she could be mixed, which makes sense if they're half sisters."

"And their noses and mouths are similar," Ellie noted. Both had long, slender noses and heart-shaped lips.

"What kind of lawyer would defend her sister's murderer?"

"Someone who really thought he was innocent," she said. "Rogan, what if this case is for real?"

"It's not, all right? Amaro's guilty. Helen Brunswick's husband killed her. And once we prove it, we can go back to catching cases off the board."

Her phone buzzed at her waist. It was Max.

"Hey there."

"Well," he said, "the moment we've been waiting for is here."

"The rapture? Because I don't think the end-times are going to work out well for us."

"The DNA reanalysis is done. And it's not good: we've got someone else's genetic marker from one of the bodies."

"We knew it was a risk. The victims were all working girls."

"Except it's not seminal fluid. It's skin, and it's beneath the fingernails of one of the Utica victims."

"Which one?"

"Donna Blank."

15

Carrie dropped the two boxes with a thud on the landing at the top of the stairs. She was surprised at the weight of the files she'd retrieved from Amaro's original attorney. She'd hauled them up four floors, and in four-inch heels no less. She caught her breath as she unlocked her front door and pushed the box through the entrance with her foot.

The other associates at Russ Waterston all lived in luxury rentals. Over drinks, they'd compare notes about doormen and various amenities: rooftop pools, in-house spas, movie-theater rooms. Not Carrie. With more than a hundred thousand dollars in student loans, this walk-up studio in Hell's Kitchen suited her just fine.

She opened the cardboard box and began spreading its contents onto her apartment floor. Every notebook and file folder was labeled in neat, handwritten block letters: lab reports, witness interviews, penalty phase. Harry McConnell was organized. Hopefully it would be worth Carrie's awkward interaction with his daughter to get her hands on these documents.

She knew she should attack the materials in a disciplined, logical order. She also knew that it would make sense to look first at the files relating to the New York City victim, Deborah Garner. Her murder was the basis for Amaro's conviction. Those materials would be the most thorough.

But she was realizing now that Melanie's concerns may have been legitimate. When it came to Anthony Amaro, she wasn't just any attorney.

She went straight to the file labeled "Donna Blank: Victim Number Four."

She flipped past several of the initial pages, summaries of random phone calls that had come in over the years. She saw photographs she'd never seen before—images of Donna's partially decomposed body. That must have been the reason why there hadn't been a funeral, just a cremation with a small memorial service at Christ the King.

Donna's mother, Marcia, had filed the missing-person report. She had waited four days to call police. End of first paragraph: "Mother volunteers that daughter has history of drug abuse and worked as a dancer at Club Rouge. When pressed by this officer, mother admitted that it was 'possible' daughter was engaged in 'prostitution activity.'"

Carrie knew from the placement of these facts at the beginning of the short report that the officer did not take Marcia's concerns seriously. Donna was just a druggie hooker who had run off for a few days to work, score, or both. Reading the report, Carrie wanted to leap back in time, into Marcia's living room, to tell that officer about the girl Carrie used to idolize. She wanted that officer to know that Donna had walked her to and from school for an entire semester in the sixth grade when she learned that kids were making fun of her and trying to steal her books for "acting smart."

When Carrie reached the final, surprising sentence of the police report, she flipped through the rest of the documents in search of a subsequent correction. Nothing. She reread the sentence, ever so slowly, and knew for certain that it was wrong.

There was a time when Donna tried to take care of Carrie, like a big sister should. But by the time Donna died, their roles were reversed. It had been Carrie's idea to try to help. Carrie's mother was never supposed to know the money was gone. Donna would go to rehab, kick her habit, and then get a real job. With regular income and no drug habit, she'd pay Carrie back long before she actually needed the money for college tuition. Carrie remembered how grown-up she had felt withdrawing the money from the bank—eight thousand dollars, nearly everything in her college account. The teller smiled as Carrie beamed, probably assuming that Carrie was buying her first car.

Carrie knew something was wrong when she went to visit Donna at Cedar Ridge. The nice lady at the front desk checked the computer and reported they had no patients named Donna Blank. Carrie asked her to try Donna Haring, wondering if Donna had used her mother's last name to conceal her identity. After all, the place was filled with people with all kinds of mental illnesses and problems far worse than Donna's. The receptionist shook her head, trying to mask her pity. It was clear to Carrie this wasn't the first time the woman had to disappoint a family member with that same reply.

No rehab. No money. Just lies.

The next time Carrie saw Donna, two weeks later, she was strung out on Sandy Avenue. She looked through Carrie like a stranger.

Carrie's mother found out, of course. Rosemary Blank found out everything. Carrie was supposed to be in her room, studying, but she could hear the phone calls and the arguments. Mom was threatening to press charges if Donna ever set foot in her house or contacted Carrie again.

Carrie only saw her sister one time after that blank-faced stare on the street. At first, she didn't hear the knock on the door. She was in her bedroom, taking a study break with her beloved TLC tape when she heard her mother yelling. Assuming it was a complaint about the volume, Carrie turned the stereo down, only to hear banging at the front door. Her mother's voice, telling someone, "Go away. You know you're not welcome here."

"Please, Rosemary. I didn't mean it—not at first. But I got to Cedar Ridge, and I freaked out. I messed up. I need

Carrie to know I'm sorry. Please let me talk to her. Pleeeeeeeeaaaase!"

She watched her mother begin to step away from the door, then leap forward again when the pounding got harder. "You can't do this!" Donna yelled. It sounded like Donna was kicking the door now. "I have a plan. I promise. I know a way to help make sure Carrie has what she needs—"

At that, Carrie's mother unlatched the bolts, yanked the door open, and planted herself in the entry like a professional linebacker. Carrie had never seen her mother so resolved. "*I* am the one who knows what Carrie needs." The only sign that she was the least bit frazzled was the strength of her Chinese accent. "*I* am the one who has gotten her to where she is, and where she will go. And the only mistake I ever made with my daughter was allowing you and your mother to have any part of her life. You're a waste of human life. You are nothing. If you had any decency, you would see the shared DNA in a girl as wonderful as my daughter and realize just how pathetic you are."

"I know. I do. And that's why I have a plan. Please, I'm begging you—"

Carrie knew better than to step from her bedroom.

"As far as Carrie and I are concerned, you no longer exist. Come here again, Donna, and I *will* have you arrested. Your father agrees. We have a friend on the police force. We will press charges, and he will put you in jail."

"Right, because you and your friends—the people *you* approve of—are so much better than the rest of the world."

Carrie flinched as Donna tried to push her way through the entrance. Rosemary slammed it shut, secured the bolt, and pressed her back against the door. "Leave now, or I'm calling 9-1-1," she yelled.

"I'm going to fix this, Rosemary, whether you accept it or not."

In the silence, Carrie braced herself for another assault on the door, but there was none. The tension in her mother's small body released, and the composure returned to her face. When she heard the sounds of her mother tinkering in the kitchen, she turned up the volume on her tape player a notch, resolving to find Donna later, when her mother wasn't around.

But she never did find her. No one did, not for another three months, when police discovered her body decomposing in Conkling Park.

That's how Carrie knew that the closing line of Donna's brief missing-person report had to be wrong. "When last seen, daughter told mom she was going to her father's house. Stepmother reports no knowledge of Donna going to house that day or since."

Had the police officer misunderstood her mother's statement? Or had he been so dismissive of the missing-person report that he failed to listen?

Carrie pulled up "Mom" on her cell but paused. She

knew her mother. She could picture her being annoyed that Donna's activities had brought a police officer to their door, not because she'd stolen Carrie's money but because she was off being irresponsible. She could imagine her mother saying whatever she needed to avoid getting dragged into Donna's drama. She knew her mother well enough to predict every word of the conversation that would ensue with a hit of the call button. She'd evade, claim she'd forgotten, and would hang up the minute Carrie pressed too hard. Rosemary Blank always knew what to say.

What mattered was the case. Only one day in, and Carrie already knew for certain that the police had made at least one error in their investigation into Donna's death.

16

Ellie was whispering to herself as she stripped off her long-sleeved shirt and wool pants.

"Be careful what you wish for, Elsa." It's what her parents used to say whenever they caught her pining for something. It happened so often that Jerry and Roberta Hatcher, like Eskimos with multiple words to describe snow, had an entire vocabulary to discuss young Ellie's desire to make her life a little better: "a case of the *I wants*," "grass-is-always-greener complex," "Little Miss Change-it."

Meanwhile, they chided her easygoing brother, Jess, as "complacent" and "apathetic," all because he accepted life exactly as it presented itself.

Two children from the same family, but entirely different cloth. Jess was dark and lean, with sharp, angled features. She was light and blond, with a heart-shaped faced and full, round lips. He barely graduated from high school, got fired from job after job, and still dreamed of being a rock star. She had worked the junior beauty pageant circuit to save money for college and had the same waitressing job for seven years before graduating from John Jay and joining the NYPD. And while Jess was the kind of person who looked around and said, "Yeah, this is fine," Ellie was always the one who fussed.

So for the last few weeks, as the thermometer had continued to read temperatures in the fifties and sixties well into mid-May, she had wished for some warmth.

Well, like her parents used to say, Be careful what you wish for, Elsa. With her bare shoulder she wiped away a stream of sweat that was about to drip from her chin.

Climate control in her old apartment had been simple. The furnace sounded like a mutant dragon on heroin, but it worked. And her only air conditioning was a window unit she had hauled home from P.C. Richard's, jamming it into the window frame and securing it with two-by-fours until she could figure out how to install it properly. It used more electricity than everything else in her apartment put together and had a tendency to whine just as she was falling asleep, but she was the one who told it when to work and how much.

Now that she and Max were in this fancy-pants building, she had lost all that control. As she'd learned three days ago from the super, something called a "chiller" couldn't be turned on because four tenants had not yet allowed the maintenance men to clean out their individual blower units because "it gets too cold." Without service, the entire system could go kablooey (his word, not hers). Something about clogs in the drains, back-ups, and floods. Four apartments out of three hundred. Now Ellie had a clear case of the "*I want*s"—as in "I want to track down these assholes and throw them from the fucking roof."

She had just changed into shorts and her favorite Pretenders T-shirt and settled onto the sofa when Max walked in, shaking a handful of mail in the air. "This was still in the box."

He had pointed out two weeks ago that she never picked up the mail from the lobby. He had also noted that she kept all her toiletries on one shelf, tucked her laptop into her bag every night before bed, and had yet to get a replacement driver's license with their new address. To him, these were all signs that she didn't truly think of the apartment as hers.

Since then, she'd been trying to remember to pick up the mail and be a little less tidy. The DMV was another issue.

"Sorry. I forgot."

"No problem. In other news, Liddy made a point of telling me to wear boxers, not briefs. Think she's losing it?"

Liddy was a very nice, very chatty woman who loved to sit in the lobby and partake in whatever conversations she could find. Ellie had never seen her without her navy-blue quilted Burberry jacket. That, combined with her tendency to warn neighbors to bundle up, placed her on the top of Ellie's list of suspected air-conditioning holdouts.

"I may have told her that my doctor said the unusually

high temperatures in our apartment could be affecting my fertility."

"You shouldn't joke around about stuff like that."

"Oh, come on, Max. It's not like my womb is going to hear me mocking my fertility and close up shop."

She immediately regretted doubling down on what was a sore subject between them. Not long before they'd moved in together, Ellie was certain Max was going to break things off when he learned she had no interest in having children. Living together was supposed to be a sign of their mutual promise to let their relationship evolve naturally. Ellie couldn't help feeling, though, that he woke up every day wondering when she was going to come around.

Now a silly joke had become an issue. "What do you want to do for dinner?" she asked, changing the subject.

"I would love a rare steak with a side of fries, but, alas, I just got a callout. Shooting in Tribeca. Looks like a gun accident, but the suspect's a lawyer. They want an ADA at the scene."

"Couldn't they call someone else? This Amaro thing's getting hot, first with the press, now the new DNA evidence? Plus I'm pretty sure one of Amaro's attorneys is Donna Blank's sister."

"You're kidding."

"No. I was hoping we could talk about the case tonight."

"Sorry, I want to, but I really gotta go." He could see

139

she was disappointed. He bent down and gave her a kiss. "The chief ADA's the one who asked for me on this. And Martin himself wanted an update today on Amaro. This is all really good for me, Ellie. I'll get home as soon as I can."

When the door closed, she looked around the apartment. It was tasteful and clean and well decorated. She removed their growing collection of take-out menus from the end table's top drawer. She saw plenty of options, but nothing she loved. She was hot. And grumpy.

She had to get out of here.

She nearly put the key in the door out of habit. She never thought of relinquishing it; Jess had always kept a key when it was her place. But she was still getting used to knocking.

"Hey," Jess said by way of greeting as he opened the door a crack. His attention shifted immediately to the window behind the living room sofa. "Damn proselytizers. Can I borrow your gun?"

"Definitely not. Not ever. Even if aliens invade."

She didn't need to look out the window to know the group he was talking about. The religious sect had been preaching on that corner long before either of them set foot in this apartment. All these years later, she still wasn't sure the basis of their belief system: some blend of Christianity, Judaism, and Hinduism, from what she could gather. All she really knew about them was that they were very, very vocal. Literally vocal. Without a license to use amplification, they resorted to screaming. She'd seen them swallow teaspoons of honey to protect their vocal cords. They were serious about the volume.

"How about a paintball gun?" Jess asked. "Is that illegal? If I played sniper and started nailing them with big splats of paint?"

"Yep. Public disorder at the least. Criminal mischief for the property damage. Assault if you hit them hard enough. Not a good idea."

"Party pooper. It's not that different from water balloons. Oh, and check your retro answering machine over there. Multiple messages from the mother."

Ellie had conditioned Jess's takeover of the apartment on his maintaining her landline and answering machine, which existed for the sole purpose of communicating with their mother. As far as Roberta Hatcher knew, Ellie was prohibited from using her department-issued cell phone for personal calls. Keeping the landline at her old apartment had the added bonus of saving Ellie from telling her mother she was living in sin, and with a man Roberta hadn't even met yet to boot.

She pushed the button on the machine and turned down the volume as she played the messages. Typical Mom: reminiscing about the old days; wondering why her kids had to live so far away; one late-night call after too much vodka, talking about "Daddy."

"How about ipecac?" Jess was asking. "If I swallow

ipecac before an evening stroll and they just *happen* to be on the receiving end of the resulting upchuck, that wouldn't be illegal, would it?"

"Well, if they could prove it was intentional—"

"Let's just forget this conversation, then, shall we?"

"Step away from the window, Jess. I haven't seen you for weeks." She opened the fridge and helped herself to the two bottles of Rolling Rock remaining of the twelve-pack she'd brought the last time she was here. A jar of Nutella was exactly where she'd left it on the counter when she'd moved. She grabbed it, too, and a spoon, and then plopped down on the couch. Perfection.

She had opened one of the beer bottles and was pulling her laptop from her bag when Jess finally stopped obsessing about the scene on the street.

"Make yourself comfy there, El."

She smiled and waved, then pointed at the second bottle of beer on the steamer trunk that doubled as a coffee table. Given that Jess had slept on this very sofa more often than not when she was paying the rent, she knew he was kidding.

On her laptop, she typed *Caroline Blank attorney* into Google and hit enter. The first listing was a brief professional bio on LinkedIn. Three semesters at Cornell University, followed, eight years later, by graduation at the top of her class from closer-to-home Cortland State. Law school was not quite as bumpy: after a first year at CUNY, she earned her J.D., with top honors, from Fordham.

She searched the Utica newspaper archives and pulled up an old article called "Tale of Two Sisters." Carrie Blank had been named the first recipient of a new scholarship called the Cyrus Morris Grant.

The grant is funded by the Dream Foundation, which selects one school per year around the country, then selects one student from that school's graduating class, to receive full tuition and room and board at the college of the recipient's choice, backed by the prestige of the award to assist with admissions.

It was a full ride to whatever college would have her. The interesting backstory: Carrie's half sister had been found murdered only two months earlier.

"Cyberstalking again?" Jess asked.

"I guess you could call it that. I've got this case, and the defense attorney is the half sister of one of the victims her client is presumed to have killed eighteen years ago."

He shook his head quickly. "Way too much information there for this addled brain to process."

She gave him a more complete rundown on the story. Helen Brunswick, the therapist murdered with the same signature as Anthony Amaro's string of killings. Brunswick's ties to Utica, where Amaro confined his killing ground until he moved down to the city, and to Deborah Garner. Amaro now seeking to set aside his conviction with the help of Linda Moreland and Carrie Blank, half sister of one of Amaro's victims.

"Utica, twenty years ago? Is this the guy who killed a bunch of prostitutes?"

"Six that we know of."

"I know a woman at the Big V who left Utica because of those murders."

By "the Big V," Jess meant Vibrations, the so-called gentlemen's club where he worked. The two of them had made a hobby of coming up with alternative names for the West Side Highway establishment: Booby Barn, Cans Castle, The Peeler and Feeler, Landing Strip Cafe. Always classy.

"You have a stripper old enough to have been in Utica two decades ago? Very, um, progressive."

"No. Mona's not a dancer—not anymore, at least. They call her the 'talent manager.' She's known the owner since way back. She's basically a mama-type for the dancers."

"And you know her whole life story?"

"Wouldn't say that, but when you work late on slow nights you end up shooting the shit. I told her the old man was a cop—how he got all eaten up by the College Hill Strangler, did himself in, yada yada yada." It was strange to hear from Jess that he'd spoken to anyone about their upbringing. Even with Ellie, he only brought up their father when it truly mattered. "And then she told me how she left Utica when she was in her mid-twenties—when she was still turning tricks out of the private dance rooms—because some sicko was killing girls left and right, and no one seemed to care."

"Think she'd be willing to talk to me?"

"If I asked her. Super nice."

"Fine. I'll pay for takeout. Then we can go?"

"Deal, but I'm vegan now."

"Don't fuck with me."

"Makes me feel better. Unclogs the pipes, if you will." He could tell she wasn't buying it. "It's for a chick."

Jess never did anything for a relationship. As in, no phone calls, no schedules, no monogamy. A surprising number of women in this world didn't seem to mind it. But now he was a vegan.

She started to ask for details, but he said, "Nope, that's all you get for now."

"Fine. Vegan takeout it is." She stuck her finger in her mouth in a feigned gag. "But your Utica stripper mama bear had better make some time for me."

17

Carrie was nearly finished reviewing one of the boxes of documents she'd retrieved from Kristin McConnell but still had a long way to go. The more pieces of paper she rifled through, the more reports she suspected were missing. She had filled nearly an entire legal pad with notes: names of potential witnesses, questions she wanted answered, gaps in the investigation.

She was about to pack it in for the night when her cell phone chirped. It was Linda. Oh no. She had told Thomas she was leaving for the day, but hadn't explained to her own boss that she was going to review Amaro's original defense attorney's documents at home since space at the office was tight. Was she calling to scold her?

"Oh, hi, Linda. I'm so glad you called. I got two big boxes of files from Harry McConnell. A lot of stuff we didn't have from the police—"

"Good. All good. But get some rest. We've got a big day tomorrow. Ten-o'clock hearing with Judge Johnsen."

Carrie had been an associate working on federal appeals. She had no idea who Judge Johnsen was.

"Okay. In the *state* courthouse?"

"Yes, of course. Carol Johnsen. We got lucky. She'll be a good judge for us."

"What should I do?"

"Be ready. For anything and everything. My source in the crime lab says the DA's office was spooked enough about the similarities between Helen Brunswick's murder and the Amaro killings that they asked for new DNA testing on their own. They found someone else's DNA."

Carrie suddenly heard her own heart beating. "Whose?"

"C'mon, dear. It's not that easy. But the DNA isn't Anthony Amaro's, and that's all that matters."

"Where? On the bodies? The clothes?"

"Under two fingernails. Index and middle fingers. Under your sister's fingernails, to be precise. She's going to be the key to this, Carrie. My gut was right. Amaro didn't do this. He's not the man who killed your sister. We're going to expose the truth."

Carrie closed her eyes and tried to focus on Linda's words. She pushed back the images that were flashing before her—Donna being pushed to the ground, Donna feeling the palm of a man's hand against her face, Donna scratching wildly at her assailant. She tried to come up with her half of the conversation.

"So, what's next?" she finally asked.

"You don't get it, Carrie. This is huge. Judge Johnsen's courtroom tomorrow. Ten a.m. It's happening faster than I thought, but this is it. This is *it*. We've got the pattern of similar confessions from Buck Majors; we've got Helen Brunswick killed with the same MO; and now we've got someone else's DNA. I cashed in chips for an expedited hearing, and I'll be calling the press."

"A hearing on what?"

"Our motion to vacate. We're ready to ask for Anthony Amaro's release. And the prosecution has no idea what's coming."

18

Plenty of cops would be troubled if a family member just happened to be friends with a former prostitute. But Jess wasn't a typical cop's family member. First, he seemed to know half the people in New York City, so it was no surprise that his cast of acquaintances was diverse. More important, given that Jess seemed most comfortable straddling a fine line between an adventurous lifestyle and the fringes of hard case crime, a friend with *past* criminal associations was the least Ellie had to worry about.

Jess breezed past the black-T-shirted doorman with a wave. As she followed, Ellie felt the doorman's gaze on the V-neck of her own shirt. Jess must have noticed, too, because he stepped backwards, blocking the view. "Dude. My sister."

Not to mention the badge and big gun, she wanted to add.

"Not a problem, man."

The darkened club was lit, here and there, in pockets of neon. By now, Ellie was familiar with the typical clusters of clientele: the young finance types, yucking it up bachelor-party-style after too many drinks; the occasional couples, the man looking on while his curious girlfriend accepts a lap dance; the regulars, staring with glazed eyes while they chew the prime rib. Two girls in thongs and pasties were working the stage to Def Leppard's "Pour Some Sugar on Me." More like pour some penicillin on me, Ellie thought.

Jess made a beeline to the bar. Ellie had no trouble identifying the woman who had to be Mona. She looked to be in her early fifties and was perched on the farthest stool. Physically petite, she came across larger than her frame thanks to a getup fit for a drag queen: blue-black hair piled high on her head, thick layers of colorful makeup, and a floor-length chiffon gown in bright turquoise. Jess signaled that Ellie should stay back. She watched as Jess greeted Mona with a friendly shoulder squeeze.

She felt her cell phone buzz. It was Max.

"Hey."

"Jesus, where are you? Is that hair metal in the background?"

She pressed her open ear shut with her index finger. "Unfortunately." —*From my head to my feet, yeah.*— "I'm at the Shake Shack with Jess. There's a woman here who might—"

"Sorry, what?"

Mona was throwing skeptical glances in Ellie's direction as she spoke to Jess.

"Jess knows a woman from Utica." A man at the next

150

table—a prime-rib chewer—glared at her like she was a child giggling in church. She traded her index finger for the next digit and let it fly in his direction. "Yeah, right—like you're here to enjoy the music."

"I just got home. Was wondering where you were."

"Sorry." How many times had she apologized to him today? "I thought I'd be back by now, but I'm with Jess."

"When are you coming home?"

She looked at her watch. It was already past eleven o'clock. "Do you mind if I just crash at his place? I can't sleep in that hot apartment."

"Yeah, okay. It's late, anyway. Love you."

"Love you, too."

As she snapped her phone back into place, Jess waved her over to the bar. Mona spun on her barstool to greet her.

"Jess mentioned how hard it was to be a big brother to a pretty sister, but he didn't do you justice." Mona had a low, smooth voice, suitable for public radio. Based on the getup, Ellie had expected something different. "What a knockout."

"Thanks to Jess, I grew up absolutely convinced that I was repellant to men. I didn't find out until I was a senior in high school that he'd been telling all the guys, 'You touch her and you die.'"

"That's a good brother, you ask me. Sorry for the evil eyes I was throwing your way, Detective."

"In my line of work, you get used to it."

"Oh no, it's not like that. I'm usually a big supporter of law enforcement. But when Jagger here mentioned the hunter, I wanted to crawl under the nearest table." She smiled softly at Jess. "Jagger. That's what I call your brother the rock-and-roller. I even have two Dog Park songs on my iPod."

Ellie happened to be a fan of Jess's band, too, but it was safe to say that she and Mona probably constituted five percent of the people who had Dog Park on their playlists.

"Sorry to bring up bad memories. You called the man 'the hunter'?"

"We all did, once we started hearing about why some of our friends were disappearing."

"And by *we*, you mean—"

"The girls. Call girls. Prostitutes. Hookers. Never cared for the term *whore*, though. I danced back then, too, but I've learned, over time, to admit that I was making most of my money doing a whole lot more. Part of what I do here for the girls is teach them the difference. Once you're bumping and grinding on a guy in the VIP Room, it feels like a small step into more . . . *intimate* contact. But, psychologically?" She shook her head. "There's a line, and I help girls find theirs. They can make a good living just from the dancing, especially with New York City tips. And if they stay off drugs and keep a sensible budget, they can build a mighty nice nest egg."

She sounded like a 1960s home ec teacher instructing young ladies on how to manage a household.

"Did you know any of the hunter's victims personally?"

"Oh yes. You have to understand, Utica is not a large city. About sixty-eight thousand people when I left; smaller now, if I had to guess. And so you're talking about a small pool of girls who were involved in the kinds of activities I was engaged in at the time. I knew Jenny Bronson real well. She had a nasty brother—one of the meanest pimps around. She wouldn't have had anything to do with the work if he hadn't gotten her into it—his own sister. And she had a sweet little son to take care of—so, one plus one, and there she went. And then I heard they found Leticia—don't remember her last name."

"Thomas. She was the third victim."

"That's right. Leticia Thomas. I didn't know her well, just to see around. But when I heard she was gone, too, I pulled back. Way back. I kept strictly to the dancing. But then when they found Donna Blank, I knew it was time to get out of Dodge."

"I can only imagine," Jess said. "Three women you knew were all killed."

"And it wasn't just that Donna was number three. When the hunter got to Donna, I knew none of us were safe."

"Why is that?" Ellie asked.

"Because Donna wasn't like Leticia and Jenny. She wasn't walking the streets or going out on calls. She stripped, did lap dances. Crossed the line when she was desperate enough to give a few handjobs behind the bar. But no way did she get in a car with a john. No way. I even tried to tell the cops that. I told them they should be doing more than just watching the streets. They needed to keep an eye on us girls at the clubs, because he was coming for us, too."

Ellie hadn't seen any mention of that information in the case files. "What did they say?"

"I'll tell you what he said—he threatened to arrest me if I didn't calm the fuck down. He didn't want to listen, but I knew what I knew about Donna. I'll go to my grave believing that, and so I believed I might go to my grave sooner rather than later if I kept working in Utica. Came downstate and never looked back."

"Did you and your friends ever have any ideas about who the killer was?"

"We know who it was: that man Anthony Amaro. Oh, just saying his name gives me the heebie-jeebies."

"Did you know Amaro before he was arrested?"

She shrugged. "Hard to say. You see a picture in the newspaper and soon enough, you start believing it's familiar. In my case, I thought I'd seen him around a couple of times, driving by in his car, looking at the girls. Guys like that: usually it's a married man, excited by the temptation, wondering what it would be like, and then they drive home with nothing but a fantasy. But maybe with Anthony Amaro, he was hunting."

"And what about before Amaro was caught? Did the girls have any theories?"

"Oh, we had plenty. Pimps doling out punishment. Johns who gave us a bad vibe. A lot of girls thought the killer would turn out to be a cop."

"Why is that?"

"Because he didn't get caught, that's why. And because the police did a damn good job keeping the rest of the public from caring about a few dead hookers. I gotta admit: when that one dude got so mad at me for telling him they better start helping us girls at the clubs, I started to wonder myself if a cop might be the one."

Ellie couldn't think of anything else to ask Mona except for her last name in case she needed it. "Winston. Jane Emily Winston to be more accurate."

Jess let out a laugh. "Jane Emily Winston? Sounds like someone who would marry Thurston Howell the Third."

She smiled, more to herself than to either of them. "Yes, indeed, that's who she was supposed to be. But I've been going by Mona since I left Utica and stopped turning tricks. Mona sounded like a strong woman, a woman who could take care of herself. Not the little broken girl whose father got to her at ten years old. Mona the Persona, is what I told myself; fake it till you make it. And *this*"—she gestured to the club around her—"for me, is making it."

155

*

In the parking lot, Jess asked if they should spring for a shared cab. It was late and still hot, and the nearest subway was a fifteen-minute walk.

"I'll pick it up since you did me a favor. Speaking of favors, can I crash on the couch tonight?"

"A blip in your domestic bliss?"

"No. The apartment's eighty-five degrees. I'm sick of sticking to the sheets."

"You know the deal. You can always crash; and the apartment's still in your name." When Max had asked Ellie to get an apartment with him, she had been relieved when Jess agreed to take over the rent on her place. As far as she was concerned, walking away from a rent-stablized residence in New York City was a more permanent commitment than even marriage. "Just say the word, sis, and it's yours again."

"Jess, I just need some air conditioning."

"Okay, whatever you say."

It seemed only minutes later when Ellie heard what sounded like a dentist's drill grinding against tooth enamel. She opened her eyes and saw chipped paint on the ceiling. She searched for the buzz and found her cell phone inching along the trunk in what used to be her living room.

She answered without looking at the screen. "Hatcher."

"How's life on your former sofa?" It was Max.

"A little too *Freaky Friday* for my tastes. I'm afraid if Jess and I bump into each other in front of the bathroom, we'll switch bodies. What's up?"

"I just got a call from Judge Johnsen's clerk. She's handling the expedited hearing docket this week, and on this morning's calendar is an emergency request from Anthony Amaro, petitioning for release."

"But we just got notice of the motion."

"I know. But Linda Moreland apparently has sources in the crime lab. She got wind of the DNA results."

Ellie forced herself to sit up and gave her spine a quick stretch. "What time?"

"Ten o'clock. Fifth floor."

"This is exactly why your boss should've held off on that DNA testing. The science is going to sound shiny and fancy. It's a distraction."

"I know, but Martin doesn't want it to look like we were trying to hide the results. I need to make sure we send the message that we're trying to do the right thing— thorough, methodical, neutral. I need you and Rogan to be there—the fresh-look team, no ties to the original investigation."

"Yeah, sure. I'll call Rogan."

She could only imagine how happy her partner would be to hear the news.

19

Max had warned Ellie that the hearing that morning would not be routine, but she had failed to anticipate the full extent of the media attention that would accompany the challenge of a criminal conviction that, in human years, would be old enough to vote. Local and national news vans lined the sidewalk as they entered the courthouse, and Ellie recognized at least seven observers in Judge Carol Johnsen's courtroom as reporters.

So far, Linda Moreland had taken the lead, laying out the grounds for her client's motion. Like the district attorney's office, Amaro had received an anonymous letter alleging a connection between Helen Brunswick's murder and the crimes for which he was supposedly responsible. The defense also had somehow managed to learn from the crime lab that, on reexamination of the physical evidence, DNA that could not be Amaro's had been discovered beneath two of Donna Blank's fingernails.

Next to Linda, a younger woman was scribbling furiously in a leatherbound book that looked more like a child's diary than a legal pad. Ellie recognized her from her Google research as Donna Blank's sister, Carrie. Behind them in the first row, a late-twentyish-looking man in a bowtie and cardigan sweater leaned forward, riveted by Linda's argument.

Fortunately, Max was armed with compelling counterpoints.

"We have been exercising due diligence, Your Honor, as should be fully expected in light of the recent developments. But to put the focus where it should be: the defendant was convicted of one, and only one, homicide—the killing of Deborah Garner. With respect to that charge, the defendant was arrested after an eyewitness identified him. Once he was arrested on the basis of that identification, he confessed. And after he confessed and was charged, he pled guilty. Ms. Moreland is trying to undermine the finality of that conviction with DNA evidence found on a woman killed a year earlier, nearly two hundred miles away, who was never named in any indictment against Mr. Amaro."

Max's words gave Ellie an idea about how to process the evidence against Amaro. She looked down at her notes with the names of Amaro's victims and the approximate dates of death.

Linda Moreland was out of her seat before Max finished his last sentence. "With all due respect, Your Honor, the district attorney's office wants it both ways. They want to say they are doing their best to find Helen Brunswick's killer and to ensure that they convicted the right person of murdering Deborah Garner. But when they take a step in the direction of accomplishing both goals—retesting the available physical evidence against my client—and get an answer they don't like, they want to explain it away. Instead of calling themselves a 'fresh look' team, it's more like the 'don't look' team. Frankly, it's disgusting."

"That's a strong term, Counsel."

"And I don't use it lightly, Your Honor. But please try to see it from my perspective. Anthony Amaro will not be the first innocent person to be exonerated. And I do believe that this new evidence exonerates him. There is a clear pattern in all these cases. We take the most compelling evidence against our clients and prove—absolutely *prove*—that it's flawed, and prosecutors simply wave it away and say, 'Well, that's never what mattered. What we *really* have is this.' And in this case, they don't *really* have anything. The identification was from a single eyewitness under unreliable conditions. Flawed eyewitness testimony has been a contributing factor in seventy-five percent of wrongful convictions. The so-called confession? It's from a detective who fancifully claims that suspect after suspect just happened to use the exact same language to implicate themselves. And the guilty plea? Anthony Amaro was terrified the state was going to execute him based on a coerced confession and a serial pattern that does not withstand scrutiny now that we have DNA evidence. Any sane person would have done the same thing to save his own life."

Next to Ellie in the first row of observer seats behind

Max, Rogan was shaking his head in disagreement. Ellie leaned forward and whispered to Max. "Take out Donna. If she's the one who's different, the pattern's more consistent."

But Ellie wasn't the only one vying for Max's attention. "And what do you have to say, Mr. Donovan, about the similarity among all of these confessions supposedly obtained by Detective Majors?" the judge asked. "'You got it right' and 'That's how it happened' and 'I didn't mean to do it.' Those three identical phrases appear in two-thirds of the confessions that Ms. Moreland has been able to compile. How does the state explain that?"

Max was on his feet now. "Again, Your Honor, this is the first we've heard from Ms. Moreland about any pattern to confessions obtained by the investigating detective. I know, however, that Detective Majors was a highly respected investigator, so much so that the department routinely asked him to give training to his peers regarding interrogations."

"Well, that's comforting," Moreland quipped.

Max ignored the dig. "What triggered this expedited hearing was the finding of new DNA evidence on Donna Blank—a woman killed in Utica—which has nothing to do with the fact that Mr. Amaro pled guilty to the murder of Deborah Garner. There are no facts in evidence to suggest that the Utica killings played a material role in Amaro's own admissions of guilt."

"Oh, come on now." Judge Johnsen was peering over

her glasses at Max. "I happen to remember this case. It may not be in the formal record, but anyone who was paying attention knows that Amaro was one of the first death penalty targets in large part because he was believed to be responsible for other killings in Utica, including Donna Blank's. How am I supposed to ignore the fact that DNA evidence now suggests another culpable party in her death?"

Ellie was frantically scribbling as Max responded to the judge's question.

"All the victims were prostitutes. They all would have had frequent encounters with multiple men. It's not surprising that one of them would have trace evidence from another man on her person." Ellie looked at Carrie Blank, sitting quietly next to Linda Moreland. This was Donna's sister — or half sister. How did it feel to have her discussed so impersonally? "We are doing what is right," Max continued. "Obviously, we asked for retesting of the physical evidence. We have two highly regarded detectives acting as a fresh-look team, detectives who had nothing to do with the original investigation."

Linda Moreland scoffed. "I wasn't going to bring this up, Judge, but, yes, they are oh so very neutral. Detective Hatcher *lives* with ADA Donovan."

Ellie was holding her notepad across the wood railing that separated her from Max.

Donna Blank—only one with non-matching

DNA. No proven prostitution ties. Only wrists were broken. She's the outlier. Deborah Garner part of consistent pattern.

But Max was too busy trying to hold up his part of an argument he was suddenly losing. "Your Honor, I am also part of the fresh-look team. I was barely out of high school when Mr. Amaro was convicted. The fact that defense counsel would even raise my relationship with Detective Hatcher shows that she is seeking to obfuscate—"

Judge Johnsen held up a palm. "Enough. If nothing else, the use of the word *obfuscate* shows that I've heard enough."

Ellie wrote yet another note and tried again to get Max's attention.

Have witness from Utica. Says Donna Blank <u>wasn't</u> a working girl.

The squeak of a door interrupted Judge Johnsen's comments, and Ellie turned to see the district attorney, Martin Overton, entering. Well over six feet tall, he had the good looks of a television anchor, with a strong chin and full head of dark-blond hair starting to grey at the temples.

"I'm sorry I'm late, Judge Johnsen. I want to make clear—both to you and to the community—that I am personally committed to seeing that my office does everything and anything to be thorough and transparent in every investigation. As I've always said, 'Better that six guilty men go free than one innocent man be imprisoned.'"

Ellie was pretty sure that the quote was either from William Blackstone or Benjamin Franklin and involved some other mathematical ratio. Regardless of the specifics, she was quite certain someone else had made the point long before Martin Overton had run for New York County District Attorney. He'd squeaked by in a contested race after the retirement of the longest-serving DA in the county's history.

Ellie tried one more time, this time speaking aloud to get Max's attention. "We have a witness. A former working girl in Utica. She says Donna isn't like the others."

She felt Rogan pulling her shoulder from behind. She turned, and he dragged a finger across his throat, signaling for her to knock it off. "Shh. Moreland is making us *those cops*."

Then Ellie saw the problem. Any facts offered for the first time this morning would only serve to fuel Linda Moreland's narrative about self-serving cops who fabricated evidence whenever convenient. And she could tell from Judge Johnsen's demeanor that she might be ready to rule.

"Look, what I keep coming back to is that District Attorney Overton wouldn't have ordered the testing of the physical evidence unless he thought it was important." *No!*, Ellie wanted to scream, Overton only ordered the testing because he was terrified of a primary challenge two years from now from a candidate on his left. "Quite frankly, I'd like to praise Mr. Overton for his clear commitment to neutrality and transparency."

"Thank you, Your Honor," Overton said. "And I know that ADA Donovan shares that commitment." Overton placed an approving hand on Max's shoulder. Ellie noticed Rogan look away.

"So here's what I'm going to do," Judge Johnsen announced. "Your fresh-look team has until Friday." Ellie could see that the judge was looking to Overton for an objection. Nothing. She continued her ruling. "Find something that changes the evidentiary picture and we'll talk. But otherwise—if you don't come up with more—I'm going to release Mr. Amaro, and prosecutors in Utica can decide whether to indict him for the killings he was never charged with. I'd say that eighteen years in prison with the questionable evidence you have is quite enough."

Ellie watched as Carrie Blank and the bow-tied male trailed behind Linda Moreland, who actually shook Martin Overton's hand as they departed the courtroom together. Ellie, Rogan, and Max followed in silence.

Three days. That's all they had.

20

Rogan was the first to break the silence. "What the hell just happened in there? It's like your boss was doing Moreland's job for her."

Max leaned his head back against his office chair and pressed his eyes closed. "I get it, Rogan. You're pissed. And you think I dragged you two into this for the wrong reasons. But Overton's trying to do the right thing. There's more than three hundred exoneration cases across the country now, and single-witness IDs are a major contributor."

"There's a damn confession, Donovan."

"You heard those excerpts in court; you're not troubled by the similarities in all of Buck Majors' confessions? The new DNA's not our only problem. I'm seeing red flags everywhere."

"Whose side are you on, man?"

Ellie had seen Rogan unleash on prosecutors before, but never Max.

"There are no sides, Rogan. Maybe you're the one who's got blinders on here. Ellie told me you've got a personal beef with Linda Moreland."

Rogan flashed a sharp look in her direction, but then

returned his attention to Max. "This isn't about personal beefs. Amaro murdered six people. For *us*, Donovan, our work is about those dead women, not climbing one more rung on the DA ladder."

"Whoa, whoa." She formed a capital T with her hands. "We're wasting time we don't have. You're both right. If Amaro's guilty, he needs to stay inside . . . forever. And if he's not, we need to fix it. We have until the end of the week to get answers. We need a plan. And whether we like it or not, Rogan, technically we're working for Max right now."

Rogan wasn't pacified, but at least he had stopped yelling.

Max shook his head. "There's too much we don't know. Who killed Helen Brunswick? Who mailed that letter? Whose DNA is under Donna Blank's fingernails? Whether she's part of the pattern or not. Whether Brunswick knew any of the victims. There is no way to tackle all of that in three days."

"You're right. But figuring out all of those things is our long-term goal. All we need to do in the short term is preserve the status quo. We want to keep Amaro inside for now. Make sure no one releases him until we're sure he's innocent, right?"

Max took in a deep breath. "Yeah, okay. Let's focus on that and see what we can do. Keeping Amaro in means addressing Judge Johnsen's concerns about the quality of the evidence. We should set aside all the mess about Helen

Brunswick and the Utica victims, and narrow in on the Deborah Garner case."

"Amaro's confession being number one," Rogan said.

Max nodded. "So find a way to cut to the chase with Majors. We need to know if he cut corners. And then we also have the eyewitness. If we can shore up the confession and the ID, we might just be okay. Then we find a way to peel away Donna Blank, like Ellie suggested. You said you had a witness?"

She told him about Mona's assertion that Donna, unlike the other victims, would not have gotten into a car with a john.

"That's thin. *Too* thin."

"I know. But Donna Blank's the only victim where we found new DNA evidence. Based on the skin beneath her nails, she seems to have fought back, and the others didn't. And her postmortem injuries weren't as severe. Only her wrists were broken."

"Maybe a copycat killed Blank," Rogan said. "That leaves Amaro on the hook for the others."

"And the copycat could also be the one who killed Helen Brunswick." She and Rogan were falling back into their normal groove. "Maybe he knew her back in Utica. Maybe all these years later, he feels some affinity toward Amaro and sends the anonymous letter to try to get him released."

"That's a lot of maybes," Max said. "Let's stick with the short-term focus and shore up the evidence against

Amaro on the Garner case. Start with the confession, like Rogan said. Any luck getting hold of Buck Majors?"

"Maybe," Rogan said. "I've been playing phone tag with him. He left a message during the hearing. Let me see what's up."

He made the call while they listened. He said a few *yeah*'s and *uh-huh*'s, then said they could be there in about an hour.

Three days.

21

According to the barebones employment files maintained by the city of New York, Buchanan Franklin Majors had served twenty-five years with the New York Police Department, first as an officer, then detective, then briefly as a sergeant detective before his retirement a decade ago. Rogan and Ellie had asked around for the more complete version. The man was a good investigator. Thorough. Patient. A pro in the interrogation room. He had a way of making suspects trust him. Of making them believe that he was their ally. That everything would get better as long as they told good old Buck the truth about what happened.

Ellie shifted her weight in the passenger seat. "How much farther?"

Rogan didn't take his eyes from the road. "You're like my five-year-old niece: *Are we there yet? How many more minutes?*"

"Your niece sounds like a genius to me. Seriously, where the hellfuck are we? We're two New York City detectives meeting a retired New York City detective. Last time I checked, New York City wasn't so . . . mani-cured." They passed a masonic lodge with a mobile sign announcing a pig roast in someone's honor. Next door, a swarm of teenagers dressed in grass skirts and bikini tops were waving drivers down for a car wash in the parking lot of a Friendly's. Nope, not N.Y.C.

"Key word being *retired*, Hatcher. Think about it: twenty-five years from now, do you want some newbie detective hauling your ass into a precinct to roll out your old war stories? No, you and Max will be enjoying your regular bingo nights, or whatever, in Long Island."

"Wash your mouth out."

"My point is, once you retire, you've earned the right to be let alone. The least we can do is meet the man on his own turf."

"So how many more minutes, Uncle J. J.?"

They passed a monument that read "Town of Orangetown," which struck her as redundant, and Rogan hit the turn signal. "We're there."

There turned out to be a parking lot for a golf course.

"I'll take Long Island bingo night," Ellie said as she got out of the car.

"You're missing out, Hatcher." Rogan paused and held a finger to his lips as they passed a golfer about to tee off. Rogan let out a whistle as the ball sailed down the fairway. "Dude crushed it."

"You told me we were meeting Buck Majors at his work."

"And that's what we're doing." He opened the door marked *Pro Shop*. Ellie felt like every person inside was inspecting them. She wanted to believe it was because they weren't dressed for golf, but suspected that her gender and Rogan's skin color might be part of it. Rogan made his way to the check-in counter and said they were here to meet with Buck Majors. As the clerk pulled out a walkie-talkie, Rogan explained: some cops took second careers as security guards or private investigators; Buck Majors now spent his days as a golf ranger.

"I don't understand those two words together. Lone Ranger. Army Ranger. Ford Ranger. Park Ranger. Got it, but no *golf* ranger."

"They keep up the pace of play."

"Still, *no comprendo*."

"So the course doesn't get all backed up. If some knuckleheads are taking too many mulligans—do-overs—or searching through the woods for a lost ball, the ranger comes by and tells them to hurry along."

"Now, that actually sounds fun."

"You make me sad sometimes, Hatcher."

Buck Majors came across like a happy-go-lucky golfer, not a cop. As they entered the clubhouse, she noticed that his eyes didn't dart around to measure up the other customers. He took the first seat at the table in the clubhouse, and didn't seem to mind having his back to the crowded restaurant. The man didn't even walk like most cops, back straight with shoulders squared. If not for the embroidered NYPD insignia on his collared golf shirt, she never would have known he'd ever been on the job.

A young waitress in a Georgetown tank top appeared immediately. "A Stella," Majors said. "For these guys, too. Just kidding. I remember the days before I could drink at work. You want a soda, maybe some ice tea? They do real brewed here, not that fake stuff."

Two teas and a Stella it was.

"Funny thing: there was a time when my whole life was NYPD. You guys are young enough, that's probably where you're still at. But to me? Now? It all feels like someone else's memories. Lost two different wives to the job, then a year after retiring, I meet a nice lady up here while shopping for books at the Barnes & Noble—you know, trying to keep myself busy? Just had our ninth anniversary and we're still going strong. Days, I spend here at the course. I don't have to pay greens fees, plus I get some extra dough to cover beers and burgers. Made some good friends among the regulars. Every Wednesday night we go to the restaurant down the street for trivia night with two other couples." He looked at his half-drained bottle of beer. "Pretty hard to beat that, wouldn't you say?"

"You had me at free golf," Rogan said.

"You said you need info on Anthony Amaro?"

"We've got a fresh body with the same MO, and now he's challenging his conviction. Linda Moreland's helping him."

"Had I known that, I would have come down to the city myself. Amaro was a true sadist. Cruel. Unrepentant. Sociopathic. And, ultimately, a coward."

"How so?" Ellie asked.

"Why break arms and legs? To inflict pain. To watch human suffering. But Amaro does it after shooting the women point-blank. Why would that be? I figure two possible explanations. Either he was too afraid of allowing a live woman a chance to fight back, so he killed them first, when they were caught off guard. Or he was too afraid of his own instincts and desires to permit another person to see them. Either way, he's a coward."

"We read all the reports," Rogan said. "You initially homed in on Amaro from E-Z Pass records?"

E-Z Pass was the system for collecting road tolls electronically throughout the Northeast.

"We were one of the very first investigations to use it to track a driver's movement. Deborah Garner was dumped at Fort Washington Park, just at the foot of the George Washington Bridge. We talked to her friends. She'd been working with another girl at the Alexander Hamilton rest stop in Secaucus. Mostly tricks right out of the parking lot, but they'd roll with the john if he insisted. Deborah got in a car and never came back. We were driving to the rest stop to take a look when one of the E-Z Pass readers at the turnpike toll plaza caught my eye. At the time, we still weren't sure what the system did, but I figured it was worth a shot. Based on the broken bones, we already thought we had a possible connection between Garner and the girls killed in Utica. We looked for cars that passed through that toll plaza that were registered to the Utica area. Turned out, one of the registered owners—Amaro—had a previous stop on his record for suspicion of loitering to pick up a hooker in Utica. We showed pictures of all the drivers to Garner's rest-stop partner and bingo, she goes right to Amaro. We had him."

"What do you remember about the confession?" Rogan asked.

"You said you read the reports." Majors held up a finger toward the waitress, and another beer appeared.

"We did," Rogan said. "But the district attorney wants us to make sure all the i's are dotted and the t's crossed."

"Well, you can check that off your list, then. My reports speak for themselves."

"No report captures the atmosphere in the box." Ellie placed her giant plastic cup of tea on the table and leaned forward. "Look, my dad was a detective. He told me how the world worked—the difference between the field and the courthouse. And as far as I'm concerned, that's the world cops will always occupy. But, like we said, we've got another victim. And just like you cracked your case by tying Garner to the Utica victims based on the postmortem treatment of the bodies, we're looking at the same situation. And here's the thing: the latest woman also has ties to Utica that go back to that era. So we just need to know: How much pressure went into that confession?"

"You're saying I *coerced* it?" It wasn't a word cops used except facetiously.

"No. I'm recognizing that I, and my partner, and you, and my father, and every other detective who has ever managed to persuade a person to give it up has to do more than say please with a cherry on top. People don't land themselves in prison for a long, long time without a little push. We're asking how hard you pushed."

"Apparently not hard enough. Never got him to confess to the Utica girls, did I?"

"No, but you got him to confess to Garner with nothing but evidence of his E-Z Pass moving through a New Jersey toll booth."

"And a witness ID. It was a clean confession. You wasted your time coming up here."

She and Rogan had already discussed the strategy for this line of questioning. With Rogan reluctant to go anywhere beyond taking Majors at his word, they eventually agreed to start with a light touch, before confronting Majors with hard questions. She looked to Rogan, wondering if he had anything else to ask Majors while he was still relatively cooperative.

"Did Amaro ever say why he had come downstate?" Rogan asked. If Majors had looked into the reasons behind Amaro's trip, the information wasn't in the police reports.

"Said he was visiting a kid he knew from foster care, but I always figured that was a cover. He was hoping to make regular visits down here for his kills, because the heat was on up in Utica."

"Amaro was in foster care?" Rogan asked. "Because these days he's playing the role of a good guy who's missed the chance to mourn his mother's funeral and play uncle to his niece and nephew."

"He's bullshitting. When he was facing the needle, he was crying about the years he spent rotating from foster home to foster home."

In the short time Ellie had been a homicide detective, New York had had a capital punishment moratorium. She'd never had the power to use death as a motivator in the box. "How much did that figure in the interrogation? The possibility of execution."

Majors looked like a mild-mannered senior citizen enjoying the links, but the laugh that escaped his lips was cruel. "There's not much I miss about the job these days, but the threat of the needle sure did make it easier to run an interrogation. You know how I got the nickname Buck? My parents named me after James Buchanan. When I was old enough to look him up, I found out he opposed the South's secession, but then waffled on the legality of the war to stop it. I was only seven years old, but I knew I didn't want to be named after someone who couldn't make up his mind. All the high-level talk about what's moral and what's not, whether the death penalty deters—I'll leave that to the politicians and philosophers, but one thing I know for sure about the death penalty: you get more confessions, which means more guilty pleas, which means fewer people getting off on technicalities.

What do you think Linda Moreland would have to say about that? Bet you anything she's got security alarms on her house, her office, her car. Takes a driver instead of the subway. Expects the hardworking people of the police department to keep her protected from the riffraff. But comes time for court, *we're* the bad guys." He spun his empty bottle on the table. "Listen to me. Guess the old Detective Dime is still in there after all."

"Did Detective Dime ever go the extra mile in coming up with a confession?" Ellie asked.

"Already told you. It was clean."

"Linda Moreland says it's too clean. *'You got it right. That's how it happened. I didn't mean to do it.'* Do those phrases sound familiar?"

Like a suspect in the box, he looked to Rogan for support. "What's your partner talking about?"

"She's quoting Moreland quoting you—quoting confessions you obtained. Count yourself lucky that she wasn't around when you were on the job, because Moreland's a real piece of work. She's got a theory that you were putting words on the page that never came out of a suspect's mouth. Turns out, those three sentences appear in most of the confessions you got over the years. We just need the explanation so we can keep Amaro where he belongs."

Majors took a deep breath, then squinted at them and smiled. He rose from the table. "You two kids trying to pull good cop/bad cop on me? On *me*? That's precious.

Have a good drive back to the city, because we're done talking."

Rogan seemed worry free as they walked to the golf course's parking lot, his gaze fixed on the balls soaring above the practice range.

"What did you make of that?" she asked.

"Seemed like most of the guys who were on the job when I started. Old school."

"Like, not above smacking-Amaro-in-the-head-with-a-telephone-book old school?"

"Sometimes I wonder if you really were raised by a cop, Hatcher. You know how it works in the box. No one gives it up easy. Sometimes you've got to suggest a path for them to get the words out."

"You can't possibly think it's okay to force innocent people to confess, telling them precisely what to say?"

"I think old Dime Majors back there would say, 'But what if they ain't so innocent?'"

"And that was for Majors to decide?"

"It is what it is, Hatcher. We've pressed for confessions, too, and you know it. When you've got the right guy, and you need to seal the deal, you do what you need to do."

"But it's starting to look like Majors had the wrong guy in Amaro's case."

"And now you're sounding like Max and his boss. We see this one different, and that's that." She started to speak, but he interrupted. "It's okay. You're in a bad position, and I get that. We get through this case, then we go back to normal."

She was struggling for something to say. She never should have let Max convince her to take this assignment.

"Seriously, Hatcher, we're cool. We got this."

They got into the car in silence, and then he started the engine.

"What next?" she asked.

"We do like we do. The best evidence was the confession and the eyewitness."

"We need to find Deborah Garner's partner at the rest stop."

"Bingo."

22

Linda had barely spoken a word to Carrie since they left the courtroom. She'd been pacing between her office, the narrow hallway, and the tiny lobby the entire time as she gave quotes to the media via her cell phone.

"Please tell Anderson," she said dramatically, "that I've always believed that the clients I've worked to exonerate were the anomalies—the few blips in an imperfect system that we must continue to review and perfect. But when I see a detective who was held up by the NYPD as a hero—as a *miracle worker* for his ability to pull self-incriminating statements from the suspects he and he alone decided to target—I start to wonder if we might not have a more systemic problem. There's no doubt in my mind that Anthony Amaro should be released. The real question is: How many more innocent people are behind bars because of Buck Majors?"

Carrie had no idea what she could possibly do to help. And she still hadn't told her mother she had quit Russ Waterston to represent Anthony Amaro. If Linda was getting this many calls, she could only imagine the extent of the media coverage in Utica. But she was certain that

the minute she dialed her mom, Linda would come looking for her. She felt trapped.

Carrie finally decided that Linda was sufficiently preoc-
cupied for her to make a quick call to her mother. Sure
enough, her mom's line had rung three times when Linda
walked into the storage room that was doubling as Carrie's
workspace, her hands laced behind her head in triumph.

"Amazing. I thought this case had the potential to
break everything open, but I never really anticipated the
power of a single narrative to capture all of the harms
I've been trying to highlight."

Carrie hit the "end" button on her phone and set it on
top of her journal on her worktable.

"You and that adorable little notebook," Linda said.
"You weren't kidding about that habit of yours, were
you?"

Carrie shrugged. She was regretting telling Linda the
truth when she'd asked what Carrie was scribbling before
that morning's court hearing. Now she felt like Linda was
questioning her efficiency.

"I'm glad the case is going well for you," Carrie said.
"But we talked about this when you hired me. I want to
know the truth about my sister's murder. I need to know
whose DNA is beneath her fingernails."

"As well you should," Linda said. "But we're not the
state. We don't have search warrants or grand juries or
the inherent power that comes with being part of the government. *This*—embarrassing them—is our only power."

"Embarrassing them doesn't tell me who killed my sister."

"Look, Carrie. I hired you on the assumption that you were smart enough to understand that identifying the real killer was only a possibility. This isn't Perry Mason. The best we can do is to pressure the state to produce the answers they should have gotten for you twenty years ago."

"So what's left for me to do at this point?" Carrie asked.

"If you think we've done anything to truly get their attention, you're giving them too much credit. We've got a clock ticking over them before Amaro's release, but that's not enough. It's all about damages now. Money."

"I thought we were supposed to be getting to the truth." She realized how naïve she sounded the minute the words escaped her lips.

"That's *their* job. Ours is to force them to do it, and money's the only way to motivate them. If it weren't for Buck Majors, they might have gotten to the truth about Donna nearly two decades ago. The DA is going to have to review every single conviction obtained as a result of one of his supposed confessions. We could keep a dozen lawyers employed full time for the next five years. We could even change the way people feel about the treatment of criminal defendants. And the first step is to convince these SOBs to finally figure out what happened to Donna. You have no idea how important you are to this case now. You're the one who knows the lay of the land. You're the one who's going to make this happen."

"And what exactly is *this*?"

"Making this a statewide case. We have Martin Overton's attention here in the city, but now we've got to start pulling in the upstate players. We need to tear down not just the Deborah Garner investigation, but Utica's complacency. Why did the Utica PD let the NYPD close their case without doing the real work?"

"I'm not sure what you want me—"

"Go to Utica," she said. "I'm sending Thomas, too. And don't argue with me about that. He's got a list of all my investigators if you need anyone up there, and you're going to want someone to drive for you, make your appointments, fetch you toothpaste from the drugstore. Trust me—the dear heart is invaluable on the road."

The lawyers Carrie had worked for at Russ Waterston had tended to be painfully specific with their requests, down to the nitty gritty of the number of pages and the preferred font for any given legal memo. Linda was terribly eager to send Carrie back to her hometown, complete with a personal assistant in tow, but she hadn't actually explained why. "I'm sorry, Linda. I don't understand what you're asking me to do."

"Find the dirt. Find our poster child. Who epitomizes the Keystone Kops who failed to figure out the truth earlier? I don't want you and Thomas back here until you can bring me Utica's Buck Majors."

23

John Shannon nearly ran right into Ellie as she and Rogan climbed the stairs at the 13th Precinct.

"Whoa, bruiser," Rogan said.

"Sorry, I'm late for grand jury. If I'm a no-show, no OT, know what I'm saying? Oh, and a heads-up: there's some guy waiting for you up there. Not a happy camper. Have fun!" He gave a chirpy wave as he continued on his way.

Their visitor turned out to be Mitch Brunswick. He leapt from his chair in the waiting area the second they hit the stairwell landing. His body language read angry, but his eyes were fatigued and red. He'd been crying in the recent past.

"When were you going to tell me?"

In the rush to react to this morning's hearing, they hadn't even thought to call Helen Brunswick's husband to notify him that Anthony Amaro was alleging a connection between his wife's murder and the crimes he was suspected of committing. By now, he would have heard about it from the news.

Rogan held out an arm to keep Brunswick back. "We're in the middle of an ongoing investigation."

"You don't think I know that? It's bad enough that I've been treated like a suspect. But you were in my home when I told you that Helen used to work upstate, right around that same time, and you said *nothing*."

If Mitch Brunswick was involved in his wife's murder, they would be idiots to talk about the case with him. If he wasn't, he would always remember this conversation as just one more indignity he suffered at the hands of police after his children's mother was killed. Until they had more information, all they could do was err on the side of caution. Cruelty was better than jeopardizing a murder investigation.

Rogan started to walk past Brunswick. "Like I said, we're working on the investigation. We promise to give you answers as soon as we have them."

"In the meantime, I have to tolerate photographs of my wife's dead body on the Internet?"

"What are you talking about?"

He handed them his cell phone. "My *kids* saw these. Some future sociopath at their school was sending it to everyone."

His smartphone was open to the website of one of the local tabloid papers. Ellie recognized the photograph as one taken at the crime scene after Helen's body was discovered. The editors had the decency to blur her bloodied torso and face, which was already gray and bloated by then, but the picture clearly depicted her broken limbs. The headline read: RETURN OF A SERIAL KILLER?

"I promise you," Ellie said. "We have no idea how they could have gotten this photograph."

His hand was trembling when she returned the phone to him.

"I was the one who identified the body," he said, staring at the screen. "She was covered with a white sheet. Her body, I mean. I saw her face, but—this." He shook the phone. "It isn't right. My wife was a person. A real person, and a good person. She didn't deserve to die, and she sure as hell doesn't deserve this."

As they watched Mitch Brunswick make his way down the stairs, Rogan said, "You know who must have leaked those pictures, don't you?"

She mumbled that she didn't know.

"Linda Moreland."

"Or whoever's leaking information to her could've sold them to the paper."

"Nope, it's Moreland. She's calling out the press, big-time. Nothing gets the dogs barking like a lurid crime-scene picture."

There was no way to be sure who was responsible for that photograph going public, but Ellie was now convinced of one thing: Mitch Brunswick had not killed his wife.

24

You the one here to see Christy McCann?"

Ellie nodded. To save time, she had made the trip alone, leaving Rogan free to work the bigger picture. It didn't take two detectives to question an eyewitness who had identified Anthony Amaro eighteen years earlier.

In movies, prostitutes are always good people with bad luck who manage through hard work and big hearts to find happiness. In the most romanticized version of the fairy tale, prostitution is fun and glamorous and leads to true love and luxury shopping sprees with men who look like Richard Gere. In the real world, prostitutes could be good or bad people, but nearly always ended up with short, harrowing lives. Jess's coworker Mona, who had managed to convince herself that she was saving girls by teaching them the difference between stripping and whoring, was the closest thing Ellie had ever seen to some kind of hooker's happy ending.

When the marshal escorted Christy McCann into the meeting room, Ellie could see that the woman who'd been turning tricks with Deborah Garner at a rest stop in Secaucus had arrived at nothing close to happiness. She was almost shockingly gaunt, with pocked skin and missing teeth. At least she'd been easy to find, right here at the Bedford Hills Correctional Facility for Women. Six years ago, she was sentenced to life in prison for forcing drain cleaner down the throat of another prostitute because she had dared to hold back money from their shared pimp.

McCann took one look at Ellie and then glanced back at the male guard for an explanation. Ellie kicked out the chair on the opposite side of the table with her foot, and McCann finally took a seat. "You're too pretty to be a cop," she said.

"Should I say thank you?" Ellie asked.

"You here about Lincoln?" Lincoln Turner was the peach of a pimp whom police suspected had ordered the drain-cleaner punishment. "Every time he gets the better of one of you people, seems I get a visit. Instead of pigs, they should call you elephants, you got such long memories." She smiled at her own joke. "But I still got nothing to say."

"I could care less about an over-the-hill pimp. I'm here about your friend, Deborah Garner."

"Ain't my friend no more. She got herself killed."

"You can drop the badass front, Christy. I read the police reports. You were beside yourself when you learned she was dead. The two of you were at that rest area together for a reason. You didn't have pimps. You had each other. She protected you, and vice versa."

"Lot of good it did us," she muttered.

"You helped her even after her death," Ellie said. "A lot of girls would have kept their heads down and their mouths shut. But when you didn't see your friend for two days, you made a call: you reached out to the police. Even after you learned that her body had been found, you kept helping her. If it hadn't been for you, they never would have known that Deborah had been working that rest stop. And they wouldn't have found the E-Z Pass records, so they wouldn't have had photographs to show you of suspects. You were the key to finding Deborah's killer."

"Deb . . ." The word was hard to make out initially, but then Christy spoke up. "She absolutely hated Deborah. Said it sounded like 'candelabra.'" Her face softened at the memory.

"Sorry. I mean, Deb. You helped find Deb's killer."

"Where were you when they were putting my ass in here for life?"

"Two different things, Christy. All I'm saying is that I know you wanted justice for your friend. I need you to tell me what you remember about Anthony Amaro."

"I know he's a killer, just like you said. Why are we talking about him after all this time?"

"There are problems with some of the evidence. But you identified him. You told police you recognized him as the man who picked up Deb at the rest stop."

"That's right. Nothing else to say."

"My understanding is that Detective Majors showed

you several photographs of drivers whose cars had passed through that area around the same time. How sure were you of the identification?"

"Maybe you should be asking your own boy instead of me."

"By 'my boy,' do you mean Detective Majors? I should be asking *him* how sure *you* were that Amaro was the man you saw? That doesn't make sense."

She pursed her lips and worked her jaw back and forth. The effect was disturbingly goatlike. "What exactly do you want me to say?"

"The truth, Christy. There's no right answer except the truth."

"You people say that, but it's never what you mean. Not with Lincoln. Not ever."

"Are you saying that you had the impression back then that you were *supposed* to identify Anthony Amaro?"

"Duh. He killed Deb. Of course I was going to identify him."

This was like talking to a windup doll. "Christy, I really mean this: Did you identify Amaro because you actually remembered seeing him, or because you thought you were supposed to pick him?"

"He was the guy. His car was in the right place, at the right time. He was a john. And he was from the same town where a bunch of girls got killed the same exact way. So I picked him."

"How did you know all that?" According to Majors,

Christy had flipped through a series of driver's-license pictures and homed in on Amaro's.

"Because the cop told me when he showed me the photo. So I said, 'Yeah, that's the guy,' and he told me I did a good job. He said that was all he needed for probable cause so he could make an arrest back where the guy lived. And then, when I called him later to find out what happened, he said the dude confessed."

"But did you actually recognize him as the man Deb left with?"

"Yeah, sure. What's the problem?"

Law enforcement knew much more now about the fallibility of eyewitness memory, but even back then, Christy should never have been told so much about the evidence against an individual suspect before viewing his photograph.

"That's not how it's supposed to work—" Ellie bit her lip. She wanted to crawl back in time and shake Buck Majors until his teeth rattled. This was his mess.

She could picture all the mistakes. Majors would have been so pleased with himself for pulling the E-Z Pass information. When he got a hit on a Utica driver with a previous record as a john, he gave the eyewitness a little push. Her ID then confirmed his certainty that Amaro was guilty, so he pushed on the interrogation, either forcing or fabricating that confession. They might never know the truth about Amaro because of his shoddy investigation.

"You want me to say I remember?" Christy offered.

"Then I remember. You want me to say something on that detective, I'm happy to do that, too. I'd do anything to help myself out here."

"Funny you should be so willing to make that offer," Ellie said. "You didn't sound willing to deal when you thought I was here about Lincoln Turner."

Christy lifted her stringy brown hair and turned to show Ellie a tattoo on the back of her neck. *LINCOLN's GIRL*. "He did it himself. Lincoln was the only man who ever loved me."

Ellie signaled to the guard that she was ready to leave.

Eighteen years ago, this woman and her friend Deb looked out for each other. They thought they could keep each other safe. Whoever killed Deborah Garner had effectively destroyed Christy McCann, too.

Ellie's cell phone flashed a new message from Max as soon as she turned it on. She called him back without listening to it.

He didn't bother with a greeting. "Are you on your way?"

"To where? I'm just leaving Bedford Hills now. We've got a problem with Christy McCann. It looks like Majors prompted her ID."

"Dammit. Okay, that makes the trip all the more important."

"What trip? I didn't have a chance to listen to the message you left."

"Rogan's on his way to my office now. Swing by the apartment and pack a bag, then meet us here and I'll lay it all out for you. We may have finally caught a break. I need you guys to go upstate."

25

As she approached Max's office, Ellie spotted Rogan through the open door, swiveling impatiently in one of the guest chairs. As she got closer, she also saw Max leaning over an unfamiliar man who was seated at his computer. "You can't get any other information?" Max pleaded.

"That's the nature of the beast," the guy at the desk was explaining. "The ISP gives us the IP address, which we can track. But the person went through our contact page for a reason."

Ellie rapped her knuckles against the door. "Adding one to the occupancy." She dropped her duffel bag at her feet with a thud.

"Hey, you," he said casually before turning his attention back to his other visitor. "Okay, thanks, Mark. I need to loop these guys in. Give me a call if you think of anything else. And, seriously, ask IT to rethink this part of the website. We're law enforcement. We need to be smarter than this."

"I'll pass it on."

He signaled to Mark to close the door behind him. "Fucking idiots," he said the minute they were alone. "Sorry, not Mark, but someone two steps up the ladder."

"What now?" she asked.

"Our website. Apparently, last year Martin had IT do an overhaul. There's a contact page with absolutely no security measures. It supposedly requires a name and e-mail address, but you can type in Rumpelstiltskin at scratch-my-ass-dot-com, and that's all the system keeps track of. Pretty obvious way for the public to send in messages to the district attorney's office with no accountability."

"Sounds like the kind of change someone would make when he's trying to be *transparent with the community*." Rogan continued to swivel. "Guess that makes your boss the idiot."

"It doesn't matter," she said, wondering how many times she'd need to play referee before this assignment was over. "Even if the site used the usual safeguards, anyone with half of a brain can open a free, untraceable e-mail account. So what exactly did Rumpelstiltskin at scratch-my-ass-dot-com send?" She took a seat next to Rogan, who at least managed a chuckle.

"You'll see why I'm so frustrated." Max handed them each a printed copy of an e-mail message.

From: Kelly Matthews, Information Technology
Subject: Fwd: A message from your website
To: Max Donovan
ADA Donovan, see below, from the website.
KM

— —Forwarded Message— —

From: A friend xx@yy.com

Anthony Amaro did it. He admitted everything to his
cellmate after he was arrested. The guy's name was
Rob Harris. Ask him what he knows.

This mail is sent via contact form on New York District
Attorney

"That message came into our website about fifteen
minutes after we left Judge Johnsen's courtroom today.
Luckily the person in IT who monitors the incoming
webmail realized it wasn't the usual kind of comment, so
she forwarded it right away. Mark—the kid who was just
here—had our website provider pull the IP address of the
computer used to post the message. But, as you heard, it
was a public computer."

Rogan reached over and slid his copy of the message
onto Max's desk. "There were reporters all over that
hearing. I'd be surprised if we don't get flooded with this
kind of nonsense."

"We can't just ignore it."

"Oh, I'm aware," Rogan said dryly. "Well, at least in
this instance, the supposed secret new evidence might
help us."

"Any possibility of finding a witness, or camera footage?" Ellie asked. "Someone who might have actually
seen the person typing the message?"

He shook his head. "The sender used one of the

million laptops on display at the midtown Apple store."

"Any idea who Rob Harris is?" Rogan asked. "We didn't see anything about a jailhouse informant in the case files."

"That's because it's not there. If Amaro made incriminating statements to another prisoner while he was in custody, law enforcement apparently never found out about it."

"But whoever sent this message claims to have," Ellie said. "What if this Rob Harris sent it himself? No, that doesn't make sense. Why use Internet anonymity just to give us his own name as a witness?"

"It could be from the same person who sent us the letter linking Helen Brunswick's murder to Amaro in the first place," Max said.

"Yeah, but the letter tried to exonerate Amaro, and this e-mail implicates him. Not to mention, how would one person know both the details of Brunswick's injuries and a conversation that took place between two cellmates eighteen years ago upstate?"

"Sorry," Rogan said, "but you two have a way of working each other up. One thing at a time. Shouldn't we be looking for Rob Harris?"

"That's why I called you guys. I confirmed with the Oneida County Sheriff's Department that Amaro was housed with one Robert Burton Harris his first night in custody. No further record since completing a drug sentence twelve years ago. Has a current address, still in Utica. Hate to ask you guys to go, but . . ."

Ellie knew why he was apologetic. Even if it weren't for their personal relationship, directing police officers for long-distance travel wasn't usually within an ADA's job description. This time, she spoke up before Rogan. "You're sending two NYPD detectives to another county to interview a jailhouse rat who might not actually be a rat?"

"You're the only ones I can possibly trust with this. I nearly had to stage a hunger strike to get Martin to approve the budget, but given the complications with Christy McCann, I convinced him that the possibility of new evidence that actually *incriminates* Amaro is too much to pass up."

She was ready for Rogan to gripe about the haul upstate, or to lob another barb about Max's boss, but instead he rose from his chair and jingled a set of keys in the air. "I'm not driving three hours without my tunes. Now grab your ratty-ass gym bag and let's hit the road, slowpoke."

He had meant what he said at the golf course. They saw this case differently, but they were still partners. They just needed to get through it, and then things would be back to normal.

"Let's do like we do," she said, hoisting her bag over her shoulder.

She didn't realize until they were out in the lobby that she hadn't even said goodbye to Max.

26

Carrie pulled her suitcase from the back corner of her bedroom closet. She wanted to cry when she saw the bright blue bikini—tags still attached—that she'd scored on a Bloomingdale's clearance rack three months earlier. She had thrown the swimsuit there as a promise to herself that the next time she traveled it would be to a white-sand beach with rum drinks and reggae music. Instead, she was packing for a sojourn in Utica.

Her hometown being what it was, she knew there was no way she could check in to the downtown Governor Hotel, the fanciest joint in the city, without her mother getting wind of it. She had to make the call.

Her mom picked up after half a ring.

"Carrie! Is that you?"

When Carrie bought her mother a digital phone two birthdays ago, her mother had complained that the "gadget" was overly complicated, its features "unneces-sary." Now she watched that caller ID screen with a hawk's eye.

"Hey, Mom. Yeah, it's me."

"I'm glad you called. There's some news coming out here. I don't want it to upset you."

In a strange way, Carrie envied her friends whose parents became less tethered to the real world as they aged. Rosemary Blank, as usual, had her finger on the pulse.

"That's actually why I was calling you, Mom. I take it you heard about the, uh, Anthony Amaro thing?"

"The, *uh, thing*? I taught you to be more specific with your vocabulary than that."

Carrie had a momentary flashback of her mother pinching her neck every time she said "like." She had left China and learned English from scratch in the United States. She wasn't about to allow her child to butcher the only language she knew. "Fine," Carrie said. "His petition for postconviction relief, to be precise."

"Yes, they've been talking about it on the networks here. I can't believe some crazy judge is going to let him out Friday. It's ridiculous."

Carrie was wondering what would upset her mother more: the fact that she was representing Anthony Amaro, or the fact that she'd been so insignificant thus far that the media hadn't bothered to notice her participation.

"There's something I need to tell you," she said. "You know who Linda Moreland is, right?"

"Of course. She's quite brash for my tastes, but is very zealous. In one of the introductions on television they said she used to teach at CUNY Law School. Did you know her?"

Carrie felt like the stars were aligning in her favor. Her best hope was that her mother would be so impressed at the level of the legal work that she would look past the fact that it related to Donna's death.

Band-Aid, Carrie said to herself. *Just rip off the Band-Aid.*

"She was teaching while I was a 1L there. In fact, she remembered me, so much so that she called me when she needed another lawyer at her firm. I'm working for her, Mom. On the Amaro case. I'll be coming up to Utica tomorrow."

"But you have a job. You don't have time to work on this—"

"I changed jobs, Mom. I'm representing Anthony Amaro."

"But—"

"No, Mom. That's it. I'll talk to you more about it tomorrow, okay? I'll be staying at the Governor."

"A hotel? For how long?"

"I don't know. A while. Until Linda thinks we have what we need."

"Why aren't you staying at home?"

"Because I'll need to work, Mom. I need wireless Internet and room service and the business center with the fax machines. And I'm going to have Linda's assistant with me, so we'll actually need two rooms, which you don't have."

"Is that—how do you pay for that?"

"It's through the law practice, Mom." Carrie's mother had pushed her so hard for so many years, but the reality is that her mother had so little for so long that, to her, an indefinite stay at a business-class hotel was the equivalent of lounging on a mattress made of money.

"I don't understand. What will you be doing?"

If only Carrie knew the answer to that question. "Figuring out if the Utica police were negligent in their investigation. If so, we can argue that they added to the deprivation of Anthony Amaro's constitutional rights."

"So you're basically trying to blame the police?"

"If that's where the blame lies. Yes, that's the strategy."

"Well, you know me. I say do what you need to do. But I'm surprised you're willing to go along with something like that."

Her mother seemed willing to look past the fact that Carrie's new job pulled her into the darkness that was Donna's life, but she still sounded concerned.

"Why are you surprised, Mom?"

"Because you're such good friends with Bill."

She was starting to wonder if her mother was totally confused. "What does this have to do with Bill?"

"Nothing, not directly. But certainly it involves his father."

Bill's father, Will, still worked at the Utica Police Department. He was the kind of cop who would never voluntarily retire. Carrie had known him since she was in the second grade, and he had given her fatherly advice innumerable times, especially after her own father passed away.

"It's not the whole department, Mom. It's just a question of why they didn't do more to solve their own cases."
She wanted to say, *Why didn't they pay more attention to Donna's murder?* but she was trying to keep the focus on the work, not the girl Rosemary Blank had refused to recognize as a member of her family.

"Right. And that's why it involves Will. Or didn't you know? He's the one in charge of the whole investigation. Linda Moreland can't drag down the UPD without taking Will Sullivan with it."

PART THREE

FREEDOM

27

Linda had warned her how difficult it would be to work on the road, but even Linda had probably failed to anticipate the demands that would be put on Carrie for her time once word got out that she was back in Utica. By the time she and Thomas checked in at the Governor Hotel, the front desk had two messages from her mother and three from Melanie. It was late in the evening—too late for her to try to make any headway with the Utica police. The thought of seeing her mother felt like a chore, but the upside of any visit to Utica was seeing Melanie in person.

She immediately regretted the decision to drop by when Tim answered the door. Last she heard, he was working the swing shift at the paper mill in Little Falls. Had he lost yet another job?

They managed to mutter a hello to each other by the time Melanie interrupted the awkwardness with a big hug. "Oh, you came! Yea! I haven't seen you since—what?—Thanksgiving?"

"Calm down," Tim said. "Not like she's the second coming of Christ or anything."

A stranger might have written off the comment as typical couples' banter, but Carrie knew all too well the complicated truth. Twenty years ago, Tim could have been a story Melanie would someday tell about a boyfriend bullet she had dodged in her youth. But instead, a then twenty-year-old Tim got Melanie pregnant while she was still in high school, and Melanie went from presumptive valedictorian to one of eleven girls whose black robes doubled as maternitywear for their walk across the graduation stage.

She still remembered how happy Melanie was the following June when Tim "stepped up," in Melanie's words, by proposing to her. "My baby will have a father. My baby won't be out of wedlock." At first, Carrie really had hoped for the best. Melanie insisted that Tim was looking for work. That he loved her and would love the baby.

There were early warning signs. When Carrie came home from Cornell for Christmas break and dropped by to see the baby, Tim, still unemployed, passed out on the sofa after drinking too much gin. As they whispered in the kitchen, late into the night, Melanie asked Carrie if she thought it was possible for a man to love a woman too much. She said Tim sat close to her, all the time, even when she was trying to find cool air in the late-summer heat when she was nine months pregnant. And since Timmy Junior was born, he was constantly accusing her of loving the baby more than him.

Then Carrie went back to Cornell, and she and Melanie had fallen out of touch. By the time Bill helped them reestablish their friendship, Melanie had tossed Tim to the curb and openly vented to Carrie about all of the many reasons he was toxic to her and their son. The on-and-off employment. The drinking. The jealousy. The petty scams and troubles with police.

As critical as Melanie was, at the time, of her estranged husband, Carrie always wondered whether she'd heard the worst of it. One night Melanie let it slip that, the previous year, she had gotten rid of a new puppy because Tim was jealous—sharing her with Timmy and a dog was just too much and she was afraid he might hurt the animal. When Carrie pushed to know why Melanie would worry about such an awful thing, she clammed up. Carrie hadn't forced her to explain. And in her silence, Melanie wasn't protecting Tim; she was protecting her own pride.

But then, five months after they had recommenced their friendship, Carrie dropped by with a bag full of groceries for what they were now calling their "family dinner night," and Tim was back. Melanie seemed sheepish about his return, but offered no explanation. How many times since then had Carrie wondered if Melanie would have been better off on her own?

To Carrie, Tim would always be the boyfriend who had become Melanie's burden to shoulder for life. And to Tim, Carrie would always be the twice-a-year visitor who made his wife silently wonder what could or should have been.

She had been in their apartment for an hour, and the mood had been stilted and awkward. She kept noticing Melanie's gaze moving toward the stains on the sofa, broken slats on their blinds, and the threadbare carpet in the front hallway. The closest they had come to a smooth conversation was when Carrie asked about Timmy Junior—TJ—who was taking classes at the community college. Melanie beamed when she reported he had a 3.8 GPA and was planning to apply to a four-year university. At that, his father let out a burp and got up to fetch another can of beer, muttering something about a "waste of money in this economy."

Then Melanie changed the subject to the last possible thing Carrie wanted to talk about—the Amaro case. "They're saying on the news that they found somebody else's DNA on the bodies."

"Just Donna's, actually. That was one of the big issues in court. The New York DA's office was saying that Donna and the other victims here had nothing to do with the validity of their case in the city."

"Well, that's dumb. It was obvious back then that they suspected Amaro of killing all of them."

"Look who thinks she's a lawyer all of a sudden," Tim mumbled.

He'd had three beers since Carrie sat down, and who knew how many before she arrived. Carrie resisted the urge to start an argument, because she knew Tim would only take it out on Melanie once they were alone. "Hey, do you know whether Mr. Sullivan has anything to do with the Amaro case?" Although Melanie had never mentioned it to Carrie, she knew from Bill that Bill's father checked in periodically on Melanie and TJ to make sure they were okay. Though they didn't have any proof that Tim got physical with his family, the suspicions of a career cop apparently matched Carrie's own.

"Yeah, I'm pretty sure he does. That's so cute that you still call him Mr. Sullivan," Melanie said. "He's been telling us to call him Will since we got out of high school."

"I can't help it." Among the panoply of manners her mother had drilled into her, Carrie had been trained to call her friends' parents "Mr." and "Mrs.," even when they insisted otherwise. "How long has he been involved in the case?" Carrie hadn't seen his name on any of the materials she'd reviewed so far.

"It was as things were winding down, I think. By the time Amaro got caught, it had been more than a year since they found Donna and the other girl."

"Stacy Myer," Carrie said.

"I think by then the lead detective on the case was about to retire, and Will took over. He told me there wasn't much for him to do at the time. He was just wrapping up the loose ends. Like, he was the contact person for victims' families, media calls, that sort of thing. I mean, I guess he told your parents, because of Donna and all."

"Yeah, they knew." She remembered her father calling her on the dorm's pay phone freshman year to tell her that there had been an arrest.

"That's gotta help you, right? I mean, that you've known the cop in charge since we were little. Talk about a lucky break."

Carrie smiled and took another big sip of her wine. It would be lucky if her job was to figure out who actually killed Donna and the other victims. But that wasn't her job, not as far as Linda Moreland was concerned. Her job was to blame the Utica Police Department for not arriving at the truth earlier, and everything Melanie was telling her supported Linda's theory that the police here had been all too eager to let the NYPD do the heavy lifting that should have been theirs. Rather than pick up the case and work it from scratch, Mr. Sullivan had used another detective's retirement as a reason to close the case for the police department's purposes, but without actually closing it with a legal conviction for those victims and their families.

Carrie stripped the comforter off the hotel bed—a blanket of germs, as far as she was concerned—and flopped down. She was exhausted and wired at the same time.

She had packed the trunk of the rental car with all of the case materials, now lined beneath the window of her hotel room. There was still one entire box of records from Amaro's original defense that she hadn't reviewed.

She removed the top of the box and stared down at the contents. The three glasses of wine she'd put away at Melanie's had left her too fuzzy for any real work at this hour.

She heard a sitcom laugh track from the adjoining room. She thought about knocking on the pass-through door to see if Thomas wanted television-viewing company, but a pop-in this late might be inappropriate. She closed her eyes and listened to the muted sounds of punch lines and canned laughter. She pretended she was a child again, nodding off in the living room as her parents watched *Cheers*. They'd catch her snoozing, but she'd shoot her eyes open, insisting she was still awake so she could stay in the living room a little longer.

Then she was remembering another moment from her childhood. There was a heat wave. She'd taken a break from hide-and-seek to fetch a pitcher of water from Bill's house. Bill had warned her to be quiet. His father was working graveyards and would be napping in the living room, the second-floor bedrooms too hot for daytime sleeping.

She opened the screen door as quietly as she could, then peeked into the living room on her way to the kitchen to make sure she hadn't woken Bill's dad. But Mr. Sullivan wasn't sleeping. He was holding a framed photograph in his hands, and he was crying. His shoulder holster was loose on the sofa next to him. She'd never seen a man cry, and she'd never seen a gun that close up. She must have made a sound, because he suddenly looked up, wiping his face immediately.

She froze. It was too late to duck into the kitchen and pretend she hadn't seen him. "It's okay, Carrie." He moved his gun away and waved her in. "Has Bill ever told you about his mother?"

He tilted the photograph in her direction. It was a younger but recognizable Mr. Sullivan with a woman in a crisp blue cotton dress, holding a baby.

"Everyone knows she died."

He set the frame down gently on the coffee table. "Three years ago today. I'm all Bill has now. I know it's hard for him."

She still remembered patting him stiffly on the back, the way her father did to Carrie when she was sad and he didn't know how to soothe her. "It's okay, Mr. Sullivan. Most of the kids only have moms, and so Bill has a dad; and you're sort of like a dad for Melanie, too. And then our moms can be moms to Bill. He'll be okay. So will you."

When she saw the tears in his eyes, she thought she had said something to make him even sadder. She didn't understand yet that a single comment—offered by the right person in the right moment—could make you cry from appreciation.

As she fell more deeply into sleep, Carrie realized the real reason she hadn't done any work tonight. She was dragging her feet. As long as she had twenty-year-old documents piled up in boxes, still awaiting review, she could tell herself she wasn't ready to confront the police officers who had done the work. The more she procrastinated, the longer it would be before she had to demonize Will Sullivan.

28

Rogan pulled the BMW to the curb, stopping behind a wood-paneled station wagon with a broken windshield, two slashed tires, and layers of graffiti, most of it gang-related. The abandoned car suited the block. A third of the houses appeared to be vacant, the paint peeling around boarded-up windows. The grass on most of the lawns was almost knee-high. It was the look of a neighborhood that probably didn't take kindly to police, especially ones from another city asking questions about conversations that took place nearly twenty years earlier.

"And I thought the Bronx was bad," Ellie said.

"Not nearly as bad as this coffee." Rogan made a pinched face and threw his Styrofoam cup out the window.

"Seriously?"

"Please. As if one more piece of litter's going to sully this paradise of nature."

She climbed out of the passenger seat, walked around to his side, and stowed the empty cup on the rear floorboard as he stepped out of the car. "You should have gotten up earlier." She tried not to gloat as she took another sip of her iced Americano. She'd had time for a morning workout in the hotel gym and a Starbucks run by the time Rogan finally texted her that he was ready to roll.

"I can't sleep in hotels. And I don't understand people who can."

She paused in front of a house two doors down. "This is it."

According to the New York Department of Motor Vehicles and the power company, this was the house where Robert Harris lived.

"We should know more about the guy before knocking on his door," Rogan said.

Amaro's one-time cellmate had kept a clean record since completing his sentence for distribution of methamphetamine twelve years earlier. But Rogan and Ellie knew that the lack of new police interactions could mean anything. Maybe Harris was a changed man. Or maybe he'd gotten smarter. No one was more dangerous than an ex-con who had vowed never to go back in. They were showing up on his dilapidated porch with no knowledge of who he was, who else might be with him, or how many illegal guns he might have.

And although Rogan didn't say it, they were here only because Max had sent them.

If the man who answered Harris's door was the same Robert Harris who had shared a cell with Anthony Amaro in 1996, he had certainly changed physically. In the mugshots they'd seen, his head was shaved, his body pumped like a beast whose only physical outlet was lifting weights in the prison yard. The man in the doorway was thin and hunched. His light-brown hair was limp, falling to his shoulders.

His eyes moved directly to the badge hanging from Ellie's neck. "You guys don't look like UPD."

"NYPD, actually," she said.

The man squinted for closer inspection, then waved them inside. "New York, huh?" He took a seat on a wooden ladder-back chair just inside his front door. There was no obvious place within reach for him to have stashed a weapon. "Guess that explains the car. No way Utica PD can afford a ride like that. You two can have the comfy spots on the sofa. So . . . I don't suppose you're here to talk about general mischief among my hoodlum neighbors, are you?"

Ellie scanned the living room as Rogan walked ahead of her. It was clean, if dated. She couldn't remember the last time she'd seen a television that came with its own wood cabinet. Close up, she now recognized their host: older, thinner, not staring at a camera like he wanted to punch someone, but the same man.

Rogan got straight to the point. "Eighteen years ago, you shared a cell for two nights with Anthony Amaro."

Harris nodded slowly. "I was wondering if that's what this might be about. I saw the news."

"So what do you remember?"

"I think," Harris said, "that you must already know, or two NYPD detectives wouldn't be in my living room."

"We're just talking to people Amaro's had contact with," Ellie said. After the mistakes Buck Majors had made, they didn't need to be accused of planting words in the mouth of an ex-con.

"I'm not stupid, Detectives. In fact, I've been told I'm quite bright. IQ of 148, according to the counselor who tried to explain to me at the age of fifteen why I was so bored in school that I was setting fires in the bathroom just for jollies. So here we go: presumably, since he was convicted, Anthony Amaro has been housed with—let's say an average of a new cellmate every five months in prison. Eighteen years is 216 months, which is forty-three-point-two cellmates, round down to forty-three. And then a year or so of pretrial custody, where turnover's higher—let's say a new person a month to be conservative. So my estimate of the number of jellybeans in that jar is fifty-five. And yet here you are in my living room."

"He spoke to you," Ellie said. "About the crimes. We need to know what he said."

"I know how this game usually works," Harris said. "In case you haven't noticed, I like to talk. Some would call it verbal sparring. It's something of a lost art form. Funny thing: a lot of cons don't want to be housed with people who talk, so I learned to spot those people and keep my mouth shut around them. But other people— they like a break from the silence. And then *some* of those

219

people do like to talk, but they don't do the kind of pedantic chatter I do. They start saying things that matter. About their families and their fears and the bad things they've done."

"And what kinds of things did Amaro tell you?"

"It started with his fears. He'd never been in before, other than that book-and-release for soliciting a prostitute, which was the bust that put him on the cops' radar, as I understand it. Anyway, he was new to the life. I wasn't. I was telling him the rules. How to stay safe."

"Why would you do that for him?"

"That's a good question. I wouldn't now. But back then, I guess I enjoyed feeling hard. Being looked up to by a man held on aggravated murder charges probably made me feel hard."

"Go on," she said.

"He told me he was scared. He was only being held on the one case down in the city, but he was afraid that the inmates would figure out that he'd killed those other girls. This is a small town. People know each other. Those women were sure to have brothers and cousins and uncles who could get to Amaro when he wasn't looking."

"He said he was afraid they'd *think* he killed the other girls?" Rogan clarified.

"No. At least, that's not how I took it. And of course I see what you're saying—that it's the kind of thing that could be misheard. But I'm very precise about language. I remember being struck that he'd said far more than he probably intended. A man who was innocent would have said something like, 'I'm scared they'll think I did something I didn't.' Or he could have left it ambiguous — as you pointed out, with 'They're going to think I killed those local girls.' But, no. He was quite clear: 'They're going to figure out I killed all five girls.' I assumed he meant the five Utica victims found in Conkling Park, since the additional murder downstate made six victims overall."

"So why didn't you trade on the information?" Ellie asked.

He stared at the television screen for a long time, even though it wasn't on. "Until a few years ago, I would have told you it was because there's a code. No snitching. Do your time. Because that's when I was still hard."

She looked at Rogan. Was this guy for real? He seemed to get off on talking like a character in a 1970s Martin Scorsese movie, so she kept feeding him lines. "So what changed?"

"My immune system. I have AIDS. And to demonstrate again my precision about words, I means AIDS, not HIV. And not that it matters, but don't start thinking I was some poor victim in prison. I assume I got infected by shooting steroids with the wrong needle. It's amazing what this disease does for your ability to be absolutely truthful. And the truth is that, back then, I did in fact try to trade on the information. I was looking at a presumptive twenty and would have done anything to cut my time."

"So what happened?"

"I told a guard I wanted to see the detective in charge of solving those murders of the prostitutes. And then I told the detective everything I just told you. He said it wasn't enough—he had the same concerns about linguistic ambiguity that we just went over."

"And that was it?" Ellie asked.

"That was it. Well, that, and he told me they already had the case wrapped up. And here's the thing: the cop didn't push me for more. He heard everything I had to say and decided, 'Thanks but no thanks.' If I recall correctly, his name was William. Last name began with an S. I remember because I tried to comment on the ugliness of snitching by throwing in a Shakespeare quote. The gist was, 'Those who are betrayed feel the treason sharply, yet the traitor stands in the worse case of woe.' Then I made some stupid joke about his name being similar to William Shakespeare. Wow, in retrospect, I suppose I realize why the man didn't want to groom me into his star witness."

"So how'd your potential for twenty years come down to six?" she asked. "You find someone else to tattle on?"

"Nope, my one attempt as a rat was enough for my tastes. Ironically, my savior was the blood test. DOC doesn't want inmates running around with the high-five, don't you know. My defense attorney never shook my hand after the news, but he did convince the judge that not even a meth dealer deserved what, at the time, looked to be a life sentence. So the judge gave me six years, assuming I'd be emaciated and oozing by the time I was released, just in time to die on someone else's dime. But by the time I got out, the science had changed. They're saying that some people will have HIV their entire lives without ever developing a single symptom. Alas, I apparently won't be one of the lucky ones, but I remind myself every day that if it weren't for the virus that made me sick, I'd still be in prison."

She didn't have a response to that. "Did you ever tell anyone else about the conversation you had with Amaro? Another inmate or prison guard, or your attorney?" Whoever sent the anonymous e-mail that led them to Harris had sent it from Manhattan. It made no sense for Harris to have sent it; and if he had, it definitely made no sense for him to travel to Manhattan to do it.

"No, just the one detective. I was shocked—and, frankly, disappointed in myself—when I realized I had basically forgotten about the whole thing until I heard Anthony Amaro's name on the news. I went to bed last night wondering if I should call someone, or whether it would only be a repeat of the conversation I had with the detective at the time. Now I can die knowing I did the right thing. Sorry, that was a joke. Too much?"

As they walked to the car, Ellie was certain that the trip to talk to Harris had been worth it, but couldn't put her finger on the reason why.

29

Carrie inched the rental car forward. If anyone needed proof that Americans loved their cars and hated to walk, one look at this McDonald's would do the trick. The parking lot was empty with the exception of a line of cars waiting for the drive-through.

Thomas had been mortified when she suggested fast food for lunch. Using his big-city biases to her advantage, she fibbed and told him that a Quarter Pounder was much better than anything else near their hotel. The truth was, Carrie loved fast food. And although she could have walked to a McDonald's two blocks from the hotel, she also loved the drive-through. Sitting in this line, listening to the radio, waiting for that familiar steamed patty with warm ketchup and soggy pickles, was the kind of ordinary thing she missed in Manhattan. The car trip had also given her an excuse to escape the gloominess of downtown, dead but for a few government buildings and some pawnshops and check-cashing shops. Here, just off the Thruway, drivers sought fuel, food, and rest among a sea of options: Denny's, Wendy's, a Best Western, and a Hess station were all within sight. It was nothing beautiful, but she found comfort in its genericness. Absent of all reminders of

Utica's once high hopes that never came to pass, this stretch of Genesee Street could be almost anywhere in America.

She used her wait time to make a call she'd been putting off. She pulled up "Bill" on her cell phone and hit enter.

By the third ring, she found herself hoping he wouldn't answer. It would be easier to break the news by voice mail.

"Hey, you."

"Oh, hey. I thought I might just get your voice mail. If you're busy, I can call back."

"Nope. Just got out of a meeting and have—wow, a six-minute break. These days, that's practically a vacation. How about you? How's life working for your law professor?"

"That's why I'm calling. I'm sorry I didn't get into the specifics when you were in the city. I wanted the night to be about celebrating your appointment," she added. "But the former professor is a defense attorney named Linda Moreland. And the case I'm helping her with is—"

"Oh my God, Anthony Amaro. I heard on the news he was challenging his conviction. New DNA evidence, right?"

"On Donna, in fact. It's crazy. Things are happening really fast. Linda sent me up to Utica last night."

"Seriously? You're home?" Neither of them had lived in Utica for years, but they would both always call it home.

"At the Governor."

"You should talk to Dad. He's pretty much been the contact person on that case since it closed. I can guarantee you he thinks Amaro's the right guy, but I assume he'd be willing to talk to you—at least to some extent. I mean, you're basically family, so you've certainly got a better crack at him than Linda Moreland. Sorry, but she doesn't have many fans in law enforcement."

"I get that. And I will go talk to your dad. But, Bill, I'm not sure he's going to like what I have to say. The truth is, Amaro's case is a lot stronger if the police in charge of the investigation come out looking bad."

"Ah, I get it. I know you, and I know what you're probably doing to yourself. Sometimes you forget I'm a cop, too. We know how the system works. Just do what you need to do, Carrie. Dad's tough, and he'll be fine."

"I'm sorry I didn't tell you any of this earlier."

"Stop saying you're sorry. It's getting painful, and my six-minute vacation is up."

"Got it. Any interest in dinner tonight, or a drink or something?"

"Geez, I'd love to, but I'm swamped for the next four days straight. Barely time to brush my teeth. That kind of busy. But I'll let you know if I free up."

"Sure thing." When the line went silent, she wondered if he was using his schedule as an excuse to avoid a person who would work for Linda Moreland.

30

That was a bust," Rogan announced as he started the engine. "The guy was a one-man freakshow."

"Meanie."

"I wasn't so taken with your new pal."

"Oh, come on, he was kind of funny. And cooperative. An hour ago, we thought he might clip us off as we took the steps of his front porch."

"You don't earn a cookie for not being a murderous meth-head scumbag. He's a guy who thinks he's smarter than everyone around him because he's spent his entire life surrounded by the bottom of the gene pool."

"But do you believe him? That's all that matters."

"Sure, what's not to believe? I think he definitely had some kind of conversation with Amaro about him being afraid of the other prisoners. But all that crap about Harris knowing the exact meaning behind the words Amaro used? Give me a break."

Rogan was proving to have a remarkable sense of direction, navigating his way back toward downtown without resorting to the GPS. He took a right onto Genesee, and Ellie recognized the old theater with the huge, beautiful marquee that they had passed last night on the way in. This stretch of downtown reminded her of Wichita, with low brown and red brick buildings, but where Wichita had torn down the theater where she and Jess used to see two-buck matinees, the Stanley Theater was announcing a showing of *The Rocky Horror Picture Show* that night. On the following block, a boarded-up house was covered in grafitti.

Her cell buzzed. It was Max. She answered using the phone's speaker function.

"Good timing," she said. "We might be getting somewhere, depending on which one of us you ask." She looked at Rogan and pointed at herself. "Me," she mouthed. "He should listen to me."

"Get there fast," Max said, "because we've got a major problem."

"What now?" she asked.

"Remember how I said I had to go to Martin to make sure we could fund you guys going up to Utica? Well, to make sure he knew how important it was, I told him that Christy McCann's ID of Amaro was a problem—that Major basically led her."

"Oh no." She saw Rogan's knuckles tighten around the steering wheel.

"He called Linda Moreland and Judge Johnsen."

Rogan couldn't hold his thoughts in. "To tell them what, exactly?"

"The new information."

"I'm a little lost here," Rogan said. "What new inform-

228

ation do you think we've gotten? We still have an eye-witness ID."

Ellie saw the problem coming and had no idea how to stop it. She had told Max as she was leaving the Bedford Hills Correctional Facility for Women yesterday that she believed Majors had stacked the deck against Amaro when showing photographs to Christy McCann. And she had brought Rogan up to speed about the interview with McCann during their drive up to Utica. But she had not told Rogan that she had criticized Majors' identification process to Max during their private phone call.

She spoke up before Max answered the question. "I'm sorry, that's my fault. Max called me as I was leaving Bedford Hills, and I told him I thought the ID was flawed."

"Don't try to take the blame," Rogan said. "My problem isn't with you sharing your opinion. It's with Donovan, for passing that opinion on to a boss who is obviously trying to help Amaro at this point."

"Rogan, I know you're frustrated," Max said. "I am, too. But it's not the kind of thing I can keep from the district attorney himself."

"You didn't even bother checking in with the other detective on this so-called fresh-look team to see if he happens to agree with Hatcher's assessment, which I don't. Majors may not have handled it perfectly, but at the end of the day, Christy McCann told Hatcher that she recognized Anthony Amaro."

"I can't even get a word in about why I called, Rogan. Ellie, will you please take me off speaker so I can tell you what's happening? It's important, and we're wasting time."

Rogan waved a hand toward her phone, indicating she should do as Max asked, but Ellie knew Max would never make the request to any other detective.

"You can explain it to us both, Max. And Rogan has a good point. I told you my worries about the ID, but it was a quick conversation. If you were going to make that official by telling Martin, we should have had a more thorough discussion—all three of us."

"There hasn't been anything thorough about this," Rogan said. "We're two people, essentially working outside the department, trying to work seven different murders across two decades in two cities, all at the same time."

"Fine." Max's clipped tone made it clear that he was fighting to keep his cool. "The process hasn't been ideal. I know that. I did what I thought was right, both in terms of getting Martin to approve your travel up there, and also keeping him up to speed, which is my job."

Rogan groaned, but Max didn't hear it and continued. "Martin, in turn, felt obliged to notify the court, because she gave us the week on the understanding that we'd be trying to shore up the evidence against Amaro. Instead, we found more exculpatory evidence, and Martin takes very seriously our duty to disclose, even after conviction."

"Let me guess," Rogan said, "in the interests of *trans-*

parency. And it's not exculpatory. Hatcher felt hinky about the ID, but the witness is still onboard. Usually prosecutors try to back up their own witnesses."

"You can yell at me all you want, Rogan, but it won't change where we are. Moreland pushed for an immediate release."

"But we have until Friday," Ellie said.

"Not anymore. You saw the judge. Linda Moreland already had her convinced this was an exoneration case and that Buck Majors went rogue. Now she finds out that instead of finding evidence that helps keep him in, we *may*—though I get Rogan's point—have more reason to doubt his guilt."

"So convince the judge to keep the same timeline." Yesterday Ellie had thought it was insane to expect them to produce new evidence in three days. Now she was clinging to every last second of time. "We're getting more evidence. We just talked to Harris. He says Amaro admitted—"

"The judge didn't care about Harris," he said. "I tried buying time by saying you were up there to interview him. Moreland went nuts that the tip came in completely anonymously. I said the tipster didn't matter if the information panned out with Harris himself. But Johnsen slammed the door on it. She said it's fundamentally unfair to justify Amaro's conviction with evidence that we didn't even know about at the time he was charged."

"But if he's guilty, he's guilty."

"Not to the judge. She said Amaro has a due-process right to have his conviction set aside if all of the government's original evidence has been undermined. If we have completely new evidence against him, the most she would do is to vacate his conviction without prejudice so we could at least retry him. Please tell me Harris is a smoking gun. At this point, we need Mother Teresa with HD photographs of Amaro burying the bodies."

"Well, not a smoking gun exactly, but he says Amaro admitted to killing the Utica victims." She did her best to explain Harris's belief that Amaro had actually confessed, not merely expressed a concern that he'd be perceived as guilty.

Max didn't even pause before writing off the information. "Not even close. The way Johnsen put it, Amaro's conviction rests on a nest filled with eggs. And each one— Buck Majors, Christy McCann, the new DNA evidence belonging to who knows who—breaks one of the eggs. She said we can break an egg or two and still have a nest, but at this point, every single egg is cracked, and we look like we're switching them out after the fact."

"That doesn't make sense," Ellie said. "A nest is made of twigs, not eggs. We should be able to switch the eggs if we need to, until we're—I don't know, breaking them and scrambling them and turning them into an omelette."

In that moment Ellie decided that metaphors were officially stupid.

"Well, the way Judge Johnsen put it, we can't prove we

got the right guy but with the wrong evidence. She signed the writ."

A writ of habeas corpus. *You have the body*, as the Latin term puts it. A petition for habeas corpus is a request by a prisoner to gain his release, claiming insufficient grounds for his detention.

"For when?"

"For *now*. She signed it. The paperwork takes a while to get processed, but he'll be getting out soon."

"Have someone sit on him. We need eyes on him at all times."

"That's why I'm calling you. He's not down here. That was part of his plea—to be housed closer to home. He's at Five Points. For now. But the release is in the computer. How quick can you get to him?"

Five Points was a maximum-security prison between Syracuse and Rochester. "An hour at least," Rogan said, more familiar with the geography than she. "Maybe an hour and a half."

"We'll go now," she said. "Damn it. We should have gotten a statement from him at the very beginning of this."

"You do what you need to do as part of your investigation. I'm just letting you know that he's getting released."

Ellie knew that the professional rules of ethics prohibited Max from contacting, or even directing contact, with a represented party. But Ellie and Rogan weren't lawyers. The only rules they had to follow came from the

Constitution, and as far as the Constitition was concerned, Amaro was fair game unless he expressly told them he didn't want to speak to them. As a result of the discrepancy between the rules for lawyers and law enforcement, it was common for prosecutors to "allow" police to contact represented parties without actually "directing" it.

"Got it," she said. They all knew the code. "We'll head to Five Points, just to make sure we keep eyes on him. We'll set up shop, however long it takes."

"That would be a lot easier if Judge Johnsen had put any limitation at all on his release: electronic monitoring, daily reporting, perhaps a *current address*. No. Once he's released, he'll be in the wind, out there in the world, with no supervision whatsoever. I put in a call to the Oneida County DA. They'll be pissed we didn't loop them in earlier, but I'm going to see if they can take what we have and get an arrest warrant for Amaro on the old cases."

"They can do that?"

"Oh yeah. He was never prosecuted in Utica, so there's no double jeopardy. I think that's why Johnsen was so willing to sign the writ. She can tell herself she's doing the right thing by setting aside a wrongful conviction, with the knowledge that Utica still has another bite at the apple if Amaro really is the guy. They can use what we have on the Garner case—weak as it is—and throw in whatever you got from that cellmate. It's not nearly enough for a conviction, but it should be enough for

234

probable cause. That's all they'll need to hold him on new charges."

"We'll see what we can do," Ellie assured him before saying goodbye.

Rogan gunned the engine. "We've got to get to this guy before he's out on the streets."

31

Thomas took the McDonald's bag from Carrie with two fingers.

"Trust me, Thomas. The taste of warm, soft pickles on ketchup-smothered meat product is way better than you're going to want to admit."

"Well, with that kind of sales pitch, how can I possibly resist?" He removed the contents and smoothed the paper bag on the hotel room's desk like a placemat. If he asked for a knife and fork, she was going to snatch that food away from him and make him starve.

"You did a great job," she said, looking around the room. She had spent the morning at the library, printing out archived articles about the case, and at the city attorney's office, requesting public records. In the meantime, he had converted the non-bedroom areas of her suite—the largest in the hotel—into a functional working space. He had pulled the desk away from the wall and scrounged up an extra chair, creating a two-sided desk, complete with both of their laptops. He had placed the various boxes and Redwelds of files, neatly labeled, around the small table in the corner.

"Linda said we can take a meeting room if we need

more space," he said. "I thought it was easier to make do here than to have to traipse down to the lobby constantly."

"Makes sense to me."

"Okay, but Linda told me to make sure you got the message: Spare no expense. This case could be worth millions of dollars. It's very exciting, don't you think? And I have to admit: this hamburger is much better than I remembered. I don't think I've had McDonald's for ten years."

Based on Carrie's experience, the people who insisted they never ate fast food had a cabinet full of Happy Meal souvenir cups. But she was starting to think that Thomas was as honest and eager as he appeared. As someone who had frequently been criticized for being "overly earnest," she appreciated his openness.

She heard the first few bars of a Journey song on his cell phone. "It's Linda!" He couldn't have been more excited if Santa Claus himself were calling. "Hi, Linda. I was just talking to Carrie about the workspace here, and she agrees that we're fine for now. We'll let you know if that changes . . . Uh-huh . . . Yes, she's right here." He held the phone in her direction. "She wants to talk to you."

"Hi, Linda."

"Are you sitting down?"

"Yeah, sure." As a hat tip to the virtue of honesty, she made a point of perching on the edge of the bed.

"I have amazing news. Amazing! Martin Overton called me first thing this morning. He has those two detectives up there. They're scrambling for more evidence because—get this—we were right. Not only did Majors lie about that confession, he also led their one eyewitness. We've taken down their entire case. And I convinced Judge Johnsen that if the only evidence they had is invalid, they can't swap out new evidence eighteen years later. And guess what? We won!"

"Didn't we basically win yesterday?" Carrie was pretty sure that their success was the reason she was in Utica.

"We made progress, but I'm saying it's not about Friday anymore. Amaro is getting out. Today. Now."

"What do you mean, out?"

"Out. A free man. No more business with the New York County Courts. We have a ton to do, but I wanted you to know as soon as possible. He'll need a ride from Five Points. Can you look up the directions?"

"Um, sure. So, you want me to get him a car or something?"

"No, silly. You're his attorney. Go pick him up. I wouldn't be surprised if other attorneys try to poach him, so make sure he understands how hard we're working on his behalf. I'll take a train up in the morning. In the meantime, you need to look out for him. I expect them to try to arrest him on the Utica charges. It's what I would do if I were in their shoes. Find a motel for him—outside the city, one that doesn't ask for names. Something cheap, so if they find him, it doesn't look like he's trying to cash in on his potential lawsuit. But pick him up now, okay? We've got to keep him protected."

To Carrie, this form of protection sounded like harboring a fugitive. "Um, are we allowed to do that? I mean, ethically, if they're trying to arrest him?"

"Until we know there's an arrest warrant in place, we can actively help him. After that, we don't have a duty to turn him in, but actual assistance gets dicier. That's why we have to act fast. Prepay the room for—I don't know, ten days. I'm wiring you cash through Western Union, but take care of that after you've got him in the car."

Carrie's head was spinning.

She had assumed this case would take years to resolve. She had expected prosecutors to fight them every step of the way. She expected the bureaucrats who ran the prison system to drag their feet, terrified that they might be freeing a killer. This case was moving faster than it would anywhere else in the country at any other time, and she had to believe it was because of the political tide that had so drastically and decisively turned against New York City law enforcement in the past year. The judge and the district attorney were worried about being reelected, and vindicating an innocent man would make for a good 30-second television ad.

But was Anthony Amaro really innocent?

"You still there, Carrie?"

"Yeah. I think my phone cut out for a second."

"Oh, another thing: the ADA told Judge Johnsen that

his detectives are up there talking to a jailhouse snitch who says Amaro confessed to him. I guess they got the guy's name from an anonymous tip. You know anything about that?"

"No."

"You didn't see anything in the old police records about a cellmate informant?"

"Not yet, but I'm still working my way through it all. Do you want me to try to track it down?"

Linda paused. "No. Let's stick with pinning blame on the police department. Any progress there?"

"Shouldn't I be leaving for the prison, Linda?"

"Yes. I just wanted a quick update on your progress."

Geez, she and Thomas had only been in Utica for eighteen hours. Linda Moreland seemed capable of moving five times faster than the rest of the world. "Well, the original Utica detective in charge of the case was in the process of retiring when the NYPD arrested Amaro. At that point, Amaro's guilty plea to the downstate case was enough to shut down the investigation here. The new detective basically just served as a contact person. That's all I've got for now."

"What do you mean, *all you've got*? That's what we were hoping to find. Some lazy cop who didn't give a rat's ass about a bunch of working girls."

Carrie felt disgusted. She needed to find a way out of this. She could quit, but it was too late: Linda would just find someone else to do the same work. Carrie decided to take a shot at changing Linda's strategy. Maybe she could try to mitigate the damage by operating from within.

"I get what you're saying, Linda, but the detective—his name's Will Sullivan—I'm not sure that throwing him under the bus is going to work. He's beloved here. A widower. Single father. He raised his boy all alone, and they're both considered huge success stories for the city. His son is Bill Sullivan . . . ?"

Linda squealed into the phone. "The boy wonder? Seriously? That's *brilliant*! The son can leverage the power of the state. Pitch into the settlement on behalf of the crime lab and the Department of Corrections. Maybe even stipulate to the release of other prisoners locked up by Buck Majors. This is *huge*. Huge! Okay, stay on Sullivan. And, oh, I've kept you on the phone too long. You hit the road now. Oh—and can you put Thomas back on? I need him to clear my schedule before I leave the city. You can find your way to the prison on your own, yes?"

Carrie could feel her french fries working their way back up as she returned Thomas's phone to him. She took this job because she'd convinced herself she'd be doing the right thing by Donna. But Linda Moreland wanted money, and she wanted to win. She wanted the celebrity lawyer reputation. Perhaps most dangerous of all, she truly believed she was saving people.

And Carrie had no idea how she could save herself from being a part of it.

32

Carrie had never been to a prison before. In law school, her study of criminal law had been restricted entirely to books. Russ Waterston didn't handle criminal cases, and the civil work she did do rarely required her to leave the firm's law library. Now she was on her way to pick up a man being released from prison. She had no idea what to expect, but she was convinced she was completely lost. All she could see was farmland in every direction.

She looked down again at the rental car's GPS system to make sure she was in the right place, and the gadget insisted she was almost there.

She took the next right turn, as prompted by the robotic voice, and pulled onto a long, narrow road. It was beautiful here, and peaceful. Up ahead, she saw a sprawling concrete complex, surrounded by watch towers and barbed wire. Now she understood. This beautiful, peaceful place was the perfect location. No one wanted a maximum security prison in his backyard. No one wanted to be near the Anthony Amaros of the world.

And yet here she was, about to serve as his personal driver.

*

A sign at the visitors' entry warned that all phones had to be turned off and could not be taken into the "hospitality area." She powered down her cell and slipped it into her purse.

A heavy woman in a flowered dress entered just ahead of her and commented that the line was short today. It didn't look short to Carrie. She counted ten people in front of her, including the flowered-dress lady, before the line turned a blind corner.

"Is the front of the line somewhere close to that turn?"

"Oh no, sweetheart. I'd say it's another thirty feet or so to the metal detectors. You haven't been here before?"

"No, I haven't."

"It's okay. I was afraid my first time, too, but my son, he needs visitors. I like to think that contact with the outside might keep him from getting too hard, you know? Who you here to see?"

"Um, my uncle." Somehow it didn't seem right in that moment to announce herself as an attorney, to declare herself an outsider.

"Oh, okay. Well aren't you a thoughtful niece."

She smiled.

A guard was pacing the distance of the line, eyeing its members. He started to pivot at the line's end, but did a double take at Carrie.

"Who are you?"

"Excuse me?"

"You counsel?"

She was wearing khakis and a white button-down shirt. Did she really stand out that much?

"Um, yes, I am."

"You here for a client?"

The flowered-dress lady was looking at her, confused. "I am," Carrie confirmed.

"You're in the wrong line. Don't worry, new lawyers do this all the time." He waved her out of the line as the flowered-dress lady commented that her uncle was lucky to have a lawyer in the family.

Carrie followed the guard past the back of the line. At the corner, he turned right instead of left, and Carrie followed. "See? Attorney window up there? Ring the bell, give the desk your client's name, and they'll get you a private room for your conference. Different from the other visitors, where we randomly monitor conversations."

She nodded. "Right, that makes sense."

"Wow, you really are green, aren't you? Tell you what: let me walk you through it. What's your guy's name?"

She noticed for the first time that the guard wasn't wearing a ring, and didn't seem to have a tanline from one either. Regardless of his reasons, she was grateful for the help.

"Anthony Amaro. My understanding is that he's supposed to be released any minute."

The guard did another double take. "Amaro? Whoa, I didn't expect that. He's been bragging to everyone who will listen about that woman from television being his lawyer."

"And I work for her. And, as you've probably figured out, I'm new to this."

"I got that." He didn't seem quite as friendly now. "Mike," he called through the window, "what's going on with Amaro? This lady's looking for him."

"He's being cut loose right now. Should be just a few minutes."

"They'll release him out back," the guard explained. "You can pull around and meet him there. You're alone?"

She nodded, and he shook his head disapprovingly. "Good luck with that."

Carrie had been resting her eyes, listening to the purr of the idling engine, but the grinding sound of the security gates jerked her to full alert.

Anthony Amaro walked out alone, dressed in a black T-shirt, blue jeans, and work boots. He carried a single cardboard box. As many times as she had looked at photographs of him over the years, she might not have recognized him in another context. He had always been physically innocuous: slightly chubby, but not fat; a receding hairline, but not bald; not ugly by any means, but certainly not attractive, either. Despite the averageness of his appearance, though, he had always looked ominous, the blank stare of his booking photo juxtaposed in newspapers with photographs of his victims.

Now, his face was puffy and sagging, like an actor made up to look older. He was balder and grayer. Whatever used to terrify her about him visually was gone. He looked harmless.

She stepped from the car, and he turned in her direction. She almost waved instinctively. She had no idea what she was doing.

She waited for him to walk within earshot. He was staring at her intensely, but it was impossible to attribute an emotion to his flat expression. "I'm an associate with Ms. Moreland's firm," she explained. "I'll get you situated in a nearby motel."

She did not offer a handshake, choosing to pop the trunk instead. He placed his cardboard box inside, and then she opened the back passenger-side door for him.

"Do you mind if I sit up front? The back feels like being in a police car or something."

"Sure, of course."

As she put the car in gear, she felt his eyes on her. "I thought Linda Moreland was representing me." He sounded disappointed, but, still, his face did not change.

"She is." Last week, Carrie was billing her time out at three hundred dollars an hour to Fortune 500 companies. Now this guy was getting her services for free, and managed to sound disappointed about it. "Linda will be arriving tomorrow. Unless you'd prefer to go back to your cell, I'm afraid I'm your contact person for now."

"Sorry if that was rude. I've been—well, you know

where I've been, since I was about your age. That's a long time. Guess I lost my manners."

"It's fine, Mr. Amaro. You just need to put your seat-belt on, and we'll get you out of here."

She watched as he instinctively reached for the right side of his waist before fumbling with the shoulder strap and securing it. He didn't speak again until they pulled onto the long road leading back to the highway. "They tell you when you go in on an LWOP that it's a living death, but it took about seven years to sink in. For my brain to get around the idea that I was never getting out. Ever. No matter what. No words to describe that kind of hopelessness. It's like someone put you in the middle of the ocean on a dinghy, and you're just waiting to die. But here I am. From the yard, you'd never know how beautiful this place was, just a few feet away." He rolled down the window and stuck his head out like a dog.

"Well, you'll get plenty more of this scenery. We're putting you in a motel pretty far out of town. Ms. Moreland wants you to have some privacy."

"The scenery in here is pretty good, too, if you don't mind me saying. You're very attractive, Miss—"

"Blank."

He pulled his head back into the car. "You're not related to Donna Blank, are you?"

Carrie felt her pulse quicken at the sound of her sister's name escaping his lips. "I'm from upstate, so I think we do share a bloodline somewhere in the past."

"But you're—what? Japanese or something?"

"Really, it doesn't matter, Mr. Amaro. Let's just focus on getting you settled in somewhere until Linda arrives, and then we'll be working on your case."

"Sure, sorry. Just been inside for a lot of years. I'll never forget the names and faces of those poor girls. It's like, on the one hand, you got to feel sorry for what happened to them. But then there's an anger, too. Like somehow it's their fault you're locked up for something you didn't do. I know it's not really, but—anyway, I know those six names and faces. You look like her in a way. Prettier, though, maybe because of your racial mix or whatever. Sorry for commenting."

"Really, it's okay." She saw the bright sun behind them flash on the windshield of an approaching car. "Get down!" On instinct, she reached her right hand to Amaro's shoulder and pushed him forward. He followed her instructions and crouched low in his seat.

"Sorry about that," she said, once the BMW passed them. "You've been released on the Deborah Garner case, but the Utica police could still try to arrest you for the other victims. We want to keep you out of sight for now, just to be safe."

He shifted in his seat. "I haven't had a woman touch me in almost twenty years. And certainly not one as pretty as you."

She looked at the GPS, already programmed for the motel she had selected to suit Linda's instructions. Twenty minutes left, driving alone, in the country, with Anthony Amaro.

Ellie and Rogan pulled up to the back gate, where most prisons processed releases. Ellie hopped out of the passenger's seat and waved down a guard walking the perimeter.

"You happen to know when Anthony Amaro's getting cut loose?" she asked.

"He pulled out of here, probably ten minutes ago."

"He's *gone*?" She looked back toward the road, wondering if they might find him hitchhiking on the main road.

"Yeah, got into a white Malibu with an Oriental lady. You just missed him."

33

The headquarters of the Utica Police Department looked a lot like Ellie's junior high school. Two floors. Blond brick. Occupied a quarter of a block. Most NYPD precinct houses were twice the size. Rogan reached for the front door, then paused. "You know this is going to blow, right?"

"As in vuvuzela-levels of blowing. Come on, Double J, let's get it over with."

They made their way to a desk sergeant at the front counter. Rogan explained they were from the NYPD and were hoping to talk to someone about Anthony Amaro.

"Yeah, sure. Let me find him."

Now that they were here, they both realized how bad this was going to look to local police. They had come here—to their jurisdiction, from New York City, to talk to a witness who might know something about five women who died right here, in this city—and hadn't bothered to make a courtesy call to the UPD. Now, to top it off, Amaro had been released, just outside their town, because of mistakes made by the NYPD.

Ellie knew Rogan had been holding back his thoughts, so she decided to express them for him. "I know. Max should have looped in Utica law enforcement, even before putting together a fresh-look team." She could see the failure as yet another signature Martin Overton move: avoid accusations that he's covering for the past by starting with a completely fresh slate. But as a result, she and Rogan were now in someone else's jurisdiction, in need of help they should have asked for a week ago. And as much as she wanted to blame the elected DA's political motivations, she knew for a fact that Max, all too happy for the career advancement, hadn't pushed back against his boss one bit.

"Too late now," he said. "How are we playing this?"

"We'll just have to tell them we've been moving nonstop. The DNA evidence. Helen Brunswick. Dealing with Linda Moreland. Rushing to Five Points. Hell, one look at you and those I-can't-sleep-in-a-hotel bags under your eyes, they'll know the pace we've been keeping."

"Please, on my worst day I'm still the finest man you'll find around this joint. You and I both know that coming here to talk to Amaro's old cellmate without going through UPD was a dis. We've been treating them like yokels."

A phone call would have been standard operating procedure if they hadn't deeply believed that UPD had basically closed up shop on the Amaro investigation.

"Maybe," she said. "But think of it this way: the fact that UPD hasn't contacted Max—despite all the news coverage of Amaro's petition for release—pretty much confirms that our instincts were right."

Rogan shushed her as the door next to the desk sergeant opened.

The man who walked out was probably in his late fifties but was trim and fit, his white hair and a few wrinkles around his eyes the only signs of age. "Detectives, I'm Will Sullivan. You're here about Anthony Amaro?"

"Have you heard from anyone in your DA's office yet?" Rogan asked. "There have been some developments this morning down in the city."

"Nope. We knew he was asking to be released, but have been assuming it's just a lot of talk. That case was solved years ago."

"Well," Rogan said, "that's the tricky part. His lawyers have attacked the most critical pieces of evidence against him—the eyewitness, the confession. It all started when a woman was killed in Brooklyn three months ago. Turns out the killer broke her limbs, postmortem. Then someone—we still don't know who—mailed letters to both Amaro and the DA, saying Amaro's innocent and the real killer's active again. Plus, the crime lab found new DNA evidence on one of the victims, and it doesn't belong to Amaro."

"Which victim?" The detective was twisting a red plastic coffee stirrer in his hands. One edge of it was flattened by teethmarks. Ellie thought of her own telltale way of holding a pen between her index and middle fingers. Will Sullivan was an ex-smoker.

"Donna Blank," Rogan said.

He nodded. "But he wasn't even convicted of killing her. It should still be fine, right?"

They were obviously going to have to rehash every point and counterpoint that they themselves had raised this week. Ellie jumped in with a quick and dirty summary of all of the arguments made before Judge Johnsen. "Look, here's the long and the short of it: we just found out that the judge granted the motion—for immediate release. Five Points cut him loose already. He's in the wind."

"Anthony Amaro is free? Right now?"

"And we don't know where," she said. "If you can put cars on the street to look for him—or if some of your guys have thoughts about where Amaro would go—we'll help however we can."

"*Help?* You said you just found out yourselves that Amaro was released. Unless the two of you know how to hyperspace halfway across the state, you came here for a reason other than to *help*."

And here it goes, she thought. "We were scrambling for something—*anything*—that might keep Amaro in. We got a tip that one of Amaro's former cellmates might have information. We came up to interview him: guy named Robert Harris. I believe you may have spoken to him during the original investigation."

Harris had mentioned that the detective he spoke to was William S-something. Will Sullivan seemed close enough. Something else seemed familiar about Sullivan's name, but she couldn't put her finger on it.

Sullivan nodded slowly. "Yeah, I remember that guy. He thought pretty highly of himself, as I recall."

The response struck Ellie as bizarre. Harris had an ego, but when a suspected serial killer's cellmate is willing to hand over even a used Kleenex, a decent detective should at least make note of it. She didn't see any use in pointing this out to Sullivan eighteen years after the fact, however. "With the Garner case falling apart, we need him," Ellie said. "One of the city ADAs is calling your DA here. The idea is to take what we have and get an arrest warrant for Amaro for the victims he was never charged with."

"Yeah, but the cellmate—you said his name was Harris, right?—he was reading something into nothing. I don't know how you do it in the NYPD, but we don't do a jailhouse snitch's bidding here."

"We just need probable cause, enough to hold Amaro while we continue to work the case."

"*We*, huh? You realize that's rich, don't you?"

"You're right," Rogan said. "It should have been both departments working together this whole time. You guys have the five victims. Downstate has Deborah Garner, and now Helen Brunswick—she's the Brooklyn victim. But she has old ties here. She was a therapist. Did some training up here as a student. We need feet on the ground in both locations. To be honest with you . . . we've got a district attorney's office that cares more about pleasing the public than protecting it."

"I don't know what kind of public you have," Sullivan

said, "but no one around here's going to be happy about Amaro being released."

"I think our DA figures people will be happy if they actually believe Amaro's innocent. Then the DA's the good guy for helping him get his freedom."

"That's messed up."

At that moment, Ellie couldn't disagree.

Rogan's candor seemed to quell Sullivan's annoyance, but something about the mention of Helen Brunswick was tugging at the edge of Ellie's brain. Some connection between Brunswick and Sullivan. "You didn't know her, did you?" she asked. "Helen Brunswick?"

"Doesn't ring a bell. Look, I see your point about working together to get Amaro into his next holding cell. I know exactly who'll be working on this at the DA's office, so let me touch base with him and get back with you. You gonna be in town a while?"

"At the Governor," Rogan said. They handed him their business cards.

He walked them to the front door, then stopped short when he saw another visitor entering. It was Carrie Blank.

"Well, what kind of surprise is this?" Sullivan howled. "Carrie Blank! Just ran into your mom at the Target this week. She didn't tell me you were here."

Ellie saw a white Chevy Malibu in the station parking lot. She pointed an accusatory finger at Carrie Blank. "Where is he? Where did you stash Amaro?"

"You do your job, Detective, and I'll do mine."

"Donna was your *sister*," Ellie hissed. "How can you do this? Who else is going to fight for her if not you?"

She felt Rogan's grip on her forearm. "Let's go," he said gently.

Ellie turned to face Sullivan. "You *know* her? She's the one who picked up Amaro from prison."

Sullivan looked at her like she was unstable.

As Ellie followed Rogan to the car, she glanced back over her shoulder. Sullivan had taken Carrie Blank up in a hug so tight that her heels lifted from the ground.

She started talking before her butt hit the passenger seat. "He's *hugging* the defense attorney? We haven't slept for days, trying to figure out what the hell's going on. And yet somehow *we're* the assholes?"

He started the engine and pulled into the street. "Do you want a hug, too? Is that what this is about?"

She flipped him a middle finger. "I like you better when you get your beauty rest. Seriously, think about your reaction to Linda Moreland, and meanwhile, Sullivan's *hugging* her associate. You don't think that's weird?"

"I don't think I know enough about it for it to be weird."

"You heard him. He still thinks Amaro did it. And Carrie Blank's sister is one of the victims. And she got the guy out of prison? And he hugs her?"

"You know how you feel about Jess? Or Max?"

"Of course I do. And that's why I don't understand

how that woman can be helping the man who at least *might* have killed her sister."

"But I'm talking about Sullivan and that hug back there. Look at it this way: I know that some part of you is—let's say, disappointed, in the shots Max has been calling on this case. And I've seen how it's tearing you apart not to say anything. It's because you still have a hug for that man at the end of the day. Hate to break it to you, Hatcher, but that's love. When even your cold, unpenetrable heart holds sway over that hard head of yours, that's *unconditional love*. Look it up."

"But Max and I live together. Are you suggesting that Sullivan and Carrie Blank—"

"Damn, woman. Not everything's so literal. I'm saying I heard the change in the man's voice when he saw that girl. He knows her. He knows her moms, sees her at the Target. There's a history there. Towns like this, people don't mind their own business. That's how I grew up, too—aunties and grandmas all chipping in. Everybody knows everybody, and the good parents mind all the other children. You ask me, he's proud of that girl, so proud he can look past her working on Amaro's case."

"He didn't even seem to care that Amaro was out."

"That's not fair, Hatcher. He didn't even know at first. Once we told him Amaro had actually been released, he was pissed. You can't measure everyone's emotions by the number of F-bombs they drop."

"I think the whole thing's weird. He obviously didn't

go out of his way back then to make sure that Amaro took his lumps up here for the other five victims. And you heard what Robert Harris said—Sullivan pretty much blew him off. And there's something about his name. It's familiar, like I already knew him when he introduced himself."

"Your self-proclaimed pedantic BFF told you he talked to a detective named William S."

"No, but it's something else. Something about Helen Brunswick. Oh, I remember. It's that crazy kid from the hospital. Brunswick had some concerns about one of her younger patients—a kid named, um . . ." Dammit, what was that kid's name? She and Rogan had talked about the incident so quickly. "You showed me that big stack of reports over the years."

Rogan was making the connection now, too. "Oh, it was Joseph—"

"Joseph *Flaherty*," she said. "He was one of the two patients Brunswick called police about during her internship. You ran their histories to see if they might have held a grudge against her. In that big stack of reports were those nuisance calls on Joseph for yelling in a cop's yard. The cop's name was William Sullivan. I remember."

"Bully for you, Rainman. You must also remember that Joseph had an alibi for some of the killings because he was committed. As in, confined and incapable of murdering women. So he and whatever beef he had with Will Sullivan is background noise."

"You don't think it's a coincidence that the kid Helen Brunswick was scared of happens to have had some kind of obsession with Sullivan?"

"Not really. It's a small city. You saw that little hut of a police headquarters. Whole department is probably twenty bodies. I could see a nutjob like Joseph Flaherty getting hassled on the beat a lot—told to move along, not to be bothering people—he gets fixated on one of them. Makes sense to me. And again, how Sullivan dealt with some crazy teenager twenty years ago isn't at the top of my concerns right now."

"Still, you have to admit he doesn't seem to have bent over backwards to have Amaro charged up here when he had the chance."

"Those calls were probably made by the DA. But, okay, I'll give the point: he's not exactly a go-getter."

"I'm telling you: it's weird."

"You have certainly told me that. Multiple times."

She pulled Jess up on her cell phone.

"So, is Utica the shithole I said it was?" he asked by way of greeting. Jess had come here to play a bar gig with Dog Park four years earlier. After someone in the audience threw a beer bottle at the stage because they looked like "a bunch of homos," Jess—straight in no other way than that one—swore he'd never go back to Utica. The episode could have happened anywhere, but Jess, as vehemently opposed to homophobia as any person could be, was holding firm on his boycott.

"We're not exactly sightseeing," she said. "Hey, I need you to do me a favor. Can you call Mona?"

"Three in the afternoon? She's probably up by now. What do you need?"

"Remember how she said she tried talking to a cop up here? She told him there was no way Donna Blank would go somewhere alone with a trick."

"The asshole threatened to arrest her."

"I need you to ask her if the asshole was named William Sullivan."

"Making friends up there, are we? Okay, let me see what I can do."

Rogan was giving her the stinkeye when she hung up.

"I'm just checking."

"Keep your eye on the ball, Hatcher. Anthony Amaro."

"I can do two things at once. What's left for us to do?"

"First of all, play nice with Sullivan, because we need that man on board if we're going to get an arrest warrant. And an alternative explanation for that DNA under Donna Blank's nails would be helpful. Since her sister's working for the defense, let's go see what her mother might have to say."

34

As Carrie felt her heels leave the ground, she wished she could enjoy Will Sullivan's hug forever. As long as she was in the air, she was a little girl getting an airplane ride from Mr. Sullivan. Anthony Amaro and Linda Moreland didn't exist. But then she felt the earth beneath her again, and Will's brow furrowed when he focused on her face.

"So, that was some scene with the detective."

"I would have preferred to tell you myself why I'm in town."

"Bill might've called a little while ago. Now, don't get mad at him for beating you to the punch. He said you were all torn up about the direction of the case—worried that yours truly might end up looking bad."

"Possibly. Yeah."

"You think this is my first time to the rodeo? I know how this works. I suppose the strategy up here will be to blame us for not figuring out for ourselves that the NYPD screwed it up—if one were to believe that claim. How'm I doing so far?"

"Spot on."

"And you know how this town works, Carrie. You don't think the city attorney's office told me you'd requested my Internal Affairs records? I can tell you all the dirt in there, if you'd like. Ancient battles. Not even battles. More like bubbles."

"I should've realized that you'd already know anything happening in Utica."

"Well, I didn't know Amaro had been released, I can tell you that."

"If it helps any, I agree. About the IA file, I mean. I'll be telling Linda there's no *there* there."

She'd found two complaints of excessive force, but that was typical for any officer who'd been around Utica as long as Mr. Sullivan. She had been surprised to find one complaint that Mr. Sullivan had helped a suspect out of a robbery charge for personal reasons. According to the storeowner, the responding officer was going to pursue felony charges until the more-senior Mr. Sullivan intervened. When the storeowner learned through the grapevine that the suspect was a friend of Mr. Sullivan's son, he ran to IAB.

The friend of Bill? Tim McDonough, who would have been Melanie's boyfriend by then, about seven months away from impregnation.

"I never realized Bill was friends with Tim back then," she said. Part of her had to wonder if the friendship had anything to do with the drug use that would land Bill in rehab after graduation. She had to assume that Tim was a bad influence, even then.

"More like acquaintances," Will said. "Tim's no angel,

but that boiled down to grabbing a six-pack of beer and throwing a drunken punch when the storeowner caught him. Tim was twenty, so no juvi for him. I didn't want to see the kid start life with a felony."

"You are so *nice*."

"Oh, that look on your face. Even when you're not saying you're sorry, you manage to telegraph it in other ways. Stop feeling guilty, Carrie. It's like you told that detective: You do your job, she'll do hers. And I'll do mine. Things will work out the way they're meant to."

Just do what you need to do, Bill had told her. *Dad's tough, and he'll be fine.*

Will Sullivan was more than tough, and he was more than fine. He was *good*.

Carrie had braced herself for a major confrontation. Accusations. Betrayal. Reminders of emotional debts never repaid. She never expected that the worst part of explaining her new job to Will Sullivan was that he would actually support her.

"If I'm not pushing my luck too much, can I ask you a question about the case?"

"I guess that depends on what it is."

"Not the case, per se, but about Donna. All the other victims were pretty clearly immersed in the sex trade. Donna had a drug problem, and she was working at a gentlemen's club, but I didn't see any real proof that she was actually turning tricks."

"Does that make a difference to the case?"

"I don't know. Maybe. Or maybe I just want to know, for me, since it was Donna."

"Would it be cruel to suggest that if you want to know why Donna was targeted, you should ask your client?"

"Not cruel. I get it. I made the decision to work for Linda Moreland."

His face softened. "Look, Donna was your family member. And there was a time, I know, when she looked out for you. I'm not saying a cross word about her, but she had a problem, Carrie, and you know that. It sounds like you've accepted the fact that she was dancing to support her habit, but you only knew that because she didn't even bother trying to hide it. In my experience, the truth is always worse than an addict is willing to say."

"But do you *know*? For sure?"

He held her gaze, and she could see the answer in his eyes.

"You saw it? Saw *her*?"

"Walking on Sandy, yeah, a couple of times. And the fact that she was found with those other girls in Conkling Park. Well . . ."

He didn't need to complete the thought. Carrie had so desperately wanted to believe that her sister was different. That she was special. That there was some other reason she had been killed. But she was just another dead hooker.

"You still look miserable, Carrie. Maybe I said too much."

"No, it's not that. It's just, I—I feel so guilty, Mr. Sullivan. I didn't know, I swear. I didn't know you'd be in the middle of this. I should've realized."

She had come here so she could tell herself that at least she'd been honest with him. He was treating this like any other case where the suspect says he's innocent, but Carrie had seen what Linda Moreland was capable of. She'd weave the tiny squares of flimsy fabric into a quilt of deception. Even one tiny Internal Affairs entry—a moment of empathy from a father, extended to his son's friend, as Mr. Sullivan had done so many times with her—would become a nefarious character trait once Linda Moreland got done with it. And meanwhile, Carrie was serving as Anthony Amaro's personal driver.

"I don't know what to do." She was starting to break down, and he hugged her again.

There she was, trying to warn him that one of the most determined defense attorneys in the country was out to tear him limb from limb, with Carrie as her lieutenant, and he was the one comforting her. "Let me tell you something, Carrie. You and Bill were competitors. I know sometimes you feel guilty about that, but look at where he is now because of it. The two of you made each other better. Don't you see that? And I know you. I know you in your heart. Maybe some other young lawyers would lose themselves to a person like Linda Moreland. But you take this experience—the way Bill took his—and you turn it into something wonderful. Because when people like you and Bill are successful, the world is better for it. And Hank would tell you the same thing. Don't you doubt that for a second. Your father was a good man, and you're every bit his daughter."

Could the man be any more decent? She felt two inches tall.

Carrie had just beep-beeped the rental car's doors when she saw Tim McDonough turn the corner. As usual, he was unshaven. His T-shirt, from the local rock radio station, was a size too small.

There were a few governmental departments housed there, but she had a specific candidate in mind: the Department of Probation.

"Tim," she called out. "Is Melanie with you?"

"She's at home."

"Makes sense, since you're the one on probation, not her."

"What's your problem, Carrie?"

"My problem is that you're still Melanie's problem." She knew she was dumping her own frustrations onto him, but she couldn't stop the words from coming out. "Don't you ever wonder where the two of you would be if you'd never gotten married? She's the best part of your life, and look what you've done to her."

"Whatever."

"If you were the least bit honest, you'd realize you've been dragging Melanie and TJ into a long, slow grave."

Two steps toward her and he was suddenly in her face. She tensed up, ready for the blow. Part of her wanted to be punched. She deserved it.

"You talk about which one of us should be grateful to Melanie? Look in your gold-framed mirror, Queen Carrie."

"What's that supposed to mean?"

He took half a step back. The bulging veins in his neck flattened. "God, this is so . . . *you*. You and your family have always treated Melanie like dirt."

"My parents treated Melanie like a second daughter."

"I'm not talking about your parents. Melanie knows you look down on her, like you don't even have time for her anymore. She sees the way you eyeball our house like it's not fit for Your Royal Highness."

She had no idea what he was talking about. "I love your wife like a sister."

"Don't get me started on your *actual* sister."

The mention of her sister seemed to come out of nowhere. "Why would you say that? Do you know something about Donna?"

"I know she was absolutely horrible to Melanie. Don't you ever feel bad that you got a shot at a fancy college and she didn't?"

Of course she did. She felt bad all the time.

"You think I got it because of Donna." Did he know that Carrie thought the same thing? What had Mr. Sullivan just said about them being competitors? She,

Melanie, and Bill had spent high school gunning for the same accolades, but in the end Carrie was the only one who applied for the big kahuna, the Morris Grant. By that time, she also had a sympathetic biography as the icing on the cake: *Poor thing's sister got murdered.* "Does it really matter anymore, Tim? That was twenty years ago."

"You don't even know, do you?" He laughed in frustration. "Melanie had just gotten the news, and was all alone, crying in the waiting room at the clinic, afraid to walk outside because once she did, it would all become real. You know her views on the subject, so she was definitely keeping the baby. In walks Donna, and Melanie thought, *Oh, someone I can trust. Carrie's big sister.* She figured, given her own problems, Donna might have some sympathy. But, nope, she was just as judgmental as you. She was horrible. She told Melanie, 'How can you go to college now? How can you have a baby and still do all that work? Won't you feel bad taking a chance away from Bill or Carrie, who actually have a shot at making it?' *That* was your sister. That's you and your family."

"I—I didn't know."

"If Melanie's never told you, it's because—like always—she's trying to protect you. But your sister crushed Melanie. She *broke* her. And worst of all, she preyed on that girl's love—for you, for Bill, for our unborn son. So think about that the next time you feel like judging us."

As she watched him walk away, she realized he might be right. She and Melanie had found their way back into each other's lives, but all this time, Carrie had felt so proud to have worked her way out of Red View—and sorry for Melanie that she hadn't. Now she was wondering whether she'd lost too much of herself along the way.

35

According to police reports, Donna Blank's mother, Marcia Haring, was sixty-seven years old, but she looked and moved like a woman in her eighties. They had just watched her shuffle from her front door to her spot on the living room sofa, favoring her right hip the entire time. Her face was marked by deep vertical lines.

She sat staring at the view through the window, a row of mismatched trash cans in a narrow alley behind the house. "He's out?" she finally said. "That's . . . shouldn't someone have told me?"

"It just happened," Ellie said. "We wanted to notify you right away." She wondered who was notifying the families of the other victims. She couldn't believe how many fires they were trying to put out on their own. "He was only convicted of the one murder down in the city, so it's still possible that he'll be prosecuted for the other cases here."

She explained that one of the hurdles was the newly discovered presence of DNA beneath two of her daughter's fingernails.

"I'd like to think she'd be the type of person to fight her attacker. Hopefully she got a big chunk out of Amaro."

"Absolutely," Rogan said. "But the problem is that the crime lab has concluded that the DNA belongs to someone else. That's why we're so eager to know whether there might be some other explanation—someone else she might have fought with besides her killer. Did your daughter have a boyfriend?"

She shook her head. "Not to mention, if anyone raised a hand to Donna, she'd take them out. My baby was tough. Well, except for when it came to her own failures. When she started smoking pot, in the eighth grade, I tried to tell myself it wasn't so different than what I was up to as a kid. But then a little pot became a lot of pot. And missed classes. And bad friends. And then it got to the point that I would've bought her all the pot in the world to keep her off the other stuff."

"That kind of lifestyle can be rough," Rogan said, "bringing rough people around. You can't think of someone she might have struggled with?"

"She seemed good the last time I saw her. Told me she was going to her father's. Guess she never got there, so maybe she changed her mind. God knows she wasn't wanted there."

"Donna was estranged from her father?" Ellie asked.

"No, but his wife, Rosemary, had no time for Donna. It was Donna's own fault, frankly. She crossed a line there's no going back from."

Marcia's eyes glazed as her thoughts went somewhere

else. She didn't want to remember the worst parts of her only child.

"I understand it's painful to talk about," Ellie said. "But, really, you never know what might help, Ms. Haring."

"The fact is, Donna stole her sister's college money. It wasn't all that much, in hindsight. But Carrie—that's Hank's girl with Rosemary—had worked real hard to save it. Carrie gave every cent to Donna to go to rehab, but Donna just used it to get high. When Hank called and told me, I think it was the hardest I ever cried in my whole life, until I lost her, of course. But Donna knew she was wrong. She was so remorseful. She swore she was going to make it up to Carrie. She had so much she wanted to say, but Rosemary absolutely prohibited Donna from seeing Carrie again. I told her when she said she was heading over there that it was still too soon. I assume she realized I was right. I always wonder if that might have put her in a low mood. Onto the streets. And someone got her from there. Someone got my baby."

"Did you know that Carrie is working for Anthony Amaro?" Ellie asked. "As his lawyer?"

The woman looked at Ellie like she was speaking in pig Latin. "I don't think that's so."

"What about a detective named Will Sullivan? Do you know him?"

She nodded.

"Do you know if Donna knew him?"

"Sure. He's got a son Carrie's age. Basically a second dad to the girl. Hank passed not even two years after Donna was killed. We've had a lot of loss in this family."

"But do you know for certain that Donna knew Sullivan?"

She could tell from Rogan's expression that he wanted to tape Ellie's mouth shut.

"I saw Donna getting in his car once. A Ford Taurus. Nothing fancy, but newer than most of the cars in Red View, so it stood out. Anyways, I figured it was another way Carrie had of trying to help her sister. I hoped it would work, but—none of us could save her. You know, maybe your lab can do some more tests. Maybe they made a mistake. It has to be Anthony Amaro, or else it means Donna's killer has been out there all these years. That's not right."

No, Ellie thought, it wasn't right.

36

Rogan was flipping through his satellite radio stations, but she knew what was coming. A Marvin Gaye song ended his search.

"Why'd you ask Donna's mother about Sullivan?"

"Instinct."

"You can do better than that."

"I think he's holding something back from us. I know I put more stock in Harris's statement than you, but you have to admit that any decent cop would have done *something* with a cellmate willing to report on a suspected serial killer."

"Or maybe he didn't give credence to a drug dealer willing to say whatever about whoever to cut his own time."

"Whomever," she corrected. "Whatever about whomever."

"How about 'whoever corrects my grammar again can walk back to the hotel'? Look, I didn't say Sullivan was a good cop, or even competent. I'm asking you why you think he's hiding something."

"I can't put my finger on it. Not yet. But I was right, wasn't I? Donna's mother saw her daughter in Sullivan's car. What's up with that?"

"Damn, Hatcher. You're the one who grew up in Kansas. Don't you see that everyone in Utica knows everyone? We know Sullivan's tight with Carrie Blank. Why is it so surprising he'd reach out to her messed-up sister? I've been trying hard not to press you on the Max thing, but do you think it's possible you're almost *looking* for something to make this case more complicated?"

"How could it possibly be more complicated than it is?"

"That's what I'm talking about right there. I think nine cops out of ten would look at this thing and say Amaro's still good for it. He confessed. You talked to the eyewitness. His old cellmate is convinced he's good for it. All this other stuff—Brunswick, the DNA, trying to poke holes in the old evidence—it's smoke and mirrors. But Max can't see it that way, because his boss doesn't want him seeing it that way. And so maybe part of you hopes they turn out to be right. All I know is, I'm having a hard time figuring out one minute to the next where exactly you stand on this case."

She wanted to tell him he was being unfair, but she knew he was right. One minute, she was seething about Amaro getting out of prison. The next, she was convinced she was seeing connections among Helen Brunswick, Joseph Flaherty, and Will Sullivan in police reports written when she was still in junior high school.

She was about to speak when Rogan turned the corner outside their hotel. The flashing lights of multiple marked cars flooded the street with color. A uniformed officer stepped forward to stop them at the parking lot entrance, and Rogan rolled his window down.

"You two guests here?" the officer asked.

Rogan said yes, and the officer waved him through.

"Impressive police work," Ellie muttered as they stepped out of the car.

A mix of uniformed officers and plainclothes police were milling around the lobby, the crackling sounds of shoulder-mounted radios clashing with the piped-in adult contemporary music.

Rogan made a beeline for the nearest uniform, but Ellie wasn't in the mood for another apology to Utica police for being in their city. She walked to the check-in desk and waved to the two clerks whispering to each other in the corner. "Sorry, but is there a problem here?" she asked. "I don't want to stay anywhere that's not safe."

"Nothing to worry about," one of them assured her. "A guest believes something may be missing from their room. I'm sure it's nothing to worry about."

Ellie heard the automatic doors opening behind her. It was Carrie Blank. She looked like she had been crying.

This really was a small town.

The clerk turned his attention from Ellie to Carrie. "Ah, there you are, Ms. Blank. Your friend has been trying to reach you."

A man rose from one of the lounge chairs in the lobby,

276

where he'd been talking to police. His once tidy hair was tousled and he was no longer wearing his eyeglasses, but Ellie recognized him as the assistant who had been glued to Linda Moreland as they left the courtroom.

"Carrie, oh my God. I've been trying to call you."

Ellie noticed the attorney check her phone and then power it on.

"I'm so sorry," the assistant continued. "That food—I think my stomach had a bad reaction. I was in so much pain. I just went back to my room to lie down. When I got back—someone had been there, Carrie. In your room. All that work I did? Everything is thrown on the floor, torn to pieces, a huge mess. I'm so sorry."

"It's okay, Thomas. It's not your fault."

Ellie didn't know Thomas from Adam, but even she could tell from his expression that, in fact, it had to be his fault.

The uniformed officer next to him explained the problem to Carrie. "Ma'am, we found the door to your hotel room ajar."

He gave a sideways glance to Thomas, who continued the explanation. "I went into the hallway for ice. Cold water helps my stomach." One hand touched his belly. "I flipped the latch so I wouldn't get locked out. I must have forgotten when I came back, and then I used the pass-through door to lie down in my own bed. I *swear*, Carrie, I'm going to redo everything. I'll get it back exactly the way it was."

"Is anything missing?"

He grimaced. "I'll figure it out. I promise. Linda's going to *kill* me."

"No, if she's going to kill anyone, it will be me for stuffing you full of McDonald's and then disappearing for three hours with my cell phone off."

"I'm so, so sorry, Carrie."

Ellie stepped forward. "If I could interrupt, Ms. Blank?"

The attorney looked at her impatiently. "What?"

"You know who the most likely suspect here is, don't you?"

"Look, I honestly have no idea."

"Anthony Amaro, or someone he sent on his behalf. Where is he, and why are you representing the man who killed your own sister?"

The attorney swallowed and immediately composed herself. "This is completely inappropriate, Detective Hatcher. You are attempting to interfere with my client's Sixth Amendment right to counsel. I will file the necessary complaint with the Utica Police Department about the break-in, but, frankly, you're a private citizen here as far as I'm concerned. Unless you have some other reason to speak to me, I'd ask you to give us some privacy."

Carrie Blank's words were firm, but Ellie could tell that the sudden transformation into a tough-talking lawyer was forced. Something about her demeanor had shifted. She had her doubts about Amaro's innocence.

Good. So did Ellie.

Ellie was channel-flipping through reality-show repeats when the word MAX appeared on her phone screen. As much as this case had highlighted some differences between them, she never would have believed that three letters could make her so homesick.

"Hey."

"You sound tired."

"Must be sympathetic sleep deprivation. Rogan was fading. I sent him away for a nap while we had the chance."

"Ooooh, a nap sounds good."

She allowed herself to shut her eyes and pretend she was home in their bed, that she'd never heard the name Anthony Amaro.

"We got another message," he said, breaking her day-dream. "This time, a phone message, left with the switch-board. She said her name was Debi Landry, calling for me about Anthony Amaro. Obviously, I called back right away. The woman who answered was a Debi Landry, but she said she had no idea who I was. She insisted she'd never heard of me and didn't call. So then I said, 'The call was about Anthony Amaro,' and she said, 'What's this got to do with *Tony*?' Get this: she was in foster care with him when they were children."

According to Buck Majors, Amaro had said he was in New York City to see someone he'd lived with in foster care. "But she wasn't the one who called you?" she asked.

"Not according to her. I pushed a little, since the last time we got a mysterious tip, it led us to Harris. I asked if Amaro had ever told her anything about his involvement in the murders. She went ballistic and said that we had no idea what they'd gone through. How Amaro protected her. How there was no way she would call a DA about him, that he was the best thing that ever happened to her as a kid. She told me not to contact her again unless she had the right to a lawyer, and hung up."

"Any way to track the original call to the switchboard?"

"Nope."

The line was quiet. Someone out there was sending them information, but they didn't know who, or why.

She heard a beep on her phone. Another call was coming in. It was Jess. "Oh, I gotta get this. Love you." She clicked over to the new call. "Hey."

"Some favor, little sister. Mona's freakin' terrified."

"Of what?"

"I asked her if the cop she remembered from Utica was named William Sullivan, and she said yeah, that sounded right. And then she asked me why. I told her that Amaro got out and you were up there, doing your whole *Cagney and Lacey* thing. She flipped when she heard Amaro was released. Now she's wondering if it was a cop all along, like her friends suspected. She doesn't want to have anything to do with this. I'm telling you, Ellie, I've never seen her this way. She's terrified."

"Please reassure her, Jess. She's not involved, and I won't let her be. You vouch for me, okay? Tell her she's just fine where she is."

Rogan had accused her earlier of making this case more complicated than it had to be, but as she hung up her phone, Ellie found herself wondering whether Mona might not have good reason to be afraid of William Sullivan.

37

Carrie was focused on the center of a pink tulip. It should've died weeks ago, but somehow this one stem lingered on at the edge of the courtyard behind the hotel.

She was outside because she couldn't stand to hear another apology from poor Thomas. He was trying to Scotch-tape scraps of torn pages from the floor of her hotel room into usable documents. She didn't think he would sleep until someone forgave him.

Her thoughts were broken by the sound of her phone. As she expected, it was Linda. She couldn't put this off any longer.

"Hi, Linda. I don't know what's wrong with my cell phone here. I keep losing my signal."

"I spent most of the day talking to Tony." When had he become "Tony"? "He's panicked. He called me collect from a pay phone. He got a call at the motel from his sister, saying that a girl he knew from foster care was trying to reach him. Her name is Debi Landry. She told Tony that an ADA called her. It was Max Donovan, and he *insisted* that he had received a message from her. He was asking her a ton of questions, trying to get her to implicate Tony. Did you see her name mentioned anywhere in the case records?"

"Not the ones I've reviewed. At least, not so far."

"You're still not done? How is that possible?"

Carrie knew the answer she wanted to give her: *Because I've been running around Utica, trying to explain myself to Melanie and my mother and Tim and Mr. Sullivan? Because you pile more work onto one attorney and one assistant than could possibly be completed? Because you're an insane woman who practices law by the seat of her pants instead of doing anything methodically and thoughtfully? Because some stranger pulled a Tasmanian Devil in my hotel room.*

The truth was that Carrie hadn't been able to bring herself to help Thomas complete the impossible task of identifying which, if any, case materials had been stolen. She'd looked through her personal belongings. The only thing that was missing was the journal she'd left on the nightstand. She realized she cared far more about that than anything relating to Anthony Amaro.

It was suddenly clear what Carrie had to do.

"I don't think this is working out."

"Well, what do you need? Would an investigator help?"

"No. I mean, it's not working out *at all*. I don't want this. I wanted to find out who killed my sister. You told me that Anthony Amaro was innocent, and that I could help get to the truth. I'm not insulting what you do. I get it. But it's not why I am here. I think you know I'm only in the way. I'm too close."

Carrie realized that part of her wanted Linda to argue with her. Why did she care so much about what people thought of her?

But she was relieved when Linda said, "Fine, take the next train back to the city if that's what you want. No hard feelings."

"Thanks, Linda." She started to add an apology, out of habit. She was always apologizing, but this time, she wouldn't have meant it.

38

It was two hours later and still no sign of Rogan. He wasn't kidding when he said he needed some sleep. Ellie had been monitoring the activity in the hotel lobby, and Carrie Blank was nowhere in sight.

Instead, she spotted Will Sullivan at the far end of the first-floor hallway. He didn't look especially happy to see her, but he didn't run away, either.

"Any progress with the break-in?" she asked.

"I wouldn't call it progress. The hotel has cameras, but only to monitor the car prowls and hand-to-hands going down in the parking lot. Anyone in or out on foot could just stay close to the perimeter of the building and avoid detection."

"What about inside the building?"

"Maybe the hotels in New York do that." It was another obvious dig. "But they don't have high-tech gear on the floors here. Hotel security has been helping us touch base with all the employees, but it's not exactly a hotbed of activity. They keep a very light staff. The house-keepers had mostly left for the day. No room service or anything. And no one reported seeing anything unusual. My gut tells me we're not getting anywhere."

"Any clear motive yet?"

"Nope, but it looks like the documents were the target. The attorney knows that at least one journal is missing."

"It has to be Anthony Amaro. He's out for the first time in eighteen years. Maybe he's worried there's something in those files he didn't want to get out."

"That's an interesting way to look at it," he said. "But in my Podunk experience, there's this thing called attorney-client privilege. It usually means the one person a criminal defendant can count on is his attorney, and I watched Carrie Blank cry today because she owes a legal duty to that man, whether she wants to or not, and it was clear she was not about to break it. There's also something called tabloid journalism. We don't see it a lot here, but you must, down in the city, with the paparazzi and all. We had Taylor Swift up here filming a music video. You would've thought it was the world's fair. Then you got the people who collect what they call serial-killer memorabilia. I think the pool down at the station house has the over-under for documents going up on eBay by the end of the day tomorrow."

"What's wrong with you?" The words were out of her mouth before she intended to speak them. Earlier, Rogan had accused her of focusing on Sullivan out of a subconscious hope that Max's insistence on a fresh look would pan out. But now she was certain that Sullivan's responses were seriously off kilter. "Don't you even want to catch a killer?"

"You really want to go there?"

"Hey, what's going on?" Rogan had risen from the dead. He did not look happy to find her going toe-to-toe in the lobby with Sullivan.

"Your partner was just accusing me of not caring about the deaths of six women."

"I'm sure Miss Congeniality didn't mean to suggest that—did you, Hatcher?"

Sullivan didn't wait for an apology. "If you want to talk about dropping the ball, I'd point out that you barely mentioned earlier today that your victim Helen Brunswick was a psychologist up here. That seemed like something that should be looked at, so I ran her. She had a patient named Joseph Flaherty. She was so scared of him that she broke confidentiality and called us. The guy's a major nut. He even turned up at my house more than a few times."

"We went through the same steps," Ellie said. "Helen Brunswick rotated through some of the hospitals up here before she quit. I figured out your connection to Flaherty as we were leaving the station house. Your names were in the reports."

"Then why didn't you say something? I thought this was supposed to be a *we* thing? Joseph Flaherty obsessed over me for a few years solid for no reason at all."

"So how come you didn't pursue charges against him? According to the reports, it was your neighbors who always called." She could tell from the expression on

Rogan's face that he was regretting having left her alone so long.

"It got to the point that he was like a raccoon under the porch, except I'm not allowed to plant poison in a trap. It seems to me that you missed the main point: Joseph never tried to harm me, but maybe Brunswick had an instinct about him that she couldn't really put her finger on. The only other patient she ever called about probably would've turned into Jeffrey Dahmer if a well-placed car accident hadn't taken him out first."

"We ruled out Flaherty for a reason," Ellie said. "He was committed to a psych ward at Cedar Ridge when at least one of the victims was killed."

"Well, here's the problem with your logic. I saw that same information. But because I'm from here, and you're not, I happen to know that half the staff at Cedar Ridge in the 1990s couldn't locate their own ass with a flashlight. We used to find patients roaming in the woods, chanting at Taco Bell, sleeping behind the churches. It was easy to wander out. Plus, here's the interesting thing: Flaherty's on a mental hold right now."

"Right." Ellie remembered Rogan mentioning that fact when he told her Flaherty's history, but didn't understand why Sullivan was bringing it up.

"Did you happen to check the dates of the hold?" Sullivan asked.

She looked to Rogan for guidance, but he shook his head.

"Joseph turned himself in—which he *never* does voluntarily, by the way—a little more than a week after Helen Brunswick was killed. You happen to remember when that anonymous letter to your DA was postmarked?"

She recited the date from memory.

"Yep. Joseph locked himself down the very next day. I may be a dumb old-timer from a Podunk town, but that's what we hicks like to call one heck of a co-inky-dink."

39

It was only eight o'clock in the morning, but Carrie's mother answered the door neatly attired in a crisp white cotton shirt and slim black pants. Even the morning after Carrie's father had died, Rosemary Blank had gone straight from the first opening of her eyes in bed to the shower into a clean set of clothes. As she liked to say: Lose an hour in the morning and you'll hunt all day for it.

"You don't knock on your own front door, Carrie."

Carrie hadn't lived here in years, but she still had her own key. Her mother led the way to the small table in the kitchen. A half piece of blackened wheat toast was still on a plate—part of the same set of dishes Carrie had eaten from as a child. Next to her mother's coffee mug was an open library book, jacket side up. The spine read: *The Opposite of Spoiled*. Her mother was always reading something.

"I was starting to wonder if everyone in Utica would see my daughter before I did." She retrieved another mug from the cabinet next to the refrigerator, filled it with coffee, and handed it to Carrie. "Mrs. Lemon told me she saw you in the McDonald's drive-through yesterday. I told her that wasn't possible. My daughter would never poison her body that way."

"Never!" Carrie said, sharing her mother's knowing smile as they both took seats at the kitchen table. "I'm sorry I didn't come earlier. We've been working nonstop. So much has happened."

"I saw on the news that he was released. Clearly, Linda Moreland hired the right lawyer for the job."

Carrie had prepared herself for all the other reactions another parent might have given. Disappointment that Carrie had helped release a man from prison without clear proof of his innocence. Embarrassment at her association with a notorious and despised criminal. Fear of public reprisals.

But Carrie's mother was proud of her.

"Why do you look so sad?" she asked. "You were hoping I might have some other reaction, so you can tell your friends how hard your mother is always pushing you?"

Clearly she had caught her mother in a playful mood. "No, it's nothing. Or everything. I don't know. I saw Tim yesterday. He was talking about Melanie. How she should have been the one to go away for school. Maybe she would have been able to cut it, even with TJ."

"Not that again. If that was anyone's fault, it was mine. You were trying to take care of me after Daddy died. Do you know how painful it was for me—after everything—to be the one who kept you from your full potential?"

She should have known that her mother was the wrong person to talk to about this. Carrie felt the tears starting again but pushed her emotions back. She had to get it together. "Sorry, Mom. It's just been a rough couple of days. This case brought up a lot of old memories."

"You'll be fine. You always are."

Carrie had been so afraid to tell her mother she had taken the job. Now she didn't know how to tell her she had quit.

"There's something I never told you, Mom."

"Oh, I'm shocked. I thought daughters told their mothers *everything*." The smile again.

"I saw you arguing with her. With Donna, that day she came to the house. I was upstairs. You thought I didn't hear over my music, but I was watching."

"Why didn't you come down?"

She stared into her mug. "I was scared. I'd never seen you so angry. And she sounded so—desperate. I thought if I came down, things would really explode. I planned to go to her later. I wanted to see her, and I wasn't going to tell you."

"If you think that's any surprise to me, you're wrong. Of course I knew you'd want to see her. That's why your father and I prohibited it. You always had a soft spot for that girl. You would have forgiven her anything."

"But that's what I'm telling you, Mom. I know you saw me as the victim, but I was the one who insisted she take that money. I didn't understand that she needed to be *ready* to stop using. She wasn't, and I pushed that money on her. I made things worse, don't you understand? When you guys shut her out, I felt like it was my fault. I wanted to see her—not to forgive her, but to apologize."

Her mother was shaking her head.

"I never got a chance to say goodbye." Carrie remembered the police report filed by Donna's mother after she went missing. "Why didn't you ever tell the police about that day?"

"I never needed to. We were only using the threat of pressing charges to keep her away from you."

"I don't mean the money, Mom. Donna told Marcia she was coming to our house the last time she saw her. According to the police report, you told the police she was never here."

"Because she wasn't. Not that day, at least. You were young. You're misremembering the timing."

Carrie was quite certain her memory was right. The day after the incident at the house, Carrie was tied up with a morning debate-team practice, followed by a full shift at the movie theater. But on Sunday, she'd gone to Donna's house. Marcia said Donna hadn't been home all weekend and she was beginning to worry. Carrie specifically remembered being grateful that she had a mother who would "begin to worry" five minutes after her curfew, not two days later.

Carrie thought about trying to explain the timing to

her mother, but took another sip of coffee instead. She didn't have the energy to argue. And it didn't even make a difference anymore. Anthony Amaro was out, and no one seemed interested in finding out who should be in prison, if not Amaro. All Linda Moreland cared about was money, and bringing down the police, and freeing more clients, and she had used Carrie as a pawn in a chess game Carrie barely understood.

This time, she couldn't hold back the tears. She hadn't felt failure like this since she had to pack up her dorm room in Ithaca. "I screwed up, Mom. It was too big. Too much. I didn't stop and think."

"About what?"

"The job. Linda Moreland. Anthony Amaro. I quit last night, Mom. I wanted to believe I got that job because I was so special, but she was using me. She wanted to hold me out there for all the world to see: *Look, even the victims' families believe he's innocent.* But I don't, or at least I'm not convinced. And Donna's killer, whoever he is? He's still out there. I'm going back to the city tomorrow to beg my way back into Russ Waterston."

Somehow her mother managed to piece together a meaningful thought buried in the words that were spilling out. "You won't have to beg for anything, Carrie. You are the smartest, kindest, most talented person I know. And you're a good person. You always have been. Anyone would be lucky to have you. You will always land on your feet. Any setback only makes you stronger.

Because that's what your father and I wanted for you."

Carrie could feel her breath becoming more even. Her mother's hushing sounds, the feeling of her warm hands soothing her back, made her feel like a child again.

"Do you understand now about the police report?"

Carrie looked up at her mother's face.

"When they asked if she'd been here, she'd only been gone a few days. Donna was always coming and going. And then, later, once they found her—what difference would it have made? Donna hurt you enough when she was alive. You didn't need to be dragged into her death. This is exactly what I was trying to save you from. Don't you see?"

40

The conference room on the second floor of the Utica PD headquarters was surprisingly modern. Ellie, Rogan, and Sullivan sat elbow-to-elbow in front of a webcam. Behind them, an Oneida County ADA named Mike Siebecker was pacing. On the large screen on the opposite wall was an image of Max, appearing via video conference.

The detectives had dominated the conversation for the last forty-five minutes, detailing all available evidence involving all of the murders. Now it was time for the lawyers to talk through the legal issues.

Siebecker took the lead. "If you look only at our Utica victims, we basically have nothing except the cellmate saying Amaro quasi-confessed, which isn't probable cause on its own. The only way to get to PC is to pull in evidence involving the city victim, Deborah Garner, where we've got the single-witness identification and the confession. It's dicey, but if you add that evidence to Harris's statement, I think I could get a judge here to sign an arrest warrant."

"That was our thinking," Max said. "At least we'd know Amaro was behind bars while we continued to investigate."

"But here's the problem," Siebecker added. "The affirmative evidence against Amaro is already thin, and then you've got to take into account what I'll call the *negative* evidence—the evidence that points to an alternative suspect."

"The unidentified DNA on Donna Blank," Max said.

"I have some thoughts on that," Ellie said, raising a hand. "In talking to people who knew the victims, there's reason to believe that Donna Blank didn't fit the profile. She worked at strip clubs. Took tips. Probably crossed the line into tricking in the bathrooms and the parking lot, but she wasn't a hard-core working girl like the other victims."

Sullivan made a coughing sound on the other side of Rogan. At least he removed his plastic chew-stick from his mouth before speaking. "I think turning tricks in parking lots makes someone a working girl."

"But she was at the fringe of that world." Ellie considered throwing in the fact that Mona had told Sullivan herself that Donna didn't fit the profile of the other victims, but she had promised Mona to leave her out of this. Instead, she said, "I would've thought you'd be in a position to know this personally. Donna's mother told us she saw her daughter get in your car." She couldn't see Rogan's face, but on the screen, she saw Max looking at her as if she had burped at the head table of the State Dining Room.

Sullivan's fingertips pressed against the table. His

voice sounded strained. "I don't know why you would say that in the tone you just used, Detective, but Donna Blank's sister happens to be one of my son's closest and oldest friends. As a favor to the family, I reached out to Donna to encourage her to seek help for her drug problem, but I assure you, that's the extent of my contact with her."

Siebecker made a time-out sign with his hands. "It's not entirely about the unidentified DNA. We also have the anonymous letter claiming that whoever killed the Utica victims murdered Brunswick. Normally, courts don't give credence to anonymous tips, but whoever wrote that letter knew that Helen Brunswick's limbs had been broken—information that hadn't been released to the public. Not to mention Brunswick's connection to the mental-health system here treating some extremely dangerous people at the same time those women were killed. Anthony Amaro has no known connection to that world, but we have one individual—Joseph Flaherty—who obviously had a negative experience with Dr. Brunswick, and who just happened to have turned himself in for civil commitment shortly after her murder."

"We don't have anything close to probable cause on Joseph," Ellie said.

"Agreed," Siebecker said. "But that's not my point. *Any* evidence against a person who is *not* Anthony Amaro is essentially a *subtraction* from the quantum of evidence we have to get us to probable cause. So, as for positive evidence against Amaro, we barely have probable cause, and then we add the negative evidence, and, alas, I don't think we're there."

Ellie looked to Max, hoping he'd find a way out of this mathematical analogy. But instead, she heard, "I have to say, I concur."

Rogan looked exhausted again. "Enough with the positive and the negative evidence talk. I may not know Oneida County, but if it's like any other place in this country, there's some judge you can call to sign what needs to be signed. It's about getting our hands on this guy again."

"The problem with that," Max said, "is: What happens when you get him? You might find evidence on him. Or he might confess. And we'll lose all of it if we don't actually have the probable cause. I hate it that this guy's on the streets as much as anyone, but we've got to do this right. Shoddy police work is what put us here in the first place."

She glanced at Rogan in her periphery, wondering if he was going to argue with that assessment. He glanced at her, clearly frustrated, but said nothing.

"So now what?" she asked.

Sullivan jumped in. "At least we know where to find Joseph. His commitment hold expired, and he's back on his meds. He's at his mother's, so I'll have my guys keep eyes on him. And we've got a BOLO out for Amaro and have guys looking—his old contacts, the motels, shelters.

My guess is his attorneys have told him by now to lay low."

"We should see what we can learn about Joseph's recent mental state," Ellie said. "And his whereabouts— whether he could have been in New York City when Helen Brunswick was killed. We could talk to his mother, maybe, as a starting point."

"We can handle that," Sullivan said. "The way she sees it, I was pretty sympathetic toward her son when he was fixated on me all those years ago."

"And us?" Rogan asked. "What role does the *fresh-look* team play in all this?"

She could tell from Max's forced smile that Rogan's sarcasm wasn't lost on him. "You'll be on the ground back here in the city; Sullivan will be in charge up there. It's time for you guys to come home."

Sullivan led the way out of the room, followed by Siebecker and Rogan. When she was alone in the conference room, she looked straight into the webcam. "This sucks, Max."

"What's wrong?"

"The whole purpose of the fresh look was to get a fresh look, right? But Sullivan's entangled. He knew at least one of the victims. He buried the info from Amaro's cellmate. He intimidated a woman who came forward to say that Donna Blank wasn't like the other girls. And he seems intent on going after Joseph Flaherty, who was a teenager locked up in a psych ward when Donna Blank was killed. As far as I can tell, the only thing Flaherty's guilty of is harassing a police officer who, oh yeah, just happens to be Will Sullivan."

"We'll talk it through together, okay? Come on home."

She nodded, and he blew a kiss and clicked offline, leaving her alone in the room. She was about to walk out when she noticed the red plastic coffee stirrer on the conference table, flattened and gnawed by Sullivan's nervous chewing.

She pulled a Kleenex from her shoulder bag and used it to scoop up the straw. She knew an analyst who would quietly do her the favor.

Couldn't hurt to check.

41

By the time Ellie put keys into her front door four hours later, she felt like she'd been on the road for a month. She let her gym bag fall to the floor.

Max appeared in the front hallway and handed her a highball glass full of Johnnie Walker Black on the rocks.

"You are a god." She took a big gulp and gave him an even bigger hug.

"You notice anything different about the apartment?"

The dining room table was set with two candles and a buffet of Chinese takeout. Then she realized this was the first time she'd walked into their home on a hot day and felt chilled.

"It's freezing. And it's *wonderful*."

"I dropped the thermostat five degrees in your honor."

At least Ellie had managed to solve one problem this week. She grabbed a spare rib from the spread and ate it with her fingers.

She was about to tell him about her pitstop at the crime lab. Michael Ma had agreed to test the coffee stirrer against the DNA beneath Donna Blank's fingernails. He'd do it fast and quietly, without even asking where the plastic stick originated. But as she started to speak, she realized how ridiculous it would sound. She could make a good case that Will Sullivan was lazy, that he had been a stone wall in the investigation over and over again, that he was oddly complacent. But to go from being an incompetent cop to involvement in Donna Blank's murder? Once she got the negative results back, she could set aside her nagging suspicions about Sullivan, and there would be no reason for anyone to know that she'd gone out on such a precarious limb.

She handed Max a set of chopsticks from the table. "Can we eat in front of the TV?"

"I've got last night's *Daily Show* all cued up."

"Perfection."

By the time she went to bed, her belly was stuffed with egg rolls, scallion pancakes, and three helpings of double-cooked pork. She felt like she'd been home for days. She heard Max's electric toothbrush running in the bathroom. She clicked off her nightstand lamp and turned his low, grateful now that he had insisted on getting the ones with dimmers. Resting her head, she realized how much smoother the sheets were here than in the Utica hotel, and how the pillow supported her neck perfectly.

As she closed her eyes, she reflected on how they had reached a new, slower place in the investigation. For days, they had been rushing from one urgent lead to the next, hoping that one would turn out to be the thing that opened the floodgates. But not every case had a breakthrough.

There were no more obvious places to turn. They'd move on to the long shots. And they'd start taking new callouts.

What had Rogan said to her? *We get through this case, then we go back to normal.* At the time, they both believed they would identify whatever person or people killed Helen Brunswick, Deborah Garner, Stacy Myer, Donna Blank, Jennifer Bronson, Leticia Thomas, and Nicole Henning. They would get justice for those victims. They would get answers for their families.

But sometimes cases went cold. Once this one did, the fresh-look team would be disbanded. They wouldn't quit immediately. They'd keep working for a few days, maybe even add more officers in a last-ditch surge of effort. But when the leads didn't pan out and no new tips came in, the team would close up shop. Things would go back to normal for Ellie, with Rogan and with Max.

By the time she fell asleep, she was telling herself it wasn't their fault: the mistakes had been made before she and Rogan had ever heard of Anthony Amaro. She was prepared to let the case go. Had she been able to admit it to herself, she was almost eager to move on.

42

For as long as Carrie could remember, she'd been working as much and as hard as possible. In school to get into
the best college possible. At Cornell to maintain the min-
imum GPA for her scholarship. Back in Utica, waiting
tables to help her mother keep the house after her father
died. Back in school again—at Cortland State, CUNY
Law, then Fordham—trying to prove she was still worth
taking a chance on. At Russ Waterston, making up in
hours and effort for the networking advantages her peers
had over her.

Carrie had spent her entire life reaching for the next
thing, but today her life was suddenly different. Today
she opened her eyes, then closed them again, and did that
several times over. By the time she got out of bed, the
clock read two thirty-four and she had violated her
mother's motto of not losing an hour in the morning
seven times over.

She kept forcing herself back into sleep for a reason:
she didn't have a job. She didn't have work to do. And,
worst of all, the confidence she used to have in her work
was shaken. She had managed to help free Anthony
Amaro but still had no idea who killed Donna and those

other women. Under the circumstances, bed seemed like a sensible place to spend the day.

But this was also the first day she could remember when she had absolutely nothing scheduled. She had no assignment to complete, no goal to meet, no clock to watch. She was one of those New Yorkers Carrie always wondered about—picking up the morning paper in the late afternoon, strolling through the city streets in tennis shoes and shorts, sunglasses on head. She forced herself to leave the apartment to get coffee and a paper. Before she knew it, the errand turned into a trek down to the High Line, the elevated park just two miles from her that she'd been swearing to see for nearly three years.

On a different day, she would never have had her ear-buds in as she crossed the street and entered the front door of her building. She would have checked the street before using her security key, searching for anyone who gave her the heebie-jeebies. If anyone suddenly appeared behind her, she would have pretended to fumble with her mail or her phone, any excuse to insist that they go ahead of her. She would have done all those things, because Carrie had grown up in a city where women were murdered, and she had internalized certain routines.

But today wasn't every other day. Today was the day she blissfully crossed the street, and entered the building, and took the stairs, all while Prince's "When Doves Cry" blasted in her ears. Today was the day she failed to notice that someone had been standing down the hall, waiting for her arrival, watching her as she inserted her key into the door.

Today was the day she didn't worry about a thing, not until she felt the first crack on the side of her head.

As she fell forward, she covered her face and skull with her arms.

Another blow, this time to a kidney. Her right arm jerked automatically to her side. She felt another blow to the head, then another, and another. It felt like a new lifetime, while thoughts of her old one flashed before her on a screen. She felt herself falling into blackness. She was getting cold. Then she felt a warm bath comforting her.

She hadn't seen her assailant. She had no idea what motivated her murder. But she knew she was being punished for helping Anthony Amaro regain his freedom.

PART FOUR

THE LAST GASP

43

Ellie knew the rhythms of an important murder investigation. When she walked into 1 Police Plaza, she could
immediately connect the energy of the environment to
what she knew to be true about the case itself. It was
big—too big for the squad room at her home base of the
13th Precinct.

Until today, the so-called fresh-look team had been
spare. Ellie, Rogan, Max. Supplements in Utica. Now
forty officers flooded a room crammed with white boards
and computers. They were working every possible angle
that could be explored without setting foot in Oneida
County. About a quarter of the team was rehashing background information from Utica: some reviewing the old
evidence; some digging up information about the reliabil-
ity of Amaro's former cellmate, Robert Harris; some con-
centrating on Helen Brunswick's former patient, Joseph
Flaherty. Then there was the focus on the victims: most
homicides were committed by an acquaintance. Even
fetish-driven serial killers often targeted a victim or two
with a personal connection. Then there were the officers
taxed with tracing the mysterious communications that
had been coming in to law enforcement—the initial tip

tying Helen Brunswick's murder to Anthony Amaro; the e-mail leading them to Robert Harris; and the telephone message that was supposedly from Anthony Amaro's foster sister.

Anyone could look at the number of bodies involved in this effort—the ringing phones, the movement from one side of the room to the other, the pandemonium—and see that this was important. But when Ellie felt this kind of energy, she had a different take. This was the moment when an institution ramped up, but when Ellie began to shut down. This was the last gasp. The investigation was intense, but ultimately narrow. This was the surge. This was the moment when the people in charge committed every possible resource, in the hope that something would break, and in the certainty that the effort could be held up as proof down the road that they'd done everything possible before giving up.

Ellie's own role was to work collectively on the profile of the victims. Was there a hidden commonality among them that they had missed? She reviewed every piece of background information they had on each of the victims. She made follow-up calls to friends and family members. This was usually her forte: imagining the lives that had been lost and figuring out where those lives had collided with danger. The entire time she'd been a detective, that skill had been facilitated by cell phones, computers, and security cameras—technology that allowed her to draw connections between people who wanted their associations to remain covert. She was realizing how much easier it had been for the bad guys to cover their tracks two decades ago.

She was on the phone with the third victim's sister, searching hopelessly for some new shred of information, when she heard a voice break through the cacophony that had become the day's background noise.

"I think I have something. Holy shit, I think I've got some*one*." She couldn't make out the responsive murmurs. "That's him," she heard from the same voice. "It's the same guy."

She rushed off the phone so she could find the speaker. He turned out to be an analyst who looked like a fan at one of Jess's dive-bar gigs: pomade in the hair, eau de cigarettes, lots of tattoos. Central casting for hipster-punk.

"What do you have?"

"I'm on the Park Slope camera crew." It was the unimaginative label they'd given to a duo of workers tapped with reviewing all available security camera footage within a ten-block radius of Helen Brunswick's office. They still didn't know if Brunswick's death was related to the older murders, but her case was the most recent, making her their best chance of catching a break. There were no security cameras in the immediate vicinity around her office, but they had expanded the radius as part of the last-ditch surge. "You asked us to look for anything that might be worth following up on."

"And?" Ellie asked.

The hipster-punk pushed back from his workstation to make room. "Right there. See that guy?" He pointed to the paused black-and-white image on his computer.

Ellie bent over and squinted at the screen. She looked for Rogan and found him hanging up a phone, his eyes simultaneously scanning the room. She waved him over.

He recognized the face, too.

"Where and when?" he asked.

"Three hours before Brunswick's murder. He bought a lottery ticket seven blocks west. Isn't that the same guy those people are talking about?" The hipster-punk's gaze moved to a rolling bulletin board parked at the front end of the room. At the center of the board was a photograph of Joseph Flaherty. The two people standing in front of it had been dubbed "the Joseph team."

"Well, I'll be damned," Rogan said.

Joseph Flaherty may not have won the lottery, but he had a certain kind of luck. There was no doubt he was the man on the screen. On paper, he'd spent his entire life in Utica. But now they had ironclad proof placing him within six hundred yards of Helen Brunswick the day of her murder.

"Wait, there's more," the analyst announced. "His face isn't even what caught my attention, because it only appears in the camera for a second."

He hit rewind. On the screen, Joseph's head tilted forward, and they watched as he appeared to walk backward to a refrigerator case, return his Snapple to the top shelf, and then continue to rotate other bottles toward him to inspect the variety of flavors.

The analyst hit pause and pointed at the screen. "See that? That's what I first noticed about the guy."

With Joseph's arm raised, the back of his jacket was lifted. He had a handgun in his waistband.

44

If there were a photograph of an alien abduction of the abominable snowman burying Jimmy Hoffa, it could not have gotten more scrutiny than this crappy video from a bodega seven blocks from Helen Brunswick's office. They had processed various freeze-framed images from the video fifty different ways. Twenty pairs of eyes had made the relevant comparisons. All twenty agreed that the man walking out of the bodega with a Snapple Peach Tea and a handgun was Joseph Flaherty.

Ellie held an enhanced copy of the photograph next to a mugshot from Flaherty's most recent booking. By now, she had memorized the details of his repeated inter-actions with law enforcement and the mental-health system. His history was typical of those individuals trapped at the intersection between the two. Busts for disruptions that were alarming enough to justify an arrest but too petty to warrant serious jail time. Stints in mental-health facilities—some voluntary, some court-mandated—but never enough to break the cycle. These were the lost people muttering to themselves beneath bridges and overpasses. They were the ones both sys-tems churned through their respective mills, until they really hurt someone, and then they made front-page news.

"We've done all we can do with one picture," Max said. "Let's make sure the Utica folks know it's time to focus in on Joseph."

"I'll make the call," Ellie said.

Joseph Flaherty was about to hit the front page. And Ellie needed to be the one to give Sullivan the credit.

Sullivan picked up on the third ring. "Ah, Detective. I hope your trip home was uneventful."

"Very much so, thank you."

"See how I knew it was you, even before you said so? We hicks way up here in the boonies have this thing called caller ID, real cutting-edge. I saw 'City of New York' on the screen and figured it was either you or your partner. I believe that's what fancy people call deductive reasoning skills."

"I get it, Detective Sullivan, and I'm calling to tell you I deserve the ribbing. We should have reached out to your department earlier."

"Glad to hear you think so. And I'm sure you're calling to remind me we're supposed to be looking for Anthony Amaro."

"Actually, no. I was—"

"Still haven't got eyes on him. I suspect Linda Moreland moved him further out from the city to make it harder for us. And I happen to know that the attorney who was here left to go back to the city."

"I got the impression you knew her."

"Since she was three feet tall. Here's the thing: Moreland's legal assistant is still at the hotel. I figure that means the big gun is on her way. I'm planning to put a tail on her. Can't imagine she'll be happy about it, but I don't plan on her finding out."

"Smart."

"I thought so, too. And you must have meant it about the change of heart. You don't even sound surprised."

She couldn't believe that just yesterday she had been so suspicious of this man that she'd carried a plastic stick covered in his saliva all the way from Utica. "You know, for what it's worth, I grew up in a place not unlike your city. Bigger, but the same, in the sense that most people are born and bred there. And I owe you an apology. I realize it's my own baggage about my hometown that made me too quick to believe that your department had swept these murders under the rug."

"That's a harsh thing to believe about any group of hardworking police officers."

"Long story. My dad was a cop. But a justified belief as to one place doesn't mean it applies everywhere else. So, I'm sorry."

"Well, okay then. Cornball hick-versus-city-slicker jokes will hereby cease. That it?"

318

"Nope. Have you had a chance to find anything new on Joseph Flaherty?"

"Not much. I tried getting the specifics of his most recent hospitalization, but they're demanding a subpoena. Guess that's the one last piece of privacy we still have. But I did manage to get some general information. For a civil commitment, even if the patient shows up voluntarily, the hospital has to certify that the person is a danger to himself or others. I know Joseph's history. He's usually just ranting and raving about delusional stuff; no evidence of danger."

Ellie had seen the pattern herself in the reports. "As I recall, he has a tendency to see Satan in his many forms." Helen Brunswick originally called police because Joseph was making nonsensical accusations that a fellow patient was the devil and had tried to kill Joseph's five wives. The complaints by Sullivan's own neighbors had been more about Joseph's general disruptiveness, but even the vague complaints mentioned Joseph's accusations that Sullivan could control people's minds and was the devil.

"That's Joseph, all right. So I'm thinking one of two things. Maybe he killed Brunswick, came back home, and had some kind of psychotic break. Or, more interestingly, maybe he faked a more serious level of crazy."

"Why would he do that?"

"Hard to get into that kind of mind, but if he just wants a little mental-health tune-up—a change in the meds, someone to watch him for a few days—he knows how to do that. But that's not what he did. He walked in on his own and wound up with an official commitment-hold, which is something that shows up in the system. Maybe he's setting the stage for an insanity plea. Or maybe he figured that if some cops on a fishing expedition started looking up every patient Helen Brunswick ever had an encounter with, they might see the hold and move on to the next person without noticing the timing."

"Worked on Rogan and me," she said.

"I was looking forward to the intense pleasure of pointing that out until you went and warmed my heart with that apology." She could hear the smile in his voice. "Right now, it's just a theory, though. I haven't been able to find anything proving that Joseph left Utica."

"Well, we can help you with that. Are you near a computer?"

"Yes indeed. We have those here, you know."

"Well, there's this modern invention called e-mail. You have that, too, I imagine." She typed his address as he recited it, and then sent a message with three attachements. "Tell me when you've got it."

"Okay, there it is. Clicking on it now. All right, I've got photo number one." It was a recent photograph of Flaherty. "And, whoa, what am I looking at here?"

"A still from the security-camera footage of a bodega near Helen Brunswick's office. Joseph may have been acting crazy for the hospital up there, but he was in Brooklyn, calmly buying a Snapple three hours before

Helen Brunswick's murder. And make sure to check out door number three. That's a close-up of the back of his waistband."

Sullivan was silent.

"You still there?"

"Sorry. I'm—wow, I think I'm actually stunned."

"Well, don't be. You were the one who put him out there as a suspect."

"Yeah but, honestly, it was just a theory."

"Well, you nailed it. Technically, it's a break in the Brunswick case here, but our ADA talked to yours. It's time to pick up Joseph. They're working on the warrant application now. You'll be in charge of executing it."

"And you and Rogan are okay with that?"

Ellie was never "okay" with someone else handling any aspect of one of her cases, but she was more okay with it under these circumstances than usual. "Absolutely. You guys have the insider knowledge on Joseph, and you've got the advantage on location. We'll come up and work it together once you have him."

"I have a past with him. Once he's in custody, I might be able to get him to talk to me. If we can get an admission as to Brunswick, we might be able to leverage that into a confession for the other victims. Geez, is it really possible Amaro wasn't the guy?"

"Too soon to tell. We'll also get a cheek swab. A DNA match to Donna Blank would . . . Well, let's not get ahead of ourselves. You and your people pick up Joseph. We'll recanvass the area around Brunswick's office now that we have a photograph to show. We can also take care of checking E-Z Pass and Amtrak to see if we can lock down the mode of transportation he used. Do you have enough manpower to do what you need to do up there?"

"We've got it. For now."

She was about to hang up when she saw Rogan rushing toward her. He looked like he had news. "Just a sec, Sullivan. Whatcha got, Double-J?"

"It's Carrie Blank. Someone bludgeoned her in her apartment this morning."

On the other end of the line she heard Sullivan let out a quiet gasp for the lawyer he had known since she was three feet tall.

45

All these years as a cop and Ellie still hated hospitals. She could handle the chaos, the sight of sick and injured people, the antiseptic smell. What got to her was the fear—not in the patients themselves, but in the loved ones left waiting for news. As they approached the emergency-room check-in desk at Bellevue, an intake nurse snapped at a frantic woman. "Have a seat! I *told* you, a doctor will be out to talk to you about your sister when he's ready." The same woman then called gently for a Mrs. Hale and told her that a doctor needed to speak to her about her husband, and would she please follow her.

Ellie wanted to tell the two women she knew how this worked. The first lady's sister was fine. Mrs. Hale's husband was not. The last thing you should wish for is kindness from the staff in an overworked emergency room.

Rogan flashed a badge to the remaining nurse at the front desk. "Carrie Blank. Brought in this morning."

At the sound of Carrie's name, Ellie saw a man speaking nearby to a doctor look suddenly in their direction. Notebook in hand. Holster on shoulder. Detective.

She nudged Rogan.

"You guys Hatcher and Rogan?" the detective asked.

They nodded, and he waved them over. "John Colgrove. Caught the case after her downstairs neighbor called the police. Blood started dripping through the ceiling." He winced at the image. "From the looks of her apartment, someone tossed the place pretty good: drawers trashed, shelves emptied, the works. Her mom told me she was Anthony Amaro's lawyer until a couple of days ago, so I figured the two of you needed to be plugged in. I'm just getting the update from the doctor here."

The doctor launched straight into her report. "The assault involved a series of blows from a blunt instrument, but the worst were to her head. She suffered a significant head injury, with some bleeding in the brain. At this point, however, she's improving, and seems to be neurologically normal or near normal."

"Can we talk to her?" Colgrove asked.

"Not yet. The bleeding impaired her breathing for quite some time, which has led to a coma-like state. We'll know more over the next few days, but a full recovery is certainly possible."

"Is Carrie's mother here yet?" Ellie asked. The last time Ellie saw her, Carrie Blank was in Utica, working on Amaro's defense. Sullivan had mentioned that she'd come back to the city, but if she was no longer Amaro's lawyer, it was news to them.

"She's on her way. She was boarding a train when I updated her a few minutes ago. But with her permission, I just allowed a family friend in to see her. The lieutenant governor, actually. He's with her now, if you'd like to speak with him."

Ellie didn't usually follow politics, but from the hallway outside Carrie's hospital room she recognized the man sitting on the edge of Carrie's bed, holding one of her hands in his. Bill Sullivan had thick, dark hair, perfect teeth, and a strong jaw. She knew that his looks had probably played a role in his anointment as a rising political star, but Ellie figured a second-generation cop was as good a pretty boy as any to run the state. She had not followed his biography closely enough, however, to have made the connection—until now—between him and Utica police detective Will Sullivan.

She was about to knock on the open door when the younger Sullivan began to speak.

"You're going to be okay, Carrie. You have to be. Please . . . for me . . . for us. There's something I have to tell you. I should have told you so long ago . . . All these years . . ."

She knew now why Will Sullivan had a soft spot in his heart for Carrie. She understood why he'd even reach out to her drug-addicted older half sister. He had known Carrie since she was three feet tall, but he also knew that his son was in love with her. She turned away to avoid interrupting the moment, but Bill must have heard her in the doorway.

"Hello?" He wiped one eye with the back of his hand.

"Sorry. NYPD. I'll wait in the lobby while you visit your friend."

"No, please. Come in." He rose from the bed and introduced himself simply as Bill.

"Ellie Hatcher. I've been working on a case with your father—involving Carrie, actually."

"Anthony Amaro," he said. "She was up in Utica, and wanted to get together. I can't believe I let some stupid schedule get in the way. At least I was in the city when Rosemary called—that's her mother. Kind of like my mother, too, in a way."

"I got the impression from your father that your families were close. When he found out what happened, I could tell he wanted to come down. Instead, I think he's working the case even harder up there."

"That's my dad."

"Carrie's mother told the doctor that Carrie was no longer representing Amaro. Do you know anything about that?"

He looked confused by the news. "You think Amaro did this?"

The pretty-boy lieutenant governor was not only a second-generation cop. He was a cop who thought just like her.

She found Rogan in the lobby, just saying goodbye on his phone.

"You got hold of her mother?"

"Yep, and the doctor didn't hear wrong. Carrie went to her mom's yesterday morning saying she had a blowout with Linda Moreland the previous night. She told her mom that Moreland was using her as a pawn. That she had used Carrie's emotions about her sister. It sounds like Carrie saw the light and walked away."

"And then today someone tries to kill her."

"And whoever did it tossed the place, and only two days after someone broke into her hotel room."

"Think it was Amaro? If he knew Carrie was related to one of the victims, paranoia could have gotten the better of him. He goes to Carrie's hotel room, throws the documents around, steals her journal to find out where her loyalties truly lie. Then, when he finds out she's no longer on the team, he comes to the city to make sure she's not a problem."

"Not on the team," Rogan said.

"Right. Meaning, she quit."

"No, that's it. It was in front of us the whole time."

"What's *it*?"

"You're the one who's been saying how weird it was that Carrie Blank would defend her sister's killer."

She saw it now. "The tips we've been getting—"

"Not the first one," he clarified. "Not the one about Helen Brunswick." He was talking about the communications the DA's office had been getting since reopening the Amaro investigation.

"You think it was Carrie Blank feeding us information?"

"Think about it: those messages gave us two names—the former cellmate Robert Harris and the former foster sister Debi Landry, and the original police reports contained neither. But Amaro certainly knew who they were, which means he could have given those names to his lawyers. *Who do we need to worry about? Who out there in the world can hurt your case?* That kind of thing. And if he had names to give Carrie Blank . . ."

She finished the train of thought. "Then Anthony Amaro is guilty, and Carrie Blank knew it and tried to tell us. Amaro slipped into the Governor to get at the evidence. He sees Carrie's journal. If she was leaking information to us, that's the kind of thing she'd write in a diary. Then when she quits, Amaro follows her to New York to shut her up and make sure she's not hanging on to anything incriminating."

"And what about Joseph Flaherty? We've got the bodega video."

They were thinking out loud, and their thoughts were flowing together, and gelling, a smooth mix of idea upon idea. This was the first time since they had heard the name Anthony Amaro that they were finally in sync. By the time Ellie spoke, she was speaking for both of them. "Flaherty killed Helen Brunswick, Amaro killed the rest. Two different killers, just like you thought from the beginning."

46

It hadn't been hard to find Buck Majors. When she and Rogan had talked to him at the golf course, he'd proudly recited the normal routine of his postretirement lifestyle. On his list was his and his wife's standing date with two other couples at a neighborhood restaurant for Wednesday-night trivia. Ellie had searched Yelp, a restaurant review website, for trivia nights in Majors' zip code. *Voilà.*

The parking lot of Christo's was nearly full. She pulled her fleet car next to an SUV with a bumper sticker boasting: "My Kid Beat Up Your Honor Student." Call it stereotyping, but she suspected the driver would not be winning any knowledge-based contests this evening.

The restaurant itself was exactly what Ellie would have imagined of a place calling itself Christo's and bringing in diners for trivia night: red-and-white-checked vinyl tablecloths, servers in oxford cloth shirts, and the glorious smell of garlic and baked cheese.

She recognized Buck Majors at one end of a rectangular table for six. Two of the couples were Buck's age—sixties—and the other was younger. They sat boy-girl-boy-girl, and were huddled together, discussing the question just announced by the bartender over the microphone: "What New Jersey punk band sang the song 'Astro Zombies'?"

A few groans came from the crowd. "New questions, Marco!"

As Ellie approached Majors' table, she overheard their deliberations. "The Sex Pistols were punk." "But weren't they British?" "What about the Ramones?"

She crouched down at Buck's end of the table. "It's the Misfits."

A guy in the next group cried out, "Hey, who's she? They're cheating!"

"You sure about that?" Majors asked.

She remembered how proud Jess had been in high school when the student Bible group had prayed for him and his first band, Sick Kittens, after they covered the song at a house party. Their mother's demand to know "Why is it so necessary to sing about astro zombies exterminating an entire race of people?" became a classic Hatcher family quote. "Final answer," she assured Majors. "No phone-a-friend needed."

"She's on our team," he announced. "Rules say we can have up to eight. Write that one down, Mindy. This is my wife, by the way—Mindy Majors. Go ahead and laugh. She knows it sounds like a stripper, and if you ask me, I think that's the only reason she took my name. Wife, this is one of the young whippersnappers I told you about the other day. Hatcher, right?"

The woman waved. "Hi Whippersnapper. How do you spell Miss Fitz?" She said it like two words.

"One word. The Misfits."

"Oh, well that means something else entirely. Got it. Bet that's a point no one else will get."

The next question came—this one about a recent change in the playing pieces for Monopoly. Her fellow teammates, as well as everyone else in the room, seemed to have a lock on the answer: something about the iron being out and a cat being in. Who knew?

"This might surprise you," Majors said, "but I'm glad you're here."

"You must really want to win at trivia."

"I've been wanting to call since that scumbag Anthony Amaro got released. I assume that's why you came?"

"I know this can't be easy for you." As a follow-up to the story about Amaro's release, the *New York Times* had a two-page article about the acclaimed Buck Majors and the problems Linda Moreland had identified over the course of his long career eliciting confessions when no other detectives could. According to Max, the DA was days away from announcing an internal review of every conviction tied to one of Majors' interrogations, more than fifty in total. "My dad was a cop. I'm not—what did you call it the other day? *Precious?* I just need to know if we're on the right track. I need to know what really happened when you questioned Amaro."

"She seems like a nice girl," Mindy said. "Just tell her

what you told me, Buck. She'll understand. And if not, fuck 'em. Sorry, dear."

"No offense taken," Ellie said.

"This is the honest-to-God truth." Majors jabbed an index finger on the table. "Amaro confessed. He was the guy. But times were different back then. We didn't parse apart the words, or videotape the sessions. It was either they confessed or they didn't. Yes or no. Simple as that. And over time, I learned that DAs and juries, they loved it when you had the exact words and the colorful phrases. It was better that way than to say, 'Yeah, he gave it up.' But I'm not a savant, you know? I don't remember all the details. I was a guy on the job who was good at getting people to give it up. And then I'd go to the reports and write down the way I heard it in my head. So, in retrospect, the exact words might have been more mine than theirs. But it doesn't change the fundamental facts."

"Amaro gave it up?"

"Damn straight. He killed that girl, Deborah Garner, and I assume that means he killed the rest of them, too. And if the papers want to vilify me, and the department wants to throw me under the bus, let them have at it. But the people I put in the can belong where they are. In fact, all day and a night's not enough. Anthony Amaro deserved to die."

What are you humming?" Max had beat her home and was cooking something that smelled delicious.

She finished hanging her jacket in the front hallway closet. Back in her old apartment, a chair in the corner of the living room had served as her coat closet. "Oh, I didn't even realize I was humming. It's something these two little girls were singing in the elevator." She did her best to mimic their singsong chant. "*We like potatoes, we like potatoes, we like potatoes . . . and Thai food.* I told them it was an ear worm. They thought the whole idea of an ear worm was pretty disgusting."

"Look at you, making friends with the kids in the elevator. They're not so horrible, are they?"

She stepped behind him and gave him a kiss on the back of the neck as he continued to chop some kind of fresh herb. "Ah, but my motive for the friendly banter was to get them to stop once the cuteness wore off. Adult curmudgeon: one. Adorable little children: zero."

The rhythm of his chopping temporarily slowed, then resumed.

"Jeez, Max. Why don't you just start taking a nightly poll. Am I ready to become a mommy yet? Because the answer's still no."

"I didn't say a word."

"No, but you were thinking it. I can't make a single joke involving marriage or a child or pregnancy or motherhood without it becoming a *thing*."

"Except it's not a thing until *you* make it a thing. It's like you're trying to convince yourself I'm the one who's unhappy, when I'm perfectly content just the way we are.

How about you stop and take a quick look around this kitchen? Prime dry-aged steak, all the way from Ottomanelli & Sons. Arugula salad. Chef Max doing all the work."

"Sorry. Thank you. It all looks delicious."

"Did you manage to track down Majors?"

"I did. And I've got to say, I believe him. Amaro admitted killing Deborah Garner."

"Any particular reason you're persuaded?"

She poured a glass of wine from the bottle he had already opened. "Your office is reexamining all of Majors' old cases. It might be better if you didn't know too much."

The chopping slowed again. "Well, I've got news I can actually share. We got another tip on Amaro."

"Today?" Carrie Blank was still unconscious in the hospital. Ellie was so sure it was the lawyer who sent them to Robert Harris.

"In the mail," he said. "Postmarked two days ago from Manhattan."

"Rogan and I think Carrie Blank might be the source. The cellmate, the foster sister—those are names Amaro himself could've given his lawyers. We think Carrie wants us to talk to these people for a reason. Is the new tip also something Carrie would have known?"

"Possibly. It's a report from child services when Amaro was only thirteen years old, and it does relate to the foster sister. Amaro and Debi Landry were removed from their foster mother for abuse. They begged not to be separated, but the state couldn't find a home willing to take both of them."

"Why would Carrie want us to know that?"

Max walked to the dining room table and came back with a manila envelope. She read the enclosed report in its entirety. If she'd had any doubts before, they were gone now.

Anthony Amaro. Joseph Flaherty. Two killers, seven victims.

47

You better get a spring in your step, or I'm telling Sydney on you." Ellie was on the fourth-floor landing of a Chinatown walk-up, waiting for Rogan to climb the final flight. Sydney Reese had been Rogan's live-in girlfriend as long as Ellie had known him. "I see another cleanse in your future."

"Don't you dare. I love that woman, but she wants a grown-ass man to eat like Gwyneth Paltrow. Sending me to work with kale smoothies the second my slim-fit shirts are snug. Tell me, how many men my age can pull off slim-fits? Tell me, Hatcher."

He took a deep breath when he reached the top step.

"All done?" she asked.

"Proceed."

Ellie knocked at the apartment belonging to Anthony Amaro's former foster sister, Debi Landry. The door cracked open, and Ellie nearly choked on the odor of ashtray. "Told you people to go away."

You people must have referred to Max, who had tried to return "her" phone call after their anonymous helper had used Debi's name and number to leave a message with the district attorney's switchboard.

Ellie stuck her foot out just in time for the door to slam against her favorite black wedge pumps. "It's us or a grand jury, Debi."

The door reopened, but the woman wasn't budging from the entryway. Ellie recognized her from her most recent booking photo for trespassing after she refused to leave a bar at closing time. Previous entries on her rap sheet included numerous busts for assault, disorderly conduct, and public intoxication. "I'm not saying anything on Tony." Her voice had the rasp of a million cigarettes.

"You don't have a choice. If you're hauled before a grand jury and refuse to testify, the DA will have you held in contempt. And if you lie, he'll charge you with perjury."

"How you gonna prove anyone's a liar? People lie in court all the time."

(Note to future perjurers: Don't declare to a police detective your intention to lie in advance.)

"Because we have this," Rogan said, handing her a copy of the report from Child Protective Services that Max had received in yesterday's mail. Debi held the document with both hands as she studied it. Like so many others Ellie had met on the job, she wasn't able to read without moving her lips.

When she looked up, her expression appeared confused. "Janet was the one who called?"

Janet Haynes was the foster parent in the home where Debi and Amaro had met. They were numbers four and five of six children in the house at the time.

Ellie nodded. "She basically reported herself. She wasn't prosecuted criminally, but she never had another foster placement again."

"Janet wasn't that bad. Like I told that DA who called, Tony always protected me."

"But Tony was always getting in trouble," Ellie said. "And he wouldn't listen to Janet. Then she called CPS, asking to give Tony back to the state."

"She overreacted. She was just mad because she loved that stupid doll collection so much. She caught me playing with three of the dolls one time, and held my elbow against a hot burner while she counted to three, one for each doll. Told me if I did it again, next time would be my face."

Rogan made a *tsk* sound. "I thought you said she wasn't that bad."

She shrugged. "I never touched the dolls again."

According to the report, Janet wanted Amaro removed from her care because he was, in her words, "a sicko." When a social worker asked the nature of the problem, Janet said the only way she could get control over Amaro when he was misbehaving was to grab his favorite child in the house, fourteen-year-old Debi, and threaten to break her limbs if he didn't behave. "Now that little sicko's obsessed with the idea," the foster mother complained. "It's not right."

"You read the whole report?" Ellie asked Debi.

She nodded.

"Janet told CPS that she noticed her dolls disappearing, one by one. She finally found them hidden under Tony's bed. He had broken all their arms and legs. Some of them were posed in what she called perverted positions, and she found drawings depicting similar images of women. When she confronted him about the dolls, he told her it was just a matter of time before he did the same to her."

"It was just talk."

"You never noticed any kind of fascination he may have had with hurting women in that specific way?" Ellie asked. "Maybe perhaps a sexual fascination?"

"Yuck, I don't think of him that way. He's like my brother."

Ellie looked at Rogan. Just as Debi hadn't denied to Max on the phone that Amaro was probably guilty, she wasn't denying her former foster mother's allegations about the young Amaro.

"You didn't think this doll episode was relevant back when Tony was first suspected of killing those women?" Rogan asked.

"I'm not saying anything against Tony. You know he's the only kid from all those years in all those homes that I'm still in touch with? And he'd say the same for me. What's that tell you?"

"I think it tells us you're not saying anything against Tony," Ellie said.

Debi nodded once, her point made.

Ellie tried a different angle. "When Tony was arrested after Deborah Garner was killed, he told the detective he had come to the city to visit someone he knew from foster care. That was you?"

"Damn straight. That's how close we are. No one I know from Utica would come here like that. Only Tony. He loves me."

"What kind of love?" Ellie asked.

"I think you have a sick kind of mind. You come here with one little report from CPS. Do you know the big picture? Do you know why Tony was in foster care in the first place?"

They said nothing.

"Tony broke the shower rod in the bathroom. His mother heard the sound, found him in there, and gave him such a beating that she broke his arm." Another broken limb in Amaro's background. "She didn't seem to care that the shower rod broke because Tony tried to hang himself from it as a twelve-year-old. So when I say Janet wasn't so bad, it's because that's the kind of parents me and Tony had. My whole life, everyone I ever met used me. Never Tony, though. We found family with each other at Janet's, and then we all got broken up to different homes. His love for me is pure, and you're trying to make it into something sick."

"And what about Deborah Garner? Wasn't Tony

using her? There was nothing pure about picking up a prostitute."

"You don't know what you're talking about. Tony told me he only gave that girl a ride because she was stranded at that rest stop and needed to get to the city. He has no idea who went and killed her. That's it. Do what you want with your grand jury. I'll be there with bells on if you make me, but I'm done for now."

They reported back to Max from the car, using Ellie's cell as a speaker phone.

"Paydirt," Rogan said. "She didn't contest a word of the CPS report. Plus, she added the fact that Amaro's mother broke his arm as a child. And get this: she placed Deborah Garner inside Amaro's car. She was trying to defend him, saying he was only giving her a ride. No way Amaro can try to pin that on Buck Majors."

While Ellie had given Max an edited version of her powwow with Buck Majors the previous night, Rogan had gotten every detail.

"That's good," Max said. "Very good. It doesn't change the plan for now, though. Utica's already got a BOLO out on Amaro. And they still need to pick up Joseph Flaherty. I'm keeping the affidavits for Flaherty's arrest warrant simple, focusing solely on the murder of Helen Brunswick." They had Brunswick's complaint about Flaherty as a teenager; his presence near her apartment, armed with a gun, just hours before she was shot to death; and a lifetime of his interactions with law enforcement to demonstrate his tendency to fixate on perceived grievances. It was enough to do the job.

Nothing to do now but wait.

48

The badge-and-gun crowd was pulling out of Plug Uglies at shift change, soon to be replaced by young bridge-and-tunnel types fresh from their first city jobs, grabbing a beer before heading back to Long Island. Jess had prepped the empty barstool next to him with a Johnnie Walker Black in front of it. It had been a while since they'd met for drinks, just the two of them. This used to be her bar of choice, located conveniently between the precinct and her apartment. Now that the apartment was his, it worked well for both of them.

He kicked back the stool with one foot. "Welcome home. Did you give Utica the finger for me when you left?"

"It wasn't that bad, Jess. People seemed nice."

"Didn't you say something about two different limb-breaking murderers being on the loose there? Seems like an awfully high madman-to-normal ratio for my tastes."

She looked at her watch. Sixty-seven minutes since the judge signed the warrant for Joseph Flaherty's arrest. "With any luck, we'll soon be down to one madman on the loose."

She took a tiny sip of her drink.

"Who the hell are you, and what have you done with my lush of a sister?"

"Sorry. I want to be clearheaded if we catch a break."

"Forty minutes late, plus you're not drinking? Might have to trade you in. Besides, you're more clearheaded on a liter of whisky than most of the stone-cold-sober detectives we knew growing up."

"Not the bar I'm aiming for, Jess. How's Mona the mama bear?"

"Slightly less freaked. Told her I'd personally lie down on the West Side Highway if you did anything to put her in jeopardy."

"It won't be necessary. I hope I didn't do anything to mess up your rep at the Rump Roast."

"Please, little sister. You got skills, but nothing close to that power."

She looked at her watch again. Sixty-nine minutes since the warrant was signed.

"I'm the one who should be looking at my watch. Shift starts in forty. That's why you were supposed to be here one whole drink ago."

"I'm sorry. I should've called. And I'm still getting used to you being a responsible person with a job and a schedule and everything." She leaned over and bumped him with her shoulder.

"To be truthful, your being late makes it a little easier to ask if you had a chance to call Mom today."

"Dammit. I keep forgetting." Freud would probably see a self-serving reason for this particular memory lapse. Ellie's mother had a way of treating every missed call as (a) a reason to fear her daughter was dead, (b) proof that her daughter didn't love her, or, (c) most curiously, both of the above.

"I think she knows," he said. "She calls the apartment. I let it ring, like you told me. But she's Mom, so a message isn't enough. She's got to hit redial and redial and redial. Last week, I unplugged the phone, and she called 911 to have someone check the apartment because the machine wasn't picking up, which had to mean that someone her detective daughter arrested broke into the apartment and was in the process of torturing her. So instead, last night, I answered."

"You didn't tell her I moved, did you?"

"No, but despite all appearances, she's not that stupid. You can't spend nineteen years with Dad and not be a tad wily."

"Message received. I'll call her."

He downed the rest of his beer and gave her a kiss on the cheek. "Off to protect the shaking boobies from the animals. God's work, you know."

Ellie had every intention of talking to her mother, but another mother's phone call interrupted her plans. It was Rosemary Blank. "You need to come to the hospital. Right now."

*

Ellie spotted a petite, older Asian woman pacing in front of the nurses' station on Carrie's floor. She wore her hair in a straight, salt-and-pepper bob clipped directly at her chin, and the kind of dress that moms of a certain type all seemed to own—made of black jersey that could be squished into a ball in the corner of a suitcase and spring back to life the following day. Ellie had purchased a similar item for her own mother two Christmases ago, only to receive it in the mail the following February with a note saying it was too "urban" for Wichita.

"Are you Mrs. Blank, by any chance?" Ellie asked.

"What are you doing to catch the person who did this?" the woman demanded.

Apparently Ellie had found Carrie's mother. "Is your daughter awake?" All Rosemary would say on the phone was that she wanted Ellie to come to the hospital as soon as possible.

"No, and I have no guarantee she ever will be."

"Mrs. Blank, you gave me the impression there was an emergency here."

"Of course there is. My daughter is in a coma. Or a 'coma-like state,' as it was explained to me, which sounds exactly like a coma. And this vicious assault happened to occur after she worked on one—exactly one—murder case, for one week in her entire legal career. Clearly there is a connection, and yet no one has been arrested, and I arrive at the hospital to find absolutely no one looking after Carrie."

She was tempted to lecture the woman about misleading a police officer, but she realized she would want someone to be as dedicated to her.

"This is a well-staffed hospital, Mrs. Blank, with its own security. They know to monitor her visitors—no one without your permission, in fact—and to call us if there is any concern whatsoever." Ellie could see an argument forming behind Mrs. Blank's eyes. "We've got an entire team of officers looking for Anthony Amaro. And the doctors here are caring for your daughter. But I understand it won't be enough until Carrie's healthy and we punish the person who did this to her."

The fight fell from her face.

"Were you close to her sister, Donna, at all?" Ellie asked. How difficult for one family to lose two daughters to violence.

"Half sister," she quickly corrected. "No, I would not call the two of us close, but she was my husband's daughter, and Carrie's only sibling. Blood is blood, but that girl was . . . troubled."

"Did Carrie say anything about a confrontation with Amaro? How did he handle the news that she was quitting as his defense lawyer?"

"She told me she found his presence unsettling, but, no, she didn't mention any kind of confrontation. I got the impression she resigned by calling Linda Moreland, not Amaro himself. If anything was weighing on her, it was the past. Coming home can be hard on her. She has a lot of guilt about being the only one of her friends to have gotten out of Red View."

"The lieutenant governor was at her bedside when I was here earlier. Seems like a success story to me."

"Exactly, which is what I tell Carrie all the time. It goes back to this scholarship they all wanted. In hindsight, it was a cruel kind of gift—selecting one child to win a pot of gold, while the rest were left scrambling for coins." Ellie remembered reading about the award when she first looked up Carrie on the Internet. "Carrie never expected to get it, but two of her friends—including Bill Sullivan—pulled out of the running. Carrie got it, and then lost it. She always says she won't consider herself a success until a news search for her name turns up more information about her legal career than stories about that scholarship and what she saw as her failure to keep it."

Ellie remembered the sight of Bill, holding Carrie's hand, ready to say something he'd been wanting to tell her for years. Had he loved her so much, even in high school, that he held back so she could have the scholarship instead? It was a sweet story—one that Ellie hoped would have a happy ending—but had nothing to do with Anthony Amaro.

"Do you know if your daughter believed Amaro was guilty? Is that why she quit?"

"She didn't seem to know what to believe. She took the job initially because Linda Moreland said Amaro was innocent. But then she started having doubts, and it became clear to her that Linda was using her. No one uses my daughter."

Rosemary Blank was clearly a force to be reckoned with.

"Do you think it's possible she might have been willing to violate attorney-client privilege to make sure the truth got out?"

"You mean revealing things she found out while she was his lawyer? Do you think that's why someone hurt her? Was it Amaro?"

"It's just a theory at this point. We did receive some information about Amaro from an anonymous source, but until your daughter's conscious, we don't know if it was her."

"That's—oh, I really don't think so. My daughter worked so hard to become a lawyer. She takes her ethics *very* seriously. If you knew her, you'd understand that she takes *everything* very seriously. I think it was difficult enough for her to quit when she felt a conflict between legal ethics and her personal ones. Leaking information? That would eat away at someone as principled as Carrie. No, I can't picture that."

As Ellie left the hospital, she thought about the way her own mother described her children. In Roberta Hatcher's eyes, Jess was a successful rock star, the front-man for Dog Park, just one catchy single away from landing the cover of *Rolling Stone*. And Ellie was a doting daughter and sister, the perfect combination of beauty and smarts, following in her father's footsteps — for now, until she met the right man and settled down to have a family. So what if Rosemary Blank didn't believe her daughter would violate the rules of professional ethics?

She could picture Carrie Blank submitting a message on the DA's website. Placing a phone call to the switchboard, using the name Debi Landry. Slipping a photocopy of yellowed documents from Amaro's file with Child Protective Services into the mail.

And those weren't the only images Ellie was seeing. She pictured Anthony Amaro, stalking the streets of Utica, in search of women whose bodies he could use to fulfill decade-old fantasies planted by an abusive mother and foster mother. She pictured him driving to New York City to visit Debi Landry, perhaps his subconscious's true object of desire, and then selecting Deborah Garner at a New Jersey rest stop to unleash his frustrations. She pictured an obsessive Joseph Flaherty, tracking down the therapist he blamed for his lifetime of insanity and shooting her in the chest.

She was finally seeing the truth that Carrie Blank had wanted them to see.

But the series of scenes dissolved when she got to the image of Joseph Flaherty, breaking Helen Brunswick's bones. Mailing letters to Anthony Amaro and the district attorney so they would connect the psychotherapist's murder to the old cases.

Why? Was he fascinated by Amaro's crimes? Did he

idolize him? Maybe once he was in custody he would tell them. Or maybe he would have reasons only his delusional mind could understand.

She looked at her watch. Going on two and a half hours since the warrant to pick up Flaherty had been signed.

As if the world was aligning with her thoughts, she felt a buzz at her waist. It was a text from Max. *UPD heading to Flaherty's now.*

Just a little longer.

49

Joseph Flaherty spread the newspaper articles around him on the bed.

He liked his bed. It was the same one he'd had since his mother took him to that parking lot off of Oriskany Boulevard, filled with furniture offered at what the signs promised were below-wholesale prices. Helium balloons floated over the entrance, cotton candy and snowcone machines drew customers to the rear. He was thirteen years old and his mother said it was time for him to have a grown-up bed. "Try as many of the mattresses as you need to," she said. "Dr. Harper says it will help if you can get more sleep."

Back then, they thought a change in the mattress might just fix him. Twenty-seven years later, the bed was still holding up fine. So was he, if people would only realize.

Joseph could barely remember a time in his life when he wasn't trying to prove that everyone didn't need to worry about him so much. He had seen pictures of himself with his mother and father and older brother when he was little. They all held him and smiled at him like they would at a normal baby, like they loved him. Even in grade school, when teachers and principals and other kids started to say he was "quiet," or "different," or "off," they were all still together at home. He just didn't like to be hugged or touched or looked at, that's all. He didn't see why that had to be such a problem.

It wasn't until middle school that he went to the first doctor. Then Dad and David moved to California to start over, without him and Mom.

Joseph began to understand he was different, because everyone kept telling him that. But he never hurt anyone— not until a couple of months ago, at least. It seemed the more he tried to tell people that he was the good one— and that other people were the bad ones—the more he got into trouble. The longer he stayed at the hospital. The less he got to be home, in this room, on the comfortable bed he had chosen for himself the last time he could remember anyone else believing his troubles were about to be fixed.

That's why it was so important to him at Cedar Ridge when he had decided to trust Dr. Brunswick with the information he had. The hero had given him some of the truth, but Joseph found out from the newspaper there was more to his story. It wasn't just one. It was five. Going to Dr. Brunswick was Joseph's single chance to show everyone that he was the hero, while the people who held themselves up as heroes were devils. He knew the truth, and had been handed an opportunity to prove his righteousness.

He tried to explain it all to Dr. Brunswick. He concentrated as hard as he could and tried to get the words out, in his own way. But Dr. Brunswick hadn't believed him. Not only that, she called the police on him. And then he tried to tell people that the police were in on it, too. That they were covering up for the false hero. And that only got him in more trouble.

His whole life got so much worse because of Dr. Brunswick.

And then Joseph had seen the hero in a new light, fooling more people, and Joseph knew he had been given a second chance to tell the world what he knew.

He couldn't just explain, not like he tried before. The pills had gotten better since then, and now he was better with his words. But he knew what the doctors had been writing about him all these years. He knew they'd never believe him. They were convinced he was delusional. Hallucinating. Crazy.

But how could someone delusional come up with such a brilliant plan? A new police investigation, with a new victim like the forgotten ones, would show the truth.

The only problem was picking the new victim. That was really the part that proved Joseph was a good person. He could have picked anyone. But justice meant that the sacrifice be paid by Dr. Brunswick. She was the one who didn't listen when she had the chance. She had blood on her hands.

He was folding up the newspaper articles, one by one,

354

when he thought he heard a knock—maybe even a voice—at the front door. If the sounds at the door were real, his mom would get it.

Many of the articles were worn from handling, nearly falling apart, but he'd been adding new ones since the local paper first reported that Anthony Amaro had asked a court to release him. Maybe one day soon he would be able to meet the man, and Amaro would shake Joseph's hand and thank him for freeing him with the truth.

He had just finished tucking the final clipping into his shoebox, right beneath the gun, when he heard the thud. A shriek from his mom. "Police. Don't move. We're here for Joseph Flaherty."

At last, they had come to him. Joseph was finally going to be able to show them. He had his box of articles all ready to go. He would choose his words carefully. He rose from the bed, prepared to explain it all.

His bedroom door opened. He recognized the detective. His being here was perfect. It was proof that even he understood the truth now. Everyone would know that Joseph was never the one they should have been worried about. He was never a threat.

The last word he heard was "GUN!" before he felt the impact of the first bullet.

Ellie checked the screen of her phone yet again. Nothing.

"You?" she asked Max, who was next to her on the sofa.

Max shook his head. Tonight's itinerary had consisted of picking at Chinese leftovers while they checked their phones for incoming calls. It had been nearly two hours since Will Sullivan told Max he had a team outside Joseph Flaherty's house, ready to take him into custody. She could've been up there if they were going to take this long.

The chirp of Max's phone broke the silence. "Donovan."

He blinked. Then winced. Then closed his eyes as he continued to listen. She could tell it wasn't good news.

"Anyone else hurt?" he asked.

No, she thought. No, no, no, no, no. They should have waited. She and Rogan should have been there.

"Okay. We'll need more information to close the Brunswick case. Rogan and Hatcher will come up in the morning."

He was about to set his phone in a container of *mapo* tofu when she caught his hand. His eyes were somewhere else but found focus in her stare.

"That was Mike Siebecker from the DA's office up there. Joseph pulled a gun when they entered the house. Sullivan fired. A clean shoot. No other injuries."

"Fatal?"

"DOA."

"What about Amaro? Did Joseph say anything about why he used Amaro's MO? Why he wrote the letters tying Brunswick to the other cases?"

"It happened fast. We'll find out more tomorrow."

Ellie didn't need to wait another day to know that their chances of learning the full story had probably died along with Joseph Flaherty.

50

They found Will Sullivan on a walnut-stained swing on the front porch of a two-story bungalow. He had a price-club-sized bucket of red licorice next to him.

"Nice car," he said, eyeing Rogan's BMW.

"Nice house," Rogan replied. He and Ellie leaned on the porch railing across from Sullivan's swing.

"Heck of a lot better than where I called home until a couple of years ago. My son finally convinced me that I'd be okay borrowing some money for a nicer place while interest rates were low. Licorice?" He offered them the bucket, and they declined. "Straight sugar, but the doctor says anything's better than cigarettes. Guess it's an oral fixation."

"One of your guys at the station told us we'd find you here," Rogan said. "Hope you don't mind."

"Nope. Funny, I think this might be the first time since I bought the house that I've actually sat here on this swing with my newspaper, the way I pictured when I decided to take it. Seemed like a real dream, the proverbial picket fence. I can't even describe the guilt I felt when I was loading up the U-Haul from my old place in Red View."

Ellie recognized the name of the neighborhood from their conversation with Rosemary Blank.

"That's where the Blank family lived?" she asked.

"Yep. Look it up in the census. One of the highest-poverty, highest-crime neighborhoods in the state of New York."

"Not a typical choice for a cop."

"I wasn't always a cop. Had a minimum-wage security job at a discount clothing store, the kind with last year's fashions, a layaway plan with worse terms than the neighborhood bookie, and cigarette butts on the dressing room floors. They called it full-time but always kept my hours under thirty so they didn't have to pay benefits. My wife waitressed, and we somehow managed to scrape by, even after Bill came along. Then Maddie died. I don't think Bill and I would've made it if I hadn't gone on the job. The feds had promised to put a hundred thousand new officers on the street. Utica got enough money to hire three new cops, and I was one of them."

"Best and worst decision of your life." It was a favorite line among cops.

"It was probably three years into the job when I could have swung a move out of Red View. Steady salary. A modest down payment. But by then, the people there liked the idea of a neighborhood cop and his son. The older residents—the ones who were afraid to walk the streets because of the gangs and the guns and the drugs—they felt a little safer if they saw my lights on. Even the ones who were up to no good had to admit a kernel of respect for a cop who at least knew the lay of the land."

Rogan and Ellie offered polite acknowledgments that they were listening. After Ellie had killed someone in the line of duty, Rogan had done the same thing for her, allowing her to go off on long tangents to avoid talking about the could-haves and should-haves that would inhabit her brain the minute she stopped talking.

"But now I'm older, getting close to retirement, and the sketchy types are getting younger and rougher. Figured I wouldn't always have the power of the badge, so now I have this place and my porch. I realized after a year or so, I'd actually stopped locking the doors. But, man, I really felt like I was abandoning those people when I left. A few neighbors said goodbye, but I saw a lot of them close their blinds as I was packing up. I wonder how they feel about me shooting a mentally ill boy while his mother could hear from the next room."

He stopped rocking on his swing. He was ready to talk about it.

"Joseph didn't give you a choice," Ellie said. "I've been in a similar situation. You can't beat yourself up over it. He was the one who made the decision. He turned you into his own weapon." The man she killed had held her lieutenant, and then her, at gunpoint. He announced his intention to kill her. If not for a lucky moment when she'd taken her chance, she knew for a certainty she'd be dead.

From what ADA Siebecker had reported to Max, Joseph didn't have a gun in his hands, not technically. He had been reaching for a gun inside a shoebox he was holding. As with any officer-involved shooting, Sullivan was suspended with pay until an official determination was made regarding justification, but Ellie had no doubt that Sullivan would be cleared. Career cop plus armed insane murderer was easy math.

"I wanted to question him," Sullivan said. "I was so sure I had a chance at somehow connecting to him. Now we may never know what really happened."

"Siebecker said they found a treasure trove of news articles about the entire case," Rogan said. "The original murders, Helen Brunswick's killing, Amaro's release. I think that makes it pretty clear what happened."

Ellie could see Sullivan's gaze move to his lap. "Our current theory," she said, "is that he became obsessed as a teenager with Amaro's crimes. He decided to kill Helen Brunswick, whom he may have resented for first calling the police on him all those years ago. He replicated Amaro's MO, giving him a basis to challenge his conviction. It would've been nice to have had confirmation — sorry, that's not what I meant. Our ADA's working on an arrest warrant for Amaro now. We'll see whether a judge goes for it, but at this point we need a warrant in place to make sure Amaro doesn't get too far."

"Someone should be watching out for the cellmate," Will said. "After what happened to Carrie—"

"Your department has a car in front of Harris's house. He knows the stakes."

"Any updates from the doctors?"

"Not yet, but they say there's no reason to believe Carrie won't regain full neurologic function. I met both her mother and your very impressive son at the hospital. You must be extremely proud."

He smiled sadly. "Hard to feel proud of anything right now. We lost our shot at questioning Joseph. And I've got to wonder if Carrie would be okay if I had found Anthony Amaro by now."

"Well, we've got a plan for that," Rogan said.

"It was a plan you first mentioned, actually," Ellie added. "According to her chatty assistant, Thomas, Linda Moreland's arriving on the twelve-thirty train from the city. We'll tail her from there."

51

In New York City, all types of people could be found coming and going on the trains in Penn Station: business commuters, tourists, runaways, group trips, con men. But as Ellie watched the Amtrak train stop in Utica, she lumped the arriving passengers in two: locals coming home, and visitors already looking forward to leaving.

Linda Moreland clearly fell into the latter camp. She wore jeans, but in an obvious I-never-wear-jeans kind of way. Her Louis Vuitton handbag and high-gloss, polycarbonate suitcase with ball-bearing wheels quickly set her apart from the authentic locals. So did the driver standing beside a black limousine with a handheld sign bearing her name.

Ellie pulled behind the limo in her Crown Vic, borrowed from UPD. She remained an average of two blocks back, staying within eyesight but varying her speed and changing lanes periodically. She followed from Main to First Street, then onto Oriskany. So far, so good. It was the route any car would take to the outskirts of the city.

She merged onto the I-90 Thruway. As expected from UPD's unsuccessful canvass of Utica motels, Linda was leaving town.

At the fork near Whitesboro, Linda's driver veered right, abandoning the interstate in favor of local Route 49. This was good. No way was Linda staying out here on her own. She was heading toward Amaro.

Ellie composed a text to Rogan. *Route 49.* Send.

Ten miles outside Utica, the limo took the exit for NY-365. The area was rural. She sent another text: *365.* According to the signs, they were in Rome.

Linda's car took a left at the fork in the road, merging onto NY-825, heading north. *Fork. 825-N.*

They were approaching a building. Ellie felt her hopes elevate. From this distance, the building up ahead looked like it could be a motel. No. The sign read "Rome Free Academy."

Linda's car turned right, away from the school. Atlas Drive, according to the street sign. The limo took a quick left. Falcon Avenue. A right onto Thor Avenue, which looped around and intersected again with Atlas. There was no development in sight. These were cul-de-sacs waiting for homes to be built on them.

Dammit. Linda's driver was verifying the tail.

Ellie sent another text: *School on left. Rome Free Academy. Stay.*

Ellie heard a buzz on her cell phone and looked at the screen, expecting a reply. Instead, the message was from Max: *Judge signed arrest warrant for Amaro. No knock.*

Excellent timing.

The limo came to a sudden stop on Atlas, and Linda

hopped out of the back seat and stomped over toward Ellie's fleet car. Another message from Max popped up on Ellie's screen: *All vics except Donna Blank.*

Max could explain the details later, but Ellie had the information she needed for the moment.

Although Ellie could hear the attorney's voice fifty feet away, she eased down the Crown Vic's window. "You lost?"

"This is absolutely unacceptable, Detective."

"Too cloudy for a road trip?"

"You are interfering with the ability of an attorney to communicate with her client. Should I add a count of harassment to our growing list of lawsuits to file against the NYPD?"

"Your client is wanted, Ms. Moreland. You're welcome to communicate with him, right after I place him in handcuffs."

"An officer-issued be-on-the-lookout is the legal equivalent of the tooth fairy, Detective."

"It's not just a BOLO anymore. Your client's got an active warrant for the murders of Nicole Henning, Jennifer Bronson, Leticia Thomas, and Stacy Myer." They deserved to have their names remembered. She didn't see any need to tell Moreland that the warrant had been approved as a no-knock warrant, allowing them to force entry into Amaro's residence without first knocking and announcing their presence.

"I didn't hear you say 'Donna Blank.'"

"Your client has a warrant out for the murder of four women and you think he deserves a pat on the back for it not being five?"

"I think it's obvious that the court knows you have a problem. Those cases were closed in the first place because whoever killed one, killed them all. Now my client has been exonerated on the Deborah Garner case, and—"

"Undermining a conviction is not the same thing as exoneration." She stopped herself before getting sucked any further into the vortex. She understood now why the cable talk shows loved having this woman as a guest.

"So, guilty until proven innocent? Thank you for the quote, Detective. I'll add that to our civil complaint. Good luck proving guilt beyond a reasonable doubt of any one of those murders. You may want to conveniently ignore Donna Blank, but juries love DNA. Plus, I hear your Utica colleagues assassinated a man this morning who looks a lot better for these crimes than my guy."

The morning news had reported the Utica Police Department's fatal shooting of a suspect in the murder of Helen Brunswick. It was impossible to know how much additional information Linda Moreland might have. *Do not engage*, Ellie reminded herself.

"Sounds like you've got your jury argument all ready to go. Think of me as helping you get your shot in the courtroom. Where's Amaro?"

366

"Goodbye, Detective. If you continue to follow, I'll head straight back to the train station."

"You have been notified that your client is being sought by police for multiple counts of murder, Ms. Moreland. If you harbor him, warn him, or give him any assistance, you're hindering prosecution."

"You're a lawyer now, Ms. Hatcher? Or perhaps you think sleeping with a prosecutor makes you one by sexual osmosis."

Ellie tucked her head back inside and put the car in gear. "You win for now, Counselor. Enjoy your drive. We'll have to catch up to your client another way."

As Ellie rolled up her window, Linda gave her a look of smug satisfaction and pivoted toward her own car. Ellie followed the black limousine to the end of Atlas and watched it hang a right, continuing on toward NY-365. Ellie took a left, heading back to Utica, giving Linda a quick *beep-beep* as a send-off.

She pulled up Rogan's number on her phone and hit dial. "You were right. She wouldn't give him up. And I officially hate Linda Moreland."

"The club will send your membership card shortly."

She saw his BMW pull out from the Rome Free Academy and take a left on 365, in the opposite direction.

She pulled a U and headed back to the school, prepared to resume Rogan's former position in the academy's parking lot. "Text me when you've got a location," she said.

"Will do."

She placed another call, this one to the Utica PD, instructing backup to start heading in her direction. It shouldn't be long.

Ellie had done her job, allowing Linda Moreland to have the last, snarky word. Riding away in the comfort of her limousine, free of that pain-in-the-butt cop from New York, the lawyer would never give a thought to the BMW behind her.

52

Carrie found herself in a dark, empty theater. The air was cold. She heard the hum of an air conditioner. The screen flickered with crackling images of white. The movie was about to start.

The film opened with a narrow shot through a doorway. It was dark inside, but even darker outside. It was the music that helped Carrie recognize the scene. AC/DC's "You Shook Me All Night Long." To this day, Carrie had to leave a room if that song came on.

Carrie felt fear infiltrating her blood as she craned her neck to see the girls on the stage. She forced herself to look away from their bare breasts. Her cheeks felt warm each time they spread their legs, flaunting the tiny triangle of fabric.

She scanned their faces, relieved not to recognize them. There was one last girl, on the right edge of the stage. Her face was obscured as she bent over, allowing the pole to rub slightly between her buttocks. Long brown hair. Thin.

At the time, Carrie had prayed for it not to be her. Maybe she had misheard her father, yelling at his ex-wife on the phone, saying one of the other drivers was gloating about Donna working a pole at Club Rouge. *Was it true?* he had demanded to know.

Even though Carrie expected what was coming, she sucked in her breath when the woman on the screen flipped her hair and turned toward the camera. It was Donna. She gripped the pole and arched her back, accepting a man's dollar bill between her teeth.

And then, just as she knew he would, another man appeared, his bulky body filling the doorway, blocking the view of the club inside. "Hey, you got ID? The boss is always looking for Chinese girls, but you're gonna need ID if you wanna work, sweet thing."

The film cut suddenly to Donna's living room, where Carrie found her sister sleeping the next day when she got out of school. Carrie, asking what was it like to have those men staring at you, exposed that way. Please don't let her like it, she had hoped. That's how I'll know she's really broken. But Donna wasn't broken. On the screen, she covered herself with a sofa cushion, as if she were embarrassed to have any part of herself in view as she spoke about the act of trading visual access to her body for money. "I hate them," she said. "The way they paw at me, dangling those singles like I should have to beg for them."

"Is that all it is?" Carrie asked. "Letting them look?"

Behind the pillow, Donna shrugged. "So far. But, honestly, what's the difference?"

"Why can't you just stop using heroin?" On the screen, she saw the surprise on her own face as Donna started to cry. Back then, Carrie had no idea how much power might reside in that simple question.

The screen cut to two still images, flashing in rapid succession. Carrie at the bank counter, withdrawing money from her college fund to pay for Donna's rehab. The receptionist at Cedar Ridge Behavioral and Psychiatric Care, telling her that Donna wasn't a patient there.

Then the film jumped to a full shot of a house. Somehow Carrie knew it was her family home, even though the house on the screen was larger, as if someone had built additions on both the left and right sides of what Carrie had always thought of as a tall, narrow house. It was freshly painted, too, and tastefully landscaped.

Again, the soundtrack brought back memories. *Don't go chasing waterfalls*. It was that last day Donna came to the house. Carrie had watched from upstairs, but now she viewed the scene from Donna's perspective as she begged her stepmother to let her see Carrie. "You can't do this. I have a plan. I promise."

The film sped up on fast-forward, the audio sounding like quarreling chipmunks, then slowed down again. "We have a friend on the police force," Carrie's mother was saying.

"Right," Donna was yelling, "because you and your friends—the people *you* approve of—are so much better than the rest of the world."

The film cut to Carrie's conversation with Will Sullivan outside the Utica Police Department. It was just a few days ago but felt like it was from another lifetime. "But do you *know*?" Carrie was asking. Had Donna really crossed the line into prostitution? "On Sandy, a couple of times," he had told her.

And then Carrie was in Tim McDonough's face outside the probation department, doing everything in her power to prompt a smack. She watched a replay of his rambling on about the past, the way Melanie had trusted Donna with news of her pregnancy when she saw her at the clinic, only to be told she couldn't possibly finish college with a baby.

In her dream, she yelled to the anonymous film operator at the back of the theater to rewind. *Go back!* she yelled. *Go back!* Something was wrong. She was missing something. But the film was over. The theater went black. She heard a voice next to her. Something about "neurologic function" and "purposeful eye movements." "Unresponsive."

The words made her remember falling forward into her apartment. The feeling of warm blood beneath her head.

She pushed the thoughts away. She wasn't ready to wake up. She wanted to crawl back into the movie theater, back into her dream. Somewhere in that dream were the answers to Donna's death.

Donna was killed for a reason.

It was all Carrie's fault.

53

I think I got you," Ellie said into her cell phone. "Gas station across the street?"

"That's me," Rogan said. He'd been keeping an eye on King's Motel since Linda Moreland's car had pulled into the lot. The motel was a two-story job, each room with its own exterior door. The sign boasted that the rooms had "Cable TV/Microwaves/weekly rates. Only best for r guest." Thanks to Linda's housecall, they knew Amaro was in room 219, first door on the second floor. The last Ellie had heard from Rogan, the curtains on the room were drawn. If they were lucky, Amaro wouldn't know they were coming.

"You see us?" Ellie asked.

"How could I miss you?"

Ellie had led the way from the south, followed by four marked Utica PD cruisers, the first of which was keeping a hundred yards' distance behind her Crown Vic. A SORT van—filled with a Special Operations Response Team on loan from the New York State Police—was in view up ahead, having broken away onto Route 60 to approach the motel from the north. Two additional marked cars were barely visible behind the armored vehicle.

The cavalry had arrived.

As planned, the SORT van stopped at the corner, out of the motel's view. Ellie recognized the voice on the radio as the team leader. "How's it look?"

They had discussed a variety of capture strategies, the final decision to be made according to circumstances on the ground. She pulled out a pair of binoculars and inspected the motel. The door to 219 was closed. Curtains still drawn. Linda's driver was at the wheel of the stopped car, engine off, reading a newspaper.

"Stay out of sight. Be ready to block the exit when you hear my word."

She pulled the Crown Vic onto a side street and began walking.

Linda's driver jerked at the sound of Ellie's knuckles against the glass. He tried fumbling with the window control, but the glass didn't budge with the engine off. She held a finger to her lips, flashed a badge, and signaled toward the door handle. When she heard the lock release, she cracked the door.

"Remember me?"

He nodded.

"Good. Your passenger probably didn't tell you your tail was the NYPD. You've got her cell phone number?"

Another nod.

"Excellent. You need to tell her that the manager of this place is giving you a hard time about having a fancy limo in his parking lot. You're scaring all the customers who think you're cops here on a drug bust. Tell her you're leaving unless she comes down and works something out with the front desk. You got all that?"

Another nod.

"And if you say one extra word, I'll have your livery license, and you'll be hooked up for hindering prosecution. Got it?"

"Absolutely. And, Detective, the warning wasn't necessary. I've seen every single episode of *Law and Order*. And I was in the high school drama club. Trust me: I got this."

She had just finished strapping on her Kevlar vest in the passenger seat of Rogan's BMW when Linda Moreland hit the motel staircase. "Don't—LEAVE!" Linda admonished her driver as she passed her hired car.

As soon as Linda entered the motel's lobby, Ellie gave the order into her radio. "Go!"

Rogan rocketed his sedan across the street into the motel parking lot. The SORT bus followed. Ellie and Rogan were out first, headed for the stairs, followed by eight men in helmets and full body armor. Ellie heard the squeal of car brakes as the marked vehicles formed a wall around the parking lot, as planned. No one was leaving through the front.

She and Rogan took either side of the door marked 219. The first SORT officer behind them held a shield marked POLICE. The second held a black steel battering ram. Ellie knew it was called The Stinger. Forty pounds, two and a half feet long, capable of shattering a brick wall. She gave the thumbs-up. The third SORT officer took hold of the rear handle of The Stinger, ready to assist the swing.

The door gave way on the second ram.

"Police!" Ellie yelled as soon as the door sprang open. "Anthony Amaro!"

He was running toward the back of the small motel room. Rogan was right behind him. As Ellie followed, she knocked over a paper bag on the floor between the foot of the bed and a dresser, then dodged two open dresser drawers.

"Closet," she yelled. She could see Amaro reaching for a bifold door in the right back corner of the room. Rogan grabbed one of Amaro's arms and swung him away from his intended target. Ellie jumped behind Amaro to take hold of his other arm. They shoved him face down on the bed, his shoulder jammed into an open Domino's pizza box. Rogan jabbed his right knee into Amaro's lower back as he forced his hands into cuffs. She felt Amaro wince as Rogan tightened the cuffs.

To the sound of Rogan reading Amaro his Miranda rights, Ellie checked the back closet that had been so important. No clothes on the bent wire hangers inside.

She stepped backwards to view the shelf above the clothes rod. She reached up with a pen and pulled out a double-action revolver by its trigger guard.

As Rogan led Amaro from the motel room, the suspect turned in Ellie's direction and smiled. "You, the blonde. You can come to my mansion and swim in my pool when this is all over. Until then, I know my rights. I'm not speaking without my lawyers."

Rogan should have kneed him harder.

Rogan was guiding Amaro's head into the back of one of the marked cars when they heard banging from inside the front window of the motel lobby. A uniformed officer stood next to Linda Moreland, shaking his head. Another uniform posted just outside the lobby's entrance explained. "She hasn't been taking orders so well." These were the two officers who had been tasked with making sure that Linda didn't interfere once she saw law enforcement swarming the motel.

Once Amaro was secured, Ellie gave a "come here" curl of her fingers, indicating it was safe to release the hound.

Linda's voice sounded like an air horn on crack. "Did you follow me? Did you have my driver call—? This is unacceptable. After you assured me—I'll have your badges."

Ellie stepped so close to Moreland that she felt her Kevlar vest brush against the woman's gut. "He had a gun. He was going for it. Did you know about the weapon?"

The attorney's eyes widened to the size of silver dollars. It was the typical response of someone who never expected her loud mouth to trigger a physical response.

"I saw the paper bag. The open dresser drawers. You warned him we were coming, even when you knew we had a warrant. That's hindering. Turn around."

"Hatcher."

She heard Rogan's voice behind her. Moreland's eyes darted to him for help.

"TURN AROUND!" she commanded.

"Ellie, don't do it. We came for Amaro, and we got him."

Moreland began to turn slowly. As if from instinct, she placed her hands behind her. Ellie could almost taste the satisfaction of throwing her in the backseat with Amaro. But then she pictured the scene, a few hours from now, after some judge made a knee-jerk decision that criminal defense attorneys were somehow exempt from the law.

Ellie released her grip from the cuffs she so desperately wanted to lock around Moreland's wrists, then leaned in to whisper in the attorney's ear. "That call from your driver was a gift. If we'd left you in there, you'd be a hostage. Your pal would've killed you."

She hopped into the front passenger seat of the transport vehicle, leaving Linda Moreland standing awkwardly in the parking lot, unsure whether she was allowed to move. As they pulled onto the street, she waved to Linda's driver, who had been watching the action from across the street.

At least someone had done the right thing.

54

With Joseph Flaherty dead and Anthony Amaro in custody, Ellie felt like Rip van Winkle crossed with the Energizer Bunny, both cranked up and exhausted. The two other people in the Utica Police Department's conference room appeared to be at each end of the wakefulness spectrum: Rogan, slumped in the chair next to her, his eyes bloodshot and puffy; Mike Siebecker, the local prosecutor, rocking back and forth on his toes, his gaze bouncing between the two detectives and the face projected on the screen.

The face on the screen belonged to Max. "Glad you two are safe." He looked almost as fatigued as Rogan. Behind him, Ellie recognized the lower-left-hand corner of the photograph she'd taken in front of the Springs General Store. She pictured him adjusting his laptop in their living room, getting the angle just so to capture that small detail.

Damn, she wanted to go home. She also wanted ten minutes alone in a cell with Anthony Amaro. A confession, even to one charge, and then she could go home in happiness.

Focus.

Rogan had been bringing Max up to speed on the scene at the motel. "He invoked the second we had hands on him."

"No surprise," Max said on the webcam. "I'm sure Linda Moreland had him rehearsing the phrase over and over again. *I want my lawyer. I want my lawyer.*"

"You guys are the prosecutors," Rogan said, "but we know the case is tough."

Next to her, still rocking nervously, Siebecker said, "I think the technical term is *disaster*."

Normally, Ellie's internal monologue would conjure up more creative synonyms for their predicament, most of them profane, but instead, she was replaying Max's impersonation of Amaro rehearsing his request for counsel. *I want my lawyer.* But those weren't the words Amaro had used, and she knew the difference was significant.

As she searched for the point she wanted to make, the others talked through the difficulty with the evidence. They were in yet another variant of the same fundamental quagmire they'd been in since the beginning. From one perspective, they had a clear case against Amaro: his ties to Utica's prostitution scene, the foster records showing his predilection for the types of injuries inflicted on the victims, a careless statement to a cellmate, the evidence tying him to Deborah Garner. Then you rotate the clear crystal and look at it under another light, and glimmers of color obscured the view: Buck Majors was a flawed interrogator, Deborah Garner's prostitution partner was a bad witness, someone else's DNA was under Donna Blank's fingernails, and the extent of Joseph Flaherty's crimes was still unknown. Not to mention, they still had Carrie Blank in the hospital, her assailant unidentified.

"Basically, we have eight women victimized," Ellie said, thinking out loud. "The original Utica five, then Deborah Garner downstate, then Helen Brunswick this year, and Carrie Blank attacked in her home. And we're pretty damn sure that Anthony Amaro and Joseph Flaherty, collectively, are responsible for all of it."

Yet as she spoke the words, she pictured Anthony Amaro face down on that sagging motel bed, Rogan's right knee in the small of his back. She remembered the flash in his dark eyes as he said he'd see her in the swimming pool of his mansion. *Until then, I know my rights. I'm not speaking without my lawyers.*

Not his lawyer. His *lawyers*, plural. Did he misspeak, or did he not know that Carrie Blank had quit? Ellie's theory that Amaro was the one who attacked Carrie rested on a motive based on Carrie's resignation from his legal team.

"But you know that's not how it works," Max was saying. "By the time we go to trial—sorry, Oneida County crimes means an Oneida County trial. By the time *Mike* goes to trial, he needs a coherent theory of the case that explains the precise roles that each person played in the entire series of events. The problem is, we have what appears at first glance to be seven murders with the same

MO, therefore one serial killer. But we're now saying that Joseph Flaherty killed Brunswick. Once you pull one card away, the entire house can fall."

"So now what?" Rogan asked. Between the two of them, it seemed like they'd asked that question a hundred times this week.

"Your job was to give a fresh look on the conviction of Anthony Amaro for the murder of Deborah Garner," Max said. He scrubbed his face with his hands. He delivered the rest of the news in a flat tone, his best attempt to show he knew this ending was unsatisfying. "That conviction has been set aside. You were simultaneously asked to investigate the murder of Helen Brunswick. That case has been cleared with evidence against Joseph Flaherty, now deceased."

Rogan actually started laughing as he rose from his seat. They were being pulled from the investigation.

"What happened to the *we*?" Ellie asked. "Two counties, working together. One case."

"Trust me," Siebecker said. "If I could keep you on, I would. But your ADA's right; your parts of the case are closed. We'll keep working it from here. And we'll see what happens. It is what it is."

And with that, Siebecker left the conference room.

It is what it is.

Rogan was on his feet, waiting for her to follow, but she just stared at the computer screen. She could tell from her reflection that she looked angry.

Max ran his fingers through his tousled hair, then returned her gaze with pleading eyes. "Come on home, Ellie."

"You're really going to leave Siebecker on his own to deal with Amaro?"

"I thought you came around on them," he said. "You said Sullivan was a good cop."

"Yeah, and he's on leave until he gets cleared for the Joseph Flaherty shooting."

"You're totally wired right now. Things will look different in a few days."

For all she knew, he was right, but she was still balancing the exhaustion and the adrenaline. She knew that once she disconnected this Internet conference, absolute fatigue would take over. She wanted to make sure she'd said and done everything possible before they walked away.

No words came out of her mouth, but she felt like something was missing.

The display on Rogan's dash read "10:02 PM" as they pulled into the hotel parking lot. "Call it," Rogan said. "Leave tonight or save the drive for morning?"

They hadn't spoken since leaving the police station. The silence wouldn't have been unusual for them. They were both dog tired, and they'd worked together long enough to share downtime in comfort. But Ellie's thoughts had been on Max, picturing him on their sofa, with the nice, pretty photographs hanging behind him. She pictured him disconnecting from the video conference and brushing his teeth. In a few minutes, he would climb into bed and send her a final text message to say goodnight. Then he would sleep.

He was at peace with this decision, no matter how it played out. And that made him fundamentally different from her.

She started to answer Rogan's question and then saw the fatigue in her partner's face.

"You don't look like you're up for a three-hour drive."

"No, I'm really not."

"I know you're not sleeping well at the hotel, though. You want me to drive?"

"Excuse me, but I haven't lost my mind yet. Besides, I think I could sleep through one of your brother's eardrum-piercing performances right now. You okay with rolling in the morning?"

"Sure," she said, trying not to sound too relieved.

55

Ellie recognized the lanky male figure entering the hotel lobby ahead of them. His perfectly erect posture was an odd match to the brown paper bag in his left hand, grease stains starting to appear on its bottom edges. Thomas, the legal assistant. It dawned on Ellie that no one had ever bothered to tell her Thomas's last name.

He did a double take as they followed him into the lobby. Then a triple.

He was what one might describe as wary.

"I want to talk to this guy," Ellie whispered to Rogan.

She could tell he was thinking about arguing. "You mind if I crash?"

"No problem. Go." As he made a beeline for the elevator, she called out to the legal assistant. "Thomas?" He stopped, as if he had no idea who was talking to him. "You work with Linda Moreland, right?"

He turned and straightened his hair, then shook her hand. "Yes, I recognize you. Detective Hatcher, right?"

"You have an excellent memory." She eyed the brown paper bag. "Late dinner?"

"For Linda. She got here today. She showed up very upset. First she said she didn't want anything. Then she sent me out, not that there's a lot of options."

If he had any clue as to what went down at the dive motel in Rome, he wasn't letting on. Ellie wanted to keep him talking.

"I don't know if you've heard," she said, "but the hospital had good news to report. Carrie showed what they called 'purposeful eye movement' today. Things like 'blink twice.' They say it's indicative of intact neurologic function, but it almost seems like she's fighting consciousness, maybe from shock. She's not communicative yet, but they hope for a full recovery."

Thomas was looking at the greasy paper bag like it was a talking dog.

"Thomas, is everything okay?"

"Carrie's in the hospital?"

"I'm sorry. I don't know why I assumed you'd know." She shouldn't have been surprised. The assault on Carrie had happened after she had quit her position with Linda's firm, and hadn't drawn any media attention. "Someone attacked Carrie in her apartment."

"Oh my gosh. No, I had no idea."

His voice was shaking. What had initially come across as wariness had transformed into outright nervousness. He hadn't known Carrie was hurt, but he definitely knew something.

"A weird question, Thomas, but do you think it's

387

possible that Carrie may have been—I don't know—perhaps *divided* in her loyalties?"

"What do you mean?"

"Conflicted. Maybe she started working for Linda with an eye toward compromising the defense?" If Ellie could prove that Carrie was the one who'd been leaking them information about Amaro, it would help prove that Amaro was Carrie's attacker. That could help Ellie keep one foot in the Amaro investigation.

"Gee. I don't think so." If this kid was playing ignorant, he deserved an Emmy. "She talked to me about the case. Quite a bit, really." He sounded proud. "And she seemed pretty happy, at least at first, about being able to nail that detective, Buck Majors. She said he planted confessions in a whole bunch of other cases, too. He was the common link that was going to let Linda tie a lot of different defendants together. All wrongful convictions."

Ellie wondered if perhaps Carrie had put on a show to play the role of devoted defense attorney. "Did you know that Carrie was related to one of the victims? Donna Blank was her half sister."

He was starting to eye the elevator doors at the other end of the lobby. She needed to hurry.

"Linda told me. And even if she hadn't, I saw Carrie's name in one of the reports. Sorry, I'm just an assistant, but the details of the cases—my God, they're so interesting. Don't you just love your job?"

"Oh, of course," she confirmed. "How could I not?

And when I found out that Carrie was related to one of the victims—wow, talk about crazy. I guess it would be natural for her to have mixed feelings. Do you think it's possible that she would have done anything to—you know—sabotage Amaro?"

His face was blank, yet sheepish, like those kids Ellie remembered from her youth, lined up for confession at Blessed Sacrament, complaining they had nothing to report, but looking plenty guilty. *Plenty* guilty in Thomas's case. *Too* guilty. But about what?

"Did *you* send us information about the case?" she asked.

"Why are you asking me that?"

Not exactly a denial.

"Sorry, Thomas. I didn't mean to sound accusatory. It's just—" *It's just* seemed to put a certain type of person at ease. "We received some anonymous messages pertaining to Anthony Amaro. It would be the kind of information that his defense team would know."

All this time, she had been sure that Carrie Blank was the leak, but Thomas was looking good right now.

"This is about the documents stolen from the hotel?"

His already fair skin became even paler. Ellie realized what she'd been missing. Thomas had been the one who left Carrie's hotel door open, supposedly by accident. And he was conveniently lying down in the adjoining room with an upset stomach during the so-called break-in.

"You need to tell me about those documents, Thomas. Filing a false police report is a crime." That should do it.

"It was Linda."

Ellie said nothing, because silence is what people like Thomas needed to keep talking.

"Linda made me do it. She told me to go through all the documents. To find anything that looked bad for the client and take it."

"Because she didn't trust Carrie with it?"

"No, she didn't. I don't know why. I was—I should have known something was wrong—I was happy to have some responsibility."

"So what did you take?"

He was staring at the fast-food bag again.

"Thomas, whatever crap is in that sack has turned into solid cholesterol by now. Carrie Blank is in the hospital, and I know you want to do the right thing. What did you take from the records?"

He sighed. "There was a memo to file from his original trial attorney, Harry McConnell. He asked Amaro whether he had admitted his crimes to anyone."

"And Amaro gave a name? Robert Harris?" Rogan's supicions had been right. It was a defense lawyer who had known about Amaro's conversation with Robert Harris. But instead of it being Carrie herself who gathered the information firsthand, she had seen the notation in the original lawyer's file.

Thomas nodded. "That's right. The cellmate when Amaro was first arrested."

"What about the report on Amaro's foster family?" she asked. "His foster mother used to threaten to break his foster sister's limbs."

"Ugh. Plus that whole fascination with the dolls?" His eyes widened dramatically. "I told Linda, this stuff not only makes him *look* guilty. It makes me think he *is* guilty. But then she told me that the weird thing about breaking the dolls' arms and legs was precisely why Buck Majors framed our client."

The only problem with Linda's theory was that Majors hadn't known the details of Amaro's foster placement. The records were sealed. Only Amaro would have been in a position to give his lawyer access to them. "Do you know why the original defense attorney had those records? Like you said, they didn't exactly help his case."

"The report was part of Mr. McConnell's—um—what's it called? For the death penalty? To save his life?"

"Mitigation?" Ellie asked.

"Yes, that's right," Thomas said. "McConnell had *mitigation* research. Background material to help save the client's life in the event Amaro was convicted of aggravated murder at trial."

"Did you find anything else?" she asked.

"That's everything," he said, "from the files, at least. The part I feel worst about is Carrie's stuff."

She was figuring out that Thomas had a tendency to

drip information in small quantities. "Her journal?" she prompted.

Thomas nodded. "I couldn't bring myself to read it, but when I called Linda and asked about it, she told me to take it."

Ellie thought about all the ways she could plead for various search warrants pertaining to Linda Moreland. And then she remembered Linda's driver, so eager to help serve up the woman who'd been barking directions in his ear for a couple of short hours.

Thomas—last name still unknown—seemed eager to be needed.

"Carrie was assaulted the morning after she left Utica," she said. "I think it's possible Linda did it."

"Oh, I don't think she'd—no, it can't be."

He was trying to tell himself that his boss couldn't be guilty, but she could tell he had his doubts.

"Would you be willing to ask Linda a few questions, just to be sure?"

Three minutes later, Ellie knocked on Rogan's door. He answered with an eye mask wrapped across his bald head like a hairband. It was the first time she had laughed all day.

"You can't read, woman?" He flipped the DO NOT DISTURB sign on the knob in a circle.

"Trust me," she said. "You want to hear this."

56

It felt like the middle of the night to Ellie and Rogan by the time Thomas knocked on the door to Linda Moreland's hotel room, but the defense attorney was hankering for her dinner. "Thank GOD," she said. "I'm STARVING. What took so long?"

From a room across the hall, Ellie and Rogan were monitoring the audio from the mic they had borrowed from UPD, hidden inside a ballpoint pen in Thomas's shirt pocket. The sound from the laptop on the little desk was clear. They were both standing, ready to intervene if necessary.

"Can you hear that, Max?" They had placed Rogan's cell phone next to the laptop so Max could listen long distance.

"Got it."

"Nothing's open this late around here," Thomas was explaining, "but I finally found something." They heard the crinkling of a paper bag. Ellie had even gotten fresh takeout for Thomas to deliver so Linda wouldn't second-guess the delay. "Linda, I need to ask you something. If you don't mind, at least."

"Come on, Thomas, man up," Rogan muttered.

"Can it wait until morning, Thomas? It's been a long day."

"Um, okay. I guess—" Dammit. He was blowing it. "I'm not sure what to tell the police if they come to me, though."

Good Thomas.

"Why would the police come to you?"

"Well, they probably won't. But that's what I need to ask you about. It's Carrie. Did you do something to make her mad at you?"

"Why would you ask that?"

"Because she called me. She's been in the hospital. Did you know that?"

There was a long pause before Linda said, "No. Is she okay?"

Ellie looked at Rogan and smiled. "Did you notice that pause?" she asked Max.

"Shhh."

There was no reason that Linda would know about the assault on Carrie. If she were innocent, she would have been more surprised to hear the news that her former associate was in the hospital. She would have said no immediately. She would have asked what happened.

"She was unconscious for two days. She's all right now. Thank God," he added. He was doing a good job. "But here's the thing, Linda. She said someone tried to kill her. And she said there's evidence tying the attack to you."

Just as they'd rehearsed, Thomas was describing Carrie's call in the vaguest of terms.

"Well, that's just ridiculous. Are you sure it was even Carrie who called? Those police detectives were following me today. They're not above playing mind games."

"Of course it was her. Look." Just in case Linda wanted verification, they had asked an NYPD officer to place a call to Thomas's cell from Carrie's, leaving the connection open for four minutes. Thomas was showing Linda his phone log.

"And she said I tried to kill her?"

"She just said that the police are planning to arrest you in the morning. She told me not to say anything. She was warning me to stay away from you. But I—I just don't believe it."

"Of course you shouldn't believe it. She must be angrier at me than I thought. She's obviously unstable. The way she just quit after three days. I should have known."

"So if the police ask me about any of this—"

"Don't talk to the police, Thomas. *Ever.* Haven't you learned anything working for me?"

"But—the documents, Linda. I'm the one who told the police there was a break-in. That was a crime, wasn't it? And you did tell me to take Carrie's journal. And to hide those documents so she wouldn't have them. Why did we do all of that?"

"Well, *we* didn't do it. You did. And you did it because

Carrie could not be trusted with the information. Hiring her was a mistake on my part, but I wasn't about to let her compromise all of the important work we're doing."

"How was she compromising it?"

"Every time I turned around, the DA's office had new information streaming in anonymously. I had my suspicions, and when you told me what you found in the files, they were confirmed. Carrie was disclosing evidence that hurt her own client. There's no greater harm an attorney can do. She owed a duty of loyalty. And releasing that evidence didn't just hurt Amaro. It hurt *everything*. Do you understand how many defendants Buck Majors set up with his fabricated confessions? Amaro is just the beginning. We're about to open the floodgates, Thomas."

"But what about the assault on Carrie? She says they have proof tying it to you."

"I don't have any idea why she would make up something so ridiculous."

"But here's the thing, Linda: she said the police have video." Thomas was following the plan to a T. It was the same kind of slow drip of information to which he'd subjected Ellie.

"What?"

"There's a surveillance camera across the street. That's all she said." It was the kind of lie that an attorney as smart as Linda Moreland would have never believed from an interrogating police officer. But from Thomas? "They're going to arrest you in the morning. And search your place."

There was another long silence, followed by the sound of Linda's voice. Would she admit to attacking Carrie? Claim it was an accident? Explain that it was Amaro? They had to hope this would work.

"Whatever happened in that apartment had nothing to do with me."

Ellie smiled at Rogan. Thomas hadn't said anything to Linda about where Carrie had been assaulted.

"But maybe we should tell the police that she was leaking information, just in case it's related."

"And if you do that, Thomas, they'll find out that you staged that break-in and filed a false police report. You don't want that, do you?"

"We could explain. It would be worth it to find out the truth about whoever hurt Carrie. I mean, it's better than them thinking you did it, right?"

"Let me worry about that, okay? I think I know who hurt Carrie. I'll take care of everything."

"But—"

"I don't want to talk about this any longer, Thomas. I just want to finish eating dinner. And thank you so much, by the way, for getting it for me. I'll figure out what's going on with Carrie tomorrow. Maybe it's some kind of misunderstanding."

"Okay. I'm really glad I talked to you about this."

From Thomas's mic they heard the sound of Linda's hotel door close. Moments later, the screen on Ellie's cell flashed a text message: "Was that OK?—Thomas."

"Aces. You rock!" She added a smiley face for emphasis.

On the speaker phone, Max was less enthusiastic. "She didn't admit to the assault."

"No," Rogan said, "but she admitted ordering her assistant to commit a theft and file a false report, all to stop Carrie from leaking more information. There was also that pause when Thomas told her Carrie had been assaulted, and she seemed to know it happened at the apartment. And then she even said she thought she knew who did it. Motive, dishonesty, knowledge. If this were a gangbanger in the Bronx, you'd agree it was enough."

"Okay. Wait for her to make a move—that'll be evidence of consciousness of guilt—then take her."

A taxi pulled in front of the hotel thirty-two minutes later. They watched, slumped in the front seats of Rogan's car, as the cabbie placed a call from his cell. Two minutes later, Linda Moreland walked out with her handbag and suitcase. She was fumbling with her cell phone.

The driver said something to her as he placed the suitcase in the trunk. His voice got a bit louder as he continued to speak. He was to the point of waving his arms animatedly when she used her free hand to remove her wallet from her purse. Despite the juggle with her cell phone, she managed to hand him what looked like a wad of cash.

Smart guy to ask for cash up front when someone wants a late-night ride all the way to New York City.

"Can I be the one to say it?" she whispered.

"I hated her first," Rogan said.

"Pretty please? Cherry on top?"

"Your lady charms don't work on me, Hatcher."

"Steak. At Peter Luger."

"Done." He turned the key in the ignition and accelerated across the parking lot, blocking the taxi's exit.

"Hey, ass—" The driver stopped himself from yelling the next syllable as he saw the badge hanging from Rogan's neck when they stepped out of the BMW.

"Linda Moreland," Ellie yelled, "you're under arrest for the attempted murder of Carrie Blank. You have the right to—"

"I know my rights, Detective."

Ellie grabbed the cell phone from her hands and placed it on the taxi's hood. She was about to continue the recitation of Linda's Miranda warnings when she noticed the sound of a voice coming from Linda's phone. She looked at the screen. It read: "Debi Landry—00:12." The line had been open for twelve seconds. She picked up the phone and listened.

"Linda?"

Ellie recognized the raspy voice of Anthony Amaro's foster sister.

"Sorry," Ellie said. "There was a commotion in the parking lot."

"You're the one who told me that bitch was screwing Tony over. You said something needed to be done. But I don't know nothing about police pinning it on you. I ain't seen them since I told them I wasn't saying nothing on Tony."

Ellie hit the disconnect button and pocketed the phone.

"That was a blatant violation of privacy, Detective."

"You said you knew your rights, Ms. Moreland. A search incident to arrest includes anything within your reach. Not my fault you left your phone on. And you must also know that Miranda warnings don't count unless they're given completely, even if the *arrestee*— that's you in this scenario—is the one who cuts them off. So, shut your sociopathic mouth while I continue. You have the right to remain silent . . ."

The recitation of the warnings was like a lullaby, the click of the handcuffs a goodnight kiss.

PART FIVE

DONNA

57

Ellie waved from the bar as she spotted Max spinning through the revolving door at Otto. He gave her a quick kiss and took the seat next to her. He also took a sip of her wine, then gave a thumbs-up to Dennis, the bar manager. "The same, please. And when you have a chance, could you find my real girlfriend? Someone replaced her with a lookalike who drinks red wine."

As Dennis poured the unpronounceable Italian varietal, he shook his head. "No, I think this is the one you're looking for. She had two Johnnie Walkers before announcing a switch."

"You pulled out of work early?" Max asked.

"As I recall, you were the one who was still sleeping when I left this morning. I've been trying to call you."

She and Rogan had decided to make the drive back to the city late last night, after booking Linda Moreland in Utica. She'd managed to slip in three hours of sleep.

"Sorry, I was swamped today."

"Any word on how our favorite lawyer's doing?"

"She's promised to sue every single guard she's encountered for one thing or another. Word must travel fast in the jails. Apparently Amaro heard the news, because he's already asking for a public defender. He wrote on the application that he had a preference for one with, quote, extensive television experience."

"You got my messages about the searches?" She and Rogan had executed warrants that morning at both Linda Moreland's and Debi Landry's apartments. They had found several of Carrie's journals on Linda's coffee table. On Debi Landry's kitchen counter, they'd found the sledgehammer that she had used in the assault. More important, Debi Landry had confessed to the attack, revealing that she'd gone to the apartment after Linda Moreland told her that Carrie was the one who had given Debi's name to the District Attorney and had done so as part of a larger plan to undermine Amaro's defense. According to Debi, she slipped into the building when another tenant entered, initially planning to confront Carrie verbally. She got so angry when she saw Carrie in person that she "lost it."

"A *sledgehammer*?" Max placed a protective hand on his head.

"A two-pound sledgehammer, to be precise."

"I'm surprised you know what a two-pound sledge-hammer is."

"I was calling it 'the badass mallet-thing' until I was corrected by a CSU officer. Now that we've seen Carrie's apartment, I think I know why she's still alive. The entry to her apartment is this tiny alcove. Once Carrie fell to the ground, there was only so much damage Debi could inflict from a bent-over position. Based on the bruises on Carrie's arms, she was protecting herself. Luckily, Debi didn't think to start dropping the weapon on Carrie's head from above, or we'd be talking about murder charges against her and Linda instead of attempted murder."

Max was swirling the wine in his glass, staring at the liquid in silence.

She waved a hand in front of his face, breaking the trance. "Why do I have a feeling there's a reason you didn't call me back today?"

"I wanted to tell you in person. The good news is that both Debi and Linda were arraigned today."

"Okay, that's what we expected, right?"

"We went with attempted murder against Debi, but Martin doesn't believe we have enough evidence to charge Linda as an accomplice."

"She *sent* Debi there."

"No. She simply told Debi that Carrie was a problem for Amaro."

"Linda's smart. She had to know Debi had a rap sheet filled with assaults, and she certainly knew how ridiculously loyal the woman is to the foster brother she sees as her only family."

"Which is all pretty reckless, but we would have to prove that she *intended* for Debi to go after Carrie. We can't do that."

"She knew exactly what she was doing; she was

lighting the match. And she had Carrie's journals—
several of them, not just the one that was stolen from
Carrie's hotel room. Debi Landry admitted tearing the
apartment apart, looking for anything that could hurt
Amaro. She grabbed the diaries just in case, and Linda
was perfectly willing to take them."

"But that's conduct after the fact. It doesn't prove
advance knowledge, let alone intent."

"According to Debi, Linda even *told* her where Carrie
lived."

"I tried, Ellie, okay? You don't think I made these
arguments to Martin? But Debi also said that she told
Linda she just wanted to talk to Carrie. So again, we
don't have enough evidence to prove that Linda intended
for Debi to hurt Carrie." He downed his glass of wine in
one swig and signaled to Dennis he'd have another.

"So what's she being charged with?"

He was still staring straight ahead. "Receiving stolen
property."

"You've got to be kidding."

"Do I seem like I'm kidding?"

"It's a fucking Class A misdemeanor," Ellie said. She
saw the customer next to Max shoot her a dirty look, and
lowered her voice. "She won't do any time."

"She'll be disbarred."

"It's not enough. She put Carrie Blank in the hospital,
just as if she'd wielded the weapon. We're supposed to be
on the same side here."

406

"Look, we have different jobs, Ellie. You know that. Weren't you the one who pointed out the other night that I shouldn't know too much about Buck Majors' interrogation tactics? You and Rogan—you . . . react. You do what needs to be done in the moment. I have to make sure the process is right. I can't charge someone unless I'm convinced beyond a reasonable doubt that they did whatever it is I'm charging them with."

"Thank you, but you don't need to mansplain the criminal justice process to me."

"Seriously? Jesus, Ellie. You really don't like it when I disagree with you, do you?"

"You never said you disagreed with me. You even said Martin made the wrong call."

"No. I said I made all these points to Martin. If you must know, he then accused me of not being objective. Frankly, I think he was right, and so was our charging decision. What Linda Moreland did was reprehensible, and it was reckless, but I am not convinced she meant for Debi to go after Carrie. I think, at most, she hoped Debi would confront Carrie and make her life difficult. Or maybe even break in and make sure she didn't hang on to additional incriminating evidence. But we can't even prove that. And it's pretty screwed up that I can't give you my honest opinion without you accusing me of talking down to you or betraying you somehow."

"You know, Rogan was right."

"Excuse me?"

"You say we *react*, like that's a bad thing. But it's just like he said: this isn't about a *process* for us. We see the bodies. We tell the survivors they're never going to see their family members again. We look directly into the faces of killers, still high from the rush, and can smell the evil rotting them from the insides. You see . . . our paperwork."

He was trying to calm her down, but she couldn't stop.

"You meet the families after they've learned to live through their grief. You see the killers after their lawyers have cleaned them up and coached them for court. We *react*, Max, because someone *has* to."

She finally stopped when she felt her cell buzz. It was Rogan.

"Hey."

"I'll pick you up in front of Otto in three minutes."

She started pulling her suit jacket from the back of her chair. "How'd you know I was here?"

Dennis nodded knowingly behind the bar. "You're always here," he mouthed, as he poured orange liquid into a martini glass.

"Because you're always there," Rogan said. "And you're especially there on Wednesdays, because you're Rainman. Some kind of mushed pea thing, right?"

"Pea and pancetta bruschetta," she mumbled.

"See? White-people food. Eat fast."

"Is everything okay?"

"Better than okay. Carrie Blank's awake."

She finished pulling on her jacket, and then threw cash on the bar to cover the tab she'd accumulated so far.

"Why are you rushing off?" Max asked.

"Because despite Linda Moreland's best efforts, Carrie Blank regained consciousness. Excuse me while I react."

58

Detectives. You're here for Carrie Blank?" It was the same physician who had originally updated Ellie on Carrie's condition after the attack.

"She asked for us," Rogan said. They were used to hospital personnel assuming that law enforcement would put its needs above the patient's.

"I'm aware. She was out a full twenty-four hours longer than the maximum I would have expected. I was beginning to fear the worst, but she went from bare responsiveness to an adamant insistence that we call police within twenty minutes."

"How did the nurse know to call me specifically?" Rogan asked.

"Because *Carrie* was very specific. She threatened to check herself out against my recommendations if we didn't call either Detective Rogan or Hatcher. She seems to be doing remarkably well, but, do you mind if I have a neurological resident sit in on your discussion with her? The substance of what she says could be medically relevant."

Rogan scratched at his temple. "I'm not sure I follow."

"Detectives, I'm used to dealing with patients who are here because of a crime. A lot of them are determined to avoid the police—gang shootings, domestic violence, drug deals gone bad. Other people—like Carrie—are eager to cooperate. But here's the thing: she didn't say one word about her head injury. It was like she didn't even care why she was in the hospital."

"Then why did she call for us?" Rogan asked.

"Well, that's why I want a neuro resident in the room, because it didn't make much sense. Something about Donna and Anthony Amaro? Do those names mean anything to you?"

They found Carrie in bed, eyes closed, her face nearly as white as the hospital sheets. Her head suddenly jerked, the tiniest yelp escaping her throat.

"Sorry if we woke you," Rogan said. "The hospital called us."

"Good, I told them to. And, trust me, if you had any idea what I was dreaming, you wouldn't apologize for waking me. They give you a hard time about coming in?"

"We swore we wouldn't traumatize you," Ellie said with a smile. They had assured the attending physician that Carrie's desire to speak to them made sense in the context of the investigation, and promised they would ask for a doctor if Carrie seemed the least bit confused.

"They're acting like I might fall into a coma any second, but they've also made it clear that I'm losing my bed, come morning. I guess unemployed lawyers don't have the best health insurance." She offered a weak laugh.

"How much do you remember about what happened?" Rogan asked.

"This?" she said, looking up at the bandages still wrapped around her head. "I feel like I remember every millisecond. Every ounce of pain. The temperature of my blood on the floor. Separating from the present. I was sure I was going to die. No, more like, I remember *actually* dying. And I remember the smell of cigarettes."

Debi Landry was a heavy smoker.

"We made an arrest just this morning," Rogan said. "A woman named Debi Landry."

Carrie blinked vacantly.

"She's Anthony Amaro's former foster sister?" Ellie prompted.

Carrie showed no sign of recognizing the name. Maybe the doctor's concerns had been correct.

Rogan looked at Ellie, and then explained. "She assaulted you when you came home and then removed several of your journals from your apartment. She gave them to Linda Moreland, who has now been charged with receiving stolen property." He managed to suppress any sarcasm as he relayed the charging decision he had only just learned about himself. "Linda also ordered the supposed burglary at the hotel in Utica, and it will be up to local prosecutors there whether to charge her with that."

"But . . . why?" Carrie was asking a question, but she sounded like her mind was elsewhere.

"Linda Moreland wanted to keep you from proving Amaro was guilty," Rogan said. "She told Debi Landry what you were doing. Debi says she went to your apartment initially just to confront you, but the fact that she went with a weapon leads us to believe she wanted revenge."

"I'm sorry. Revenge for what? Quitting?"

"No," Rogan said slowly. "For the leads to new evidence."

"What new evidence?"

"An old cellmate of Amaro's?" Ellie said. "Plus some information from his time as a foster child that showed motive?"

Carrie's expression was still vacant. If only Ellie's own poker face were so good.

Ellie stepped in closer. "We know who sent the information to the district attorney's office, Carrie."

More blankness, followed by impatience. "So who was it?"

"It's okay," Ellie said. "We know."

"Yeah, but *I* don't. Am I missing something here?"

Dammit. Ellie was so sure that, once alert, Carrie would give them more helpful information. But now she saw the problem: of course, Carrie couldn't admit to sending the anonymous tips without risking disbarment.

"We don't want to get you in trouble," Ellie said. "But

it's important that we be able to establish the motive for your assault. And if you have any other evidence against Amaro—"

"Wait, you think I—? Absolutely not. I was his lawyer. That would be a blatant ethical violation."

Carrie wasn't bluffing. She was genuinely confused by the entire discussion.

"If you weren't the anonymous source, and you didn't see who attacked you, why did you have the hospital call us?"

"Because I think I know why Donna was killed. And I don't think it was Anthony Amaro who did it."

59

Tell me why everyone's so sure Anthony Amaro killed my sister."

Rogan started walking out of Carrie's room. "There are limits to what we can tell you, Ms. Blank. I suggest you call the ADA in the morning."

"Wait! I'm sorry. I'm—I'm trying to help, okay? But— I'm—I want to make sure I'm on the right track. Let me put it this way. I think Donna was different."

Jess's friend Mona had said the same thing.

"She wasn't into the life," Ellie said. "Not like the other girls. She worked at a strip club—"

"Club Rouge," Carrie said. "I know about that."

"And she had a drug problem. But we don't know of anything firmly connecting her to street prostitution."

"And I saw the autopsy. Her fractures weren't nearly as severe as the other victims. Plus, there's the skin beneath her nails. She fought. There's no evidence the others defended themselves. They must have been knocked out or incapacitated first. I think Donna was killed by someone else. I found an oversight in the police files. When Donna's mother first reported her missing, she said Donna was on her way to my house."

Ellie and Rogan both nodded.

"My mother said she never got there," Carrie said, "but she did. She came over to apologize." She sounded frustrated as she tried to make them understand a conflict that had meant everything twenty years earlier, but probably sounded trivial to her ears today. "There was this whole drama where I gave Donna money from my college fund, but instead of going to rehab—"

"Her mother told us," Ellie said. "Go on."

"So when she was at the house to apologize, she kept promising that she had a plan to make everything better. She was going to make sure that I got the opportunity I deserved. I heard her crying—screaming—she meant it. Donna could be determined when she wanted. That was why I thought rehab would work—"

Carrie's voice started to drift, but Ellie needed her to focus.

"You don't think—your mother?"

"Oh, God no. My mother can inflict more damage with words than force. What I keep coming back to is Donna's insistence that she had a plan to pay me back. It was only eight thousand dollars, but to my family it was a fortune. She couldn't make that dancing at a crummy strip joint in Utica."

"So you think she had some other income in mind," Ellie said.

"Maybe stealing it, or selling drugs. I don't know, but something that could have put her in danger. I keep thinking that whatever she was saying to my mother about having a plan is the reason she was killed."

"You wound up getting that scholarship," she said. "It had to have been much more than the money Donna stole."

"You know about the Morris Grant? So you probably also heard that I blew it. It figures. Two of my friends were much more likely to get it. Everyone—including me—knew I was basically third in line. But by the time the committee picked a winner, I was the poor kid whose sister got offed by a serial killer. I always assumed that's why they picked me."

"Sorry," Rogan said, "but how is any of this connected to the bodies found at Conkling Park?"

Ellie hadn't mentioned her conversation with Rosemary Blank because it hadn't seemed important at the time. Now she was reconsidering.

"Am I correct in understanding that your two friends withdrew from consideration?" she asked.

Carrie nodded, then winced in discomfort. "Down the road, I realized they both had their reasons—one was pregnant, and one had a drug problem."

"Didn't that strike you as odd that they thought that far in advance? I'd expect most kids would go ahead and apply, and then deal with the fallout later. Is it possible Donna knew about your friends' problems?"

Carrie blinked vacantly and then opened her mouth in sudden realization. "Yes, that's it. When I was back in

Utica, I saw the husband of the friend who got pregnant, Melanie. He said Donna had found out that Melanie was pregnant and basically bullied her into withdrawing. Melanie obviously told Tim about it at the time. And I know Tim has violent tendencies. Oh my God. It was about the scholarship."

Rogan had his eyes closed, trying to process all the new names and facts that were coming in. "I'm not sure I see why this guy Tim would target your sister. Your friend was still pregnant. Her secret was coming out one way or the other."

"It could have started out as a fight and escalated from there," Carrie said, "which would explain the skin beneath Donna's nails."

Ellie pictured Donna Blank pleading for another chance to be part of her father's second family. She imagined Donna bullying Carrie's friend to drop out of a life-changing competition. She tried to force her mind to leap to the idea of the friend's boyfriend shooting Donna, and then staging her body to resemble a victim of Anthony Amaro.

She couldn't make the leap. Ellie had seen the Utica Police Department's records. They had managed to bungle a lot, but she couldn't imagine some random hothead discovering insider knowledge about the case.

But Carrie was competing with *two* friends.

"You mentioned a second friend, with a drug problem?" Ellie asked.

Carrie nodded. "Bill Sullivan. He's the lieutenant governor now."

"And he was in rehab?"

She nodded again. "Back then, I didn't realize how bad it was. I mean, I'd seen him drink to the point of blacking out, and he was smoking weed. But that was nothing at our high school. Then when he went to rehab after graduation, I just assumed he was holding the bar higher for himself since his dad was a cop. But he's been remarkably open about the truth."

"Which is what exactly?" Ellie had a vague recollection of Bill Sullivan's backstory but couldn't remember the details.

"I think the way he put it was 'human garbage can.' He was using anything he could get his hands on. Heroin, speed. Meth was brand-new. I think the main problem was crack. But look at him now."

Something about the timeline didn't sound right. If Bill was too addicted to compete for a scholarship, why did he postpone counseling until after graduation? And how many kids skipped college for rehab when their own friends hadn't even noticed a problem?

"This may sound like an odd question," Ellie said, "but are you sure he actually went to rehab?"

"You mean, did he pull a walkout like my sister? No. I visited him, so I know for a fact he went."

"Where did he go?"

"Same place I wanted Donna to go. Cedar Ridge. A few months of inpatient did the trick."

Ellie was mentally replaying the conversation with Carrie Blank as they made their way to the hospital exit. The sound of Rogan's muttering pulled her from her thoughts. "Five victims," he was saying to himself.

"Now who sounds like Rainman?"

"That's what Amaro told his pedantic cellmate, Robert Harris—that he was afraid that the other prisoners would figure out he killed *all five victims*."

Ellie opened her mouth to speak, then paused as she realized his point. By the time Amaro was housed with Harris, he had already been charged with killing Deborah Garner in the city, and five bodies had been found in Conkling Park. Harris had insisted that he was a stickler for wording. If Amaro had feared that the other inmates would realize he'd killed the local women in addition to Garner, he would have referred to all *six* victims.

"It's just like Carrie said: Donna was different," Rogan said, hitting his clicker to unlock the car doors. "If she was killed because of whatever plan she had to pay Carrie back, that would leave only five total victims, including Deborah Garner. We know Donna Blank had a drug problem, and that Utica's a small town. Wouldn't take a lot for her to find out Will Sullivan's kid was a fellow addict."

Ellie hopped in the passenger seat, pulled up a contact on her phone, and hit enter. Michael Ma picked up his line in the crime lab.

"M and M, it's Ellie Hatcher."

"Hey, Ellie Belly. Where are my cookies?" As far as Ellie could tell, Michael Ma had three favorite things: his work, nicknames, and the peanut-butter cookies he thought Ellie made for him from scratch as a token of appreciation when he bent over backwards for her in the crime lab. Ellie Belly might lose her favored-cop status if M and M ever found out that her "homemade" Nutter Butters came from Bouchon Bakery.

"That plastic coffee stirrer I brought you the other night? Do you still have it?" Ellie was now glad she'd forgotten to cancel the request.

"Is that how we're playing now? You used to show up, treats in hand, before you even asked for something. Now I need to produce results before I get . . . *yummy cookies?*"

His Cookie Monster impersonation wasn't too shabby. "A double batch, Mike, I promise. This is important."

"Yeah, I'm working on it. Compare coffee stirrer against Donna Blank fingernail scrapings. It's DNA, from a fucking swizzle stick. I'm a miracle worker, but miracles take time."

"When?"

He let out a pained whine. "Tomorrow. I can get back to you tomorrow."

"What time?"

"I remember when I used to like you. Morning. Okay?"

"As in barely before noon, or *real* morning?"

"Morning!"

Ellie had a lot of practice detecting when people were about to hang up on her. She yelled "*Wait*" to keep him on the line. "With the DNA, if it's not a true match—you can still tell if it's a family member, right?"

"Don't they teach biology in Kansas? Of course."

"Be sure to check that too, okay? And thanks, M and M. Extra cookies, and love, and appreciation, and world peace, and *namaste*, and you are so awesome."

"You can stop now. We're good."

Rogan started the engine as she hung up. "God help me," he said, "but I think I actually followed that entire conversation. Do I understand correctly that you brought home one of Will Sullivan's gnawed-on, nasty coffee stirrers as a souvenir?"

"I was having a particularly dubious moment."

"And you didn't bother to tell your partner you were comparing his DNA against the Donna Blank samples?"

"You would have tried to stop me," she said.

"Because you were wrong about him."

"Maybe so, but we could be right about his son."

He pulled away from the curb. "Where am I dropping you?" Rogan asked. "Back at your restaurant, or home?"

Ellie briefly pictured herself sprawled on the sofa in her old apartment on Thirty-eighth Street. "Home."

"You mean the new place."

"Of course. Why would you ask that? That's where I live. Home."

"No reason." Sometimes it scared her how well Rogan could read her.

She opened the apartment door to find Max asleep on the couch, the light of a muted *Seinfeld* repeat providing the only light. She placed a hand on his shoulder. "Come to bed."

He turned on his side and let out a deep sigh.

She rocked him gently. "Max, come to bed."

He groaned and pulled a cushion over his head. She turned off the television and walked alone to their bedroom, knowing he would follow in his own time, and knowing she could have tried harder to wake him.

60

The Roosevelt Hotel in midtown Manhattan struck just the right tone as a forum for a politician who appealed to the working class. It was elegant, but not the least bit trendy. Refined, but not snooty. From the original Gatsby-era architecture to the Grand Central Station–style clock overlooking the lobby to the namesake's presidential portrait (Teddy, not Franklin) hanging from a bathroom wall, the place was steeped in history. It was the perfect spot for Bill Sullivan's town hall on public safety, which doubled as a fundraiser for the generous supporters who had enjoyed his company at a banquet breakfast earlier this morning.

Carrie took a seat in the back row. About half of the folding chairs were occupied, mostly by retirees and younger parents, many with children in tow. A few attendees carried signs with handwritten messages that appeared evenly split between the "Support the Police"/"NYPD Heroes" types and the "Kids Aren't Criminals"/"End Stop and Frisk Now" types.

An African-American woman around Carrie's age asked what the moderator had announced would be the final question. She read from a sheet of paper, but her voice was loud and clear: "I live in the 40th Precinct with my two teenaged sons." Someone in the crowd called out a supportive *South Bronx, Boogie Down!* "We want our streets to be safe. We want the police to protect us. But what are my sons supposed to think when they and their friends are regularly asked to explain their presence on the sidewalks, while the drugs and the gangs and the guns are still everywhere they look?"

"Thank you for the very thoughtful question," Bill said. "What is your name?"

"Nicole. Nicole Watson."

"I know you're not alone in how you feel about these stop-and-frisk practices, Ms. Watson. You want to be safe in your neighborhood, but too often you see good kids—the ones you want to go on and become civic leaders and fathers—treated like criminals, while the real criminals continue to rule the streets. As a result, an entire community distrusts the police. Both federal and state law are clear on this point: police need an actual, articulable reason to stop a person from going about his or her own business. And, separate from that, they need a reason to suspect the person is armed in order to do a frisk. Every police department in the state—the NYPD included—should be following those requirements. But the public should understand that, lawfully implemented, investigatory stops keep them safe. They make New York a safer place to live. No one wants to go back to the days where robbers and thugs behaved like they owned the streets. And there's a lesson here for law enforcement, too. I was a cop, and I'm the son of a cop, so I speak from experience. When police start acting lawlessly—when they are the ones who act like they are unaccountable, when they stop people for no reason—or, worse, for discriminatory reasons—it undermines the rule of law. It risks the legitimacy of law enforcement. And it invites entire communities to disengage from the social contract. That doesn't make anyone safer, including the police. At the state level, I've been working with the governor to provide training assistance to local police departments all across New York. We need them to understand that we support stop and frisk, and want to make sure they know how to do it lawfully and, hopefully, with the support of the affected communities. Thank you, everyone. You've been a terrific group. I always learn something new when people like you show up and give me a few minutes of your time."

Carrie watched Bill work his way through the crowd— shaking hands, grasping forearms, leaning forward to listen to a comment. He didn't talk down to his constituents in clichés and platitudes. He treated them as equals. He had real-world experience, movie-star charisma, and a deep knowledge of how government worked and its powers and limitations. Her best friend had the potential to go on to become governor of New York, maybe even find a place on the national ticket.

She saw him notice her when he was five rows away.

He smiled at her and, for the first time since Linda Moreland had called her about the possibility of a job, she believed everything would be okay.

61

Dude, I thought we had a pact: DNA, coffee stirrer, Donna Blank." It was officially noon—no longer morning by any definition—and yet Ellie's call to Michael Ma at the crime lab had gone straight to his voice mail. "It's important. Give me a call, okay? And, oh yeah, this is Hatcher, so don't pretend you don't know."

"Hate to point this out," Rogan said, "but the Donna Blank murder case isn't ours anymore."

She jabbed her spoon of Nutella in his direction. "Say it again and I'll flick this at you."

"I'm serious. You know as well as I do: we were working this case on loan to the DA's office. Last I heard, the fresh-look team closed up shop."

"Right, like Utica PD is going to entertain the notion that their golden boy Bill Sullivan murdered someone. Admit it, Rogan, you feel it, too."

"Since when do we go by *feelings*?"

"You know what I mean. Even before Carrie told us about the scholarship, we thought her sister didn't fit the pattern. And it was the DNA under her nails that's been the biggest hurdle in keeping Amaro locked up. Now we find out that the last time anyone saw her, she was on a tear to make sure her little sister got a prize other people were in line for?"

"It's a solid theory."

"It's more than a theory. For someone to make Donna appear to be one of Amaro's victims, he'd have to know about the broken bones. Bill's father would have known." She thought back to all of the horrific, supposedly non-public facts about the College Hill Strangler that she had memorized as a child. "And Donna's mother said she saw her daughter in Will Sullivan's car. She assumed that Will was trying to help Donna, but Donna could just as well have been seeing *Bill* in the car, not the father."

"And you think a high school senior pulled this off by himself? Killing the girl? Staging the body? Finding the right dump spot?"

Motive. Who had motive? "I think Bill killed Donna— probably in a panic, maybe even by accident. And I think Will Sullivan loves his son more than anything. Like you said, unconditional love. I think he was the kind of father who would internalize any possible shortcoming in Bill, convincing himself that it was because he was a single father, or hadn't been home enough." Ellie saw the scene playing out. Will Sullivan in tears as he replicated the postmortem injuries he'd seen in Amaro's victims. Disposing of the body. Protecting his son, but then insisting that he go straight from high school to Cedar Ridge as some form of rehabilitation. Repentance. "It would also explain why Will didn't seem to have the least bit of anger toward Carrie when she was representing Amaro."

"We already had an explanation for that: he cares about the woman."

"But we didn't have an explanation for why Joseph Flaherty was so fixated on the Amaro killings, or why he kept showing up at the Sullivan house, yelling about the devil. It all goes back to Cedar Ridge. Helen Brunswick originally called the police on Flaherty because he was obsessed with another kid at Cedar Ridge. Then after his release, the kid starts making a fuss at the Sullivan house. Will Sullivan made it seem like Flaherty's beef was with him, but what if it was all about Bill? What if Flaherty *knew* what Bill had done, and tried to tell Helen Brunswick about it. Instead of believing him, she saw him as obsessed. Take those facts and combine them with Flaherty's mental illness—"

"Too bad we don't have any proof, *and* are supposed to be working another case." He threw a file folder full of photographs at her. They'd gotten the callout in the middle of the night, just as Max was crawling into bed with her. She'd already seen them all ten times, the crime scene at a liquor store robbery gone bad.

"We put the suspect photos out. Now we wait."

Rogan tapped his Montblanc against the desk. "Cedar Ridge," he said, nodding. He could feel it, too.

"Yep. But like you said, we've got another case to

work," she said, slowly scooping up another heap of Nutella.

"I hate you right now, woman."

She smiled.

"Hold tight," he said. He picked up the handset to his telephone, dialed a number and asked for a listing for Sandra Flaherty in Utica. They both waited as the call was connected. She listened as Rogan explained he was calling from the NYPD and offered condolences for the loss of her son. Then he asked the question they'd both been asking themselves: Had Joseph known a boy named Bill Sullivan?

Rogan muttered *Uh-huh* and *I see*, then thanked the woman and hung up.

"So? What did she say?"

He broke into a wide smile. "Bingo. She didn't even hesitate. She said of course they knew each other. They met when they were just teenagers, at—you guessed it—Cedar Ridge. And then she told me that, in his own way, Joseph must have been proud of his old acquaintance—the way he went on to become such a success."

"And why did she think that?"

"Because her son saved so many pictures of Bill over the years."

"Obsession. Does she still have the pictures?"

"Nope. She said the Utica PD took them all when they searched the house after the shooting, along with the articles about those *horrible murders*. But she assured me she saw them. And she wanted me to know they meant that, at heart, her son was a good boy."

"Why do I have a sudden image of Will Sullivan on his porch swing, burning those pictures one by one?"

"We need to get Donovan on board," he said. "Utica PD can't be the ones to work this. Think he'll back us up on that?"

A week ago, she would have been certain that Max would back her up on anything. Now, all she could say was that she hoped so.

62

Carrie was surprised by the effort it took to rise from her chair in the back of the town hall meeting. All those days of inactivity had taken their toll.

"What are you doing here?" Bill asked. "I was planning to go to the hospital for a visit."

"Bellevue kicked me out—thank you, HMO. And, frankly, I had a panic attack when the cab pulled up in front of my apartment."

"That's only natural."

"Seriously, I might need to call a real estate agent. I can't imagine feeling safe there again." He gave her a hug, gentle at first, but then she pulled him in tight.

"Why don't you get a hotel room until you feel up to dealing with your apartment? Here, or anywhere else you'd be comfortable."

"I was actually thinking of going up to Utica for a while. Any chance you're heading back to the capital? I can train it from there."

"How does door-to-door service sound? Dad called last night. I thought I'd spend a couple days with him, so I scheduled some last-minute local meetings."

"He's having a hard time with the shooting?" So much had happened in those days she had lost.

"He's acting like . . . Dad. But it's got to be rough."

He waved away the driver who started to step out of the black Town Car as they approached, and they both hopped in the backseat.

"I have no idea why," she said, "but with all these thoughts I've been having about the past, the idea of watching television with my mother and sleeping in my old bed feels really comforting."

"You just described your mother as comforting. Maybe that hit to your head did more damage than you thought."

As the car pulled away from the curb, she blurted out the real reason she had told her cabdriver she'd changed her mind, to take her instead to the Roosevelt Hotel.

"One of the nurses told me she saw you visiting me at the hospital. She said you were crying and holding my hand. You said you'd always meant to tell me something, but then one of the detectives came in." She wanted to hit the rewind button. Maybe she had brain damage after all. "I'm sorry. I obviously wasn't there, not in a real sense. And the nurse could have misheard. I shouldn't have brought it up."

"Don't be sorry. And she didn't hear wrong. That's exactly what I said. I don't know that I'd describe myself as *crying*, mind you—" He started to laugh, but then stopped himself. He looked serious as he grabbed her hand.

She waited for him to say something. Anything. She had spent three full days in a quasi–dream state. Was she there again? She was staring at his hand entwined in hers. They'd been here before, with much more physical entanglement. But not like this. Not in the middle of the day, sober, as two grown-ups. Not with this intensity.

She was about to break the silence, when he gripped her hand more tightly.

Ellie's cell buzzed.

"That better be Donovan," Rogan said from the driver's seat as she unclipped her phone. She nodded confirmation, then hit the speaker button.

"Did you get hold of Siebecker?" she asked. There was no time for a greeting. They'd just passed a sign saying they were seven miles from Utica.

"Yeah. He called as soon as he was out of court. It took a while for him to process the connection between Joseph Flaherty, Bill Sullivan, and Flaherty's obsession with both the Sullivans and the park murders. The way he reacted, we may as well have been accusing Joseph and the Baby Jesus."

"But he's on board?"

"He is. You are officially authorized to act on behalf of the Oneida County district attorney."

Ellie had feared another round of debate with Max, but to her relief he had not only agreed with their assessment of the evidence, but had come up with the idea of asking Siebecker to authorize them to act on his office's behalf within Oneida County.

"He did tell me to relay one thing: he prays you guys are wrong."

"Wouldn't be the first time prayer came up short," Ellie said.

"Seriously, you guys. Be careful." Even through the tiny speaker in her cell phone, she could hear the concern in Max's voice.

"Always," she said. "And, Max . . . thanks."

"Anything for you guys."

She hit the end-call button.

"Sounds like you two are doing all right," Rogan said.

"Well, at least he came through with Siebecker."

"You mind me saying something on those lines? I mean about you and Max."

Ellie considered Rogan one of the most important people in her life, and she assumed he felt the same. She also assumed that part of the explanation for that strong connection was the fact that they never talked directly about their feelings. She couldn't remember a time when Rogan wanted to comment on a strictly personal matter.

"Sure, we've got a few more miles."

"This case is just a case. It's not worth blowing whatever you've got going at home."

"You're the one who tried to explain to my significant other that for us it's never just a case."

"Okay, it's not 'just a case' in the same way an ADA

might see it. But compared to stuff that really matters? Your health? Your family? Hell, yeah, this case—and all the rest of them—they're just cases. I know you, Hatcher. You've got your back up. He pressed you to move in. I saw it when you were looking at apartments—finding this and that to complain about, trying to drag me into it to validate all your nitpicking. You don't like to be pushed, and that man is pushing you."

"So maybe he's the one you should talk to."

"I could have written that line for you before you said it, Hatcher. You don't think Sydney pushes me? I've got palm prints on my back from all the pushing. And I'm better for it. Pushing isn't the same as changing. She puts me on those stupid cleanses because she knows how angry I'd be at myself if I started looking like the Michelin Man—a much darker version, mind you."

She smiled at the notion.

"All I'm saying is, we all need someone to call us out on our shit. You've got to learn how to let people into your life, Hatcher. Okay, I've said my piece."

She thought about Max cooking dinner for her in their kitchen, telling her she seemed to be searching for evidence that he was the one who was unhappy. She thought about the worry in his voice just now when he told her to be careful. It had made her want to turn back the clock to the previous night. To wake him up and apologize for her outburst at Otto. To take back all that anger. To tell him that they'd get past these conflicts about work.

Now Rogan was verbalizing a fear she'd never wanted to acknowledge, not even to herself. Maybe she was one of those people who couldn't do what came so simply to other people.

"You devising a clever retort?" he asked. His smile was almost daring her.

"Nope. I'm figuring out how to thank you for caring, without grossing us both out."

"Stop right there—I'll consider myself thanked."

They passed a sign marking the Oneida County line. "Hey, look at that," she said. "We're in our newly appointed territory."

"First we were the fresh-look team, now we belong to Siebecker's office. We've been passed around more than a joint at a Phish concert."

"Since when do you know about Phish?"

"Never pigeonhole J. J. Rogan. Jeffrey James knows all."

Rogan had just hit Genesee Street when Ellie's phone rang again. She recognized Michael Ma's number because she'd been dialing it all day.

"Mike, you said you'd get back to me this *morning*."

"I know. I got called out. I've been on my hands and knees in a parking garage four levels below ground—and not in a fun way, in case you're wondering."

"Please tell me you've got the Donna Blank results."

"Give me two seconds. I literally just walked into my

438

office, but, yeah, it's right here." She heard paper rustling and hit the speaker button on her phone so Rogan could hear, too. "Well, whatever secret spidey senses you were testing were right: I've got a familial match between the DNA on that straw you brought me and the skin cells beneath Donna Blank's fingernails."

"Yes! Does it tell you the genetic overlap? Is it consistent with a father's saliva on the coffee stirrer, and his son's skin under Blank's nails?"

"Both male. Fifty percent DNA overlap, which is consistent with father-son. Wait, can you hold on a second?"

"I gotta run, Mike."

"No, not you." He was talking to someone in the background. "Can't you see I'm on the phone? Yeah. About Donna Blank . . . No, with NYPD . . . What are you talking about—Utica?"

"Mike," she barked. "Is there a problem?"

"Um, unclear."

"What do you mean?"

"Depends on why you were keeping this on the down low. Promise you won't kill me. I was underground. Like, *literally* underground. Not figuratively like most people—"

"Mike! Focus!"

"I wasn't here when it happened."

"When *what* happened?"

"I've got an eager-beaver numbskull of an intern here. Apparently he saw the results come in, and figured he'd

439

take it upon himself to notify the investigating detective. Lo and behold, that apparently isn't you anymore. Did you know the case got moved to Utica?"

"Yes, but—oh no, please tell me you can stop it."

"It's all by e-mail. The results already got sent. But don't worry—no one but you knows who that straw belongs to, right? Just call the detective in Utica. It went to someone named Will Sullivan."

"When? Ask the numbskull intern: When did he send it?"

"He says fifteen minutes ago."

She hung up without saying goodbye and pulled up the number for Mike Siebecker at the DA's office.

Rogan flipped a mid-block U-turn and opened up the engine. They had to get to Will Sullivan's house fifteen minutes ago.

63

Parked down the street from Will Sullivan's house, they had no way of knowing if he was home. The driveway was empty, but the attached garage was closed.

Ellie's cell phone rang. It was Mike Siebecker.

"Hatcher."

"Still nothing," he said. Siebecker had left an urgent message on Sullivan's voice mail, supposedly about his testimony in a pending gang shooting case. The plan had been for Siebecker to have the detective come to his office at the courthouse. Instead, they were still waiting for him to return the call.

"You made it clear it was important?"

"Yes, as much as I could without tipping him off."

"It's been almost twenty minutes since you called him."

"You never know," Siebecker said. "He could be in the middle of something."

"Right, like tracking down a forged passport for his son to get the hell out of Dodge."

"I'm working on the affidavits for an arrest warrant as we speak. Jesus, I still can't believe it. Bill Sullivan. A killer. And Will, covering it up."

"It could be more than covering up, Siebecker. Will

was the one who flagged Flaherty as a suspect in Brunswick's murder in the first place. Why would he do that if Flaherty knew the truth about Bill and Donna Blank? If we had questioned him—"

"So you think Will was *planning* to shoot Flaherty?"

"Just call as soon as you hear something?"

"Of course."

She shook her head as she disconnected. "So now what?"

Rogan pulled his key from the ignition. "We knock on the door."

Carrie hadn't been inside Mr. Sullivan's house since two Christmases ago, when she and her mother joined Bill and his father for supper. She'd never had occasion to lie in any of the beds.

She let out a giggle.

Next to her, Bill rolled toward her and draped one arm across her exposed chest. "I think I nodded off."

"Me, too," she said.

"That laugh was a nice sound to wake up to. Please tell me it wasn't about—*this*."

She turned to face him. "Definitely not. I was just thinking about that time we were at your old house, when I came home freshman year for Christmas." She giggled again, and he kissed her on the lips. "Remember? When I was supposedly helping with your college admissions essay?"

His smile grew larger. "Dad got off work earlier than I expected."

"We were in your bedroom, but my clothes were in the kitchen."

"I managed to throw them in the oven."

"And I hid naked in your closet for two hours until he fell asleep. I don't think I ever got the burnt pizza smell out of my T-shirt. Speaking of which, where is your father? Should I be scoping out my hiding spot?"

"Honestly? I'd like to think Dad would be happy about this by now."

"What do you mean, *by now*?"

"Nothing. Just, in a lot of ways, this is something we should have figured out a long time ago."

"You make it sound like your father hasn't approved in the past?"

"It's nothing like that. I mean it, Carrie. I'm tired of us pretending we're just friends. We wind up like this for a reason."

"You don't think I know that? It was always you who was pulling away, and I never understood why. I assumed you weren't ready to settle down, or maybe I wasn't exactly the ideal political partner or something."

He gave her a sad squint. "Don't you know me better than that?"

Part of her wanted to go back to his comment about him wanting to think his father would be happy for them after all this time, but she didn't want to ruin the moment.

She jerked at the sound of the doorbell, then covered her mouth. "Oh my God," she whispered. "I feel like two teenagers getting busted by your dad again!"

He was out of bed, stepping into his pants, when his cell phone began to buzz against the nightstand. "Nope, must be some kids selling magazines, because speak of the devil." He held up the screen. It was his father. "Hey, Dad . . . I'm actually at your house. It was supposed to be a surprise . . . That close? Okay, I'll see you in a couple of minutes." He made a funny, panicked face and pointed at his bare wrist. Time was of the essence.

The doorbell rang again as she pulled her dress over her head. She didn't need to live here to send whoever it was away. She could still hear Bill's voice on the phone as she headed into the hallway.

"Sure . . . No, I'm not going anywhere . . . Dad, what's wrong? . . . Just tell me."

She started to turn back to make sure everything was okay, but there went the doorbell again. She'd get rid of these nuisances and then find out what Bill's father had called about.

Ellie craned her neck, nearly pressing her right ear against the front door. She hadn't been sure after the second time she pressed the bell, but with that last chime, she'd definitely heard footsteps.

This was a stupid move. They had taken a gamble that Will Sullivan was a good enough man not to take a shot at them, though they'd strapped on Kevlar to be safe. It was an educated guess, but one with deadly consequences if they were wrong. She unholstered her Glock.

She listened as the footsteps approached the front door. She held the Glock at her chest and took one step away from the entrance, using the exterior of the house for cover. She saw the doorknob begin to rotate. No sounds of locks turning. That was good. If he was holed up in there, expecting the police, the bolt would have been secured.

The door opened and Carrie Blank's head peeked out. She said hi automatically, then stopped herself at the sight of Ellie's drawn weapon. "What in the—"

Ellie felt herself exhale and lowered her gun. "Is Will around?"

"No, but he just called. Is everything okay?"

"Where can I find him?"

"I don't know." She turned, and Ellie saw a long corridor inside the doorway. "Let me see if Bill—"

"Bill Sullivan's here?" Ellie asked. Carrie looked back toward her from the hallway. Just as her eyes widened at the sight of the Glock pointing past her through the door, an arm grabbed her across the front of her chest and spun her in Ellie's direction. Bill Sullivan was now behind Carrie, using her body as a shield. His left arm was wrapped around her, pinning her own arms to her sides. His right hand held a chef's knife to her throat.

Carrie's eyes darted to her left, as if she was searching for something down the hall. Someone.

445

"Drop the gun," Bill ordered.

Carrie sucked her breath in. She hadn't realized that her lifelong friend was the person who had grabbed her.

"I can't do that, Bill. You know that." Ellie was still on the porch, just beyond the doorway, but tried to project her voice to the back of the house.

Carrie's entire body stiffened as Bill pressed the flat of the blade hard against her neck.

"Do it!" he yelled.

He doesn't have a gun, Ellie told herself, or he'd be holding it to Carrie's head. She couldn't let that equation change. She slowly lowered her weapon. When it was at her side, she threw it into a hedge beside the porch, and then raised her hands in front of her.

"Keys!" he said.

"What keys?"

"You got here, didn't you? Give me the car keys. Now!"

"They're in the car."

"Stop lying."

"I swear I'm not lying. Look at what I'm wearing. Pants without pockets. I took off my jacket for the Kevlar. Where the hell am I keeping keys? I'm parked two houses to the south. Gray BMW." She was saying too much. He was going to realize she hadn't come alone. "I'm not even on duty. This was my own hunch. Keys above the visor. Take my car and go." She recited the license plate from memory, because those are the kinds of details that stuck in Ellie's head.

"Get in here. On the sofa. Sit." He pulled Carrie one step back into the hallway. "Slow."

Ellie did as she was ordered, moving carefully. As long as Bill felt like he was in control, they were going to be okay. Coming to the house without backup had been a risky move, but the plan had been for Rogan to wait at the back door while she'd knocked on the front. They'd remembered Will Sullivan's comment about living in a house where he didn't lock up. The only question now was whether Rogan was already in the house, or whether he would wait to take Bill down at the car. Everything would be fine. She sat in the center of the sofa, hands still in front of her.

Carrie was trembling so hard that Bill was having a hard time keeping the knife steady against her throat.

"Your duty belt. You've got cuffs, and don't try to tell me you don't, or I'll kill her. Put them on."

Ellie had no choice but to comply. She had to hope that she'd thrown her gun without enough force to bury it in the branches.

As Ellie clicked the second manacle around her own wrist, Carrie began to whimper. "Why are you doing this? Bill? Please. Stop. Please."

No, no, no. The only way they walked out alive was to remain calm. "Carrie, take a breath," she said.

"Why, Bill, why?"

"Please, Carrie, I need you not to hate me."

"Bill," Ellie said firmly. "How can you tell her not to

447

hate you when you're treating her like this. You're scaring her. I'm cuffed, like you wanted. Just let her go, and you can walk outside. Take the car and leave."

This wasn't working. Carrie started to cry, and Bill tightened his hold on her. She was going to get them both killed if Ellie didn't find a way to shut her up.

"He's doing this because of Donna," Ellie said suddenly. "You were right about Donna having a plan about your college fund. She made sure your friends didn't apply for that scholarship."

Carrie looked confused and then let out a cry. Ellie had hoped that the shock of realizing her best friend was a murderer might scare her into submission. Instead, she began to cry uncontrollably, the weight of her sobbing body pulling against Bill's embrace.

Now it was Bill trying to calm her. "Carrie, stop. It's—I don't want to hurt you. Please. Donna—that was an accident. She—she knew I had a problem. We'd used together a couple of times. She was going to tell everyone. I was just trying to keep her from leaving. We fought, and we were both high out of our minds, and then I grabbed one of dad's guns, just to scare her. She reached for it. It went off. Dad came home from graveyard and found me curled in a ball on the closet floor. She'd been dead for hours. What was I supposed to do?"

The more he talked—the more he tried to get Carrie to understand—the more inconsolable she became.

"Don't you see—I've tried to do the right thing from

that moment on. I didn't go for the scholarship. I never used a single drug again. I went away to Cedar Ridge. And I had to learn how to forgive myself. But then I made the mistake of telling Joseph Flaherty, just to hear myself say it out loud. I figured he was too insane to understand."

Carrie was wailing now, but Bill kept talking. He didn't seem to notice the sound of feet stomping up the stairs of the porch. *No, Rogan*, she begged, *not now*.

But it wasn't Rogan who appeared in the open front door. It was Will Sullivan, pointing a Sig Sauer pistol at his son. "Don't do this, Bill. It's like you said. You've tried to make up for what you did. That's all anyone can do."

"I got that doctor killed, Dad. Don't you see? Flaherty trusted Helen Brunswick. He told her what he knew about me, and she didn't believe him. He came to one of my town halls, the one in Utica the week before her murder. He said Brunswick had labeled him, that she'd gotten him in trouble with the police and made his illness worse. He was fixated on both of us. He said he'd find a way to make sure the truth came out. She's dead because of me. And I nearly got Carrie killed. Plus, Anthony Amaro is free because of me. It's all my fault."

Carrie was catching her breath. Her eyes were locked only on Will Sullivan as she spoke to his son. "You're a good person, Bill. Everyone in this room knows this. What happened with Donna was a long time ago," Carrie said. "You were a different person then."

"No, I'm not. I'm the same. I have to make it right."
He grabbed Carrie tighter and adjusted his grip on the knife.

Rogan suddenly appeared at the rear of the living room, his Glock trained at Bill's forehead.

"Drop it!" he yelled. Two guns versus Bill's one knife.

"They have my DNA." Bill's eyes pleaded toward his father. "You said so yourself. I was eighteen, and I was a crackhead. And I've been hiding my crime ever since. I'll spend the rest of my life behind bars. I was a cop. And the son of a cop. You know what prison will be like for me?"

"Son," Will said, "you're making things worse. You're terrifying Carrie, of all people."

Ellie saw something change in Carrie's stance. She had been trying to melt away from Bill's body, but now she stood erect. Her face, no longer contorted with fear, appeared confident. "Everyone, stop! He won't hurt me. He won't. He *wants* you to shoot. But he won't hurt me."

I have to make it right. I was a crackhead. I was a cop. Bill was right: he would spend the rest of his life in prison, and his imprisonment would be a living hell. He'd be better off dead.

"Dad, come on," he pleaded. "You need to be the one. You know it."

Ellie saw the father's finger stiffen against his trigger.

"No!" Carrie yelled, pressing her body against Bill's. "He won't do it. Don't shoot him."

450

"Dad, please," Bill begged. "I can't spend my life that way. Do it. Please."

Will's face was red. His arms were beginning to shake. She could see father and son silently exchange a lifetime of memories and confidences. She could almost hear their plan: Bill would push Carrie to safety, and Will would take the fatal shot.

"Amaro will go free," Ellie said.

Bill jerked his head in her direction.

"Your DNA is beneath Donna's nails. He'll say you were the one who killed all of those girls found in Conkling Park. You'll be his reasonable doubt. He'll put your father on the stand and call him an accomplice. He'll accuse your father of murdering Flaherty to cover up your crimes."

Confusion flashed across Bill's face.

Ellie began to rise slowly from the sofa. Even in handcuffs, she could take a running charge at Will Sullivan if she had to.

"No! No, that's not true. Dad meant to take Flaherty in. He was going to try to get him to see that Amaro really was guilty, that I wasn't the devil, or whatever. Dad would never have taken that shot if Flaherty hadn't had a gun."

Ellie knew right then they'd never be certain what had been in Will Sullivan's heart when he walked into Flaherty's bedroom, but she remembered his rocking on his porch swing, cradling his bucket of licorice sticks the morning after the shooting. His regret had seemed sincere. He had even mentioned his belief that he would have been able to connect with Flaherty had there been any opportunity to speak.

She had to convince Bill he owed it to Carrie and his father to stay alive. "That's why you can't take the easy way out. You have to make this right, but that can't happen here in this living room. You're the only one who can tell the truth. You're the only one who can keep Anthony Amaro behind bars."

Will Sullivan lowered his weapon, but Rogan still had his gun fixed on Bill.

"I forgive you," Carrie said. "I forgive you."

He dropped the knife, and Carrie turned to embrace him. Will Sullivan placed his weapon on the end table next to Ellie and then headed for his son. Rogan lowered his gun to his side while he unlocked Ellie's cuffs with his other hand.

They had to pull Will and Carrie away to make the arrest. As they walked Bill out the front door, Ellie heard Carrie consoling his father.

Rogan escorted Bill to the backseat of the BMW, then clicked the locks shut while Ellie called 911 for a proper transport vehicle. Ellie heard sirens in the distance, growing louder. Bill was staring out the window, knowing this was the last time he'd see his father's house.

"Did you see that?" Ellie asked. "The way she was reaching for him?"

Rogan nodded. "For the man who killed her sister. Pretty remarkable."

"She meant it when she said she forgave him. She forgave him instantaneously." That, Ellie thought, was unconditional love.

"I had a shot," Rogan said. "When he turned toward his father, I had him. But then you said Amaro would go free. He jerked, and the window closed. You saved his life, Hatcher."

As she watched two Utica detectives move a boy they had known since childhood into the backseat of a marked car, she was certain that Bill Sullivan would disagree.

64

It was another two days before Ellie and Rogan returned to New York City. Ellie came home to find Max already asleep, the nightstand lamp left on at her side of the bed.

"You're back." He blinked at her sleepily. They had spoken multiple times a day while she was in Utica but she had missed seeing his face. She climbed into bed, and he wrapped his arms around her. She took a deep breath. He always smelled so good, like truffles and damp wood. This smell always made her feel safe.

"I've missed you," she said, crawling into the nook between his chest and shoulder, her favorite place to sleep.

She was surprised when he adjusted his body to face her.

"There's something I've been wanting to tell you, but I wanted to wait until you were home. You were right."

"Well, of course I was. But about what?"

"The fresh-look team. The case. From the very beginning, you said I was putting you in a bad position."

"We already talked about this. It's all good." In her very first call to him after leaving Will Sullivan's house, she had apologized for the arguments they'd been having about the case. They both promised not to let work come between them.

"But from the outset, it was my decision to put you and Rogan on the case that caused the problem. I may have picked you for all the right reasons, but I should have realized there would be issues."

"Everything worked out, though. Truth, justice, etcetera."

"But we fought more in one week than we have the entire time we've known each other. You think I liked having you sleep at your old apartment?"

"I'm sorry. I should have come home that night."

"I know you, Ellie. Sometimes you overthink and undertalk." He smiled and kissed her gently on the lips. "And I accept that. But we can't keep going through this. I can't keep *putting you* through this. You could have gotten killed up there, and it's because I sent you off on some mission outside the department."

She shushed him. "None of that was your fault. It's fine, Max. Let's just go to sleep."

"I spoke with Martin today. I won't be handling homicides anymore."

"What? That's ridiculous. He's totally overreacting."

"No, it was my decision. And it was the right thing to do. I should have done something about this when we first moved in together, but since we were saying it was just an experiment . . ." The thought trailed off. "Anyway,

I've solved the problem. I'm just sorry I didn't see it earlier."

"There has to be an alternative. You could still handle murder cases. We could agree not to work on the same ones."

"Not good enough. With the NYPD's murder cases split up by county, our office really doesn't handle that many, which means for me it's only a few a year. And if it's not one of yours, it's still going to involve a coworker or a friend or one of Rogan's former partners. It's cleaner to draw a clear line."

"But your career—"

"You're more important. Besides, this is Manhattan. The real bad guys are on Wall Street. Martin agreed I can start handling more financial crimes. If anything, it's a promotion, as far as stature's concerned. It could even lead to something at the U.S. Attorney's office. I think he was impressed that I took the initiative."

"But I don't want you to resent me."

"I did this, Ellie, because to me you're not an experiment. I'm not waiting every day, like you're convinced I am, hoping you're going to change. I know you've spent your whole life taking care of your mother and Jess, and, frankly, taking care of yourself. I just needed to know that you were also willing to take care of me. The last few months convinced me you are. So this is what I want to do."

"I don't know what to say."

"Don't say anything. And please don't overthink it. I'm not dumb. I saw how relieved you were when Jess said he could swing the rent on your apartment. And I know why you insisted that one of us pay individually for every purchase we made when we moved in. And, for the record, if you leave, the nightstands are yours."

"No, it was because—"

"Stop, Ellie. It's who you are. Part of you will always be thinking about the day you might need to be on your own again. What I'm trying to say is, I accept it."

She wiped a tear away from her cheek. "And what happens when I don't change my mind about kids? I know I said I'd keep an open mind, but I don't see it happening."

"Look, I happen to think any kid would be lucky to have you as a mother. I've seen how you take care of Jess. Hell, you help random strangers with their luggage on the subway. Whether you know it or not, you are naturally caretaking. And don't stick your tongue out like it's gross. But I'm not as dead set on kids as you've made me out to be. I just don't want you to write off the option for the wrong reasons."

"Someday you're going to regret sacrificing for me. Kids. Your job."

He furrowed his brow and then gave her a squeeze. "I will never, ever regret a single day I've spent with you, or a single thing I do to make those days with you better. That's what I mean when I say I love you, Ellie."

457

He was saying that he loved her unconditionally. As she returned his embrace, she truly believed that she felt the same way about him, at least to the extent that she knew how.

65

One Month Later

Carrie scanned the three-judge panel for any follow-up questions. For better or worse, they looked like they'd heard enough.

"And for those reasons, Your Honor, the appellant respectfully requests that you reverse the district court's decision certifying the class action and remand for further proceedings consistent with the Supreme Court's decision in *American Express v. Italian Colors Restaurant.*"

The amber light on the lectern switched to red. Perfect timing.

"Good job," Mark Schumaker said as she placed her legal pad into her open briefcase at counsel's table.

She had just finished her first oral argument in front of the Second Circuit Court of Appeals. It wasn't a sexy constitutional law topic, and the case wasn't even particularly close, but she expected to score a win for her client in one of the most prestigious courts in the country.

Andrew Gold, the other associate who had worked on the appellate briefs, was full of praise for her performance, but she knew he would have preferred the chance to present their arguments himself. A month ago, Carrie had been crying at the Governor Hotel in Utica, feeling like a failure for quitting her position with Linda Moreland and wondering whether anyone would ever give her a job again. As it turned out, her old firm, Russ Waterston, had been delighted to take her back. The firm had even agreed to let her take six weeks of vacation at the end of the year so she could finally go to Europe.

Other than Mark Schumaker, no one at the firm was entirely sure of the details of her very short leave of absence, but the rumors had made her something of a rock star among the other associates.

As they hit the bottom of the courthouse stairs, she spotted a familiar face. Carrie waved, but the woman suddenly turned and ducked into the clerk's office.

"I think that's what the kids call a *dis*," Mark said. When he saw her serious expression, he added, "Maybe she just didn't see you. Or perhaps it's not who you thought."

But Carrie was positive the woman was Kristin McConnell, the daughter of Anthony Amaro's original defense attorney. And she was sure Kristin had seen her, too. The duck into the clerk's office—where lawyers would rarely go themselves—had been a clear dodge. It was strange; the woman had been perfectly pleasant when Carrie had gone to her office to pick up the files Kristin's father had kept in storage.

Then she realized the only reason the attorney would avoid her.

Mark was leading the way to the chauffeured sedan waiting at the curb, one of the perks of representing big business. "You guys can take off without me," she said. "I have to deal with something."

"That's right," Mark said. "Linda Moreland's sentencing is today."

Kristin McConnell was on her way to the courthouse elevator when Carrie walked back inside.

"Kristin," she called out.

The woman turned at the sound of her name. Busted. She gave Carrie a quick wave, then jabbed at the elevator button three times. The light above the doors indicated that the car was on the tenth floor.

"I know you meant to help," Carrie said.

"I'm not sure what you're talking about."

"The tips you were sending to the District Attorney about Anthony Amaro. You knew your father had represented a guilty man."

"I'm sure you're mistaken, Ms. Blank."

"Amaro had told your father about the incriminating statement he'd made to his cellmate in Utica. And your father had the records about Amaro's mistreatment in foster care so he could try to present a sympathetic case during the penalty phase if the case went to trial. Only Amaro's defense lawyer would have had that information. That's why the police thought I was the one sending it. That's what Linda Moreland

461

thought, too. I almost got killed because of that belief."

The elevator had stopped again, this time on the sixth floor.

Carrie saw Kristin swallow. "My father had very strong feelings about what sort of life I was cut out for."

"Let's just say I can empathize, but I don't understand what that has to do with leaking information to the prosecution."

"When I tried to tell him I wasn't cut out for defense work—busting my butt for guilty people, all based on some abstract principle—he told me he was disappointed in me. That I was *wasting* my talent."

"Guess I wasn't cut out for it, either. I quit after two days, then got knocked in the head for my trouble." She tapped her knuckles to the top of her head, the way she'd learned she could evoke a smile when the awkward subject was raised.

She didn't see any point in telling the woman that she was still working on the criminal-defense side of the table in one respect: the Sullivan family. She was helping Bill's lawyers identify possible defenses. The hope was to get a plea agreement for manslaughter, with his sentence served in protective custody. For a couple of hours she had believed the two of them might spend their entire lives together. Now she knew they would never be together again—not like that—but she truly believed he deserved a chance at some kind of future down the road.

As for Will, Carrie had drafted a motion to dismiss obstruction charges on the grounds that the statute of limitations had long expired. To convict him now, the government would only be able to rely on recent events. She predicted that the case would be settled by forcing Will to resign without his pension.

"You've got quite a sense of humor about it under the circumstances," Kristin said.

She didn't, but she was becoming a better faker than in the past. "If it makes any difference, I'm pretty sure Anthony Amaro would still be on the streets right now if someone hadn't sent that information to the DA." Regarding other hypothetical scenarios, Carrie had stopped asking herself whether it would have been better for the truth about Donna's death to have remained hidden.

The elevator finally came to rest on the ground floor. "And just so you know," Kristin said, stepping inside, "if any attorney sent those documents, he or she would be disbarred." The elevator doors closed, leaving Carrie on her own. She looked at her watch.

Linda Moreland would be sentenced in twenty minutes, but she saw no reason to give that woman another second of her time. Carrie had the rest of her life waiting for her.

66

Ellie opened the courtroom door carefully, hoping to slip in quietly. Once inside, she realized that the judge hadn't even taken the bench yet. Ellie was pleased to see a large reporter presence.

Linda Moreland glanced toward the sound of her foot-steps down the galley, but she avoided eye contact.

The lawyer at the opposing counsel table was happier to see her. "You made it." Max rose and gave her a quick hug over the railing that separated the viewing area from the lawyers and the bench.

"Rogan said he'd finish up some lingering reports." Given that Linda Moreland had been an indirect cause of some rough moments between them, it seemed fitting for Ellie to be here. She knew the work Max had poured into this plea agreement, the final step in putting last month's saga to rest—at least from their perspective. It would be up to Oneida County to deal with Bill and Will Sullivan.

The bailiff stepped to the front of the courtroom and announced, "Please rise for the Honorable Judge John DeWitt Gregory."

The judge was only halfway to his own seat before waving them to sit down. "I keep insisting that these

464

bailiffs dispense with that particular formality now that it takes me an eternity to make my way up here, but who listens to me?" He looked out at the courtroom and then focused on Linda in obvious alarm. "Ms. Moreland, I understood from the docket that we were here for you to enter a plea of guilty and proceed directly to sentencing. Please tell me that I am having a senior moment with my eyesight and am simply missing the appearance of whatever attorney you have arranged to represent your interests."

Linda rose to speak. "Your Honor can rest assured that your vision is fine. I am representing myself."

"I'm well aware of your reputation and talents in the field, but you know what they say about a woman who is her own lawyer having a fool for a client."

"Actually, Your Honor, the original quote was that a *man* who is his own lawyer has a fool for a client. I'd like to believe that might be a distinction with a difference in my case."

A few of the observers giggled.

"Very well, then." The judge asked Linda a series of questions to confirm her decision to act on her own behalf. "Now, I understand we have a plea agreement, Mr. Donovan."

"We do, Your Honor. The defendant has agreed to enter a plea of gulty to both charges in the information." Although Linda had originally been charged only with receiving Carrie's stolen diaries, Max had persuaded his

465

boss that an additional charge of reckless endangering was appropriate. It was also only a misdemeanor, but it at least reflected the role that Linda had played in putting Carrie at risk. The charge also set the stage for what was about to happen next.

"Very well. And has the government agreed to dismiss any other pending charges or forgo future charges in exchange for the defendant's plea of guilty? It's not often I'd expect to see you here on a misdemeanor, Mr. Donovan."

"Yes, Your Honor. After joint discussions with the Oneida County district attorney's office, it was agreed that Ms. Moreland would not be prosecuted for conduct occurring in Utica that was related to this prosecution."

The judge looked curious but nodded. It was the agreement not to prosecute Linda for fabricating the burglary at the hotel in Utica that had persuaded her to change her plea. A conviction for persuading her assistant to file a false report to the police would have been clear grounds for permanent disbarment. Max knew that Linda's ultimate goal was to save her law license.

"And is there a sentencing recommendation as part of this plea agreement?"

"A year of probation and forty hours of community service," Max confirmed. "But a further condition of the defendant's guilty plea is a process we are proposing for Your Honor to ensure that there is a sufficient factual basis."

"New York law always requires a factual basis for a guilty plea."

"Indeed. And typically that showing is satisfied by the defendant's own allocution. What we have agreed to, if it's acceptable to Your Honor, is that Ms. Moreland will provide her rendition of the facts, and then the court may follow up with questions as it deems appropriate before ruling on legal sufficiency."

Max had suggested this option in the face of Linda's resistance to the reckless endangerment charge. In theory, the process would enable her to avoid an express admission of guilt and to try to persuade the court that the state had brought charges inappropriately.

"I must not be completely senile yet," Judge Gregory said, "because I believe I understood that. So let's hear it, Ms. Moreland. What are the facts?"

Just as Max had anticipated, Linda made herself out to be a hero, beginning with the letter she had received from Anthony Amaro requesting her assistance. She described her hiring of Carrie Blank as a brilliant epiphany, enlisting a bright young lawyer with an interest in finding her sister's real killer. In her telling, Carrie Blank was the obvious culprit behind the leaks to the prosecution. Linda was struggling to strategize a reaction when her client's former foster sister, Debi Landry, called her office, wondering why prosecutors and police were hounding her.

"I'm eighty-three years old," Judge Gregory interrupted. "Will I still be alive when this story is over? The court reads the newspaper and takes judicial notice of the fact that Anthony Amaro has been cleared as a suspect in the killing of Ms. Blank's sister but recently pled guilty to killing four other women in Utica and received a twenty-five-year sentence." Mike Siebecker had made the call to offer Amaro a deal of twenty-five years. If Amaro could live into his seventies, he might see freedom again. Siebecker had decided he'd rather take that chance than risk an acquittal at trial. Those were the realities of plea bargaining. "The woman you mentioned—Debi Landry—pled guilty to . . . what was it, Mr. Donovan?"

"Assault One, Your Honor."

"Now, what does any of this have to do with you, Ms. Moreland?"

"In my attempt to explain to Ms. Landry how her name had gotten to law enforcement, I'm afraid I revealed my belief that my associate was betraying client confidences. Honestly, I was just trying to end the conversation as I was juggling an ever-growing number of wrongful-conviction cases."

Judge Gregory rotated one hand in a "get on with it" gesture.

"Long story short, Your Honor, after my conversation with Ms. Landry, she assaulted Ms. Blank and then stole personal belongings from her home. She came to me afterward, and she had my former associate's journals with her. I realized immediately I made a terrible mistake when I agreed to take them from her, but, at the time, I had absolutely no idea the extent of Carrie's injuries, and my desire to expose her ethical violations was over-whelming. I agree that the above facts are sufficient for the receiving stolen property charge, Your Honor, but do not agree with the state's decision to charge me with reck-less endangerment."

"I see. I can ask questions before I rule?"

"That's what we've agreed to," Moreland said.

"And why aren't you asking the questions, Mr. Donovan?"

"Because Ms. Moreland objected. Apparently she trusts you to be fairer." More giggles from the courtroom.

"I see."

This was where Max was hoping that his superior knowledge of local practice would outmatch Linda Moreland's reputational heft. Linda's recent expertise was in appeals and post-conviction relief. She didn't know the ins and outs of state court procedure, let alone the idiosyncracies of individual judges.

But Max did.

"Well . . ." Judge Gregory leaned back in his chair as if thinking to himself. "You say that you made this offhand comment about a potential leak in your office in a rush to get off the phone with Ms. Landry. Do you know how long that call lasted?"

She did, because Ellie had pulled the LUDs. Debi's call to Linda had lasted more than ten minutes.

"The state produced records in discovery indicating about ten minutes."

"Uh-huh. And did you refer to your former associate simply by her job title, or did you refer to her by name?"

Linda knew that Ellie had listened in on Debi's side of the conversation the night Linda had called her to see if she'd spoken to police. She also knew that Debi had confessed when she was arrested. She could only stretch the truth so far.

"I believe by name, Your Honor."

"First and last name?"

"I believe so, yes."

"And if I were to ask Mr. Donovan here what Ms. Landry has said about that conversation, what would he say?"

Linda's cockiness had convinced her that she could talk an octogenarian judge into the quick, Solomonic conviction on one charge and dismissal of the other, but she didn't know Judge Gregory like Max did. Max had steered the plea to this judge because he was a former law professor who got his back up when lawyers underestimated him.

"I—I'm not sure that's for me to speculate."

"Very well, then. Mr. Donovan, would you care to answer that question?"

"With all due respect," Linda said, "that's not the process we agreed to."

"Ah, but this is my courtroom, and I just asked the

defendant a question she won't answer, but which I expect Mr. Donovan certainly can. Please proceed."

Max already had the relevant reports in front of him. "In a call from the defendant to Debi Landry that was intercepted by police, Ms. Landry said, quote, *You're the one who told me that bitch was screwing Tony over. You said something needed to be done.*"

Ellie noticed some of the reporters shifting awkwardly in their seats. The beloved celebrity lawyer had clearly crossed a moral line, if not a legal one.

"Aha," the judge said. "Ms. Moreland, did the prosecutor misspeak when he said this was a call from you to Landry? Or was this intercepted call different from the ten-minute call you referred to earlier?"

"It was a different call."

"Can you please stop acting like you're in a deposition. You're a good enough lawyer to know what I'm about to ask you next, so go ahead and answer, please."

"It was a call that I placed to Ms. Landry."

The judge stared at Linda impatiently.

"I called her because my assistant—in cooperation with police—led me to believe that I was a suspect in the horrific assault against Carrie, so I called Ms. Landry to make sure she was not fabricating some kind of false story in an attempt to garner favor with a prosecutor's office that would like nothing more than to see me go down."

"And would you say that Ms. Landry is close to your

former client, Mr. Amaro?" Linda started to answer, but the judge immediately realized that his question left too much wiggle room. "For example, if I were to check Mr. Amaro's visitor logs at the prison, would this person he met in childhood have visited him?"

Ellie could see Linda's confidence fading. "I'm not certain about that fact specifically, Your Honor, but, yes, I suppose it would be fair to say the two are close."

"Mr. Donovan, please save me the trouble of having my clerk run the search for me, and tell me what criminal convictions Ms. Landry had prior to any conversations the defendant had with her."

Ellie noticed that the judge was now referring to Linda as the defendant instead of Ms. Moreland. She watched his frown grow deeper, and more reporters shaking their heads in disgust with each conviction Max rattled off from Debi's lengthy rap sheet. The picture was clear: Linda was careful to avoid any explicit directives, but she had waved Carrie Blank like a chewtoy in front of an unpredictable offender with a history of violence.

"I've heard enough," Judge Gregory said. "I not only find a factual basis for both counts of the information, but I'll be writing a letter personally to the state bar association to ensure they receive a transcript of these proceedings. And before the defendant even asks if she can perform her community service through pro bono legal activities, I will answer with a resounding *no*. You will pick up trash or paint over graffiti or whatever else the county conjures for you, just like anyone else. If you ask me, Ms. Moreland, you're lucky the state didn't charge you as an accomplice to Ms. Landry's deeds, but I imagine they concluded that you had successfully abused your legal knowledge to obtain in result what would be unlawful for you to do or ask for directly. I'll be certain to point that out to the bar as well."

Max glanced back at Ellie. She tried to suppress a smile that might be construed as vengeful, but she knew her face was filled with pride that Max had found a way to do the right thing.

Ellie knocked on her former apartment door. Jess was pulling on a Pixies T-shirt, his hair still damp from a shower, when he answered.

"Whoa, you've gotten skinny," she said. "Does this mean you're still dating the vegan?"

"Indeed," he said, making his way back to the bathroom. Interesting. Jess had a tendency to correct her vocabulary from *dating* to *hooking up* when it came to his romantic life. "Gotta say, I feel good. Skinny like Sid Vicious, but without the heroin."

"When do I get to meet her?" Out of habit, she walked toward the spot on the kitchen counter where her jar of Nutella had once lived, but then remembered finishing it the last time she was over.

Jess emerged from the bathroom, running some kind of muddy substance through his hair. "You free tonight?"

"Seriously?"

"Sure, why not? If she doesn't like you, I'm going to have to kick her to the curb, so better sooner than later."

"As if anyone doesn't like the Hatchers."

"Where's Max?" Jess had referred to Max as "Captain America" until two weeks ago. The name change was probably as close as Jess would get to an express endorsement.

"DA happy hour. Should be called DA *unhappy* hour, if you ask me. Bunch of people worried about how their conduct will look if photographs turn up at their judicial confirmation hearings."

"Ah, and yet when I take you to my hangouts, you're afraid to go in the bathroom because you're likely to see something you'll have to call in."

"Goldilocks, forever searching for a bar that's just right. You said you got the paperwork from the management company?"

"Right there on the coffee trunk, awaiting your signature."

Two weeks ago, Ellie had asked Jess to see if there was a way for her to legally transfer the apartment's lease into his name.

"Got a pen?" She removed the documents from the mailing envelope. Jess had already signed.

"You sure about this?" he asked, handing her one from a kitchen drawer. "I mean, you know I would always give it up if you needed it back, but, still . . ."

She signed her name and handed him the agreement. "I'm absolutely positive."

She only needed one home, and it was no longer here.

Acknowledgments

All Day and a Night is my tenth novel, which means it likely contains the millionth word I have written with the support and guidance of my wonderful editor, Jennifer Barth, and agent, Philip Spitzer. I have never been much of a team player, but these two pros have taught me what a difference the right combination of bright minds and good hearts can make.

Rounding out the team are Lukas Ortiz and Lucas Hunt at the Spitzer Literary Agency; Amy Baker, Jonathan Burnham, Ed Cohen, Heather Drucker, Michael Morrison, Katie O'Callaghan, Katy Schneider, Leah Wasielewski, David Watson, and Lydia Weaver at Harper; and Angus Cargill at Faber and Faber. Offering quiet but helpful publishing-related whispers from the sidelines are Anne-Lise Spitzer and Richard Rhorer.

That's more than enough with the sports analogies, but I also owe a big thank you to NYPD Lieutenant Lucas Miller, Dr. David Newman, and Nic Wolff for their helpful expertise. Any mistakes are mine, but I will still try to blame them on you. For helping me keep it real from the minute I decided to try to write about New York, I will always remember and cherish retired NYPD Sergeant Edward Devlin.

Thank you to the readers who go the extra mile, serving as the online Kitchen Cabinet. You named Carrie's fictional neighborhood and some of its institutions. Though I can't thank each of you individually, you may recognize a few character names that I randomly selected from your membership. All the lamentation about changes in publishing can make it hard to focus on the work and craft of writing a book. I try to block out the noise, tell the best story I can, and hope it works. Knowing that I've got a few readers cheering me on (oops, sports again) helps me do that. If you're reading this and want to meet a pretty darn likable group of booklovers, pop in at *https://www.facebook.com/alafairburkebooks* and *www.twitter.com/alafairburke.*

Finally, I am thankful, as always, to my family, friends, and mostly my husband, Sean, for . . . everything.

This novel is a fictional account of one fictional case involving one fictional wrongful conviction claim. I.e., it's made up. To learn more about the causes of wrongful convictions and the more than three hundred exonerations that have been made through post-conviction DNA testing, a good starting place is with the Innocence Project. *http://www.innocenceproject.org/*

If you enjoyed this, then follow Ellie Hatcher's first case

ff

DEAD CONNECTION

DATING CAN BE MURDER . . .

'A sleek and utterly riveting thriller.' **Tess Gerritsen**

ELLIE HATCHER'S FATHER SPENT MUCH OF HIS LIFE
PURSUING A NOTORIOUS SERIAL KILLER. SO WHEN,
YEARS LATER, A NEW KILLER EMERGES TARGETING
SINGLE WOMEN ONLINE, ELLIE, NOW AN NYPD
DETECTIVE, AGREES TO PLAY VICTIM IN AN
ATTEMPT TO TRAP HIM . . .

In her first Ellie Hatcher novel, Alafair Burke
unnervingly explores a world of stolen identities, a
world in which no-one is who they appear to be.

'Absolutely riveting . . . Burke delivers a first-rate thriller, as
a rookie detective investigates the dark side of internet
dating while trying to survive the mean streets of New York.'
Lisa Gardner

'Engaging characters, dark subject matter and a compelling
story. A suspenseful and entertaining read.' **Kathy Reichs**

'*Dead Connection* deserves every accolade . . . These are
characters I'd follow forever!' **Tess Gerritsen**

Also by Alafair Burke

ff

IF YOU WERE HERE

YOUR PAST CAN CHANGE EVERYTHING

'You know you're in good hands.'
Gillian Flynn, O *Magazine* summer pick

WHEN A MYSTERIOUS STRANGER RESCUES A YOUNG
PICKPOCKET FROM THE TRACKS OF A SUBWAY
STATION, SHE SPARKS A MEDIA FRENZY. WHO IS
THIS HEROIC WOMAN?

On seeing the footage, magazine journalist McKenna
thinks she recognizes her as Susan Hauptmann, an old
friend who introduced her to her husband, Patrick. But
Susan disappeared over a decade ago. As she goes on
her trail, McKenna is forced to ask questions about all
their pasts, questions which could destroy their futures.

Sublimely plotted and devastating on marriage,
friendship and the stories we tell ourselves, *If You Were
Here* will keep you mesmerized to the very last word.

'*If You Were Here* is a winner: a suspenseful, tightly plotted
story of friendship, lies, and betrayal. Alafair Burke writes
deftly about secrets buried close to home.' **Meg Gardiner**

'In the style of Harlan Coben and Linwood Barclay . . . Burke
knows how to keep her readers guessing.' *Guardian*